MONSTER'S OBSESSION

MONSTER AND ME, BOOK 2

C.R. JANE

MILA YOUNG

JOIN OUR READERS' GROUP

Stay up to date with C.R. Jane by joining her Facebook readers' group, C.R.'s Fated Realm. Ask questions, get first looks at new books/series, and have fun with other book lovers!

https://www.facebook.com/groups/C.R.FatedRealm

Join Mila Young's Wicked Readers Group to chat directly with Mila and other readers about her books. enter giveaways, and generally just have loads of fun!

https://www.facebook.com/groups/1407946459316639

DEDICATION

To all of us who love the color morally grey…

*This book is for you because we know you've come
for all the monster smut…*

And you won't be disappointed.

Monster
LUM!X, Gaby Ponte

Karma
Taylor Swift

A Friend
Lavina Hope

Lost Myself To You
Besomorph, Mougleta

Anti-Hero
Taylor Swift

10:35
Tiesto, Tate McRae

Run
Thomas Lizard, Steven Coulter

A New Drug
Aesthetic Perfection, Chris Pohl

Listen to the Spotify Playlist:

MONSTER'S OBSESSION

The monsters already own my body…but do they want my heart…

Left to die in a monstrous land, I'm saved by the monster I least expect.

He hates me. But he loves what my body can do for him.

I shouldn't want to keep him.

I shouldn't want to keep all of them.

I'm just their plaything after all.

But one by one, they find their way into my heart.

And even as the world falls apart around me…

I realize that I've become just as obsessed with my monsters…as they are with me.

BEFORE YOU ENTER...

Trigger Warning

Please Read…

Monster's Obsession is a paranormal romance where the heroine ends up with more than one love interest. It may have triggers for some as it has darker themes, sexual scenes, blood-play, violence, sexual assault, torture, and mention of non-consent.

WYL
N
E
S
N
E
S
MONSTER CASTLE
REALM: S

CITY
APE
CLIFFS OF DOOM
PARIAH
GRAVE CAVES
HUNTING LANDS
OWBURN

PROLOGUE

BLAKE

BEFORE

"Crawl to me, Pet," my monster king purred as he sat on his gold throne in front of me.

He was lounging there, his wide shoulders and pumped-up muscles calling to me. Everything about him called to me.

And he was mine. Everything about him was mine. At least in this moment.

He crooked his finger towards me, the long-clawed tip glinting in the pale light of the room. My insides flickered, my panties wet simply from seeing him there in all of his glory. I was voracious for him.

He was completely nude, his long red cock jutting out to his stomach, the two heads glistening with liquid that I knew first-hand was delicious. I couldn't wait to feed on it. To take each head in my mouth in the only way that I could ever own my king. His pleasure. It was all mine in these dreams.

But it would have to do.

His posture was relaxed, but I could see in his gaze how much he wanted me. The feverish glint that those golden eyes got when he was aroused. They told me he was wild and worked up, and it gave me the courage to slowly crawl towards him, the silver silk robe I was wearing trailing down my shoulders as I moved across the room.

I was aware of *their* gazes too.

The rest of my monsters.

My sweet monster was in his human form, leaning against the wall, slowly stroking his swollen cock, up and down, up and down. His eyes were closed, and a lock of his dark hair had fallen in his face, but I knew he was aware of every move I made, every breath I took. He was always aware of me, more so than the others, like he lived to *see* me.

My violent, violet-gazed monster tracked me as I crawled. "Dirty little angel," he growled, his voice a low whisper that wrapped around me, tightening around my skin. He was my dirty talker, preferring to stay on the edges of our play. But his voice was the soundtrack to my orgasms.

And my last monster…his shadows flickered in and out of focus in the dark corners of the room, nowhere and yet everywhere at once. He was terrifying. There was a dark energy to him, darker than the others. Like every time he fucked me, he hated to do it.

But he still fucked me well.

His emerald eyes hungrily stalked me as I crawled.

I wasn't sure whether it was real or imagined, but the distance to the throne seemed to get longer. Every move I made never got me any closer to my king.

My breasts were aching, my thighs slick with wanting him. Wanting them.

They'd all taken me night after night. And still, it was never enough. When I woke up, I'd be all alone again, my body pulsing with need, desperate for more. Always more.

A tongue suddenly slipped through my folds, and I screamed in surprise as it darted away. I glanced behind me, only to see the wisp of a dark tendril folding back into the shadows.

I stuck my tongue out at the asshole for teasing me and then turned back towards my monster king, whose dark chuckle caressed my skin. "Do you want more of his tongue, Blake? Does your greedy pussy need it?"

I gasped again as his hot tongue separated my folds, dancing around my entrance…before darting away again.

I growled in frustration and crawled faster, desperate to get some relief.

Suddenly, sharp claws were pulling my thighs apart, and he was covering the seam of my sex with his mouth. He sucked and licked voraciously, a clawed fingertip pushing into my clenching core.

I moaned…loudly, my front dropping to the ground as he held my ass up…and feasted. He forced his face into my core, sucking rhythmically…messily on my folds and clit.

"Please, please, please," I sobbed when he abruptly stopped.

My king clucked his tongue sympathetically. "What do you need, Pet?"

I trembled as I lifted myself back to my hands, shaking my head and trying to clear the lust-ridden fog clouding my head. "I need a fucking orgasm," I shot back at him.

"Then keep coming…"

There was a challenge in his glinting gold gaze, and a promise. If I just played his game, I would get everything I wanted.

At least as much as could fill my sleeping hours.

I took a careful…hopeful look behind me before I crawled toward him again.

And then *his* mouth was there again. His tongue spearing so far inside of me, it felt like it was pressing against my womb.

"Fuck," my shadow monster growled against my folds. "Fuck. Fuck. Fuck. I could eat this fucking pussy forever."

His teeth scraped against me gently as he ate at me wildly, his growls vibrating on my tender core.

My desperate cries filled the hall. Out of the corner of my eye, I saw milky cum jetting onto my dark-haired monster's tan stomach, his vibrant, milky blue eyes bearing down on me.

The sight of that had pleasure tearing through me violently, convulsing over my skin…tremors wracking my insides.

I locked eyes with my king, his forked tongue slipping out like he was tasting my lust in the air as I came.

And still, my shadow monster ate at me. I reared back against him, riding his mouth as he continued to lick and suck. The pad of his finger rubbed against my asshole, the twin sensations so strong, my head was rocking back and forth, hoarse screams scraping against my throat.

A little more pressure and another rush of pleasure was rocking through me, painful in its intensity to the point that my vision flickered around the edges, like his shadows were invading my head and not just my body.

"Enough," the king's calm voice sliced through the air.

His mouth and tongue instantly disappeared. I whined and glanced back, and this time I saw him before he disappeared. His emerald green eyes almost looked…longing as he stared at me. This was sex. Jaw-dropping, incredible, irreplaceable sex that I hoped would continue in my dreams forever.

But that was all it was.

Dream monsters weren't supposed to look at you like that.

I blinked, and he was gone.

"Blake." The monster king's voice was like a beacon. He never got jealous of his friends playing with me, but when he decided it was his turn…he expected it to happen immediately.

And evidently…he'd decided it was his turn.

I turned my attention towards him, my breath hitching at the sight of his sharp-tipped claws squeezing one of his crowned heads like he was trying to hold off his own impending orgasm.

Licking my lips, I began to crawl again…but this time, the room slipped away and I was at his feet just a few seconds later.

I fucking loved dreams.

"You look hungry, Pet," he murmured, his eyes heavy-lidded and sensual, like twin sparks of candlelight in a dark room.

"I'm starving."

"Fuck," I heard my dark-haired sweet one murmur. I glanced over and saw he was erect again.

I was just as hungry for him.

"Eyes on me," the king growled, an edge of savagery in his tone.

"Always," I purred, sitting up on my knees so I could rest my hands on his massive thighs.

"I want to suck on you," I murmured, leaning down to slowly lick a line up his stomach. "I want to make you cum. I want to taste you."

"How much do you want it, Pet?"

I moaned in response, pressing my chest against his legs.

"You want me to fuck your perfect mouth? Shove it down your throat until you gag?"

"Yes," I whispered desperately, really wanting that.

It was freeing, these dreams of mine. I didn't have to worry about what society wanted. I could just feel. I could just be. I could have whatever dirty thing I wanted and feel no shame. And what I wanted right then was his massive cock fucking my mouth.

"Take it," he murmured.

His movements were slow as he slid his ass forward, his enormous cock jutting forward like an offering. I stared at his cock worshipfully, feeling a bit like one of the strung-out junkies that resided in the psych ward with me. Maybe this was my brain taking my observations of them and putting them into my dreams. I was always trying to do that…make connections…but they never seemed to make that much sense.

His red cock was long and thick, with ridged veins running the length of it. I knew from experience how smooth it felt against my skin. The tip was leaking moisture. I licked my lips and leaned forward, my mouth watering.

This craving I had for him, every night no matter what horror I'd experienced that day, it never ebbed. If anything, it grew. I curled my fingers around him, unable to make it even close to all the way around. And then I touched the tip of my tongue to one of his heads, moaning softly as the salty musk of him rolled over my taste buds. I squeezed lightly and another burst of liquid fell on my tongue.

I wanted more of it.

I wanted all of it.

I sucked on the tip, like it truly was candy I wanted to savor. Soft pressure indicated that his tail had joined the picture. It trailed down my spine as his length pushed into my mouth, the other head softly hitting my cheek. I tightened my grip, knowing exactly how he liked it. I squeezed and explored even though I'd done this a thousand times before.

"Fuck," he growled, throwing his head back as he bit his lip with his sharp incisors.

The sound reverberated through me, and combined with the fact that his tail was now softly rubbing between my folds…I was on the precipice of cumming once again.

He wrapped his hand in my hair, the sharp tips of his claws pressing into my skull as he gently guided my head up and down until I was feasting on him, taking him as deep as his other head let me before I switched to going back and forth.

His thighs were trembling beneath my hands and suddenly, he was ripping my head off his dick with a roar that echoed around the room.

"I love your mouth, but I want your cunt, Pet." Before I could blink, he was gripping me by the waist and spinning me around so he was pressing his glistening heads against my center, my thighs shiny with my own cum as I faced away from him.

He pushed slowly into me, and it was such a tight fit. So tight...it felt impossible every time. But like every other time...he somehow made it in. Inch by inch, he slid inside, the two heads massaging different parts of my walls as he filled me.

"Such a tight pussy," he groaned as he thrust his face into my neck and bit down almost savagely into my skin.

"It hurts," I gasped...but like usual, he didn't offer to stop. His tail slipped between my legs and gently massaged my clit while he pushed inch by inch into me until he was fully seated.

I. Couldn't. Breathe. That was all I could think for a second as I tried to relax. There was a buzzing sound in my ears, enormous pressure in my core. My lashes fluttered against my cheeks, and I was faintly aware of the other three enormous monsters hovering a few feet away from me, but I was too out of it to be able to focus on their features.

His tail continued to press against my clit, slowly, until my inner walls began to relax.

"Such a sweet girl, taking all of me," he whispered roughly against my skin, his tongue licking at the sweat dotting me.

I whimpered, and his answering dark chuckle sent a slow,

rolling orgasm through my insides that had me clenching him even tighter.

"I'm going to take such good care of you," he said as his clawed hands slowly lifted me until just his two heads were stretching my hole…before he slammed me down again.

I screamed, locking gazes with the three beings in front of me, their cocks out, their tails and claws fucking themselves.

My king licked at my pulse and then he sucked on the pressure point as he bounced me up and down. Every move stretched and stimulated. There was no rhythm to his movements, and that made it even more intense. Sometimes he'd withdraw slowly to the tip and pause. Other times his strokes would be rapid, my orgasm building quickly before he'd cut it off.

He was so deep inside of me, I could imagine his heads pushing into my cervix, his monster seed flooding my insides.

"Give me your fucking perfect mouth," he growled, a claw-tipped hand yanking my gaze away from his three… friends and bringing my attention back to him. His tongue pushed into my mouth, his tongue fucking me with the same erratic rhythm as his dick.

"You're soaking my big cock, Blake. I can feel your juices coating my balls."

Wow. His mouth.

"I want this forever," he whispered against my mouth, and my eyes flew open as I met his gaze.

Why did my dreams have to torture me like this? I was all alone all day, and at night I had this. More pleasure than I knew what to do with. I didn't need my brain to imagine more…

I moaned, ignoring what he'd just said. I leaned back against his chest and reached up to fist his horns.

That seemed to do the trick of distracting him because he lost control then, pounding into me violently.

Every thrust hurt, and every thrust brought me closer to yet another orgasm.

"You're going to cum for me, Blake. Your cunt is going to choke my cock."

His tail slid down my folds until it reached my slick rosebud. It pressed inside at the same time a flutter started low in my insides, turning into a violent crescendo that coursed through me.

I was screaming, my gaze locked on the monsters in front of me.

I came and came until the edges of my vision darkened… and eventually everything disappeared.

NOW

H

ave you ever wanted something so badly that it promised to destroy you? Where nothing you did would shake it off. And no matter how hard you fucking tried, you were going to fall flat on your face?

That was me with Blake. The human I hated who we'd been feeding on for years in her dreams, fucking her every which way. Then Creed had to go and bring her into Wyld to feed our population. Many called her our savior. The guys were obsessed with her to a fault.

Why didn't any of them see that she could be our destruction?

Or maybe it was just me. I was obviously broken in the head, because even looking at her got my cock so hard it hurt. That was all she was to me though. A fuck.

I sat atop the lofty stone of our city wall near the entrance gates, legs dangling over the edge, where the world stretched outward into a never-ending maze of sand, where the blood-red sky burned bright.

Blake stood outside the city, at least half a mile away,

glancing around, appearing completely lost. I was pressed up tight against the side of the gates in case she gazed my way, but she was too busy frantically running toward the city gates to notice me.

The longer I watched her, the more convinced I was that I could taste her honeyed scent on the back of my throat.

It buzzed in my nostrils, the impression of her body burned on my hands. The moans she made in my ears from all the times I ruined her as I took her—fuck, I was becoming as tormented as Creed and the others around this human. This was another reason I had to get rid of her once and for all.

Open-mouthed, she clutched her middle, her head swinging left and right with fright, a small cry on her lips. She was completely lost and terrified—fuck yes, I was a bastard for enjoying her this way.

Would I change it?

Absolutely not.

I put her outside the city walls for the taking, after all.

There was more than one way to save what little sanity I had left—getting rid of her once and for all had seemed the best of those options.

She turned toward the metal doors, pushing at them, slamming her tiny fists against them. No one would hear her when they were too busy dealing with Steele's return—the Red Queen's killer. Even the guards must have left their now empty stations to help capture him.

Turning my attention to Blake once more, I studied her from up here.

Her absurd pink hair, fluttering over her deflated shoulders, glinting in the sunlight. The ridiculous loose dress that hung off her small frame. She was barefooted too.

I assumed that once we took her from earth and brought her to our world, I'd be able to put her in the back of my mind. I'd fuck her when we needed to feed, then do my own thing. But I realized I'd never get enough as long as she was in my face day in and day out.

Grinding my teeth, I raised my head just in time to catch sight of the sand moving like a rippling sea in a storm, promising the arrival of real danger.

I should be relieved she'd be out of my hair.

Blake's piercing scream had me grinning. She'd finally noticed her fate coming from behind her, and she frantically beat on the doors, terror pouring from her throat.

Anticipation rose, my pulse hammering.

Running a hand through my hair, I stretched the agitation in my back, shoving it away. I gripped the edge of the wall harder as I peered down at Blake in tears as the Gazen approached.

Time to enjoy the show.

In the distance, the Gazen creature threw itself out of the sand, then back in like an enormous worm with clawed feet. It dug deep, then came back up. Curved horns broke the surface, tossing sand in every direction, its screech flooding my ears. The next time the Gazen came back up, its mouth gaped open, revealing two rows of long teeth. Dark leather skin glinted beneath the bloody sun, then it vanished underground again.

Fucking ugly things.

Blake was screaming madly, but the girl wasn't completely stupid. She'd found herself two large stones, one in each hand, resigned to the fact that no one was coming to rescue her.

"Come get me!" she screamed, and fuck me but my cock just twitched seeing her in warrior mode.

It all happened too fast after that. The Gazen burst out of the sand mere feet from Blake. She might have screamed, but she wasn't a helpless maiden either. She hurled the stones to her right, sending the creature in a mad dive after them.

She in turn swung left and bolted, keeping close to the

wall, scanning it, clearly searching for grooves or something she could climb onto.

Oh, pretty little thing, there's no way in for you.

Still, I was on my feet in seconds, rushing across the top of the thick, stone wall to follow her just as the creature returned. She didn't stand a chance.

And yet something tightened in my chest, something so painful that I starved for breath. I pushed it away, knowing this had to be done.

The creature burst out of the sand right on her heels, the force lifting her into the air and propelling her forward in a throw that saved her from being eaten alive right away…that would come soon enough.

She hit the sand with a grunt, and it was only then that the red smear of blood across her arm became obvious. Something shifted inside me.

Adrenaline pumped in my veins. My pulse quickened, and it felt as though someone tightened their grip around my heart.

Boom. Boom. Boom.

The Gazen was coming back to finish off its prey, thundering through the sand. It made one last explosive burst out of the sand, towering over her, teeth bared, a screech in its throat.

Her scream was loud enough to rival the Gazen.

This was the final blow. The moment I'd get what I wanted.

Except, was it?

A feral, predatory obsession came over me. As did images flashing in my mind of Blake's smile, the submissive glances she'd give, her laughter, the moans, her gorgeous tiny body cradled against me. Everything about her stole my breath away.

I fucking hated that she had an effect on me.

Yet a territorial obsession burst through me at the very last fucking second. It slammed into me so fast, I lost my head momentarily.

Then I went and leapt right off the wall before I could make sense of it, my blade pre-dipped with venom already gripped in my outstretched hand.

Silently I fell through the air, coming down fast.

I smacked into the back of the worm's neck, the impact rattling through me up to my teeth, but the sand-muncher wasn't exactly prepared either. My strike threw the beast off balance, and it landed with a splat on the sand, inches from Blake's feet.

She cried out and backpedaled, calling my name in shock at realizing she wasn't alone.

I, on the other hand, desperately scrambled up the enormous, leathery neck, taking the opportune moment I'd gained.

The thing shuddered beneath me, ready to dive back under. I threw myself forward, landing on its huge brow, then drove all my strength behind my arm. I drove that blade so deep into its one eye that it might very well come out its ass. I chuckled at my own sick joke.

Green blood spurted from its eye, and my nose scrunched up as the scent of rotten food assaulted my nostrils.

Gagging at the smell, I wrenched my blade back with a sloshing wet sound, then hurled myself off the creature just as it slumped onto its side, convulsing. In order to kill these fuckers, you needed to destroy its brain, or gut it, and I wasn't in the mood for getting putrid intestines all over me. So I let it die slowly.

The moment I hit the sand, Blake rushed into my arms, her small body curling around my middle, her beautiful silvery eyes crammed with fear behind them as she stared up at me like I was what humans called guardian angels.

I hated myself for saving her. But...I couldn't kill her. Apparently, my emotions and cock had taken over. What the fuck was I supposed to do now? Play loving boyfriend like the rest of them? Fuck that!

Her body radiated heat, and she was so soft that I curled around her, embracing the curves of her body against me. Her chest rose and fell quickly. I should let her go and get the fuck out of there, but something about having her in my arms when she was hurt and vulnerable had my insides roaring with a primal need to protect her.

"You saved me," she murmured, her cheeks still wet from tears. "I was positive I was going to die today." She trembled in my arms as I kept her tightly against me, and I followed her gaze to the Gazen.

The hideous thing had stopped having seizures and lay dead. It wouldn't remain there too long as those on the black market from the city always found a way to sneak past the walls and collect the dead creatures for healing potions, for selling, for whatever the fuck they wanted. We turned a blind eye to it for the single reason that we didn't want the dead reptilian things.

Blake whimpered against me.

"Hush now." I curled my hand gently across the back of her head, my other hand still gripping the blade. The thought crossed my mind that, out here, I could easily finish the job I started.

But when I glanced down at her terrified face, I felt something deeper stir within me–a raw obsession I detested.

"I don't even remember how I got out here." She breathed heavily, while a terrible urge came over me to kiss her, to settle her nerves, which I resisted. There were things she brought out of me that no one else had ever done…not even the Red Queen. Though to be fair, the queen had been a sadistic bitch.

"I want to get out of here," she mumbled under her breath.

I tightened my arms around her, and she moaned.

"Fine." I collected her hand, my gaze falling to the blood dripping down her arm, the torn fabric of her dress revealing an open gash from where the Gazen must have got her with its teeth. She stumbled, and I knew she wouldn't make it far. In truth, her time was running out fast.

The worms carried venom in their saliva, and a small cut was all you needed to get infected. Then death came knocking pretty damn fast after that.

"I know you may not trust me, but I need you to, okay?" I'd never been the nice guy to her, never wanted her to see me as anything but the monster I was. She was our meal ticket. But fucking someone every night for years did something to my head. It twisted me, made me crave her as though she'd become part of my soul, and I didn't need that in my life.

She blinked at me, the color in her face already fading. "I never said I didn't trust you."

I wasn't a fool and understood when I was being placated. I'd been nothing but a jerk to her.

"Tempest, I'm not feeling too well." Her voice came out hoarse, and a weird sensation hit me right in the chest at her words. Her body slackened against me, and I caught her.

"You've been poisoned by the Gazen and you won't last much longer." The venom of a Gazen was deadly. I'd seen a few survive with healing, but the method was like tossing a coin—she might survive or she might not.

With shaky hands, she held onto me. "I've got you." The venom was claiming her fast.

Her eyes widened, her vulnerability like a whisper across my skin.

Tucking the blade into the sheath on my belt, I released my monster. It rushed over me, stealing my human form, while a mixture of regret, anxiety, and anger lashed at my insides.

One second I'd tried to kill her, and now I raced against

the clock to save her from the venom… because if she was going to die, I wanted it to be by my hands.

The world around me seemed to shrink as I grew in size until I was at least three feet taller than my human form, my jawline buzzing from the razor-sharp teeth extending, a tightness across my head intensifying as horns emerged. My body lengthened into shadows, bits of me stretching outward, darkening the land around us.

Blake gasped, but the brave human didn't back away. She'd seen me many times this way, especially in her dreams.

I extended my long arm, my clawed fingers unfurling toward her as wisps of darkness whipped around my hand.

"Come to me," I rasped the words with a growl.

She surprised me by quickly accepting my offer and curling against me. The rational part of my brain twinged that I'd finally done the right thing. At least for now.

I swept her into my arms, and she wrapped her arms around my neck just as the booming sound of another approaching Gazen made itself known.

"Hold on, we're going to move fast."

She lowered her head against my chest, and I took off, moving like the wind with the ease of stepping over it. For me, it was a breeze, and once I landed on the other side, I hurried as I felt her weaken in my arms.

Time was running out, and there was only one place that I knew of where I could extract the venom from her body.

CHAPTER 2
STEELE

"Just kill him already," Seven growled, his words booming through the thick air of Wyld city. A place I hadn't called home for a long time, and if these idiotic bastards had anything to do with it, I'd never call it home again.

Creed held me by the throat, my feet dangling off the floor, and I eyed the blade on his belt seeing the way his hand lingered over the hilt. For a split second, I contemplated playing weak, showing them I'd be willing to surrender if it meant we could talk like a fucking family.

Huge mistake on my part because Seven, in his usual style, was out for blood. Ash lingered in the background like a hellish guard dog ready to rip into me the moment he got a chance, and Creed was the big chief, all puffy chest and fangs on show. Nothing had changed all these years I'd been away from my home, right down to that asshole, Tempest, vanishing during every fucking important event.

I slammed my hand into Creed's arm, over and over, but he was stone and unmovable. His body was already shifting into his monstrous form, growing to his eight-foot height, horns pushing out from his temples, his tail whipping behind him, side to side, showing his growing agitation, like a wolf about to attack.

"How could you?" he spat in my face, speaking in our native Wyld language, and I wasn't sure if he was referring to me returning home or supposedly killing the Red Queen. Either way, nothing I said would make him less stabby toward me.

"He's ready to die. What's the damn hold up?" Seven whined, all worked up. It almost felt like I'd stepped back in time because so little had changed. Well, except for Creed going and bringing my baby girl to Wyld City. Of course I'd followed her to collect what belonged to me.

I never made a sound, not that I could speak while he practically suffocated me. But hey, I'd been tortured enough times during my miserable life to know that a bit of choking would tickle my dick before it killed me.

"Let me do it already," Seven snapped, coming at me like a shadow, still dressed in all black, including his hook, and covering the bottom half of his face. Those eyes carried pure hostility. "I'll cut off his head, just as he did to our queen."

Creed's blood-red eyes narrowed on me.

Irritation slid down my spine, wrapping around me like barbed wire, and I threw my arm out, my fist smashing into the idiot's face. Then I kicked Creed in the fucking balls because I wasn't above fighting dirty.

A slip in his grip was all I needed, and he gave me that. I threw all my weight behind me and slammed my fists into his arm, then ripped away from his grasp.

Ash flew at me, but I leapt up and over him. He was running at me like a fucking bull, but that also made him slower to react. I spun instantly behind him and kicked him in the back, then recoiled, just as Creed rose toward me, Seven at his side.

I had my hands out in front of me, in some form of semi-peace offering...if one could call it that. "Let's talk," I proposed, gasping for air. "Maybe it's time you finally listen to my side of the story before you automatically assume my guilt."

I stumbled back, quickly taking stock of the three monsters in front of me, the castle to my left and the city to my right. I was in a tight squeeze, but I did love a challenge.

"You're still spinning lies," Seven crowed, his nose creasing with disgust.

Ash snarled to my left, hot air misting from the corners of his mouth, his sharp teeth bared.

"I was once your brother. We were unstoppable. Creed, you know me better than anyone; what reason would I have to kill the queen? It's fucking common sense… none of us would benefit. I never killed her… if you knew me at all, you'd know this."

Ash grunted, his head shaking, those curled horns that protruded from the sides of his head, absolutely huge with sharpened tips, casting shadows over us. His lipless mouth with too many teeth stretched the width of his face into a frightening frown. He might have no eyes, but he knew exactly where everyone was, and even their emotional state, better than those with sight. The bastard was a fighter, and rarely missed his mark.

"You were the last one with the queen the night she was butchered," Ash growled. "And you just happened to conveniently run away afterward. Why run if you weren't guilty?"

I grizzled, keeping my cool because I'd gone over this in my head hundreds of times, with the decisions I made and how quickly everything had escalated. "Because I found her dead, and when her guards came and discovered me over her body, blood on my hands from trying to help her, what do you think it looked like? They came at me with aggression, with accusations."

"Stop fucking lying," Seven snarled. "Really, I've had enough of listening to his voice. He disgraces us."

"You've had years to convince us, but instead you hid on earth. That screams guilty to me," Ash chided. His eyeless face turned my way like he could see more than the others.

I tensed, my patience thinning because I'd lived for years hiding on earth after losing my home. What had fucked me up the worst though was that the monsters I'd once called brothers…they'd turned their back on me without a second thought.

I'd made an attempt to connect with them and explain my side of the story a long time ago, but they wouldn't listen. It turned into a witch hunt for me. They blamed me for her death, for the city starving, for the chaos that spread afterward.

I guessed they needed a scapegoat while the real killer still lingered somewhere in the realm, getting away with it, while I got all the damn blame. One day I'd find that fucker and skin him alive.

That was when I came to the decision that trying to make peace would only end one way for me—my death.

Creed paused for a moment, actually listening to my words for a change.

Hope trickled in my veins that reason would win out for once, and we could talk about this once and for all.

But it was only a second of calm that crossed his gaze before fury lit in his eyes like the burning sun glinting overhead.

Run. My mind screamed, Creed's next move easy to spot. I'd seen it hundreds of times. The wheels in his head spun with his prepared attack.

I threw myself to the left, bolting along the bridges that connected the towering homes in the city. Anyone that might have been around us, watching us, scrambled back inside, slamming doors and windows shut.

Monsters I once called friends darted behind me madly,

growling for my death, but ahead of me, their fucking sheep of an army was also racing toward me. Fucking great.

Half a dozen guards resembling oversized spiders scurried toward me on long, thin legs, bulbous bodies, and a streak of red across their heads to acknowledge they were part of the city's army.

Well, dealing with them just wouldn't work for me.

I pivoted to my left and propelled myself onto the bridge's railing, then bounced outward, across the lava below that would burn me to a crisp. Its heat swallowed me in unbearable waves.

But my sights were set on the tower just ahead of me, and I slammed against the railing, smacking it hard across my middle. I groaned, but shoved myself forward, the motion pushing me into a roll. Then I was on my feet and I took off.

A quick glance behind me showed the three monsters had split up, coming at me from different angles, Creed right on my heels.

I just needed to shake them off long enough to catch my breath and find Blake. I'd take her back to earth and I'd do my fucking best to make her life perfect. I'd lost enough in my life already that I sure as fuck wouldn't lose Blake as well. I wasn't a murderer, but I'd become one if anyone stood in our way.

A ripple of possessiveness rolled over me, knowing Creed and his men had been fucking her night after night, stealing her from me. I'd been dying without her, so I'd risked everything to come collect her.

That thought alone pushed me faster, to duck and weave among the city towers and bridges, through back lanes, until by some miracle I found myself free of my pursuers.

I slipped into a small home where the door lay ajar. Shutting it behind me, I pressed my back to the wall, my breaths heaving as I stood in silence in an empty room that appeared abandoned. I inhaled the foul taste of stale air, but pushed past it and tried to work out my next steps.

Stay low.

Watch their every move.

Track down Blake.

Then…steal her back.

Sounded doable with some planning ahead of time.

Darkness stilled around me, and in my head, I traced the streets and mapped all the danger points, where I'd keep away.

Most of them were guarded from what I remembered. It had also been a long time since I'd been home, so things could have changed. But one thing I was certain of was that no one lingered in the Hunting Lands. It was a place where everyone kept to themselves and hunted. And I had no issue with laying low there, taking out anyone who crossed my path. At least until I bought myself some time and could get Blake away from them.

I listened for noises outside, the bridges quieter than normal, but word would have spread fast of my return, of the king putting out a death call on my head. Which was fine. I was used to hiding in plain sight, and I could take different forms. But first, I needed to get them off my fucking tail.

Fate.

I remembered the queen once told me that fate determined our death, that there was no stopping it if it was your time.

But sometimes even fate could be swayed into your bidding.

That was the thing about our queen, she'd been a fucking sadist with a dark streak who got off at seeing others suffer. We'd had many of our staff in our castle mysteriously vanish, and there was that one time I walked in on her taking a bath in blood. She'd called it her "beauty regime" and told me it wasn't my concern where it had come from.

She'd had many haters as well as admirers, but I'd never

wished for her death. Even if I should have with everything I suspected she'd done to her citizens and those in the royal palace.

Muffled words echoed somewhere in the distance. I stilled, dread lingering in my chest like a burning flame threatening to encase me in infinite darkness. When the sound faded, I scanned the large room for another way out, realizing very quickly there wasn't one.

It also happened to be the exact moment that a tremendous explosion boomed behind me, the door flying off its hinges and right past me, slamming into the wall.

With my heart in my throat, I whipped around to find Creed striding into the house with fire in his eyes. On his heels, Seven and Ash burst their way in, taking out a wall completely. The whole tower shook, dust falling over us from them ripping it apart in their entrance.

I was royally fucked. So I did the only thing I had left—I lunged at them, fangs and claws out.

We crashed in a thunderous battle that could easily topple over this building for good. The fight turned real nasty when all three piled on top of me, punches and kicks tearing into me.

I gave just as good as I took, biting flesh, tearing it, slamming my fist into faces and ribs. I had no idea where I started or ended, but I soon found myself outside. Creed stood over me, his fist coming down so unexpectedly and fast that when it collided with my face, my head flung back, smacking into the metal bridge we stood on.

Stars danced in my vision, pain ricocheting across my skull. I groaned, the world tilting on its axis around me. The next thing I knew, I was being dragged by a leg across the bridge, my body jostling, my head hitting every bump we passed.

It was only when the castle shadow cast over me that I blinked open my dazed eyes, craning my head up to stare at the three figures glaring down at me. They were talking, but I couldn't make out what they were saying with how loudly the blood thumped in my ears.

Every inch of me hurt.

"Creed--," I started, then turned my head to spit out the blood in my mouth. That made them grin.

Creed snatched my throat once more and wrenched me to my feet, his face twisted into a pained grimace. Even in his monstrous form, he looked in pain. Perhaps he hadn't been the only one to get a few good punches in.

I caught my reflection in the glass doors of the castle entrance, my face all busted up, me hanging from Creed's hand around my neck. Hatred flared across my mind.

"I really am sorry that I have to do this. We were close once," he growled under his breath. "But what you did is unforgiveable. Our city *will* have justice for the queen's death."

He was really going to kill me. The threat flared behind his gaze, and I realized the ache on his face had nothing to do with physical pain. A shiver licked down my spine at the reality.

"Get it over with already," Seven barked. "Then we'll display his body in the middle of the city for all to see, hanging him by his toes."

My blood ran cold at the viciousness in his voice. I didn't have a death wish, but I'd also never feared it. The only thing I feared was being without Blake. "I didn't fucking kill her," I snarled, my brain running with ways to escape, to get out of this mess. To get back to my sweetheart. I wasn't one to give up, not now or ever.

But when no one said a word, and only the heavy ominous promise of my death sang on the breeze, I raised my gaze to Creed. "If you're going to do it, then do it in front of Blake. Let her see the real you. The monster who'd kill an innocent friend instead of taking his word."

Creed's face paled slightly at my words.

Then a faint cry caught on the breeze. Something almost feminine.

I glanced around, finding no sign of my sweet Blake.

An icy touch slid down my back when the sound ended, my thoughts flying to where she'd gone. A cruel silence followed, which I broke. "Bring her to me," I demanded, a foreboding sense flaring through me. "Now!"

Ash just stood there, while Seven glanced around, having heard the scream too.

My heart raced as someone emerged from within the castle. Freddy, Creed's servant, still leaving a trail of slime everywhere apparently. I sure as fuck didn't miss his blob-like appearance and eyes that seemed to move around his face when he stared at you.

"Your Majesty," he called out with panic in his voice, slithering toward us rapidly, the outline of his gray-like mass jiggling crazily.

"Not now," Creed snapped, never taking his eyes off me.

"I must insist," Freddy continued. "You see, the human girl seems to have gone missing."

The air rushed out of my lungs, the acrid air stifling, ripping the life right out of me.

"What did you say?" Creed swung around, shoving me at Ash and Seven who snatched me, their grip like iron bands.

I might have fought them, but my attention was on Freddy. "What the fuck does that mean? Gone missing?"

The blob appeared to be sweating under Creed's stare, something I didn't know his kind was capable of doing. Yet beads of it rolled down his gelatinous body, leaving pale streaks behind.

Freddy shook his head, continued to jiggle. "After you took off, I'd been searching for her, along with some of the guards, but she's nowhere. Not in the castle, not on the bridges. I'm sorry, but I can't find her."

"Are you fucking kidding me?" I spit, the splintering ache of her absence carving through me. "How the hell did you lose her?"

"She has to be somewhere in the castle. She wouldn't take off on her own." Ash released me in seconds and darted into the castle, moving like a madman, smashing right through the glass doors and not stopping.

"Fuck!" Seven growled, his grip on me tightening. "We need to find her. She's not safe in the city alone. Fuck, fuck, fuck." Seeing Seven was currently stuck repeating only one word, I shoved an elbow back into his ribs, then ripped free from his grasp with all the force I had left.

"Creed, if anything happens to her, it's on you," I snarled, breathing heavily, my threat loud.

He snapped his attention toward me, a feral expression crawling over his features. A low snarl rumbled in his chest, then he headbutted me with fury.

The sharp pain split across my head, hurting like shit. The world around me faded so fast, that I only heard a few of Creed's words before darkness claimed me completely.

"Lock the fucker up. We're tearing down the city until we find her."

CHAPTER

BLAKE

The world was spinning around me. Dark specters darted in and out of my vision, and I was faintly aware that I was screaming.

What was happening to me?

When I'd been locked in the asylum, I'd thought about death a lot. I'd thought about what it would feel like. If it would hurt. I'd wondered if it would give me any relief from the fucking hard life I'd been placed in.

Was I dying? Is that what was happening? Was the excruciating pain lacing through my bloodstream how it was going to end for me?

"You're not going to fucking die," a voice growled, and my eyes flew open to see Tempest staring down at me, an edge of panic to his words.

"You're a grumpy, grumpy goat," I mumbled nonsensically, because evidently my brain had melted and that was all I was able to say. If he even could understand my words. Because I wasn't sure that I'd spoken out loud. I wasn't sure if I was even capable.

"Keep your eyes open!" he snapped as my lids flitted closed. It was all I could do to try and pry them open again.

The world was a reddish blur around me, and my eyeballs seemed to have gained a thousand pounds because keeping them open could have been one of the hardest things I'd ever done.

"That's it, sweetheart. You're doing such a good job," he purred.

Nope, that wasn't Tempest. That was Steele's voice I was hearing in my head.

Was he here too?

"Fuckkkk," Tempest muttered as he leapt in the air.

My head lulled to the side, giving me a view of the literal lava underneath us as we soared. There were skeletal hands reaching for us from the searing orange and red liquid, and I was really hoping I was tripping. I tried to open my mouth and scream, but it got caught in my throat. The best I could do was to try and hold on to Tempest tighter. The air smelled like sulfur...and the heat coming off the lava was almost unbearable.

We landed on a rock, and the jolt had pain shooting through my already aching skull.

I couldn't hold in my whimper, even though I was really glad we hadn't fallen into the lava where all the scary creatures were. Tempest cursed again.

His next jump was much softer...but it still hurt. I buried my face into his neck to try and block out the pain... and the sight of the lava, and the demonic hands I was convinced were going to reach out and grab me at any moment.

Sparks of light flickered under my eyelids, answering pain exploding in my skull. I was more than whimpering now...I was sobbing. It felt like every nerve in my body was plugged into a light socket and my body was made up of nothing but pain.

"Almost there," he murmured, sounding almost like he was reassuring himself more than he was reassuring me.

I tried to nod…but my body was cramped up, unable to move. A frozen living corpse, stuck inside my own body.

I'd never imagined anything could ever be like this.

Cool air hit me as Tempest made one last jump, the blazing inferno from the lava river from hell replaced by icy fingers.

I couldn't open my eyes, though, to figure out where we were. I was still stuck inside my skull, my world somehow still managing to spin even with my eyes closed.

Tempest lay me down softly on the moist ground, and I heard the sound of him moving away.

Was he just leaving me here? I couldn't even fucking call after him. He couldn't leave me here like this.

I couldn't imagine a worse way to die than being trapped in the dark, the never-ending pain driving me mad.

My insides shivered as something freezing cold suddenly pressed against my face. I hadn't even heard him come back thanks to my dark thoughts.

"You're burning up," he murmured, and I relaxed…as much as one could in this state…because he hadn't left me. "It's going to take a minute to get the antidote ready. I'll be right back."

I didn't want him to go away from me. He felt like my lifeline, the only thing keeping me alive, and the irrational part of me was sure that as soon as he stepped away from me again, I'd die.

But I couldn't speak or move…so I couldn't exactly tell him that. All I could do was listen to his footsteps fade away and pray he'd come back.

There were a pair of eyes staring at me underneath my eyelids. Rationally, a part of my brain realized it wasn't possible, but everything else in my hellscape of a mind was telling me it was real. The eyes transformed into my father's and then my mother's, flickering back and forth between the two, except with the same hate inside both of them…the same disdain that always made me feel like a flea they desperately wished to squish. Self-loathing flushed through me, sharpening the pain in my veins. Dark thoughts swamped my brain.

I should die. I deserved to die. I was nothing but a waste of space. The whole universe would be better off without me.

Thoughts I kept locked up tight stayed with me, refusing to go back in their box. This was worse than scary demons trying to drag me to hell. Or hearing voices…or seeing shadows. This was the truth about me flayed open so I was forced to absorb it into myself.

I didn't want to go on. Please, let it end. I begged and shouted my pleas inside my head, and just when I thought it was truly the end, that my brain couldn't possibly keep these thoughts for a second longer without my whole body just exploding…

My mouth was wrenched open.

"This is going to stop the pain, Blake. This will make everything better."

A warm liquid was poured into my mouth, salty and bitter at the same time. He tipped my head back and then held my mouth closed so the liquid was forced to flow down my throat. It was a miracle that it somehow didn't end up choking me.

The effect of the liquid was instantaneous; it acted like a balm to my fucking soul as it shot through my vital organs, and veins…replacing the nightmare pain with a numbing, drugging sensation that felt like I was being dunked in a warm bath. Everything in my body felt exhausted but almost pleasurable, like the aftermath of an intense orgasm or adrenaline rush.

And it felt like a fucking miracle when I was able to blearily open my fucking eyes and move my fucking fingers.

A fucking miracle.

I stared at my surroundings in wonder…was I still hallucinating?

The sky was sparkling above me…but I could clearly see grey-tinged rock everywhere. We were in some kind of cave. But the ceiling…even though I could see the rock formations hanging down, above that I could see what appeared to be a cascade of stars, more brilliant than I could ever remember seeing in my life. There was a slice of red up there, almost looking like some kind of symbol. Was that a crown?

I tried to squint and make out what it was, but then Tempest's face appeared in my vision, blocking out the beauty above us. Although his face was a different kind of beauty…no less majestic despite his assholish ways. "You're going to live," he announced…but why did he sound so conflicted about that?

I tried to speak, but my voice came out as a raspy whisper. I needed water…desperately. After failing at first to get the word out, I eventually squeaked it, and Tempest immediately darted away, returning a second later with a clay cup full of water that I was sure had dripped straight from the gods.

I'd never tasted anything so good in my entire life.

I guzzled the entire cup. "More," I demanded, and he immediately took the cup and refilled it. This time I stared after him, and saw he was getting the deliciousness from water flowing down the wall of the cave.

He brought it over to me and I again drank it almost in one gulp. It took four refills before my throat stopped feeling like I'd stuck a flaming torch down it.

I finally sat up more and stretched. Everything was sore, like I'd run a marathon—not that I knew what that felt like from experience…but I could imagine it, thank you very much.

My gaze caught Tempest's. He was leaning against the wall, that same conflicted gleam in his gaze as he stared at me, looking at me, but at the same time…not looking at me. More like looking through me.

"I'm feeling almost normal," I offered…and he winced… but still said nothing.

Shaking my head because…males…I clumsily stood up, a wave of nausea hitting me from how much water I'd just guzzled down.

Irrational anger hit me. I'd been dropped outside the city by some unknown force. I'd been almost eaten by a worm from my worst nightmares. And then I'd almost died while suffering pain beyond comprehension.

Why the fuck was *he* being so moody?

"What the hell is wrong with you?" I snapped, my hands on my hips in frustration.

He growled, a definite warning sign, but I couldn't be stopped.

I stalked towards him, waving my hands in the air like a crazy person. I got up right in front of him and pushed on his shoulders. His massive form didn't move an inch, so it was completely ineffectual, but maybe he was getting the message that I was done with his over-the-top moodiness.

"Tell me what your problem is? You have no problem fucking me. But everything else about me you seem to royally hate."

That got his attention.

"No problem fucking you?" he snorted, his eyes lowering as hate and distrust blared from their depths. "I have a problem with everything about you. You're nothing but a disappointment. Just like *her*. And just like *her*…no one else seems to notice. Their heads are too wrapped around your cunt."

"Who is *her*?" I asked, forming my fingers into mock quotation marks.

"The Red Queen. Her majesty. Eruthria the cunt."

I paused, biting on my lip in confusion, not understanding anything that was happening right then.

He turned away from me and paced the cave, flickering in and out of the shadows like he was too upset to be able to keep himself fully formed.

"It was my understanding she was the group's 'long lost love'…enough that when she died, you encased her freaking head in a museum so you could stare at her loveliness whenever you wanted." I wasn't proud of the jealousy in my voice. I knew they'd never love me like that. Steele claimed to love me in my dreams, but in reality…well, he was a murderer, right? So I wasn't sure how far *that* love went. He'd once loved *her* too, and he'd still killed her.

"She was not my 'love'," he snapped, ferociously.

I arched a brow, my mind whirling as I tried to think back on everything they'd ever said about her highness

"She was a poison to our land. Just like you." My gut churned at the way he'd said "poison." I hated that word coming out of his mouth.

He had stopped his aimless pacing and was now standing there, his emerald green eyes piercing into me as his shadows swirled around him like a tornado…like a tempest.

"At first, I was as obsessed with her as the rest. I thought she was everything. I gave her everything." His fierce voice faded into a pained whisper. "And then the curtain began to fall, and I saw who she really was. A selfish plague on our land who cared no more for our people than she cared for a speck of dust on the ground."

"I don't understand," I murmured. "She fed the people. Just like I do. You fucked her, and the kingdom prospered."

"It started slowly, slowly enough that it could be explained away. She'd just had a bad day. There was a lot of pressure on her. She was in one of her moods. But then her cruelty continued to grow. She began to play favorites. She refused to heal Seven—"

"She refused to heal him?"

His answering smile was all sharp teeth and the promise of destruction and pain. "He came to her, sliced all over by our enemies, and she could have made it all go away. Instead, she sent him away. And now he has those scars forever, a reminder of how the Red Queen cared so little for her lover that she tossed him aside like common trash."

Well…Seven was making a lot more sense after that story. It was amazing that he'd deigned to have sex with me at all with that horror story in his relationship history. A wave of possessiveness wound its way through me. What a fucking bitch! For a second I wished she was living, just so I could kill her all over again.

But really make it hurt.

"And then I found out that she was plotting behind all of our backs with our enemies. She had a plan to slowly starve the city, and once she'd weakened us all enough, she'd let them in the gates to take over."

"You obviously never told the rest of them that," I snapped sarcastically. "She's encased in a freaking shrine, for fuck's sake."

"I attempted to. But she had Creed and the others by the dick so hard, that he wouldn't even listen to anything I had to say negative about her. To him, she was perfect. She was his queen."

The jealousy frothing around inside of me only continued to grow thinking about her with Creed. About him taking her with his perfect body. About him moving in and out of her with his perfectly unique cock.

"So what did you do after he wouldn't listen?" I asked, even as the knowledge of what he was telling me started to sink into my thick skull.

"I killed her. I sliced that bitch's head clean off after Steele left her room. When he returned and found her, it made it so much easier to blame him."

"You killed her," I said slowly. "And then you decided to blame Steele for it?" My voice dripped with distaste.

"I did. He made it easy for me by disappearing that night after finding the queen's dead body. I knew there'd be a mourning period…"

"And a starving period! Creed said that your people starved after her death!"

"They were already starving before that, thanks to her! He was just too blind to notice! But they would have been dead if I hadn't acted. All of them would have been dead. Temporary pain is better than death." He sighed, rubbing a clawed hand wearily down his face. "I knew there'd be something to replace her…someone. I obviously didn't anticipate it would be a mere mortal," he sneered in disgust, and I bristled even though that was probably the least offensive thing he'd said thus far.

Tempest was emanating a dark, dangerous energy…practically vibrating with it as he stood there.

"You have to tell them the truth," I said slowly. "You can't keep the blame pinned on Steele. They're going to kill him for that. They could be killing him right now!" My voice became hysterical at the thought.

"They're never going to know the truth. They would never forgive me. They are all so completely irrational around pussy, I'm the only one who can protect this city." His hands were trembling. "I'll do anything to keep my people safe."

While I could get behind his patriotism, he wasn't allowed to do it at the expense of Steele. My heart was hammering just thinking about what they could be doing to him that very second. I'd have to be smart about this though. I couldn't exactly run out of the cave and try to get back into the city myself. I'd most definitely be eaten this time…wait a minute.

"You were the one who left me out there?" I gasped, my eyes widening as realization struck me.

He smiled then, and it may have been one of the most terrifying things I'd ever witnessed.

"Why would you do that? I'm definitely *not* planning on destroying the kingdom! You fools were the ones who brought me here!" My voice was coming out in a screech that even hurt my ears.

"I have no intention of letting history repeat itself. We were able to find one replacement. We'll find another. Once my brothers get to the point where they're in love and unable to see what's right in front of their faces—"

"No one is in love with anyone," I snapped.

"Surely you aren't fool enough to believe that," he drawled. "You could say jump, and all of the idiots would ask 'how high'?"

Strange how you could be in a completely terrifying situation but somehow still be getting the warm fuzzies at the same time. My brain must have cracked under all the pain I'd just endured. That was the only explanation.

"Tempest," I murmured, holding out my hand in front of me like you would with a feral animal. "I can assure you I mean your people no harm."

He was prowling towards me now…every inch the predator. It made me wonder how we'd gotten to the point where I was now the prey.

I tried to stay there. I really did. I knew retreating from a predator was never the wise thing to do. But as his power began to build in the cavern…and his monster fully came out to play…I couldn't help it. I had to take a step back, and then another, hating how his green eyes gleamed with pleasure at my fear.

"Where are you going, poison?" he purred as he matched me, step for step.

"You're making a mistake. You think they won't realize that it's you this time?" I was proud that my voice only came out with a slight tremble.

"Their grief will cloud their mind, just like it did last time."

"Who are you going to blame this time? It obviously can't be Steele."

His lips curled in displeasure. "I'll figure it out," he growled.

I squeaked when my back hit the cold, hard wall of the cave. Wide-eyed, my gaze darted around the room. Which tunnel was the exit?

But then he was right in front of me, ensuring I wasn't going anywhere. His hate-filled eyes bored into me, no sign of sympathy or regret of what he was about to do anywhere to be found.

A tear dripped down my face. I hated that I was allowing him to see it, but I couldn't help it. I couldn't help feeling betrayed. I'd given him my body...over and over again...for years.

And it was clear that it meant nothing to him.

"How can you do this? How can you have been inside of me, yet kill me like it was…"

"Like it was nothing?" he purred.

His gaze tracked my face, a flash of heat in his eyes suddenly.

"Does it feel better if I tell you you're the best fuck I've ever had?"

A hitched sob forced its way out of my mouth, but I didn't answer the asshole. What could I say?

His gaze moved from my face, tracing the lines of my body like a lover's caress. "It would be a shame…" he murmured, his voice fading away.

"A shame to kill someone you've known intimately and who has never done anything bad to you…yes, it would be."

"Might be awhile, if ever, that I find someone who gets me off like you do."

"Don't you dare," I hissed, pressing myself back against

the wall like there was a chance it would open and I could disappear inside of it. Was he really thinking about fucking me before he killed me?

I swung out and caught him in the side of the face, but he didn't even blink.

"Don't be even more of a monster than you already are," I pleaded.

He pressed against me as if he hadn't heard anything that I said, his dick hard and ready. And my body, as traitorous and insane as it obviously was…began to respond to his presence.

It was like a Pavlovian response. He'd been inside of me so many times that I was programmed to get hot for him. To get…

"I can smell how wet your pussy is for me," he said, his tongue darting out to lick across my lips. "Even knowing what's going to happen…you can't help but want me. Because you know how good I always make you feel."

"Please…" I whimpered. And fuck, I'm sure by the sound of my voice, it was unclear to him whether I was begging him not to kill me…or begging him to fuck me.

"One last fuck before I kill you. I'll let myself have that," he murmured, almost absentmindedly as his clawed hand came forward and he ripped what little scraps of clothes were left after the Gazen attack.

The cold air hit my nipples, pebbling them into hard points. He took his time looking at me, as if he really was memorizing this scene for later…when he didn't have my body anymore.

"Your people will starve again," I reminded him desperately, my chest heaving under his gaze.

"It's a price we'll all have to pay to protect ourselves from your betrayal."

Fuck! He was so exasperating. I wasn't her. I'd never do what she'd done to them.

Not in a million years.

He roughly moved me, until his thighs were between my legs, our chests flush together…his cock wedged against me. His eyes had dilated, the round pupils turning into vertical slits…like a pit viper.

My breaths were coming out in gasps, as his nose rubbed against mine…almost lovingly.

"Why don't you just kill me? What have I done to deserve being humiliated before you do it? Just throw me back to those worm monsters. I'd rather die like that, than have you touch me…"

"We both know that's a lie, little poison." His hand moved between my legs and he rubbed on my clit in that expert way of his. "You're like a bitch in heat when it comes to me. Don't you want a little pleasure…before the pain?"

"I hate you," I whispered as his snake-like gaze swept over my face.

"The things I'm going to do to you." Hunger replaced the scary, smug arrogance, and suddenly his lips caught mine in a kiss that had my insides twisting. His forked tongue slid between my lips, tangling expertly with mine.

I didn't move my lips, but I didn't push him away either…I knew it wouldn't do anything to change what was happening.

What I didn't admit to myself…not even a little bit, is that a part of me wanted this. I wanted his ruin.

"Kiss me, poison," he rumbled against my lips as I tried to bite him instead.

He fisted my hair and I whimpered. "Kiss me."

Suddenly I found myself sucking on his tongue, his fingers pressing expertly on my swollen, throbbing clit.

His licks against my mouth were aggressive…and filthy. Every swipe echoed in my desperate pussy.

"Sure you won't miss this?" I purred, not recognizing the sass coming out of me. Something in his eyes sparked at my words, and I wondered if he was really capable of killing me.

He'd saved me from the worm creature when it would have been much easier to let me die.

There was a guttural noise in his chest at my words and he deepened our kiss. His tail wrapped around my neck as he ate at me.

It was always like this with him. He pleasured me like he owned me. Like he owned me, but he hated it.

My fingers dug into his thick shoulders as violent, disgusting arousal grew inside me.

I was embarrassed at how horny I was acting in the face of this murdering asshole. But he'd trained my body for years to respond to him. They all knew how to touch me expertly. They all knew how to make me crazy for them.

Before they'd come to my dreams, I never would have thought I wanted it painful…or rough.

Now I was desperate for it.

His breaths were heavy against mine as his tail tightened and my breathing turned into gasps. His finger moved from my clit to stroking leisurely through my folds until tears were running down my face because I was so desperate to cum…

"Poor little poison. Do you want me to let you cum?" He asked the question wickedly…but his tail was too tight around my neck for me to respond with anything but a moan.

"You want to be my good girl, don't you? You're desperate for it."

He abruptly pushed his fingers deep inside me, and I hiccuped a sob as he briefly loosened his grip around my neck to let me gulp some oxygen down before he tightened again.

"You want my cock. You want my cock more than anything. Don't you?"

I felt like I was going insane. He was edging me over and

over. Every time I got close to falling over the edge, he'd stop me.

And there was no escaping it. The world would start to black around the edges as he cut off my oxygen…and he'd release me right before I passed out.

Sweat and tears were dripping down my skin.

"You're dripping," he murmured, taking his claw-tipped hand and licking my juice off of it. He pretended to savor it… or at least I thought he was pretending.

"Maybe you're right, poison. Maybe I would miss the way your cunt tastes…"

He swiped his finger through my folds again and this time brought it up to my lips, forcing it into my mouth so I had no choice but to taste the salty, earthy flavor of myself

"Maybe I would miss the way your cunt chokes my dick," he whispered. He moved his wide crown to my opening, his reptilian gaze locking with mine…and then he surged into me, eliciting a sharp scream.

He was huge.

For a second I lost all thought. There was only the feeling of him inside me as my pussy worked to accommodate him.

He gripped my hips, his sharp claws digging into me, making small cuts in my skin that had rivulets of blood running down my legs and ass.

It was the ultimate mix of pain and pleasure. There was something freeing about a hate fuck, about the loss of blood and oxygen. My mind was soaring high, my attention fixed on the thick column of flesh currently wedged tight in my body.

"Maybe I would miss how wet you are for me. Or your pretty, desperate little screams." He bent over and licked between my breasts and then around each nipple in a torturous figure eight.

His tail was tightening around my throat with every word

that came out of his mouth, like he was furious he was even saying them.

"Maybe I would miss how well you take me. Better than any other lover, poison. Maybe I would miss how you actually are…my good girl."

My eyes widened at his words…but then he was lifting my hips and thrusting into me so hard that what little air I was getting—thanks to his tail—disappeared.

I cried and he laughed, all sharp teeth and shadows.

Suddenly, something whispered against my asshole. I was confused, wondering if I was imagining it. His tongue was on my skin, his hands were gripping my hips, his dick was barreling in and out of me…his tail was still wrapped around my neck.

Whatever it was, it softly circled the beyond sensitive rim. A shocked, scared yelp burst from my lips, the sound cut off by the tightening of his tail.

"Shhh, little poison. It's only me," he whispered. Shadows curled in my vision, and I thought I was passing out for a moment…before realizing that it was him. It was his shadows pushing into my ass in the perfect mimicry of his thrusting cock.

I was sobbing by this point. There was so much pressure. His fucks were desperate and hungry.

They were not the fucks of someone who didn't care at all. Who was just getting his rocks off before he dumped my body into lava or something like that….

I was catapulting off the edge—finally—the starlight ceiling of the cave multiplying as sparks filled my vision. This was the hardest I think I'd ever cum.

"Maybe I would miss the sounds you make," he rumbled before his tongue went back to laving at my nipple.

His shadow dick and his cock were working in sync, pressing in at exactly the same time. Sharp pleasure emanated through me with every hard thrust. My hands were holding his horns like a lifeline, like they were the only things keeping me tethered to the earth.

His sharp incisor teeth bit at my skin, pinpricks of pain just like his claws. And then blood was running down the front of me as well.

And still, he continued to move, his tail loosening like he could read my fucking mind, catching me right before I passed out.

"Maybe I would miss you too much, little poison," he finally whispered as he came with a loud roar that echoed around the cave, bits of rock falling around us.

And then his tail strangled me, and this time it didn't let up.

As the word faded around me…even as I came one last time, I thought I heard him murmur to me…

"Forget."

CHAPTER 4

BLAKE

"This way." Tempest grabbed my hand to guide me across a thin, rickety bridge. It stretched out between two towering buildings that could easily be mistaken for alien pods from a movie. Though the monster realm of Wyld might as well be fiction considering that such a place shouldn't exist.

And yet, there I was, living amongst monsters, falling head over heels for them too.

We'd been walking for ages through the city, and for the life of me, I couldn't remember where we'd come from or what I'd done beforehand. Was it strange that I'd forgotten? Everything felt foggy in my head.

I kept glancing over my shoulder at the lofty towers, the endless bridges that connected every building like the veins in a body, keeping everything together. And that strange feeling sat on my mind that I'd forgotten something important.

When the bridge wobbled beneath me, I released a small squeak, my hand desperately seeking Tempest's. We walked on metal panels linked together by chains that were only three feet wide, and they made a terrible racket. The surface was rough though, like someone had glued sandpaper to it, which my feet gripped onto, thank goodness.

Tempest's large hand slid across my lower back, stealing my attention, drawing me to stand in front of him. "Keep walking. We're already halfway across the bridge."

I blinked at him over my shoulder. There was something strange about Tempest—the times I'd spent with him in the past tended to result in him growling at me, making it clear he didn't love my company. So why was he being helpful now?

Had the world gone topsy turvy, or was this another of my crazed sex-induced dreams and we were about to have incredible sex while hanging from this bridge? Did I mention things felt fuzzy in my head?

With a nudge of his hands at my waist, we were moving forward once more on a bridge that had me feeling like we were in a circus walking a tightrope.

A few wrong steps and I'd fall over the edge to where the drop went on forever. The faint orange glow far below us was the lava the city has been built over. And the longer I stared down there, the harder my heart pounded and my feet slowed.

"What if we fall? And why in the world doesn't this stupid bridge have a railing? Oh my god, why are we on this bridge and where did we come from? I feel so lost." A manic sensation came over me, fear of falling, or was it feeling lost, all culminating into a huge ball of me freaking out.

Tempest, his breath feather soft on my cheek, whispered, "In Wyld, it's said that fear is an indicator that you're about to do something really brave."

His words played on my mind because it wasn't something I'd ever expect to hear from him.

"Now, get moving."

Exhaling deeply, I tried to embrace the confidence in myself, which I clearly lacked in that moment. "Just so you know, I'm not a giant fan of heights at the best of times, and nothing you've said is calming me down. But being carried might be my new favorite thing in the world." My words were on fast-forward while sweat dripped down my back.

His chuckle only irritated me. I'd made it out this far across the bridge before I came to my senses. What was another fifteen feet forward?

The bridge suddenly jiggled and jumped beneath me. My brain hit all the panic buttons, adrenaline shooting to the sun and back.

I screamed, backing into Tempest, shuddering. "What the fuck's going on?" I cried out, my fear so heavy that tears filled my eyes. I was about to tumble into the abyss.

With Tempest's tight grip on my waist, I twisted my head around to him, only to find him staring at something behind us. A blue bug with at least a dozen feet, standing as tall as a Great Dane, stepped onto the bridge, not pausing either as those long, spiky legs struck the bridge.

The hideous creature unleashed a screech, its three black eyes blinking at us in unison, mouth opened and filled with serrated teeth that he snapped at us.

What in the world was that, and why was it moving so fast toward us?

"Oh, you better get moving," Tempest warned, his voice darkening. "The Tylepede has just challenged us to a battle if we don't get out of its way. And the challenge involves wrestling it."

"But…I-I. What?" I couldn't get words out, yet the bridge kept shaking, and when the thing started charging, something came over me.

Panic.

I lunged forward and ran, finding bravery and energy where seconds before I had none.

Leaping off the bridge, I swung around, recoiling to give it space. My mouth dropped open when I saw Tempest and the giant blue bug strolling across the bridge, shoulder to shoulder, swaying like two drunk friends as they laughed at me.

That fucker. He'd tricked me. I rubbed at my chest, my heart still racing from getting across that death trap.

Once they reached me, the bug made another noise that sounded more like it was blowing a raspberry at me, then it scuttled away.

"Real funny," I called out after it.

I raised my gaze to Tempest, who grinned like the devil, and I wanted to shove him off the bridge.

"You lied!" I accused him.

That evil grin on his human face shouldn't do anything but anger me, but his conflicted expression confused me.

"It got you to cross the bridge, didn't it?" He snorted the smart-ass comment.

I tensed all over. "That's not the point, and–"

He didn't even wait for me to finish talking before he swept me off my feet so fast that I lost my breath. With me cradled in his arms, he murmured. "We need to move faster and you're too slow."

My face heated, my head and body warring because after all these years of having sex with him, I couldn't get my body to stop craving him. He didn't say a word though to imply he was similarly affected; he was just his usual aloof self.

He took off and we moved at lightning speed, heated air buffeting against me, tugging at my pink hair. And I couldn't stop wondering what had brought on this change in him... Tempest was never kind to me.

When we finally came to a stop, my head spun. "We're back home," he stated, setting my feet back down right in front of the enormous monster castle, its lofty towers, with the balcony circling it, casting a shadow over the city.

A terrifying growl pierced the air from behind me, and I jumped, bumping into Tempest.

I twisted around.

"Blake!" Creed called as he burst out of the front doors that lay smashed open, his eyes wild with panic. "You're safe."

Before I got the chance to respond, let alone think through a response, I was in Creed's arms, being swung around, his kisses peppering my face. He seemed to have missed me, but where had I'd been? The longer I remained attached to him, inhaling his deep masculine scent that drove me crazy, I started to remember things.

A huge battle outside the castle, my monsters furious, and attacking… "Steele," I gasped. Then it came back to me how they tried to catch him, to kill him. My heart splintered.

"It's okay," Creed hushed me, still holding me close to him, even if my feet were now on solid ground. "Steele won't hurt anyone for now. I thought I lost you."

"He'd never hurt me." I pushed off Creed, wincing at the hatred behind his voice. "Why would you lose me?"

But Creed didn't seem to hear me as he turned abruptly toward Tempest. "Where'd you find her? Did you take her?" The accusation rang through the air, but it left me desperate to know too, considering I couldn't seem to remember what happened after the battle.

Tempest stepped closer, his face serious, and he kept glancing at me cautiously as if he was searching for something. "I found her wandering aimlessly down by the Hunting Lands. Poor thing was lost and couldn't even remember how she got there."

"How the fuck did she make it past the walls?"

He was running a hand through his hair, eyes wider than normal. "Beats me, but luckily I found her before she started wandering into the woods."

"Fuck." Creed slapped a hand on his shoulder. "It's good you found her, but I need to know every damn detail."

"Why don't I remember any of this?" I squeaked.

But before Creed or Tempest could respond, large arms

wrapped around my middle, and Ash's laughter sliced through the air. "You found her. It's a miracle she's intact."

"Why does everyone think I was dead or something?"

He had me twisting around to face him in his human form, cupping my face, and his lips were on mine, the kiss so passionate, so intense, my toes curled in my sandals.

"I can't lose you," he breathed against my mouth. "Ever. You know that, right?"

"Ash, I'm so confused. I don't remember getting lost. I can't remember where I was, or how I got there. And I'm worried about Steele. He's still alive? Please tell me he is." A sob hitched from my throat just thinking about him dead.

His milky blue eyes pierced right into my soul, though I knew they couldn't see me. My monster, Ash, was blind. I studied his gorgeousness, his lips curled up with worry, his unkempt hair falling over his forehead. Those sharp cheek-bones and beauty that made him a god in my eyes.

"Steele is safe for now," he said, disgruntledly. "But what's the last thing you remember?"

My gaze wandered upward, where those vulture-like Avis birds flew overhead, as I attempted to recall the details clearly. How Ash, Seven, and Creed fought against Steele. How I'd discovered the man I'd fallen in love with on earth was here in the Shadowburn realm, and it turned out he was a monster this whole time.

My stomach tightened thinking of the memories of them tearing each other apart, of seeing their blood slice through the air. These men—or rather monsters—had somehow crawled into my heart. To witness them trying to destroy each other… destroyed me.

I glanced over to Creed and Tempest who had stepped farther from us in a heated discussion.

"The last thing I remember is something hard hitting me in the back of the head," I said, glancing up at Ash as my hand moved to the spot on my head and I winced at the bump. "Then the next thing I knew, I was traipsing through the city with Tempest."

We were in a city of monsters, so while my heroes were busy fighting like animals, someone could have dragged me away for their own intentions. That in turn sent a shiver up my spine of what they could have done if Tempest hadn't found me.

It was at that exact moment that I caught movement to the right of Ash.

Seven. He marched past a creepy spider guard, arms swinging by his side, coming right for us fast.

His eyes were immediately on me, his mouth parting with shock. He was next to me in seconds, embracing me, his body shuddering, his soft words in my ear. "I'm so thankful you're okay. We were about to burn the city down to find you."

My heart fluttered to hear the ache in his voice. He'd missed me.

"It's a miracle," Ash added from behind me, not missing out on the chance to join in the hug, though Seven did pull back suddenly. It felt as though he remembered that things between us hadn't exactly been smoothed out since he'd forced an orgasm out of me against my will.

I still wanted answers why he was acting like such a fucking jerk, and something inside of me hurt to have him pull away. Every inch of me begged for his touch, for him to do something to eradicate this void between us. The urge was so overwhelming I almost raised the point of our discussion then and there, wanting to find out what his problem had been. It was obvious he cared, and yet he'd pushed me beyond my limit.

The thought left me more confused about my emotions, my missing memory, my worry for Steele.

Creed's and Tempest's footsteps drew my attention as they returned to my side, and I found myself surrounded by all four monsters, their warmth embracing me. I noticed Tempest had stepped back, glancing out elsewhere like he'd rather be anywhere but here.

"You were all so worried about me, it almost makes me feel special," I murmured, pushing a smile on my face even though I was more than a little overwhelmed and confused. "But maybe someone can take me to see Steele now?"

No one rushed to respond, but by their disgruntled expressions, I didn't expect them to. Creed's powerful hands grasped my waist and twisted me around to face him gently. His jawline tightened, but I didn't want to hear what he had to say. I'd seen them fight to kill Steele, and I suspected it had everything to do with them believing he decapitated their queen. I'd learned from the others that Steele had once been part of their inner circle, it would have been the worst betrayal to them that he'd killed their queen.

I refused to believe that he'd do that though. It would go everything against what I knew about him.

Which admittedly…wasn't exactly that much.

"I know what you're going to say," I admitted, holding my arms tight by my side. "But that doesn't change that I want to see him, that I'm asking you not to kill him."

His shoulders rose and fell heavily, then he licked his teeth with obvious agitation. Ash's hands were clenched by his side, Seven remained silent, and Tempest studied me with a dark demeanor, much like his usual asshole self. He never said a word.

Creed's large hand cupped the side of my face tenderly. "We'll talk about it later. First, I want to celebrate that we didn't lose you."

God, he was frustrating the hell out of me.

"My king," someone yelled in the distance, though in truth, it sounded more like a screech.

We all turned in unison toward the closest bridge that led away from the castle, manned by huge spider guards. I shivered looking at them.

My attention was quickly diverted to another guard, who appeared more humanoid, if you ignored the bald, round head covered in blinking eyes. His nose and mouth were tiny in comparison.

"My king," he announced, falling to one knee before Creed, glancing up, and every eye honed in on him. Well, except for the one above his ear, which turned to stare at me.

Was he doing that to everyone around him or just me… because it was freaking me out.

"Speak," Creed barked, which had the wandering eye swinging back to his king.

"Incredible news. Rachidra has given birth to the city's first baby since we lost our queen. It's healthy and everyone is cheering. Some are already celebrating."

The news struck me as I remembered them talking about the monsters' inability to fall pregnant for so long, so this was a miracle.

All the men around me gasped, and within the span of a few seconds, everything spilled into pandemonium.

CHAPTER

BLAKE

It was chaos on the streets as we made our way to Rachidra's home. News of the first successful birth in Wyld since the Red Queen's death had spread rapidly. The monsters had given up hope… Creed had said the celebrations would most likely last a week. In the human world, I knew a lot of new mothers wanted some peace and quiet initially after a birth, but that was evidently not the case in Wyld. Almost immediately after the birth, one of Rachidra's men had come to the castle asking…for me.

So here we were, headed through the streets filled with raucous monsters, about to meet my first monster baby.

The monsters were…interesting and terrifying on a normal day, but watching them right now…it was a miracle my eyes didn't fall out of their sockets with how far they were bulging out as I stared at the world around me.

We'd just passed a mutated locust monster, except a locust from your nightmares because it was at least three times my size with four sets of pincers. It had a long, string bean type appendage between its legs which I assumed was its dick. And it appeared to be extremely intoxicated. As were all of its companions—smaller, round groundhog-looking creatures with short spikes instead of fur and razor-sharp incisor teeth that extended down to their stomachs. The locust monster was swaying around in a strange dance…urinating…as the groundhog monsters danced around it…like the urine stream was actually a water sprinkler and they were children running through it on a hot summer day. It was both fascinating and disgusting to watch.

Seven caught me staring and chuckled lowly, the sound of it reverberating through my insides, straight to my core. I was glad to see the spark of life in him. He hadn't been the same since that moment with his…other self? It was hard to characterize the personalities residing in Seven, some much scarier than others. As if he could read my mind, his smile slipped away and he went back to staring morosely at the streets laden with creatures.

Shaking my head, I turned back to monster watching, jumping when I saw a giant Venus fly trap creature burst from the ground a few feet away from me, a coiled black vine reaching out to snap up one of the groundhog creatures. I waited for it to spit it back out, but a minute later I realized that wasn't going to happen.

"Ash," I murmured anxiously. He was walking next to me, holding my hand, occasionally swaying it back and forth playfully like we were out for a casual, romantic stroll.

"What is it, sweetheart?"

"That giant pod thing just ate one of the groundhog creatures. Is that allowed?"

I knew Ash couldn't see what I was gaping at, but his senses were so evolved to make up for his blindness, it was as if he could see.

"Mmmh. It's very much allowed. The *bellistones* are pests. They breed like your rabbits do on earth, and the *chamataras* keep them in check." He sniffed the air. "There must have just been a birth. They don't usually gather in packs like that."

The *chamatara* burped loudly just then, and I jumped again. Ash snorted. "Want me to kill it?"

"No!" I squeaked, nestling into his side as it scooped up another *bellistone*, this one emitting a loud screeching sound before it was gobbled up by the *chamatara*.

The city, Wyld, was fucking crazy.

I'd known that before, but it was reinforced on the daily.

"What's the praying mantis thing called?" I asked, glancing behind me to see that somehow…it was still peeing all over the *chamataras* who must not have realized yet they were being systematically eaten.

Ash frowned. He was in his human form today, I think to be a comfort to me because he could sense I was nervous about visiting the new monster mother. But I found myself wondering if I could ask him to turn back into his other form.

He was terrifying…and I'd come to find it very sexy.

"I don't think I'm familiar with the 'praying mantis,' he mused. "Creed?"

"Isn't it that the bug that eats the head off its mate after they fuck?" offered Creed, turning his attention from a pack of small devil-looking monsters that were doing some sort of synchronized dance.

I snorted. "That would be the random bug fact you know….but yes. It's that one."

Creed searched the monsters around us until he found the one still…peeing. "Mmmh. That's a *qualime*. Disgusting things. But they're fun to party with."

"Please tell me allowing someone to pee on me isn't some weird kind of ritual here I'm expected to participate in someday soon," I drawled, shivering at the thought.

"I'll take whatever you can give me, baby," joked Ash…or at least I thought he was joking.

I hoped.

Ash let go of my hand and wrapped his arm around my waist. "I'll protect you from the big bad *qualime*." He brushed a kiss across my forehead, and I shivered at the way the tender move made my heart flay open and bleed.

I was feeling too much.

That wasn't what this was.

That wasn't what this was ever going to be.

A flicker of a dream…or memory ran through my head, of moments where I'd wished for more during all the orgasms.

Sometimes it felt like Ash wanted more.

"Rachidra's home is right up there," announced Tempest, pointing to a scraggly black tower stretching towards the blood-soaked sky. Dark crimson banners with a gold ball symbol were sticking out of the walls all the way to the top.

"Fertility banners," murmured Seven, awe in his gaze as he stared up at them. "It's been awhile since I've seen those."

There was a reverence to all of their demeanors that grew as we approached the entrance. The monsters gathered around this tower were also quieter and more respectful than their counterparts we had passed on our walk earlier.

I froze. "What if they ask me to hold it?" I whispered frantically, tugging on the front of his shirt.

"Ask you to hold the baby?"

"Yes," I practically screeched, prompting a weathered rock-looking monster to make something that resembled a shushing sound, like I'd wake the baby inside.

"Then you hold it…" Ash answered, his forehead wrinkled in confusion.

"Is there any special way I'm supposed to do it?"

Ash was gently moving me forward as I freaked out, and we were now at the immense, onyx-colored door that led into the tower. The same gold symbol had been painted on the middle of the door.

"You just hold it," he offered…unhelpfully as Tempest raised his hand to bang on the door. Before his fist could even touch the door, it was flying open, and there was the closest thing to a cyclops I'd seen in Wyld standing there in the doorway, staring worshipfully at my...the monsters around me.

He was a dark forest green color with a large emerald eye taking up the majority of his bald, perfectly round head. The eye was beautiful, with at least five different shades of green in it and long dark eyelashes that would make any human woman weak with envy.

I was definitely envious.

He murmured something softly in a language I didn't understand. Creed and the others all said a single word back to him that sounded like "asham."

Then his gaze blinked to me. His eye widened…and tears began to stream down his face, so copious that they completely soaked the brown robe he was wearing. "We are so honored," he sputtered through his tears.

I shot a panicked look at Ash, wondering what I was supposed to do, but he just squeezed my waist...again, unhelpfully.

"I'm so happy for you," I murmured, and then panicked even more as he sobbed harder, pressing his hand across his chest like he was having a heart attack.

"You're happy for *me*? After you've done so much for us. The rumors are true. You are…"

Before he could sob out even more, a mottled grey-colored monster with tiny yellow horns and a long snout appeared behind him and slung an arm around the cyclops guy, pulling him back against his chest and laying his chin on his head affectionately. "Cyprus, darling. I know the baby is making us all emotional, but you're going to scare our honored guest."

Cyprus wiped his eye with thin grey fingers and long black nails. "I'm sorry. Please come in. Rachidra will be so happy to see you."

The grey monster moved Cyprus out of the way so there was a path for us to walk. Creed walked in first, ever the king, and then Ash led me after him. Cyprus and the grey monster were both watching me closely as we passed, and I gave them a small smile that had Cyprus bursting into a fresh round of tears.

I didn't have much time to think about the odd encounter because the hallway we were in was very short...and just beyond it was a giant grey room with a red marble swirl ceiling and red stone walls...and the baby.

The female I assumed to be Rachidra was seated on a squishy, red chaise lounge cradling a crimson silk-wrapped squirming...baby tightly to her chest. "Your highness," she murmured to Creed, before her gaze immediately flicked to mine.

"Blake?" she asked, my name rolling awkwardly off her blue-tinged lips. She was beautiful in a monstrous way, dark blue tendrils falling to her waist, moving like there was a breeze blowing. She had four long fangs peeking over her full lips, and her eyes were the same blue as her skin. She reminded me a bit of Raven in the *X-Men* films.

"Rachidra?" I answered, her name sounding just as awkward on my lips. We both grinned and giggled, and immediately the panic that had been flooding my veins dissipated like waves receding from the shore.

Cyprus and the grey monster appeared in the doorway. Cyprus had managed to stop crying but upon seeing Rachidra and the baby, he was tearing up again. The grey monster rolled his eyes affectionately and shot Creed an apologetic glance.

"Drakon, I'm sure you've done your fair share of crying as well, knowing you," jested Seven, sounding more...happy than I'd ever heard him. I turned to stare at him, shocked to see he was staring at my stomach, his violet eyes gleaming. What in the world?

Drakon chuckled and led Cyprus over to Rachidra, bending down to kiss her...a kiss that quickly escalated to the point that I was half expecting Rachidra to be pregnant again.

Cyprus was swooning as he stared at them.

It was fucking adorable.

The swaddled baby made a slight cooing sound and Rachidra and Drakon finally separated, their attention going to the squirming bundle.

Rachidra murmured nonsensical things, which seemed to be a common trait between monster and human mothers to their offspring, and moved the red blanket to reveal…

The cutest creature I'd ever seen.

The monster baby was lime green with a full head of fuzzy blue hair sprouting all over his cute little head, and oddly, tiny yellow horns. I'd have to ask about monster procreation capabilities, because that baby seemed to have traits from all three of them. His two eyes were the same incredible green as Cyprus's.

I was obsessed.

I gasped when he opened his cute little mouth and yawned widely, and his gaze seemed to track me.

"He's perfect," I murmured, and then all three of the new parents were crying. I glanced at Creed anxiously, but he seemed to be enthralled by the sight of the baby, his gaze laser-focused on the tiny bundle.

"Would you do us the honor of holding him?" Rachidra asked through her tears.

Creed

I was a king. I didn't make it a habit of withholding things from myself; I didn't have to. If I wanted something, it was done.

Usually.

Watching as Rachidra handed her miracle to Blake was testing every cell in my body. I was desperate. Desperate to fuck Blake. Desperate to breed her. I wanted her stomach rounded with our child, I wanted her breasts to leak her milk. I could see myself suckling on her rosy-tipped nipples, drinking from her. They were already sensitive without pregnancy, and I could just imagine the little cries she'd give me then.

I wanted to fill her with my cum, again and again until she was so full of my life source that it was gushing down her legs, her pink pussy flushed and plump from me taking her over and over.

She'd have my baby. I'd make sure of that.

It was just about timing.

If she knew how obsessed I was with her, how every thought I had, every breath I took was for her…she'd run. She was definitely what the humans called a flight risk.

I glanced over at Ash, noting the amused smirk on his face. He could obviously sense how petrified she appeared holding the baby. She was completely stiff, her eyes wide and terrified as she stared down at the child. Monster babies were extremely resilient. If she dropped it, absolutely nothing would happen to it. Quite different from their human counterparts.

Rachidra was patiently trying to arrange Blake's arms so it was more natural, but after a second, Drakon gently pulled her away…probably because of the crazy eyes Seven was giving her for daring to touch Blake.

We were all possessive of her, and it was growing every day.

I tried to discreetly adjust my raging hard-on. Seeing her hold a monster baby was almost too much for me to handle. I bit down hard on my lip, trying to keep out thoughts of her pink pussy plump and overflowing with my seed. I was desperate to fill her up, for her to milk all the hot cum out of me. I needed to breed her.

It wasn't a desire anymore. It was a fucking necessity.

Blake would have my baby.

I just needed to convince her of that.

———

Seven

Blake was killing me. Watching her hold that baby had all sorts of images in my head. And all of them involved her heavy with my child. Our child. Images of sharing her with Ash, of pumping her full of our seed…they were on constant replay.

Her initial terror at holding the baby had faded after a few minutes. Now she was gazing down at it, her eyes misty as she stared at the baby lovingly. I could just see her with our baby.

Getting her pregnant would serve another purpose as well…keeping her here with us forever. Willingly.

There was always the chance one day she'd wake up and decide that a life full of monsters was too scary for her tastes…or she'd be done with our bullshit…my bullshit. And then things would get really complicated because none of us were willing to let her go. If we could breed her, maybe she'd never get to that point. Maybe she'd be so wrapped up in our child that she would forget we were monsters. If I could only get the demons inside of me to cooperate.

I noted Creed adjusting himself and I felt that pain. Since the first night we'd come to her, I'd been a horny bastard. All I could think about was pinning her down, licking her slowly, tasting every inch of her body. I could never get enough.

I imagined her down on all fours, her stomach huge and rounded, her lush hips firmly in my grip as I fucked her…her soft mewls filling the room.

"Down boy," Ash whispered, nudging me with his tail, the only monster part of him today.

She's ours, he whispered. *He* didn't like other males in the room. *He* did like the sight of Blake with the baby though, and he pushed for dominance…I'm sure to try and mount her right then.

Not today, asshole, I seethed, gritting my teeth to try and stay in control. Blake glanced up and her mouth dropped, I'm sure seeing the strain on my features.

"Get it together," Creed murmured, and thankfully *he* decided to heed our king's warning and once again retreated back with the others.

I could see the indecision on Blake's face, wondering if she should come towards me. I hated that I was so messed up. I could never be whole for her. And while the other six demons inside of me were relatively harmless…*he* was not. She'd never be safe while I had no control over him. I couldn't repeat what happened the other day, when he'd taken control and…

I could never be with her like I wanted.

I turned away from the sight of her holding the baby. The scene had gone from sweet torture to painful torture.

And I'd had enough of that for a million lifetimes.

———

Blake

The monster baby, Luco, was nuzzling into my chest, and I swear my freaking heart had melted into a puddle of goo. He yawned, and my eyes widened when I saw rows of tiny incisor teeth.

"Um…he doesn't use those when he's feeding…right?" I asked tentatively, blushing when Rachidra and her mates all chuckled.

"He retracts them…most of the time," she said with a slight wince. I shivered just thinking about the times when he didn't. The baby made a soft gurgling noise and began to nuzzle more into my chest.

"Looks like he's getting hungry," Rachidra murmured,

casting a cautious glance at the guys before she reached out for the baby. I awkwardly handed it over to her, admiring how she made it look so easy. She settled back onto her lounge chair, popped her boob out, and began to nurse. It was still a shock how "free" everyone was with their bodies here, but this was something I could definitely get behind. I thought a mother feeding her baby was one of the most beautiful things I'd ever seen…even if I wasn't so sure I could ever be that confident in the act.

I gazed over at the guys and took a stutter step back when I realized all their attention was on me. And the looks on their faces were so…hopeful? I wasn't sure what that was all about.

Drakon took that moment to step forward, carrying a small jewelry box type item in his hands. The material of the box resembled red stained glass. It matched the rest of their decor perfectly.

"There is no way for us to repay you the gift you have given us," he murmured, Rachidra and Cyprus's rapt attention on the two of us. "But we'd like to give you this gift as a token of our appreciation." Drakon slowly undid the lid, revealing a gold knife with a ruby-encrusted hilt. It was gorgeous…and extremely expensive looking. "This has been in my family for thousands of years. It is said to give good luck to whoever bears it." I opened my mouth to object to the gift. All I'd done was have really good sex with my monsters, not anything to deserve this overwhelmingly beautiful gift.

I felt Creed's dark, overwhelming presence behind me. "Accept this gift, Pet. You would put shame on his whole household were you to reject it," he murmured.

Oh fuck. I definitely didn't want that.

I reached out my hands for the box and all three monsters' shoulders slumped with relief.

"Thank you so much for this gift, and for inviting us into your home. Your family is beautiful," I said softly, my voice thick with emotion.

Cyprus burst into tears, lightening the mood as everyone chuckled at him—well, Rachidra, Drakon, and I chuckled; the rest of my monsters just looked a little less scary.

Or maybe that was just in my head.

"We need to be on our way," Creed said in that demanding way of his, as he nodded at Drakon and placed his hand on my back to usher me toward the door. Rachidra's face fell at his pronouncement…and then Cyprus began to cry hard.

"I'll definitely be back if you'll have me," I spit out quickly, overwhelmed with how happy their expressions were after I said that.

I didn't think I would get used to this…people—creatures—actually wanting to be around me. I mean, it was mostly about sex and the lust energy I was providing everyone, but hey, to have anyone liking me at all felt good.

Creed led me to the entrance and then out into the street, which had filled with even more monsters, and all I could think was…so this was what happiness felt like.

The only thing that could make it better was if Steele was here.

I was going to have to work on that.

CHAPTER 6

BLAKE

"Hi baby," Steele's voice murmured as my eyes opened. I cried out when I realized I wasn't in my bed where I'd fallen asleep wrapped around Ash…I was in a small pool of water surrounded by lush palm trees…

And I was completely naked, the warm water a soft, perfect caress against my skin.

"Just a dream," he said, coming up behind me and wrapping his arms around my waist.

Right…because he was in a monster prison in real life.

I turned in his embrace and threw my arms around his neck.

"Steele! I've been so worried about you! Are you okay? Are they torturing you down there?" I asked urgently, searching his face for any signs of trauma.

We had so much to talk about. He had a lot to explain. But before all of that, I needed to make sure he was alright. He'd been the one source of light in my life for many years.

That didn't change overnight.

"I'm fine. It takes more than a dungeon to take me down, baby." His voice sent shivers through my insides. I reached up and pushed some of his raven-colored hair out of his face, those arctic blue eyes staring at me as if I held his soul in my hands.

"You're so beautiful, Blake." His lips grazed my shoulder and a soft moan slipped from my lips. I shook my head, trying to concentrate…but it was hard when his every move seemed intent on trying to seduce me.

"Creed won't talk to me about you at all. Every time I mention your name, he closes off."

"Mmmh. I have a plan," he replied, his tongue joining his lips as he moved them from my shoulder to my neck…and then made his way up.

"Well, do you need any help?"

Steele's hands slid down my back until they were gripping my ass, his fingers sliding between my cheeks and stroking from my asshole to my core. I moaned louder this time.

"What I need help with at the moment, sweetheart, is getting inside your tight little cunt."

"We should probably talk," I whispered, my words coming out half-hearted and weak. His hands moved to my waist and he shifted me gently towards my back so my chest was arched up to him like an offering. He kissed my breasts, nuzzling my nipples for a moment before he sucked on one. "Steele. I have a million questions," I breathed.

"We will. You'll know everything about me someday soon." He moved to the other breast and suckled on the tip harder, his teeth grazing the skin, my breath coming out in sharp gasps. "But I need to taste you right now. The worst thing about that cell is not being able to touch you. I tried to give you some space in your sleep…but I couldn't stay away."

His tongue moved lower, lapping at my skin as he traced a line from my breasts, around my belly button, to the apex of my thighs. Steele moved me back further in the water, and this was quite the dream…because the water seemed to cradle me as I reclined, holding me in place so I stayed afloat with no effort.

He pushed my thighs wide, and then his mouth was on me. He took his time licking me, like he was savoring my cunt. "You're mine, Blake. You'll always be mine. You taste like fucking heaven."

I whimpered as his dirty mouth went to work, his tongue dipping inside of me, fucking me slowly until I was a mindless mess. I gripped his thick, silky hair. The water melded over my breasts, plucking at my nipples in time with Steele's tongue.

What the fuck kind of water was this?

I wanted something like this for my room.

I obviously wasn't thinking clearly.

Steele sucked on my clit, his fingers back around my ass again, dipping all over as he feasted on me.

I erupted, his tongue and the magical water fingers too much for me to handle.

"I love you. I love you. I love you," I screamed as I shook my head back and forth, shattering into a million pieces.

"What was that, baby?" he asked in shock, moving his head away from my folds.

It took me a second to realize what I'd just said…very loudly. "I—"

"I know you love me, Blake. There's no way that the gods would make me this obsessed and in love with you…only for you not to feel it too."

Before I could say anything else, try to explain it away or something, he reared back and pushed his massive cock inside me. He stretched me, his thickness taking away my breath. The vibrating I'd experienced before with him started again, pressing against every pressure point inside of me until I was screaming my devotion once again as he chuckled darkly, those incredible eyes of his boring into my soul.

He drove into me, every move belying his possession. I wrapped my legs around him, moving with him as best as I could as he spiked the flames inside of me.

"Fucking obsessed with this cunt. You're so beautiful, baby. I'm so in love with you," he groaned as his strokes grew more and more powerful with every thrust.

The orgasm this time was a spiritual experience. And a tear fell down my cheek as he thrust into me, because it felt like he was connecting with my soul.

And I hated that.

I hated how vulnerable that left me, that he could seal himself to me like that. He was wrapping himself around my heart.

And when he ultimately broke it—because how could a lying monster not—it was going to destroy me.

Steele fucked me through my soul defying orgasm, rutting in and out of me until my voice was hoarse from my screams, and I was at the tip of what I could handle.

"You're mine," he growled, as he began to cum, my insides flooded with his heat as I came right along with him, my body squeezing and drawing as much of him inside as I could take.

I passed over the precipice then, my body finally falling into darkness, all the pleasure wrung out of me.

"I love you, Blake."

I sat up, blinking slowly, half expecting Steele to be there in bed with me…but of course, he was nowhere to be found.

Determination flooded my veins. I'd get answers. Today. Screw Creed and whatever he had to say about it.

I quickly got dressed, scowling at my pink hair in the mirror as I scrubbed at my face. I was not in a "pink" mood today, and it made me look far more cheerful than I actually was.

Taking a deep breath, I left the bathroom and opened the door of my bedroom to step out into the hallway.

I froze when I remembered I couldn't just jog on down to where they were keeping Steele.

Because I had no idea where in this place that was.

Which meant I had to ask Creed about it, and I was sure he would be a huge asshole about my request.

Taking a deep breath, I started off down the hall, hoping

Creed was eating breakfast or one of the others could tell me where he was.

I walked across the bridge where Tempest had wrapped his tail around my throat, a fluttery sensation building inside at the thought. I'd been terrified that night…but also a bit turned on when I thought back on it and was honest with myself.

Wasn't sure what that said about me.

Remembering the flying monsters I'd seen outside before, I hustled across the bridge, not interested in seeing one of them up close again.

As I made it near the dining area, voices ricocheted along the hallway, nervous and frantic. A shiver slid across my skin as my steps slowed in anticipation of what was ahead.

Turning the corner, I found a group of servants gathered around something I couldn't see. None of my monsters were around, but as soon as the servants noticed me standing there, they moved, making a path for me to walk forward. I hesitated, not sure if I wanted to know what they'd been looking at…but eventually, I womaned up and walked through the crowd.

I frowned when I saw they'd all been staring at a large puddle of goo.

It took me a second to realize what exactly it was.

But the floating shark-like teeth finally tipped me off.

The pile of goo was Freddy. Or at least it had been Freddy.

There was a commotion, and suddenly Creed was pushing through, his golden gaze tracing my features a bit obsessively.

"Blake! What are you—" His words cut off when he saw Freddy. He obviously recognized the goo at once and shock flashed across his face before it went suspiciously blank.

"Take a step back, Blake," he ordered in a too-calm voice as he pushed me back and then crouched down, pulling something that resembled a thermometer out of his pocket and sliding it carefully into the goo.

The device immediately flashed red, and the fervor of the small crowd gathered around us turned into a low roar.

"What does that mean?" I murmured nervously as Creed stood back up, his lips curled up in concern. "What happened to him?"

"He starved to death," Creed answered, and dread flared in my chest.

Because that was supposed to be the whole reason I was here. My lust was supposed to be feeding the city.

And if that wasn't working...what would happen to everyone?

What would happen to me when they realized I wasn't useful anymore?

CHAPTER

BLAKE

I was pacing in my room, my stomach in knots, unable to get the puddle of Freddy out of my mind. I assumed the crazy amount of sex we'd been having was doing its job to feed the city's population. But evidently, it hadn't been enough.

Creed told me to stay in my room while he and the others headed into the city to find out what was going on, so here I was, close to losing my shit. If we couldn't feed the population, would they even want me here? Would they send me away or worse yet, search for someone else to replace me?

A small gasp grazed my throat at the thought, and my chest burst into a fiery jealous mess.

Frustration needled through me too; I couldn't just sit around not knowing. I was going crazy.

Unable to take it a second longer, I stepped out of my room, deciding I had to find one of my monsters and get answers.

The hallway stood empty and eerily silent. I entered the elevator and confidently said, "Balcony." The location might give me a vantage point to spot their whereabouts.

A raspy voice from within the walls stated, "Bakehouse."

I was startled. "Wait, no. Balcony." I emphasized the last word carefully. But I was suddenly lurching sideways, and we were moving. This elevator never listened to me, and I suspected if a monster was living in the wall, running on a hamster wheel to move this tin box, he hated me.

We were moving too fast, and my insides lurched.

I pressed my back to the wall to stop myself from falling over, my heart racing because it felt like I was suddenly on one of those spinning rides at a fair.

I cried out, "Stop!"

When we finally came to an abrupt pause, the contents of my gut were in my throat. I rapidly stumbled out, trying to escape the sensation of the world turning around me.

The sliding sound of the doors shutting left me standing alone in a hallway that I could only imagine was the basement, considering the lack of windows and its dingy feel.

The dark stone walls in front of me were chipped, fiery torches hung from the ceiling, and there was a really musty smell in the air. When I stepped forward, the soles of my shoes made a sucking sound from the stickiness. I didn't want to look too closely at what covered the stone floor.

I didn't want to be here at all actually, so I hit the elevator button on the wall.

Then I waited and waited.

And I waited some more.

Groaning under my breath, I was convinced the elevator monster was fucking with me. "Fine, I'm sure there are other ways to get to the balcony."

Turning, I wandered down the eerie hallway, picking up speed, and checking out every corridor I passed. Most led into darkness, and with no signs, I didn't want to get lost.

Finally, I paused in front of arched, double doors. Curiosity getting the better of me, I knocked, and when someone grumbled *enter*, I pushed on the handle.

The door swung open to a long, narrow room with a

counter running along the one side, with an oversized deep sink. All kinds of kitchen knives peppered the wall. Shelves covered the other side, filled with bowls. They appeared to be flowing with slime in various colors. Gross.

Movement at the end of the long room called my attention to a shadow shifting, and someone emerging.

A sliver of fear rippled over my skin, and I held onto the door handle with a death grip.

What in the world was that? I couldn't take my eyes off the skeletal monster that stepped forward. Long arms with gnarled fingers dragged on the floor, its head round with orb-like eyes and two horns sticking out of the side of its head. They bowed outward with the tips touching higher over his head.

"I was wondering when I'd get the honor of meeting you, Blake," he said with a gritty voice like he was chewing on rocks.

"You know my name?" I gasped.

He threw his head back and made a terrifying sound of teeth chattering. "It's all everyone's been talking about. The little human who has enough power to feed monsters. It must be quite unusual for you to be in Wyld."

"*Unusual* is a good way to describe it," I murmured, still standing in the doorway, which made me comfortable as it gave me an easy escape. Well, as far as the elevator since the knobhead hated me.

"Your essence has been extraordinary to feed on, so fresh and slightly peppery." He reached for something on the shelves and came back with a bowl overspilling with tentacles. I might have assumed it was an octopus, until he dumped the contents on the counter, revealing a snail-like creature with tentacles running along its sides.

Slime stretched from the bowl to the mammoth snail, and I gagged.

"Well, that is until the last couple of days or so," the

horned monster said casually, pulling a butcher knife from the wall, sounding slightly disgruntled. "There are all kinds of rumors flying around about it, of course."

"Like what?" I found myself entering the kitchen out of pure curiosity.

Despite his terrifying appearance, he studied me with soft eyes when he twisted in my direction. "Many are saying that perhaps as a human, you are not strong enough to keep up with the king and his men to feed us all."

He spoke so casually, while panic and a sliver of anger laced my blood. What if that was true? Did I want to face the reality of that? But...it had worked so far, so why had it changed now? With the thought came a scorching determination to show them I was every bit as good in the role.

"Of course, they blame me," I blurted out, my breath catching in my throat. "Maybe it's a temporary glitch, and I just need to do more."

The corner of his mouth curled upward. "Yes, you need to be fucked more."

Narrowing my eyes on him, I couldn't tell if he was being sarcastic or playful. But when he returned to his work, I guessed he was being serious. Monsters in Wyld fed on the energy created by Creed, Aspen, Seven, and Tempest when they had sex with me. I didn't fully understand the mechanics of it, and sure, the whole thing was strange, but so was a different realm where creatures of nightmares lived in a city built over a lava pit. There was no such thing as normal in this world.

The skeletal monster suddenly brought the knife down hard, carving halfway down the snail, and I flinched at the slurping sounds. The thing fell apart in half, more slime pouring out of it. I kept swallowing back the gagging reflex pushing forward.

"Give me a moment to finish this dish, then I'll show you something that might help."

I nodded, my heart hammering as fast as the monster was chopping that snail until all that remained were tiny cubes of the grey gelatinous thing. Which in turn reminded me of Freddy, and I was left feeling like crap that he was dead…or probably dead. You couldn't be sure of anything in Wyld I supposed.

Grabbing an empty plate from the shelves, he swept the cubes into it with his hand. Setting the plate down, he wiped his hands on a filthy dish rag, then offered me a smile, full of blunt teeth and a pale gray tongue.

When he stretched his back, he stood at least seven feet, not counting the horns, and I blinked up at him, feeling tiny in comparison.

"Bane is my name," he stated proudly, grabbing the dish and patting my back.

Already I felt the sticky slime seep through my shirt where he touched me, and I shivered. I'd have to burn the top.

"Nice to meet you, Bane," I finally said. "It's good to talk to someone new in the castle. So, you're a chef? What's with the dish of…" I wasn't sure what to call it. "I thought your kind didn't need physical food?"

"They're called vexlings. These pests are all over the city, chewing through everything—cords, walls, clothes, even our ears when we sleep—so we eat them as a delicacy There's no nutritional value to them for us, but we love the sticky texture." He made a slurping sound with his tongue, which wasn't helping my revolting stomach.

"This way," he muttered, lifting his chin toward the other end of the long kitchen.

I followed him, shadows gathering around us to the point where, for a few seconds, everything went dark, then we emerged into another room, which surprisingly wasn't half bad. Gone was the filthy kitchen and slime, replaced with what I could only describe as a monster cafe.

Tables and stools littered the oversized room with vibrant green shrubs and tangled vines covering the walls. In the middle of the room stood a spiral metal staircase which ascended to a small platform where half a dozen monsters were talking and drinking something out of long horn-like cups.

Overhead, more greenery spread over the ceiling along with huge globe lights that lit up the room. I'd never seen anything like it, but it would make a good spot to enjoy reading a book while sipping on hot chocolate. As long as there was no snail slime in my drink.

A strange humming song played in the room, soothing the atmosphere, and there were fluorescent green moths fluttering around the place. I batted one out of my face when I caught a man with two heads staring at me, all four eyes blinking at the same time. Was he judging me for not feeding them enough?

"This way," Bane said to me, and I stayed close.

"What is this place?" I asked, moving fast to keep up with his long strides.

"An escape for everyone who works at the castle to catch up with colleagues, to enjoy a small treat, or simply to get away from their boss." He made that teeth-chattering sound again…laughing at his own joke, I assumed.

I decided then I liked Bane. Just because he appeared terrifying, didn't mean he couldn't be nice too.

He set the plate of snail cubes in front of a young couple who at first glance could be mistaken for humans, with green hair and bright emerald eyes, but the moment the plate slid onto their table, thin, long tongues jutted out of their mouths and snatched up a morsel, reminding me of lizards.

Loud chewing and lips smacking was kind of revolting, so I was glad when Bane moved on quickly. I followed him up a set of steps at the back of the room and came to an area tucked away in the corner. I gasped at the sight because the little section was encased by a massive birdcage. We stepped in through the open door, the space taken up by two leather sofas with a round table in the middle. Vines grew all over the birdcage, entwined around the metal bars. Across from the doorway stood a circular window that overlooked the city.

Bright light spilled into the cage, its warmth relaxing.

Something giddy rose through me at this little hideaway.

"This spot is gorgeous. I could see myself hiding up here," I admitted, rather liking the vibe.

"Good, and now that you know the location, I recommend making use of it with the king and his men."

I kept turning the words over in my head, 'make use of it.' Surely, he didn't mean having sex in the birdcage?

"This seating is reserved for our king and his royal party only. No one else is permitted to use it, so it's yours, and you also have privacy from the rest of the room." He was folding his long arms around his middle, which looped all the way around and back again, his weird version of folding his arms.

"Another reason for this escape room is to let those working at the castle also experience a powerful feeding when the king and queen visit this Cage Room."

"Oh," I gasped, and I suddenly didn't want to sit on any of the furniture, thinking that Creed and the others had sex with the queen in here. It was strange to feel jealousy for someone I'd never met and who was long gone. But for all I knew, they still missed her…craved her.

"Thank you for showing me this place," I said softly, inching toward the cage door, figuring I might try my luck with reaching the balcony once more to spot my monsters. "But I should be heading back."

"Nonsense, you just arrived," Bane insisted, unraveling his arms and taking my hands into his long skeletal ones, his touch icy cold. "I will bring you a cold beverage while you relax."

I might have almost vomited at the thought. "You're very

kind, but I'm not thirsty or hungry. Please, I don't need anything." I didn't want to be rude, but I couldn't eat or drink anything from this place after seeing the snail.

"There are books you can read in the drawers under the table too," he exclaimed, making his way to the doorway where he paused. "Please do me the honor of staying here a little while as it will calm those downstairs if they think you might be here waiting for our king to feed them."

"B-but I don't know where Creed is and—"

"Yes, yes." He waved me to quiet down. "But they don't need to know that. Everyone has been so on edge the last couple of days with the lower food supply, and unrest is spreading through the city, so I'm trying to bring some calm where I can. But you need to hurry and spend more time with the king and his men." There was a dark desperation behind his voice, the hunger everyone must be experiencing, leaving me feeling horrible.

I nodded, figuring I'd go along with it. It was the least I could do, seeing as I felt absolutely terrible about starving people. What I needed was for my monsters to get back already.

Bane gave me a thankful smile, ducked his head through the doorway, and stepped out of the cage.

Sitting on the edge of the couch, I gazed around, trying really hard not to overthink how chaotic my life was becoming. To distract myself, I pulled out the drawer beneath the coffee table, thinking it was an odd place to keep books. It turned out that these weren't exactly books, but more like magazines. I grabbed the top one that had a photo of a blue monster with deep blue dots all over her body and her tail curled around her middle, her long golden hair draped down her body, falling to her knees. She was quite beautiful. Though her hair would take a lot of work to keep it so shiny and perfect.

I started to flick through it, deciding that I'd leave after a few minutes as there had to be an easy way out of the cafe that didn't require patrons to go through the kitchen or the elevator.

When I landed on a page where the blue female was being bent over and someone else's tail was pushing between her spread thighs, I dropped the magazine instantly. Mostly out of shock that I was flicking through a monster porn mag. What the hell!

But as if on cue, the moment it hit the floor, someone cleared their throat from the doorway. My gaze shot up to where Creed filled the entrance to the cage.

Raven black hair dangled over his shoulders, glowing red eyes that screamed predator, and a face sculpted so perfectly, he could be a god. I couldn't deny that even in his monster form, he turned me on. He wore tight, black pants and shirt, and his chest was ripped with sculpted muscles and calling for my touch.

Butterflies burst through me at seeing him, at the thought he'd found me, and with an audible gulp, I jolted to my feet.

"You're back," I murmured.

His eyes gleamed, his nostrils flaring, taking in my scent. "You've missed me, I see," he stated, his gaze sliding to the magazine at my feet. It was only when I also glanced down that I realized the page had flipped over to one of a minotaur monster holding the world's biggest cock and a tiny snake-like monster kneeling in front of him with her mouth gaping open.

I flushed all over. "I-I wasn't looking at that." God, could I sound any more guilty. I picked it up quickly and stuffed it back into the drawer. "Anyway, what did you find out?" Was it suddenly really hot in here?

"We have a big problem," he announced, sauntering across the cage and to the window. He held out his hand to me. I accepted it, my fingers curled with his, and he drew me to stand in front of him, both of us staring out the window. It didn't take me long to notice smoke curling upward from three spots farther across the city.

"Are those fires?" My muscles strained because I feared the worst.

"Protesters," he muttered, his voice darkening. "Families are starving, so many are furious and lost about what to do. They're angry at me, threatening to burn down the whole city if I don't fix this now."

Every single nuance of feeling in my body seized up, and fear twisted inside me. I tightened my hand around his and glanced up at my king. He ran a clawed hand along the side of my face, and I didn't need words. I knew exactly what he was thinking.

I pushed myself up on my toes, twisting around to reach his face. I kissed him softly at first, then I licked his lips, the sharpness of his teeth cushioned against mine.

"Let's head back to our room and give the city what it needs." I stepped back, his hand in mine, and I tried to draw him with me across the cage.

"We're not going anywhere," he murmured from behind me, his voice low, hunger already in his tone. He stood still, pausing my attempt to guide him. Before I could get a word out, his woodsy, masculine scent slammed into me.

My knees weakened, and an inferno unfurled in waves through me. It was a small miracle that I didn't just throw myself at him.

He flashed me a grin, and I might have melted. This was the thing that didn't make sense to me... there wasn't a lack of sensual arousal between us or sex. Just thinking of my dream with him the other night sent my heart racing, but if the city demanded I get fucked more often by four sinful monsters, I guess I'd take one for the team.

There was no time to feel shy about Creed intending to do it here in this cage, not when he drew me back to his side, our bodies clashing. I squeezed my thighs together, flaming the building ache.

I took a deep breath, and on the exhale, whispered, "I'll do whatever it takes to help the population."

Before I was aware, Creed lifted me off my feet, his mouth crashing to mine, my heart thumping. Not a single thought beyond the way he kissed me with a sinful mix of gentleness and forcefulness, his tongue exploring every inch of my mouth. He knew how quickly his kisses left me weak-kneed and utter putty in his hands. When he captured my lower lip into his mouth, sucking on it, he gave it a light bite with his teeth.

I moaned, so lost to the arousal consuming me that I tugged on his shirt, which he peeled off and tossed aside. He pressed me against him once more, his huge monstrous body solid, powerful, and scorching hot to the touch. My panties were drenched in moments, sharp jolts of pleasure shooting through me.

"I don't know how much more I can wait," I murmured, my voice raspy, my body on the verge of bursting.

"You're beautiful when you beg for sex." He swept his tongue across my mouth possessively. "You have no idea what you do to me, Pet. I think about fucking you dozens of times a day, and the time I get with you is never enough."

Our mouths clashed once more.

I moaned, pouring all my tension into my kiss where Creed tasted sweet and dark. He had me pressed up against the side of the sofa, grinding his groin into me, his erection impossibly hard.

His mouth was on my neck, teeth scraping my skin, leaving a blaze of kisses trailing to my collarbone. "You're everything to me. I'll never let you leave my side."

He curled his fingers into the low neck of my dress and roughly tugged on it, the top buttons ripping and freeing my breasts. They bounced out, to which Creed growled with delight, his eyes practically fucking my tits. His long, forked tongue lapped at my hard nipples aggressively and roughly, as he pushed my breasts together for him to tease them both simultaneously.

While sucking on them, he grabbed my ass and kneaded it, grinding me against his cock.

I felt a sharp piercing sting over one nipple, and I yelped, staring down at the two lines of blood rolling down my breast where he'd bitten me. With an excited groan, he licked my blood.

My breaths grew to short pants, my hands combing through his wild dark hair, my fingers curling around his two long, black horns. They were cold to the touch, and so smooth, they felt incredible when the rest of me burned up.

He tore his lips from my breasts, lust burning behind his eyes.

A sound somewhere downstairs caught my attention, and I glanced at the open birdcage door. "What if someone comes up and sees us?" I gasped.

"Does it make a difference when they're already feeding on our lust, and soon they'll hear you scream? We aren't shy in Wyld; we don't hide the pleasure of sexuality."

Nothing in this world was rational, I should have known that, but I hadn't lived in this realm long enough to become accustomed to such differences just yet.

When he pinched my nipple, I cried out, slick dripping past my panties. His touches short-circuited my brain, leaving me unable to think beyond needing his huge cock inside of me. Nudging his leg between mine, I took the chance for some relief because I was beyond frantic with need, practically humping his thigh to intensify the friction on my aching clit. I was going crazy.

On the inside, I was aflame, and I gripped onto his powerful shoulders to bring him down to me.

I'd completely lost control, stroking myself back and forth over his thigh. "It's not enough," I whined.

"I promise it will be very soon." His words danced in my mind while he bunched up my skirt, pushing it to my waist. His fingers hooked across my hip, then ripped my panties off without pause. He balled them in his hand and pushed them into the pocket of his pants. Then he removed his thigh from between my legs and replaced it with his hand.

Thick fingers slipped over my slick folds, dragging across them. My hips rocked over his sinful touch, needing him to hit the right spot, but he was teasing me still, I knew that. He was dragging out the feeding, but there was only so much a girl could take.

"Please, Creed. Because if you won't play nice and give me what I want, then I'll have to make you wait too." I started to shift my hips to show him I meant it.

A hardness gripped his face, and he pushed one of his fingers into me, drawing me closer to him.

I mewled, my back arching, my nipples hardening. "That's it."

"Whose pussy am I fingering?" he growled, his tongue licking my lips.

"Mine," I answered with a moan.

But when he pressed two fingers inside me, then pushed and pulled out, his thumb on my clit, he held me in a place of complete control over me. We both knew it. Arousal was roaring within me, and I craved more.

"Tell me again, Pet, whose pussy is this?" Unrelentingly, he fingered me, slick slipping down the insides of my thighs with the things he did to me.

Pressure gathered as he stroked faster in and out of me.

Moaning, I held onto him to keep me upright, the shocks of pleasure intensifying to the point where I could barely stand on my own. Then he pulled out completely.

A small growl rubbed on my throat, a fiery hunger coming over me, overriding all my sanity.

"Let me hear it," he insisted.

"Yours. Fuck, Creed. My pussy is yours."

He made a slow pass of his thumb over my mouth, then pushed his two fingers inside, the ones covered in my slick.

"That's a good girl. Now turn around for me and let me make you scream."

With his fingers licked clean, I twisted around to look away from him.

"Is this how you want me?" I wiggled my rear at him.

He slid his hands over the curves of my ass, his clawed fingers pressing against my skin. "My beautiful pet, you're fucking perfect."

He dragged his fingers over my drenched offering, sliding over my swollen lips and all the way up my ass, over my puckered hole.

"You're ready for me."

When he withdrew his hand, I glanced over my shoulder as he pulled his pants open and dropped them, revealing his huge red dick with two heads.

A jolt of desire licked over my pussy at the promise of pleasure he offered, and as much as I attempted to gather myself, I failed miserably. I lifted my ass higher, so eager for him, I was about to cry if he didn't hurry the hell up.

"Your smell is my addiction," he admitted as he rubbed his tips over my drenched pussy, pausing at the entrance. "Are you ready for me, Pet?"

"Yes," I gasped. "Please don't make me wait."

He laughed, deep and throaty, then pushed both heads into me.

I dipped my head forward, gripping the couch as he worked into me slowly at first, making me feel every inch of him. I absolutely loved knowing he had me dripping for him, that he could turn me on enough to take his huge cock.

He was stretching me, and it felt so incredible I cried out for more, rocking my hips for friction.

"Fuck me, my monster. Fuck me hard," I begged, my insides gripping his heads tightly.

He growled, his clawed hands grasping my hips, their sharpness biting into flesh. He pushed forward; the sloshing sound from how drenched I was had become music to my ears.

Sinking all the way in to the hilt, I cried out at how fucking huge he was, leaving me completely undone. He fucked me, nothing soft about the way he claimed me...

My king was rough, slamming into me to the point where I bumped into the couch, our force driving it slightly forward with each pounding.

Groaning, I rocked my hips to meet each of his slaps, both of us moving in a manic rhythm. It was an act of discipline in itself that I hadn't exploded yet...I held back as much as I could to lengthen the sensation, so I could keep feeling like I floated on clouds while he completely ruined my pussy.

Our grunts escalated, the couch scraping the floorboards with each pump—something everyone in the castle could probably hear.

I glanced over my shoulder to where Creed in his monstrous form threw his head back, howling as he fucked me with his monster cock. He moved unbelievably fast, that friction I craved close to lighting me on fire.

"That's it, Pet, take my cock like you were born to ride it."

At this stage, my knees had given up, the couch taking all my weight. But Creed wasn't having that when he slipped an arm under my stomach and lifted me higher, holding me against him as he kept on hammering into me.

I'd lost thought over everything. Unrelentingly, he kept on taking me again and again, my hands steady on the couch.

And before I knew it, my climax crashed over me, coming so hard, it destroyed me.

I shuddered in his arms, a scream scrapping my throat raw, my body completely giving up. Creed wrapped an arm across my chest and lifted me up so my back sat flush to his chest, his massive cock still buried deep inside me.

But he wasn't finished, he kept on fucking me as I shook with my orgasm. He wasn't far behind though, and snarling, he trembled as he shoved himself balls deep, and burst with his orgasm.

Spilling his seed into me, he kept on pulsing, filling me to the point that cum started to run down my inner legs.

I kept crying out from the magic that tingled over my body, my voice turning raspy, both of us riding the pleasure train to fucking Nirvana.

I didn't know how long it was before we finally settled, but I was completely full of cock and cum.

Sucking in sharp breaths, I tried to calm myself after being fucked roughly enough I knew I'd be sore tomorrow.

"How are you feeling, Pet?" he whispered in my ear, his tongue on my neck.

"Like I'll never walk again," I joked. "But it was incredible. You're always so much rougher when you're in your monster form."

"Not too rough, I hope," he asked, a tenderness in his voice that I adored.

"The perfect amount. Though I seriously don't think I can stand on my own for a little bit."

His kisses melted over my neck and shoulder, his large, clawed hand holding onto a breast as he held me up. I was under no illusion that this was over. I still felt him inside me, hard as a rock.

Our rushed breaths started to slow, and with it came the reality of where we'd had sex and that I had no idea how I was supposed to leave this cage without leaving a puddle of cum behind me. One thing was certain though--I was completely lost to my monsters, unable to get enough.

"How do we get back to our room without me flashing the world? My dress is torn and, well, we're both a bit of a mess…"

"Blake, I have no intentions of stopping fucking you. I'll carry you back to your room." He blinked at me, his voice matter-of-fact, and a ripple of arousal rolled through me. He set me on the couch, then went to collect the shirt he'd discarded and offered it to me. "Put this on to cover yourself."

"Thank you." Dragging the shirt over my head, I was about to stand up, when Creed lifted me into his arms.

"I've got you. If you're sore, I'll carry you everywhere you need to go."

I laughed at him because I was capable of walking. What I was experiencing was more a case of feeling a sweet ache from how hard he'd taken me, how much he'd stretched me.

I wasn't going to complain though if he wanted to carry me back to my room. I was all for avoiding the walk of shame through the café. They all knew what we'd been doing. I wasn't really interested in everyone knowing what I looked like when their king fucked me hard.

Cringing on the inside at that last thought, it was too late to do anything about it, so I wrapped my arms around his neck and tucked my head against his chest.

To my surprise, Creed didn't head downstairs, but rather took a small corridor in the opposite direction that eventually brought us out to a doorway. He placed his palm against a panel near the door, and it opened for us instantly.

We were suddenly in an elevator and rushing upward.

"I'll soothe your sore pussy with my tongue once we reach your room," Creed informed me, staring at me. "Then I'll claim you again from your sweet ass, and bring you to orgasm at least three more times."

I gasped aloud at that, already out of breath from one.

He kissed my forehead. "I want to keep you happy while I feed my city."

I was in a haze from the amazing sex, but it was hard to miss that this terrifying monster sounded like he almost cared. My pulse sped up, convinced I'd swoon right off my feet if he wasn't carrying me.

We left the elevator, and excitement flared across my skin that we were about to tear down the castle to my screams. Every instinct inside me yelled this was exactly where I was meant to be. And with a grin, I prepared myself to have my brains fucked out.

Again.

CHAPTER 8

CREED

My gorgeous, little pet was ravenous in bed, her sweet pussy greedy for my cock. She couldn't get enough, and I gave her everything she pleaded for and more. I bit her, licked and sucked everywhere, and even now, that intense wave of desire raced through me, calling me back to her side.

My cock throbbed, adrenaline pumping through my veins in memory of her beauty, of how deeply obsessed I'd become. I'd never experienced such a powerful need for a female before. Never felt this overwhelming hunger even for our red queen…What had awakened inside me for Blake was fucking intense and new.

She'd fallen asleep in my arms after her fourth orgasm, completely spent, so I let her rest and came out onto the main balcony.

She'd begged me to take her to see Steele several times, but I couldn't bring her more heartache because once we got rid of Steele, she'd be devastated. It was better she kept her distance from him. Even if she hated me, I needed to protect her, and one day she'd understand my actions. Maybe even forgive me.

I sighed with the heaviness settling over my heart.

In front of the castle gates, a crowd was protesting, calling for an explanation, wanting us punished for starving them. Guards held them at bay for now, but for how long?

I could feel a thin layer of the feeding energy I'd generated with her. I'd drawn it inside of me. Except...normally after sex, our power rippled thickly in the air, and now it was barely enough to keep people from dying.

It did my head in because it made no damn sense.

The hours we'd spent fucking, her orgasms alone, should have fed the entire city two times over. So, what in the world was going on?

Smoke rose across the city in the distance where the Wyld residents were burning buildings in protest over the past day. My army was dealing with them, but my stomach hardened with worry that nothing I did was enough.

I'd been struggling with keeping them well-fed since we lost our queen, but I honestly believed we had a solution with Blake. For a while there, the energy we supplied had been bountiful, but then overnight it seemed to have faded.

I gripped the railing of the balcony, my knuckles turning white as my thoughts tumbled over one another. My heart broke to hear the cries from my people. I felt fucking useless.

Someone had done something to block the energy. That was the only explanation I had.

It seemed to start after a certain unexpected asshole returned to Wyld. I didn't believe in coincidences, and I sure as fuck wasn't going to let him get away with it. He'd killed our queen, attempting to starve us back then, so it wasn't a stretch to assume he was back to finish us off.

I twisted around, fury on my mind as Ash and Seven appeared, both in human form and looking disgruntled.

"It's not working," Ash pointed out the obvious. "It was barely a taste, let alone to satisfy the people. How long before they revolt by storming into the castle, demanding our heads?"

Seven stood there, wearing all black as normal, saying nothing. He'd been distant lately, which was unlike him, but with every muscle in my body coiled with stress, I had to focus on our major problem first.

"I suspect Steele's responsible," I stated, already marching back inside and heading to the elevator.

Ash and Seven followed on my heels.

"Then we kill him," Seven murmured without hesitation. "He's killed our queen, and he's back to do it again? Fuck that. He needs to die." His words echoed off the walls, mimicking my own thoughts.

Inside the elevator, I growled, "Prison." We started descending, and I turned to my men. Ash said nothing, but his brow furrowed, and rage ignited behind Seven's gaze.

"It adds up," I stated. "He came back for Blake, hating that we claimed her every night for years, while he tried to steal her back on earth. What better way to achieve this than distract us with the city going into total bedlam."

Fury thickened in the elevator, but I could still smell the sugary sweet scent of Blake's slick, fogging my head to a state of utter madness. I was desperate to fix what the fuck was going on because I wasn't giving her up, now or ever.

Once we reached the basement, we stormed into the underground tunnels.

Heat poured upward from the stone floor, as we had built the dungeon as low to the lava pit as possible to ensure our enemies suffered. Each breath stung my nose and dried the back of my throat.

Darkness rose around us as we left behind the lights. Down here, there was nothing but shadows.

We passed a single lit torch cradled in a metal basket on the wall, and Seven snatched it, carving through the dark with it. The heavy stench of sulfur deepened, and sweat trickled down my back, bubbling across my forehead from the heat alone.

Thick chains hung off the walls, bugs scuttling out of our way

It was unbearable at the best of times, but today, it felt oppressive.

The light from the torch stole the darkness, revealing a cell built into the wall, and inside, Steele hung from the ceiling by chains around his wrists. Seven set the torch in a metal basket near the cell.

The floor trembled, and I glanced over to a monstrous beast, round as ten barrels, over eight feet tall, with four arms, each grasping an ax, and a plaited beard that reached halfway down his belly.

"My king," he rasped, his voice darkening. "I wasn't expecting you today."

"Neither was I," I answered truthfully, prepared to leave the fucker down here for as long as possible. "Open the door," I commanded.

He gave a slight bow of his head, drew out an oversized skeleton key, and unlocked the door. Then he retreated into the shadows, watching just in case Steele broke free. Not that he'd get past the three of us.

My boot kicked the door open right as a creature with three horns the size of my fist scurried across the floor in front of us.

The thump of my footsteps echoed, rebounding off the walls.

Perspiration ran down Steele's face, his clothes sticking to him. He hung there in his monster form, but these cells were built to withstand even the strongest of us.

His eyes opened, almost glowing against the light. He growled at our presence, then barked out a raspy, dry laugh.

"Couldn't keep away from me. Tell me you've brought my Blake."

"She'll never be yours," Ash spat, hurling a fist into his gut before I even got the chance.

Steele sneered at us, his upper lip curled over sharpened fangs. I snatched him by the throat, holding him close.

"If it wasn't for Blake, you wouldn't be breathing right now," I barked in his face. "But that can change in a heartbeat, and Blake *will* find out the truth of your betrayal and lies, about you murdering our queen in cold blood!"

He never flinched once, but licked his dry lips, his eyes narrowing on me. "Fuck you, Creed. All this time and you still don't believe me. We were like brothers once. It baffles me you still haven't worked out the truth of how broken and corrupt Queen Eruthria was. She sure as fuck had plenty of enemies. We all know this, so why are you so damn determined to pin this on me?"

"You keep saying the same shit," Ash snarled, while Seven lingered close, crazy desperation in his eyes to attack. *Soon*, I thought.

"If you want to start proving your innocence, then remove the curse you placed on the city," I stated abruptly.

He blinked at me, then at Ash and Seven. "What the fuck are you talking about?"

Seven lunged at him that time, shoving him out of my grasp and hammering into him. Steele thrashed and kicked, and I knew he'd been dying for this moment.

Blood splashed, primal grunts filling the space. Ash lingered near, wanting his chance. But the more I watched Seven beat Steele, the more I suspected he wasn't going to break. The bastard had never broken once; even when he'd been captured by an enemy city and tortured for a week…he still gave nothing away. He'd later told me he was prepared to die before he shared anything.

There was only one solution then. Kill him and the curse should die with him.

"Enough," I snarled.

Throwing a last strike to Steele's face, Seven retreated, blood dripping from his balled hands.

Steele swung in the middle of the room, blood running down his face, which hung forward, and he groaned…before chuckling maniacally.

"Is that your plan?" he grunted. "Blame everything that goes wrong in your city on me? You're going to feel like a real fuckhead when you discover how wrong you've been. Then I'll make you grovel before I consider forgiving you lot."

"You're so jealous that Blake wants us, you couldn't stand it. You'd rather starve the whole city than lose her to us." Hatred laced Seven's voice.

Steele spat blood on the floor, then stared at Seven with a twisted glare. "I didn't put a damn curse on the city. Why the fuck would I want them to starve? I've grieved so much in the years I've been away from my homeland, from the people I considered family. I wouldn't put them in danger, you fucking psycho." He heaved for breath, his words fast and loud.

Seven's shoulders curved forward, staring at him with daggers in his eyes.

One word from me, and Steele would be dead.

One word that would also destroy Blake, but this was bigger than all of us. Without feeding our city, everyone would die.

Anger rose through me, at the fires and protests, at nearly losing Freddy, and most of all, at the heartache I was about to bring my beautiful pet.

"This ends now. We kill you, then the curse is lifted," I growled, furious at Steele for making me do this. I grabbed a blade from the sheath on my belt and approached him.

Panic blanched his face. "Creed, don't do this." He

thrashed, wrenching at the chains keeping his arms above him.

As if on cue, Ash and Seven lunged to his side and grabbed hold of him to stop his kicking legs.

"I don't take pleasure in this, but I also won't be fucking betrayed by someone I once considered a brother." My chest constricted, fury bubbling over my mind. I snatched him by his hair, forcing his head to the side, exposing his neck.

The sting of grief suffocated me, the hurt-filled resignation clawing at my insides because killing someone who was once a friend was going to ruin me. But as king, there were hard decisions I had to make, ones that would save the city. They needed me.

That meant doing the shit work I wouldn't wish upon anyone else.

I lifted my hand, my fingers grasping the leather hilt, and I met Steele's terrified gaze. "Any last words?" I growled, the ache in my chest deepening. Ash and Seven didn't say a word, but their silence darkened my thoughts.

In this situation, there was no light. No savior. Only the need to finish what had started all those years ago when our city had been thrown into chaos from the death of our queen. This ended now.

A drop of perspiration ran down the side of Steele's face, his mouth opening with what I could only imagine were well-calculated words at his last attempt at survival.

"I call for a Red Battle," he commanded.

"Fuck that," Seven stated. "We destroy him now and the curse will be lifted."

"And if it doesn't?" Steele blurted with a growl. "I never killed the queen, and I didn't curse the city. You know me better than this. Give me the chance to prove my innocence. And if I'm guilty, then kill me in front of everyone."

I drew in a sharp breath, part of me wanting him to be guilty so we could finally end this and move on from the shit-storm of our past. But another part considered his request. He'd been like a brother to me growing up. We shared everything, and fought side by side. To have someone I trusted infinitely kill our queen, it felt like he'd gutted me and destroyed a part of me that day. Blake came to mind…if I allowed this…she'd see his guilt firsthand.

"Maybe it's not a bad idea," Ash muttered, pushing to stand alongside me. "We're all unsure, so this will give us concrete knowledge. The truth needs to come out, so what's another day to wait?"

Seven roared his protest.

I stilled with the word *truth* in my mind. Something I'd been wanting since the queen's death. Killing Steele now would never give me absolute closure to her murder. But maybe the Red Battle would.

So I reluctantly nodded, giving the man I once protected with my life his last chance.

"Agreed. We hold the Red Battle. And if you're found guilty, Steele, you will be killed in front of Blake once she discovers who you really are." My arms dropped by my side, my tense muscles across my back knotting.

"That's all I ask," Steele stated with relief in his voice.

My stomach clenched, and bile spilled into the back of my throat that I still had no solution to my starving city.

Without another word, we marched out. The cell locked with a click and we left him hanging in there.

"Are you sure about this?" Seven grumbled.

"Why not?" Ash retorted before I got a chance. "How could he possibly cheat his way out of this?"

"If anyone can find a way, it's Steele," Seven answered with a growl.

"I don't think he'll be cheating his way out of this," I murmured under my breath. I hadn't once considered the Red Battle because, in my mind, Steele had been guilty of the queen's death. "Whatever happens, we'll get the truth and finally settle this. Get preparations underway for the Red Battle as soon as possible."

Time was running out to find a solution to our city before everyone tore it into the lava…with us in it.

But with that thought, an idea came to mind…

CHAPTER 9

ASH

Just visit the Cliffs of Doom to set up the *Mad Battle*, Creed had said. *It'd be fun*, he insisted. "Like fuck it is," I groaned under my breath, hearing the thump of footsteps behind our beast-drawn carriage, the hissing breaths of the creatures tracking us.

The hot breeze speared through my hair, bringing me their scents, and I shifted in the front seat of the carriage, whipping the reins over the animals drawing Seven and me faster through the dusty deadlands.

I inhaled the dry, dusty-scaly smell, telling me we were dealing with reptilian fuckers. By the sounds of it, I calculated there to be at least half a dozen of them and they'd been following us for a while.

Seven and I raced through the worst part of the city where only the most dangerous and desperate lived. Considering everyone had been starving for the past couple of days, many residents were at a breaking point. Of course, if they attacked us, it would mean their immediate death, but when you were already so close to dying, what did you have to lose?

Everyone was pissed and wanted revenge for their suffering, and in truth, I couldn't blame them.

"Stop whining like a fucking baby," Seven growled, shifting around in his seat, whipping his reins over the several Derins who drew our carriage, large creatures who snorted fire. Tempest once told me that the Derins had eight legs and constantly walked around with a hard-on, hence their name meant *nine-legged beast* in our language. I suspected he was bullshitting me, but I also wasn't going to touch them across their underbelly to find out if it was true.

With so many of the staff at the castle struggling to carry out the most menial of tasks, Creed didn't trust them to set up for the upcoming Red Battle. So guess who got roped into doing a servant's job?

"You whine too much," Seven continued.

Sometimes, it was really hard to like my brother when all I wanted to do was choke him to death.

"To hell with that. Shouldn't we be with Blake, fucking her brains out and helping provide more food to everyone in need?"

"Yeah, well, I still think we should have lopped Steele's head off, then I bet we'd suddenly have the food resources flowing easily to everyone." He sounded more bitter than usual and wasn't whining about being with Blake, which was unlike him. "And I don't mind being out here, just getting my hands dirty, doing something other than feeling completely useless."

"What's up your ass, brother?" I asked, furrowing my brow. "You've been acting strange. Since when did you want to be anywhere but near Blake?"

Silence swept between us, and I tightened my hold on the reins.

"Are you going to say something, or is this like the time we had to travel into the Hunting Lands to search for escaped prisoners and you were giving me the silent treatment?"

He sighed loudly. "We were only fourteen at the time. Shoot me for being scared and blaming you for getting us into that situation after *you* accidentally released them. How about you focus on our trip and stop talking about shit."

Frustrating the hell out of me, I threw my fist out, catching him hard in the arm and sending him lurching sideways.

"You're in a pissy mood," I growled. "What's wrong? Are you stressing about the city starving? We'll find a solution for it, but–"

"Fuck, can you shut up? I just want silence. I feel like absolute shit over what I did to Blake." His breath hitched with the indication that he hadn't meant to blurt that out.

I stiffened and twisted in his direction. Even if I couldn't see him, I wanted him in front of me so I could strangle him if he didn't speak fast. "What did you do?" I snarled.

"Calm the hell down," he snapped, his voice more sorrowful than rageful. "I didn't mean to, but sometimes I can't control which one of my personalities comes forward, and it was *him* who finally met Blake."

My blood ran cold. "Are you kidding me?" My brother had seven personalities. He was twisted in the head, and, well, most personas we could handle, except for the darkest one who enjoyed torturing everyone. There'd been times when we locked him in the dungeon until that asshole returned because we'd find him hurting the staff in the castle.

I gripped the leather reins in my hand tighter, thinking about how Blake had to face him.

I sucked in the bitter, hot air as Seven spoke.

"I tried really hard to hold him back." He licked his lips. "I can tell he's as obsessed with her as I am, but he tried to show her he didn't care about her."

My breaths were picking up, and I wanted to body slam him over my knees from just hearing his words.

"He pinned her to the window and brought her to a forced orgasm. When I saw the tears in her eyes, the asshole slipped back into me, leaving me to face the mess he'd created. Fuck, I haven't been able to talk to her since. I feel like a piece of shit. I want to make it up to her, to make her understand I'd never hurt her. But I fucking did." His voice broke, and he swallowed hard.

My muscles tightened, my hands forming into fists. Every inch of me demanded I hurt him exactly as he'd hurt my Blake. With sheer strength I stopped myself because I knew my brother and how much he'd suffered with his multiple personalities, how deep inside the real Seven would never harm Blake.

And yet I struggled to sit next to him when I wanted to destroy something. I longed to swing the carriage around and race back to the city to collect Blake into my arms To kiss her all over and remind her that I'd walk on fire for her.

"I don't know how to make this right," he murmured, grief lacing his words.

"You have no idea how much I want to smash your face right now," I grumbled. "But I'm guessing nothing I do could hurt you as much as you torturing yourself. You need to go talk to her and set this straight. Get on your fucking knees and grovel for forgiveness."

He huffed a breath. "And if she doesn't forgive me?" he asked gruffly.

"Then…" I paused for a moment, feeling the sting of his anguish. "Then we'll deal with that when we get to it. But you need to make this right, and fast."

"I know," was all he said, as we continued on, my mind in meltdown at the fury I couldn't do anything with.

"Promise me this stays between us until I fix it?" He spat the words, and I felt the spittle on my face. Fuck. I wiped it away with my sleeve.

I ground my teeth, hissing my response, "I give you my word, I won't say anything, but if you do nothing about it, I'll come after you and fuck you up. You got it?" A growl rumbled in my chest, fury beating into me.

"That's fair," he conceded under his breath.

The carriage gave an abrupt shudder, then another, rocking about too much to be just the uneven ground. My pulse kicked up, and I stiffened, the stench of the cockheads following us flaring heavily in the air. They were furious about their lack of food and wanted to make us pay for their suffering, no doubt.

"They're on the carriage, aren't they?" I rasped.

"At least four of them."

"Good. I need something to smash. On three, let's break some necks."

"Fuck yeah!"

I wrenched back the reins, the Derins screeching their protest at the sudden halt.

"Three," I stated, and we both whipped out of our seats, lunging at the assholes who had no idea how terrible their timing was. I was fucking burning with rage…and they were about to find out.

———

Blake

I stepped out of the shower to find Creed sitting on the bed in my room, leaning back on his arms, completely naked and his cock erect with two red heads. We'd just finished a marathon of sex, and I assumed we were done considering he got up and left the room right afterward.

But evidently, he was back. And by the Cheshire Cat grin he wore, he wasn't close to being finished with me.

"Where did you go?" I asked, removing the towel from my head and letting it fall to my feet. Wet, pink hair tumbled over my shoulders and down my back. I roughly used my fingers to push it off my face.

He groaned, his gaze sliding over my naked body as his eyes practically fucked me. So much for having a cold shower. I'd become so in tune with my monsters' arousal that slick drenched my folds almost instantaneously when they gave me any kind of sexy look.

And Creed's look was definitely sexy.

It was sinfully seductive to have a monster look at me like he could eat me up.

"Come to me," he said gruffly, his nostrils flaring with his inhales. "You smell like you're ready for me again. Let me see how wet you are."

"You never answered my question," I pressed, moving toward him, my gaze on that gorgeous mouth and the devious things it had done to me.

"You'll see soon enough, Pet." Even while holding his human form, his tail slid from the bed and down to my feet before the naughty thing curled up my inner leg, his touch tender.

I held his gaze, my breath speeding up as his tail traced the seam of my pussy. It was a feat in itself that I still stood on my feet.

"Just looking at you naked could bring me to my knees. You're so fucking beautiful." He took my hand, drawing me to stand between his legs.

Creed's tail pressed in between my slick folds. I groaned and teetered on my feet, pressing my thighs together.

"Down, boy," I teased, pushing away at his tail.

"Don't resist me, Pet," he said.

"You know that's close to impossible, right?" A surge of arousal came over me in waves, my breaths rough with the way the soft tip of his tail teased my entrance once more. I was well aware he could morph it into various shapes. My sex quivered with need.

He sat back on the bed, lost to his own lust, his breaths quickening, the bulbous tips of his cock seeping with pre-cum.

I knew exactly what he craved, and what I desired.

I didn't hesitate and lowered myself to my knees in front of my king.

"You're so captivating kneeling before me," he purred, and I yelped when his tail pushed into me. I should have panicked, but I'd done wilder things with my monsters, so what was a bit of tail fucking between lovers?

His hand slid through my hair to the back of my head. "Taste me," he managed in a husky breath.

I leaned in and swirled my tongue across both tips, enjoying his salty tang. His hand tightened behind my head, fisting my hair as I sensed him tense at my touch. He pushed his tail in and out of me over and over, making a wet sound from how drenched I'd become. My hips rocked back and forth, desire building inside me. I started to lick him from the base and up to where it split into two tips, my inhales and exhales growing raspy with each passing second.

He stroked my swollen folds, teasing me, while I repaid the favor by pushing his two heads into my mouth, which was a miracle in itself. The trick was to take one, then slip the other from the corner of my mouth. Sure, I might look like a chipmunk with too many nuts in my mouth, but I was one deliriously happy chipmunk.

His groan flooded the room as I worked my lips up and down his shaft, his length bumping the back of my throat. Fingers tangling in my hair, he pushed it off my face, then pulled it into a ponytail that he held to guide me. I cupped his balls, kneading them softly, wanting to drive him insane. Just like he made me feel every single day.

"I love seeing your lips wrapped around my cock. Suck harder," he growled while I was panting from his tail circling my clit.

Pumping my mouth over him, I felt him tensing, his balls drawing in, his cock somehow harder.

He was about to explode in my mouth, so I went faster.

But he suddenly tugged my hair back, pulling me off his

cock, his tail slipping out of me. That was when I noticed him staring up at something behind me.

I did the same, quickly understanding we weren't alone.

I hadn't even heard anyone enter the room, but a group of guards had Steele by the arm, shoving him inside, all of them watching us. A blush warmed my cheeks, and I closed my legs immediately. How long had they been watching me give Creed head while his tail fucked me?

I shot to my feet, suddenly feeling vulnerable being naked. Invaded. Shaking.

Creed barked something at the guards to leave, and they scurried out of the room fast, shutting the door behind him.

Steele's gaze burned over me, and I stood there feeling lost and torn. "What's going on?"

Before I could move to grab something to cover myself, Creed wrapped an arm around my middle and drew me down to sit on his lap, his cock nestled against my ass.

Steele had just stepped out of the shower, hair wet, clean clothes, but the blushing red scars on his face were fresh.

"Creed, what's happening?" My gaze swung from him to Steele, who watched me carefully, then back at Creed.

"Pet, I've tried everything to feed our population, and maybe the missing element has been Steele. He returned to the city when the change happened, so what if his presence disrupted the energy? He used to always participate in feeds, so he's going to join us now and we can discover if this works."

I blinked at him, unsure if I heard right. "You were trying to kill him not long ago, and now you want to share me with him?" Trying to make sense of everything was hurting my head.

"Sweetheart," Steele said softly from across the room, drawing my attention to him. "I'm not being forced into doing this. I agreed to help. Are you comfortable with both of us fucking you?"

By the way his pants tented with his erection, I had no doubt he meant every word.

Simply staring at him sent my tummy into a fluttering mess of butterflies.

I loved the guy, even if we had so much to talk about. Everything had happened so fast between us that we never got alone time. And I doubted this would be the ideal spot to talk about our emotions or that he forgot to tell me he was a monster too. Especially not with Creed possessively holding onto me.

Steele stared at me with piercing eyes that carried a hungry determination. I missed him so much it hurt.

"Of course I'm ecstatic to be shared," I murmured, desperately wanting this to be the beginning of them mending their ways too.

Steele smiled, the flawless proportions on his face looking like he'd been carved out of marble into one of those angel statues.

"Thank you," Creed murmured in my ear, his warm breath flaring over my neck, his hands sliding tenderly under my breasts, igniting my arousal tenfold.

I nodded, caught up in a strange sensation of desire, confusion, and worry that these two powerful monsters might end up in a fight again. I didn't miss the way they glared at each other like they knew something I wasn't privy to.

It was a bizarre thing to be between two men I adored, and yet they loathed one another. Should I kiss them, or get them to open up and talk about their differences?

But everything faded into the abyss of my mind when Creed's hands slid down my body, pushing my legs apart, his fingers stroking me.

I moaned, my spine arching, and I somehow managed to grow wetter. Perhaps I shouldn't be as turned on as I was, except the way Steele studied me, licking his lips, made me feel like a goddess.

I'd barely recovered from my morning session with my king, but here I was again moaning, my hips rocking for more.

"Approach, Steele," he commanded, tucking my legs over his, so he could spread me wider as I sat on his lap. "She needs us, so taste her, show her how much you've missed her."

My handsome lover stepped forward, tearing his shirt up and over his head, his gaze never leaving me. He never once protested at kneeling before Creed and me.

"Don't look so worried," he said with a smile. "You're spectacular, and between us, we'll make you feel things you've never experienced before."

I grinned at him, struggling to balance how ridiculously turned on I was, how I wanted to cry for the bruises on his face, and how I contemplated asking them to finally tell me what the hell was going on between them.

"Just remember, sweetheart, I love you," he whispered loud enough for me to hear his words. Then his tongue swept up over my swollen folds, stealing all my thoughts. "You're so wet, so perfect," he murmured, his eyes on me, staring up from between my spread legs. Fuck, I could never tire of the view.

He flicked my clit, and I moaned my response. Creed pinched my nipples, bringing them to life. I found myself pleading for more punishment.

"Harder," I gasped. "Make me hurt."

"You're doing well, my good girl, letting him eat your pussy like that." Creed trailed his hands over my breasts, kneading them, then pinched my nipples harder, pulling them. All while Steele sucked on my engorged lips, devouring me, making deliciously slurpy sounds that I loved.

Everything about these two monsters made me unbearably horny. They smelled of sex, of musk, of sin. And I wanted them to break me, to make me scream.

Steele pressed open my slick folds and plunged his tongue into me.

Shuddering, I gasped with each breath. Creed's mouth pressed to the back of my neck, leaving me covered in kisses. "You are going to sound so beautiful when I make you scream."

His hands were on my hips, lifting me slightly off him, his cock now fully nestled between my ass cheeks. I was drenched with my slick, which made it easier for Creed to press the tip of his erection into my ass.

I tensed at first, but it was hard to think of anything but elation when Steele never released my pussy from his mouth, his teeth gently biting around my clit.

His moves left me spasming in response, while Creed slowly worked to get into my rear. I felt only one of his cock tips, and I appreciated him retracting one back, seeing as I was a lot tighter back there. That was the thing about his cock —it was magical like that. But even with one head, my monster king was huge.

"Are you sure it'll fit?" My voice came out breathy and rough, and I was curling the bed sheets into my fists to hold onto something as I sat on Creed's lap.

"Let me show you how well you can take me," he purred in my ear.

I mewled, leaning my weight against him as he pushed into my ass inch by inch, Steele, on the other hand, was going to town on me. But once Creed thrust all the way inside, his growls matched mine, and I was on the verge of exploding.

My body quivered and my legs trembled.

It just so happened that in that same moment, Tempest barged into the room, finding us all tangled in our carnal pleasure, bringing us all to a halting stop.

Steele pulled back, glancing at the newcomer, and they both exchanged a hissing growl.

"Took your time," Creed barked at him.

"Wait, you invited him to join us too?" I gasped because I didn't realize we were having an orgy. I half expected Ash and Seven to pour into the room next. I only had so many holes though.

"I want as many of us building up the energy, seeing if we can push past the damn barrier blocking our feeding," Creed explained like he'd given this a lot of thought.

"Well, don't stop on my account," Tempest stated as his dark gaze swept over my body and he kicked the door shut.

He started to undress, setting his top aside before toeing his shoes off. He tugged at the zipper on his pants. Someone was eager, weren't they?

He kept watching me though. I didn't understand Tempest lately, but I also knew that with Creed around, he couldn't push me to the limit of hurting me either.

"Are you alright with all three of us?" Creed asked.

While I appreciated him asking, it also felt like I didn't have a choice. I had to help the city. And I was so horny. I'd cry if I didn't come soon.

"Yes," I answered quickly, then it all happened.

Tempest climbed onto the bed, crawling toward us butt naked, me captivated by his sharp cheekbones, full lips, and beautiful face that easily masked the monster lurking inside. His bright green eyes were like a serpent's, never leaving its prey, and it shouldn't be surprising that he stared at me that way.

Steele was on his feet too, stripping off his pants. His huge cock popped out, and I might have gulped a bit too loudly because he paused and glanced at me.

My gaze locked onto his erection. "Wait, why does your cock look different?"

It was silvery blue with raven-black ridges running in

circles around his shaft. I'd had sex with Steele before. I would have remembered if his blue penis came with built-in speed bumps.

A corner of his mouth curled upward as he lowered his gaze to where he palmed himself. "I couldn't show you the real me and have you freak out, sweetheart."

"Well, I'm still freaking out about you being a monster and not telling me all this time. And now this! We really need to talk about this."

"Let's keep going," Creed murmured in my ear. "You've been doing so well."

I contemplated disagreeing, but I also wasn't exactly in a position to argue when I was dripping wet with slick and horny as hell…not to mention Creed's erection in my ass.

Steele offered me a soft smile, a knowing look that told me he understood my frustration, that he had shit to explain.

"I promise," he muttered, lowering his hand to my offering, his fingers playing me like a piano, knowing exactly where to press and stroke, driving me close to my orgasm. "First, let me feed your hungry pussy, shall we?"

I was drooling, wanting him inside me…wanting all the dicks inside me.

Apparently, that was who I'd become…A cock magnet.

"Please," I moaned.

Creed's tail raised in front of Steele like a viper and curled around his dick instantly. He groaned, looking disgruntled, flinching back, but he wasn't fast enough. The black tail grabbed him by the cock.

"Fuck," he hissed. "Get that thing off me."

But when Creed tugged him toward me by his erection, practically guiding him into me, I nearly laughed out loud at how my king had to control every situation. Even how my other lover was about to have sex with me.

"Lay back with me," Creed whispered in my ear and drew me to lay on the bed, with him beneath me.

Heaving for breath, I laid there, spread, my ass completely full, and Steele didn't fight it, but rather he gripped my thighs and settled in front of my spread legs.

"Make her feel amazing," Creed ordered, his words raspy, almost sounding like a threat.

I bristled because that wasn't what I wanted to hear, but when Steele slid his cock across my slick, I raised my hips, which also had me tightening my ass around Creed. He growled in my ear, his hands cupping my breasts.

"You want to be fucked hard, right?" Steele asked with a grin, fully knowing the answer already.

Tempest huffed loudly, in clear agitation at Steele's flirting.

"Please," I moaned. "Bury yourself into me balls deep, so deep that I'll forget everything else."

"That's it, Pet." Creed held me against him. "I love how tight your ass is." And somehow, he managed to push deeper. "I want you to think of us when you walk tomorrow as your pussy and cute rear ache."

Steele finally eased his fat tip into me, and I prepared myself for his size, for accommodating him.

My breaths sped up while he slid in, the ridges rubbing my sides in ways I could never have imagined. He pressed all the way in, seemingly in a rush while a growl rolled in his chest.

And it was only then that I sensed something vibrating inside my core channel.

I froze, startled, and cried out with my body quivering, lost to the sensation of rising pleasure. I craned my neck, staring at a grinning Steele.

"Is your cock vibrating?"

He nodded, smiling, so proud of himself. "Oh sweetheart, I haven't even begun to show you the pleasure I can bring you."

"My god, you've got a ribbed vibrator as a dick."

He laughed, sliding in and out of me, heightening the tingling pleasure. "I'll fuck you like you've never been fucked before."

"Okay, we get it. You got a fancy love muscle," Tempest growled. "Can we get started already?"

Those people who said they saw stars during sex were onto something. These two monsters hadn't even started thrusting, but my head was dancing with arousal, lights blinking in my vision.

"How are you doing, sweetheart?" Steele asked softly, his hand reaching over to cup my cheek. I turned my head to kiss his palm.

"Absolutely incredible."

"I've got you," Creed breathed in my ear, his arms wrapped around me. "I'll hold you, Pet. Now, are you ready for Tempest?"

"He's hardly needed," Steele spoke over him. "I can show her things she's never felt before."

"Things she's no doubt already experienced with me." Creed's response grew snappier, more aggressive.

"Okay," I cut them off right as Steele was about to respond. My pussy and ass constricted around them both, making them growl in response. "I get you're competitive, but right now, I'm stuffed with two cocks, and I want to be fucked, please."

Creed chuckled behind me, kissing me behind my ear. "You're adorable when you get mad."

Steele in turn grinned wickedly, a knowing gleam in his eyes, one bursting with love for me. Then they started their beautiful assault on my body, cocks pulling in and out, hands all over my skin.

Between them, I felt completely exposed and vulnerable, and at the same time, the luckiest girl in the world.

Tempest laid a soft hand across my jawline and drew me to turn my head toward him. He leaned over and kissed me, tenderly at first, then we were animals, tongues tangling, my libido on overdrive.

"Ready for me?" he breathed against my mouth, the question sending jolts of desire through me because I could never deny my monsters. I had sex on the brain when it came to them, a connection between us that I could never ignore.

"Yes." Because it was true. I was ready for each of my holes to be completely wrecked.

He massaged my throat and pulled back, offering me his huge cock. Shuffling closer, he gripped the base of his shaft and I reached over to hold its strength, feeling more like steel covered in velvet. I slid him past my lips, taking him gradually into my mouth, and god have mercy, but I loved the way he smelled, the taste of his cock in my mouth.

When I lifted my gaze, there was something almost familiar in the way his features morphed into someone who could be described as happy…an emotion rarely seen on his face.

Then all three monsters moved in unison, grinding into me, claiming me, taking everything I offered.

They kept drawing out and plunging into me over and over, until I could barely take it, but that was when they sped up, turning animalistic. Tempest's cock pushed to the back of my throat, my eyes tearing up from how deep he pushed himself.

Creed was kissing my neck, Steele stroking my clit as he fucked me. If there was such a thing as heaven, I was convinced I'd found it.

Panting, I moved my body with their rhythm, the four of us on a chorus of moans, my pussy soaking wet with each of their thrusts.

They went so deep, that I doubted I'd ever forget this fucking.

I floated, groaning for more because it was euphoric. They owned me, and they knew it as they hungrily claimed my body, hammering into me, tugging at my breasts, their teeth on my neck, and their grunts resonating through me.

I was tight all over, rocking with them, all of us sweating and panting for breath. I had Creed embracing me, his whispers in my ear with filthy words.

"You're so tight. I'm going to lick you everywhere it aches after this. But fuck me, Pet, you're going to be mine forever."

He growled and pushed me closer and closer to the edge. All the while, I held onto Steele's ravenous gaze as he pumped into me. I drowned in him, the love he gave me.

I didn't miss how Tempest kept massaging my throat to take him farther, to look up at him only. Talk about possessive men.

And as they hammered into me, an orgasm took me over the edge. White light blinked behind my eyes and I groaned, my body convulsing. Somehow I didn't manage to choke on Tempest's cock, but he moved faster now.

I was soaked, climaxing so hard, the room spun with me. But the monsters never paused, and I kept coming. It didn't stop, and I could barely breathe as I drowned in pleasure.

They fucked me faster too, as if they planned it. And they shoved into me one last time before pausing and bursting with their own high. Their cocks spilled into me, filling me to the brim with cum.

Swallowing Tempest's seed, he guided my hair off my face, and I could officially say, I'd never had so much cum inside me at the same time as I did then.

Tempest pulled out of my mouth, and I swallowed the last drops, smiling up at him with satisfaction as I collapsed back onto Creed. Perspiration ran down my neck. Then I broke out laughing at how amazing that was, how blown away I was that I just had three dicks inside me.

"That was insane, and intense, and we should do it again." I tried to move and groaned at the soreness settling in. "But maybe not right away," I panted.

"Fuck yeah," Tempest snarled.

"I'm game." Steele grinned.

"Let's prepare you a hot bath first," Creed said softly, and somehow we all disentangled from one another, slick and cum running down my inner legs. I'd need another quick shower before the bath. I might have liked cum inside me, but I didn't fancy it floating in my bath.

"Do you think it worked?" I asked. "That we fed everyone?"

"I really hope so, but I'll go find out for sure." My king collected me into his arms and kissed my lips. "Rest, and I'll get a tub brought up to your room."

When he climbed off the bed, I grabbed a pillow, hugging it to my chest. Tempest was collecting his clothes off the floor and offered me a lopsided smile. "Well, I'm off then." The distance bothered me, and you'd think after all this time of him pulling away, I'd be used to it. Except, lately, he confused me with the conflicted look always on his face, something that made no sense to me.

Once Tempest wandered out of the room, I pushed myself to the edge of the bed. "Can Steele and I talk for a bit privately? Can you give us some time?"

"I think it's time," Steele admitted, heartfelt emotions whirling behind his eyes. He moved toward me, and my heart fluttered because I had a million questions for him. Things I needed to understand that only he could answer.

But Creed already grabbed him by the arm, dragging him to the door. "Maybe later," was all he said before hauling him out the door.

I got to my feet. "Creed, that's not fair," I called out. "I need to know what's going on. Please."

But he didn't seem to hear me, or perhaps he chose not to, because they were gone in a flash, and the door shut behind him with a bang.

What the hell was that about? I screamed out of pure frustration.

I was getting really fucking tired of being kept in the dark, and I rushed to the door, wrenching it open to find the hall completely empty. Not even a sound to let me know which direction they'd gone.

Fuck!

CHAPTER 10

BLAKE

Later never came.

Instead, I awoke abruptly to someone shaking my shoulder. Opening my eyes, I stared at a woman with the palest face and what appeared to be white tentacles flowing from her head as though they were dreadlocks. My initial impression was that she was a cross between Medusa and a ghoul.

"Do I know you?" I asked croakily, slightly alarmed. Monsters in the Shadowburn realm never went about anything in a way I'd consider common sense. So there had to be a reason for her being in my face and in my room.

"Girl, you must get up, the carriage is waiting for you outside." She spoke in a sing-song way that sounded almost soothing, and maybe that was why I felt calmer than I should.

I blinked at this beautiful monster with golden eyes, my mind and heart racing. "What carriage? What's going on?"

Before she responded, I shoved the blankets aside and scrambled out of bed, realizing very quickly I was completely nude. So with one of Creed's shirts still discarded on the floor, I grabbed it and slipped it on as I hurried to the window that overlooked the front of the castle. His musky, sexy scent from the shirt overwhelmed me, and it also reminded me that I was still pissed at him for dragging Steele out of my room when I begged him to let us talk.

From my window, I spotted an old-fashioned carriage in front of the castle. Black as the night, it had spear-like decorations protruding upward from around the roof, and in front of it, four oversized beasts beat their hooves into the stone floor. They were stocky and the size of water buffaloes, their pelts the color of a stormy sky.

Twisting back around, I quickly noticed there were actually two women in my room, both identical, and they had no legs that I could see. Only dozens of white tentacles that they stood on, while others moved across their bodies like slithering snakes, and every now and then I caught a glimpse of something flesh pink underneath. The taller woman slinked across the room and pushed open the bathroom door.

"I hear humans have a need to relieve their bowels after waking. I suggest you hurry up as you may not get the chance to once we leave."

My head spun with too many questions, while fear zipped down my spine. "Where am I going? Where's Creed?" For all I knew, I was about to be kidnapped by angry Wyld monsters for not feeding them enough. Except, would they really care about me using the toilet first?

"It's the Red Battle, human girl," the smaller woman said, sounding slightly disgruntled. "It begins shortly, and many in the city are rushing to the Cliffs of Doom to find out if he's guilty or not."

"The what? Who's guilty?" My gaze swung between them and landed on the woman holding the bathroom door open, one of her tentacles tapping the floor impatiently. "Hurry into the bathroom and I'll tell you," she said with exasperation.

I took the chance and moved fast into the bathroom. I didn't need a shower, considering I'd had a bath right before I went to sleep. But I would brush my teeth and, as the monster put it, "relieve my bowels".

As I went about my morning routine super quickly, I listened to the woman's musical voice from the door she hadn't fully shut.

"Steele, who used to be one of the royals from the royal circle, has finally been caught, and today he will be held responsible for his treason."

Her words startled me, and that earlier dread I tried to calm squeezed around my throat like a noose. If I wasn't sitting on the toilet, I might have marched right out of the bathroom to force her to tell me everything. Instead, I called out, "What does that mean? Is he being punished? Is that where the carriage is taking me? I really have to speak to Creed. You need to take me to him." I spoke frantically, starting to have a panic attack on the toilet.

"No punishment yet," she explained. "You see, there are three stages for someone who breaks our laws. One, we need a confession. When the guilty refuses to provide one, they enter the Red Battle, an arena that will reveal if they are truly innocent or guilty of their crime. Then they must accept their fate, and lastly, they will be made to pay by something we call, *head for a head*."

"I-I think we call that eye for an eye." I was suddenly moving with speed through the bathroom, terror gripping me.

"Tell me more about the Red Battle, please," I begged as I emerged into the bedroom. I had to get to Steele, to see if I could help him because I didn't for a moment believe the man I'd fallen in love with would murder his queen. He wouldn't.

"First, I must get you into the carriage or Creed will have my head if you're late. Then I'll explain everything. Our king is already there."

"He left without me?" I gasped, then shook my head.

"Fine, then let's go." I was already marching across the room when both women came to my side, tugging at my shirt.

"You cannot go out looking like that. You will be at the king's side, and you must appear perfect for your part in the Red Battle."

I choked on a small cry, my eyes already watering because I didn't care about these theatrics, not when Steele might die today.

"I can't wait another second. I have to go now." My voice trembled, anxiety swirling in my gut.

At that stage, they literally ripped the top off me, and one produced a red dress for me to wear. I'd lost all my patience, and I snatched the gown that felt like water in my hands slipping through my fingers. With the women's help, I slid it up and over my head.

The silk-like dress cascaded down my body, falling to my ankles. It was cool to the touch and had an almost wet sensation as it clung to my body. It followed the curves of my breasts to the point that it even accentuated my areolas. Dipping at my narrow waist, it traced my hips all the way down my legs. I could just imagine how revealing it was from behind, following my curves.

Splits raced up both sides of my legs to my hips, and the top part of the gown had a high neck and long sleeves. Golden buttons adorned my wrists, and more ran down from one shoulder to the opposite hip, slicing diagonally across my body. They were fake buttons but glinted in the light.

If I wasn't on the verge of crying, I might be in awe of the dress. But I was too worked up and had already pulled open the door to go to this Red Battle.

The shorter woman placed a pair of high, golden boots in front of me, pausing me. I stepped into them as the other woman leaned down to zip them up to mid-thigh.

I ran my fingers over the fabric across my stomach, unable

to shake off how much the fabric felt like water. "What is this material made of, anyway?"

"Of tears, magic, and blood, all spun together with the finest spider web," the golden-eyed woman told me, both of them studying me with awe in their gazes. "And you are spectacular in it."

"Tears?" I guess it kind of fit considering I was ready to burst out crying. "It's very pretty, but maybe too much for such a devastating occasion."

"Quite the opposite," she said. "The queen would wear this gown at every Red Battle."

My mouth dried, and I hoped "this gown" wasn't literal and I wasn't actually wearing that bitch's dress.

"We need to go," I said frantically, my throat squeezing, having wasted enough time. I had to reach Creed.

In a flutter, we rushed downstairs, me starting to hyperventilate as every worst-case scenario rolled over my mind of how they would hurt Steele so they could finally confirm their accusation of him killing the last queen.

Downstairs, the beasts attached to the carriage turned in my direction as if even they could tell I didn't belong in this realm. A tall, bony monster in a black cloak sat up front, grasping the reins with skeletal hands. He didn't even glance at me.

The animals attached to the carriage had nine legs each, most decorated with bells on their ankles, which made a loud ringing sound. But it was only when I narrowed my eyes, did I notice one of the legs on each animal wasn't touching the floor, which was strange. Then they moved and the bulbous tip on each of the shorter legs poked out and I gasped. They weren't legs at all, but full-on erections.

I might have vomited in my mouth a little.

"Oh, gross!" I hoped they weren't having that reaction due to imagining my gruesome end, considering how they stared at me with death in their eyes.

Nostrils flaring, one of them suddenly snorted flames.

I flinched, screaming out of pure fright, which set off the animals who screeched their surprise, shooting out more flames. The skeletal man was suddenly frantically whistling at them, tugging on their reins.

"Hurry, girl, get inside," the woman urged me, pressing a tentacle to my arm to shove me forward.

"Are you sure? I think they're going to kill me," I murmured, never taking my eyes off the strange horses. "And why do they all have hard-ons?"

She laughed, pushing me forward until I climbed into the carriage that might as well have come right out of Bram Stoker's *Dracula*. Everything screamed gothic--windows trimmed with short lace curtains, two sets of long benches facing each other, covered in a soft, velvety black fabric.

The woman was suddenly in the carriage with me, sitting across from me, her snow-white tentacles spreading outward, taking up her whole side…they stretched across the seat, up the walls behind her, and one reached out to pull the door shut. And then she slouched, exhaling a long breath.

"I will be joining you for the journey," she said, matter-of-factly. "Those animals are called Derins, and they run wild in the Hunting Lands but can be tamed. And yes, they are extremely horny beasts." She chuckled. "Always out and ready in case the chance presents itself."

"Guess that's not too different to most males," I teased, thinking of how absolutely horny my monsters were constantly.

She laughed once more, and I noticed that when she did, the double row of suckers on the underside of her tentacles jiggled.

I liked the ease that she spoke with compared to back in my room, and the tension she held onto earlier seemed to have melted off her shoulders.

The carriage suddenly lurched forward, and the force

pushed me back into my seat. We were off, leaving behind the castle, and my stomach was in complete knots. I stared out at the landscape, the bridges we crossed, the towers, the monsters glancing our way from their homes.

It was only when I felt the slight tug on my hair, that I jerked back around to find several tentacles, gripping brushes that were combing through my messy pink hair.

"Now that we have time, I will style your hair and fix your makeup."

"You really don't have to," I murmured, pushing strands of hair out of my face.

"Nonsense. When the king asked me to care for you, I swore on my life, and I take my job seriously. I can only deliver you to him when you are completely perfect." She smiled, wrinkles deepening at the corners of her eyes. She was such a beautiful woman with an octopus body, which didn't feel as strange as it should. A testament to the fact I was acclimating to this realm.

"Did Creed say anything else, like why he had to leave so early without me?"

"Oh, the king doesn't share such things with me," she said loudly, then leaned forward, whispering, "Some of the maids overheard him saying that he wanted to personally take the prisoner to the Cliffs of Doom for the ceremony, and he wanted you to turn up right as the event was about to commence."

I bit my lower lip, mostly from frustration and anxiety. He was doing everything damn possible to keep Steele and me apart.

"It's for the best," she said, gesturing to the outside world with a tentacle. "It's dry and arid out there near the cliffs. Better if you don't spend too much time there anyway. It's full of reptilian creatures who'd try to suck the marrow from your bones the first chance they got."

I shivered at the thought, while she combed the knots out

of my hair, then commenced pulling strands off my face before she braided them. I twisted sideways in my seat, to give her easier access to my hair.

"What's your name?" I murmured, feeling slightly rude for not asking until now.

"Hopaka," she answered with a smile, like she'd been waiting for me to ask. "It was my mother's name, and her mother's, and so on. In my family, the females take their mom's name, you see, and the males take what name they please."

"Wouldn't that become confusing after a while?"

She shook her head. "Oh, but our names are differentiated by the way it's pronounced. You say mine as Hopaka, while my mother's is Hopaka."

For the life of me, I couldn't tell the difference in the way she said it. They sounded identical. But I nodded regardless and kept staring outside.

My knees bounced, my heart pulsing harder as I thought about losing Steele. How furious…and heartbroken I'd be if they killed him. I'd never got the chance to talk to him and find out the truth. Everything inside of me said that Steele would be honest with me.

I remembered the times we'd spent together back on earth, his affection, his promises, his devotion. I thought I'd met the perfect man, but I guess even the most angelic guy hid secrets...like the fact he was a real monster who was hiding on earth.

That didn't mean he deserved to die though.

I guess the world was unfair like that though…no matter what realm you were in.

A soft sigh pressed against my throat as I thought about my family, and how I didn't deserve their rejection, or being shoved into an asylum. Anger came over me whenever I wasted time thinking about them.

I pushed those thoughts aside, left only with silence and its whispers inside my head of my mother's last words to me.

We all have to live with our own demons, dear. Enjoy yours.

If only I'd known back then how right she'd been.

I didn't recall how long we'd been traveling, but outside, the city had turned into an open dried land, peppered with boulders, dead trees, and the occasional rock formation that came complete with doorways, I guessed where the locals lived.

"Done," Hopaka finally announced. "Let me look at you."

She studied me, her tentacles adjusting things in my hair, when she finally said, "Absolutely remarkable." She reached into the drawer under her seat and pulled out a handheld mirror, holding it up for me.

Three braids ran from my forehead and back over my head, while whole snippets of loose hair remained to frame my face. Amid the braids were tiny white bones, clipped in place. The rest of the pink hair tumbled over my shoulders in soft waves.

I might as well have just stepped out of a fantasy movie because even I had to admit, I was freaking stunning.

"Are they real bones?" I asked, reaching up to finger one, but she rapidly pushed my hand back down.

"Of course. Nothing but the best for you. No expense was spared."

I didn't have the stomach to ask what creature they came from but smiled at her anyway. "I love it, and you have extraordinary skills." Especially considering she did all of it with tentacles.

"Oh, you wait until I finish with your makeup. Close your eyes and leave the rest to me. I do need to be quick. We are almost there."

I instantly glanced outside, seeing only flat, open land, and nerves tightened in my gut. I closed my eyes, asking, "What can I expect at the Red Battle?"

"Well, the place will be full," she began, and I felt the softness of her touch as she applied my makeup. "It's been a long time since anyone held such an event, so everyone will try to cram close to watch."

"And who is Steele battling?" My voice squeaked even as I said the words.

"It's unknown. That's the beauty of this place. There's magic in the mountain itself from our ancestors, and every Red Battle is unique. We won't know who he must defeat, but the accused will be proven innocent if he wins the fight, and guilty if he fails."

My eyes snapped open to a makeup sponge in my face, then I quickly shut them again. "That sounds insane. How is that proving his real innocence? What if Steele faces someone four times his size? It's a battle of the strongest then." My hands were shaking as I pictured it in my head. "How different is it from the witch hunters in ancient times proving a female was a witch by throwing her into a river, while tied to a rock? She gets out, she's a witch. She dies, she's innocent. Utter madness."

"I don't know what a witch is, but it's not that cut and dry. It's said the first king and queen settled in the Cliffs of Doom when they created the city of Wyld, and the queen was known to carry magic in her veins. When she died, she was buried in the Grave Caves, a place steeped in magic minerals, which are often used during the Red Battle to ensure the truth always came out in the fight, one way or another."

My head hurt, not really understanding how the battle was going to happen. But I still held onto the belief that Steele was innocent, so if the fight was as fair as Hopaka insinuated, then he should be safe, right?

But if I'd learned anything since arriving in the Shadowburn realm, it was that nothing was simple, or even made sense. I tightened my hands into a ball in my lap. Terror twisted in my chest. I hated having no idea what to expect.

When I felt the lurch of the carriage, my eyes shot open, my heart hitting the back of my throat.

Hopaka had just pulled back, studying me with a grin. "Done. Just in time too." She lifted the mirror, and I stared at my reflection, not recognizing myself at first.

Thick red stripes had been drawn under my eyes, curling upward at the edges and decorated with what resembled studded rubies. Three more stones sat in a downward line on the bridge of my nose, while black makeup gave my eyes a smoky appearance. I batted my eyelashes which appeared longer than normal, and each strand was tipped with red glitter.

I pouted my ruby lips, the colors perfectly blending to match my cherry red dress and my bright pink hair. "Wow, I actually look beautiful."

She laughed, placing a tentacle on my hand. "You have always been beautiful; the makeup has only brought out your female fierceness."

Which it did, but the moment the door to the carriage swung open and steaming hot hair rushed inside, my anxiety went through the roof.

The driver stood there, holding the door, which I guessed was my cue, so I climbed out.

Hot air pressed down on me, my nostrils burning with each inhale as I glanced back to Hopaka, but she wasn't getting out.

"Sorry, this is where my service ends. But remember, you are fierce. Go and impress them."

"Impress *them*?"

Suddenly, the driver shut the door, and climbed back onto his perch before leaving me behind.

My stomach dropped, and I called out, "Where are you going? Where do I go?" But they never stopped. They just left me in the middle of freaking nowhere.

That was when I glanced up and really took in my

surroundings. At the ginormous stone mountains ahead of me, where the top of the cliffs had been carved to resemble a terrifying skull appearing to be mid-scream with a gaping mouth filled with sharp teeth and long fangs.

I trembled, my chest seeming to squeeze in on itself because I suddenly felt so lost, that I feared for my life. At the base of the mountain stood a gaping cave opening with two spider guards out front.

My skin crawled. "Well, this is just great, isn't it."

"Are you lost, beautiful one?" Ash's voice came from behind me abruptly, and I could have cried.

I spun and threw myself into his monstrous arms, hugging him, so relieved I wanted to scream. He stood there in his hideous form, with thick leathery skin, those enormous horns, and a mouth filled with incisors for teeth, but I didn't care. I adored him all the same, and I sure as hell didn't want to approach the spider guards alone.

"Thank god you're here." I drew back as he ran a thumb over my chin.

"I'm not a god, gorgeous, I'm so much more," he teased with a grin. "We need to go though. Creed asked me to wait for you as he's getting the match started."

"I have so many questions."

Ash didn't wait to hear what they were. He just lifted me into his arms and moved us toward the mountain.

I swallowed hard, fear pummeling into me that there was nothing I could do to save Steele from the upcoming fucking, stupid Red Battle.

CHAPTER

BLAKE

The moment we burst into the mountain cave, the explosive cheer of monsters became deafening.

Ash never stopped moving. I was cradled in his arms, and we rushed through the crowds who parted away from us, jumping out of the way like their life depended on it.

We traveled through lofty tunnels carved out of the stone, voices and cheering echoing around us, and everyone stared at me, mostly with glares. I didn't want to see their anger. I felt like shattered glass on the inside, ready to fall apart, able to focus on one thing only—stopping this ridiculous battle.

When we finally left behind the masses, I breathed easy, saying to Ash, "This is insane."

"So many have waited for the queen's murderer to be brought to justice, and this is their moment for that. Many blame Steele for the beginning of the city's hunger ever since they lost the Red Queen."

"And do you believe he killed her?" My voice raised, emotions tightening my lungs.

Ash didn't respond right away, breathing quickly instead, and I watched the conflict play across his face. "I've known him for so long, trusted him, shared so much, and I want to say he didn't. It destroys me on the inside because he's family, but innocent people don't run from the scene of the crime."

"He was scared, and I'd be just as terrified if I was accused," I answered, defending him even if I didn't know the truth, but I felt his innocence deep in my soul. The man I loved couldn't be a killer.

"The truth will reveal itself today," he answered, pushing through a narrow doorway.

"And what if it's wrong and Steele is killed in the battle?" I murmured, my chest hurting.

"The Red Battle doesn't lie. All you need to do is watch the outcome because we're not talking about a normal fight during the Red Battle. We won't even know how it plays out until it begins."

He reminded me of what Hopaka said in the carriage.

Every Red Battle is unique.

It wasn't what I wanted to hear, because going into something blindly added to my bubbling anxiety.

Conflicted, I was left shaking, and Ash set me on my feet, his huge clawed hands on my waist. "If Steele has nothing to hide, he'll be safe. But if he killed the queen, then the city will demand retribution."

"And what if he had a really good reason for it? What if —" The words choked from my throat.

"He'll be given a chance to explain. We're not complete barbarians, gorgeous."

I couldn't bring myself to answer because I didn't necessarily agree, especially when a sickening sensation stretched through me. I was certain Steele had already tried to explain before now…and it hadn't worked.

"We need to hurry." He ushered me forward, collecting my hand into his, and we made our way through the narrow tunnel where no one else wandered.

When we finally emerged through an arched doorway, the bright light from flaming torches blinded me momentarily.

Not to mention, the chattering and hollering were ear-piercing.

I blinked, slowly taking in my surroundings, finding myself on a stone balcony. We were inside the mountain still, in an oversized cavern to be precise, where the surrounding walls were carved with holes and other balconies for other monsters, and where the wall was empty, it had been carved into terrifying monsters. Red fabric hung from the ceiling in loops, reminding me of dripping blood.

Our balcony wasn't far from the arena, if one could call it that–a circular platform in the middle of the cavern, secured by dozens of chains, suspended over a gaping hole seething with lava.

Surrounding the pit were ascending stone steps, cram-packed with monsters, with not a single empty spot left.

But where was Steele?

Everything around me was too much.

The shouting.

The deadly fighting ring.

Ominous feelings like I'd stepped back to ancient monster times.

The floor seemed to move with me, and I suddenly didn't want to be there.

"I'll be right back," Ash whispered in my ear, then walked into the tunnel. But it was only when I glanced back to stop him from leaving me alone on the balcony, that I noted I wasn't alone at all.

Seven and Tempest stood on either side of the entrance.

I swallowed hard.

Both of them couldn't look more disgruntled if they tried, but they weren't concealing the way they stared at me either, their gazes sliding up and down my body. Neither was in monster form; both were dressed in red suits, which made me wonder if it was a royal thing to stand out among the city's population.

"Well, isn't this fun," I said over the shouting, though I doubted they heard me.

Seven said something, I could tell by the movement of his jaw, but with the bottom half of his face covered, I didn't hear a thing. Only his eyes were visible, which was enough to see exactly how he felt. And right then, I got the impression he wanted to reach out to me.

I moved closer, wanting to hear what he had to say, desperately needing to talk to him. Since our last time together, there hadn't been a word between us. Since I was possibly about to lose a man I loved, an urgency came over me to prevent him from ignoring me...and try to work out our differences. I couldn't bear to lose any of them.

When I stepped closer, his eyes smiled, even if behind them, he seemed to carry the heaviest of burdens.

Strong clawed hands suddenly gripped me by the waist and spun me around to face Tempest, stealing me away from Seven.

"Red isn't exactly your color," he muttered, while I huffed and twisted back toward Seven only to see the back of him as he left the balcony. My lips curled upward at Tempest taking that moment away from me only to insult me.

Snapping back toward him, I pushed his hands off me. "What do you want?"

"The dress doesn't suit you," he remarked, eyeing me head to toe.

I was getting really sick of his insults. "Yeah, well, by the bulge in your pants, I'd rather think you love the way I look."

Pushing away from him, I went to stand in the corner of the balcony, staring out at the masses. I felt sick to my stomach waiting for this stupid fight to start, and the hot prick of tears burned my eyes.

Tempest's shadow fell over me, his hands gripped the balcony railing on either side of me, trapping me inside. I spun toward him, my eyes teary from how high-strung and stressed I felt.

"I can't do this today with you," I stated. "Insult me another day, but right now, I'm so scared for Steele that I'm going to pass out."

He studied me for a long moment, and to my surprise, he shuffled backward, giving me space. I'd like to think he felt sorry for me, but I was certain it was related to me not making a scene, seeing as I expected Creed to join us any moment now.

"You get used to it after a while," he said, loud enough for me to hear.

"What's that?"

"Tragedy. If you learn to expect it, then it doesn't hurt as much when it happens." Turning from me, he went to stand at the other end of the balcony, staring out at the arena.

His words caught me off guard. I couldn't remember Tempest ever saying anything so profound before. It made me wonder what had happened to him to feel the need to conceal his pain. Though I shouldn't be surprised because most of my monsters were just as broken on the inside as me.

Words spilled from my mouth. "Maybe the tragedy isn't the problem, but the parts of ourselves we allow to die because of it."

I didn't wait for a response, I didn't want one. Instead, I stared out at monsters everywhere, some piled so close they might be sitting on one another. The corners and entrances behind the stone steps around us were crammed The entire cavern seemed to shudder with their guttural sounds.

Surveying the place, I searched for Creed and Steele, coming up short. When I turned to the balcony entrance, figuring I might pop into the tunnel to see if I could see anyone, something small on the wall caught my attention.

I frowned, squinting for a better look.

It was a small red crown painted onto the stone. I'd seen

that before, I knew I had, but for the life of me, I couldn't remember where.

Right then Creed, Ash, and Seven entered the balcony, and the soul-splitting dread curled under my ribs.

With Creed's presence, a hush fell over the arena. He stood tall, shoulders square, and his expression dark. Dressed in deep red, he wore a tight-fitting army jacket with half a dozen buckles across his torso, and matching leather pants with heavy boots that could kill with a single stomp.

Long hair framed his gorgeous face, and when he glanced down at me, something light crossed his face, a brightness behind his eyes that moments earlier were suffocating.

"Pet, you've just stolen my heart. You look every part a beautiful warrior goddess," he murmured, taking my hand in his.

"I'm really pissed at you," I answered. "How could you let this go ahead when I never got a chance to speak to Steele, and then you left me behind this morning. Can't you call it off?" The words spilled from my lips as quickly as the anger building inside of me.

Tightness pinched at the corners of his mouth. "I know you won't accept my apology that I had to keep you at a distance, but it has been a long time coming for us to finally discover the truth of what happened to our queen. Our city has suffered for years, starved, lost loved ones, and I owe them an answer."

"And I deserved to speak to Steele and not be blocked by you." My voice strained, tears leaking from the corners of my eyes.

Creed reached over and collected them with his thumbs before they spilled. "You're breaking my heart," he croaked.

"And you're destroying me." I choked up. "I might lose someone today who I couldn't even say goodbye to." My words sounded brittle because they were like ice, shattering, and I couldn't even look at Creed any longer.

A monster resembling a porcupine rushed onto the balcony, carrying several golden chairs he set down for us in a line.

I turned toward the arena right as a siren suddenly went off, echoing off the walls, and I cringed at how much it hurt my ears. I couldn't move away from the railing; my hands were curled around it so hard, they hurt.

I hated how little control I had, hated how I understood Creed's decision but didn't want to, hated that everything around me was darkening, my life becoming madness.

Ash was suddenly at my side, his hand on my back. "I'll stay with you," he offered, and my heart melted, tears blurring my vision. I leaned against him because, right now, I was so angry, so heartbroken, I trembled. Everything had become too complicated, too painful, too much.

I wasn't ready to live in a world without Steele, that was clear as I stood there and watched a lanky monster dressed in a gold bodysuit cross the stone bridge and onto the platform, which didn't sway as much as I'd expect.

He had wild, golden hair that seemed to flutter where there was no wind, his face long, and when you stared at him sideways, he almost vanished from how flat he was.

Drums started to play, the tempo slowly picking up, my heart matching its speed.

And goosebumps raced up my arms.

Before I knew it, a beast of a man with four arms and covered in fur, shoved through the crowds to my right. They in turn went ballistic, and at first, I assumed he'd be Steele's challenger, until I noticed he held onto a thick chain that was latched around Steele's neck, and he hauled my lover behind him.

Bone-crushing heartache carved through me, and I winced. Ash held me tighter against him, not saying a word. My knees weakened, and I leaned forward, watching Steele being led onto the platform. There the monster unlatched the metal bracket from around his neck and released him, then walked away. Steele remained in his human form for now, wearing torn clothes, no shoes, his hair a mess.

Everything about him appeared vulnerable, but I'd seen him fight, and I knew he was a lot more powerful than he appeared.

He turned to take in the crowds who had come to see him perish. Suddenly, he paused, staring right in our direction.

My breath hitched, my heart bleeding to see him in such a condition. I didn't care what anyone said, I refused to even give thought to him being guilty.

The golden man cleared his throat, the sound projecting across the cavern.

"Welcome." His voice boomed loudly.

The crowds burst into hoots and shouts, screaming out, *death for Steele.*

A part of me died on the inside to hear the hatred, to know that so many of them believed he'd killed their queen.

Then the announcer continued, "Monster sistren and brethren, we have assembled to bear witness to the undeniable guilt of the accused. The charge is the regicide of our queen. Despite indisputable evidence, the felon insults us further by requesting a Red Battle. As per our rites, the accuser must face the accused in a battle to assuage any doubt of guilt. For this trial, the accuser is the queen's guard, Captain Vero, who failed to protect his queen's life. As by agreement, Vero's life was forfeited when he failed in his duty, but not before vowing to return to meet judgment on the queen's murderer. By pure strength of vengeance, back from the unending tortures of Darkevers, I present former guard Captain Vero!"

"Darkevers," I muttered under my breath.

"What humans call Hell," Ash whispered in my ear.

"And did he just say he's summoning a dead guard?"

"With ancient magic, he has the power to do so."

I blinked up at Ash, my body shaking. "What's wrong, gorgeous?"

"If he can summon the dead guard, then that's perfect. They can ask him who killed the queen, and everyone will see that Steele is innocent." A thread of hope flared over me.

A pitiful expression twisted Ash's face as his hand on mine tightened. "I wish I could say it'd be that easy. Except, bringing anyone back from the dead is complicated, and a spell that has been in the making for the last couple of days. But those who return are not themselves. They can't speak and don't hold memories from the past. They are simply prime animalistic creatures who go ballistic when torn from the afterlife and brought back here."

I shuddered, his response welling in my chest like forming ice, numbing me all over. "So does Steele stand any chance of winning?"

Ash shrugged. "If he's innocent, he should."

"Should?" I squeaked, but Ash drew me against him, and that was when Creed stood and joined me on the other side. As much as I was furious at him, I took his hand in mine as well, needing the strength that was wrecking me from the inside out.

With a single wave of the gold monster's hand, he tossed a fistful of golden powder into the air that took on a life of its own, swirling into a vortex, expanding in size. The monster started chanting something in a tongue I didn't understand.

The golden storm grew, blowing against us with unbearable strength, knocking me into Creed.

He rapidly embraced me and turned us around so he shielded me with his body. I tucked myself against him, the howling cry of the wind sounding like someone stood right behind me, roaring.

The storm flatlined in a heartbeat.

Followed by unbearable silence.

I untangled myself from his arms. Tempest and Seven had taken cover by ducking.

The crowds exploded into cheers and hoots.

Frantically, I pushed past Creed to see what was going on, finding Steele facing a hideous creature who resembled a troll. Greenish in color, long wiry hair hung down his back and from his chin, and muscles rippled, looking ready to burst out of his soldier's uniform.

That had to be Captain Vero.

Light glinted off the curved blade he grasped, and terror filled me. I clenched my fists at seeing this monster tower over Steele. But not one to sit back, Steele unleashed his terrifying form too.

Black mist spun around him, his body expanding with thicker muscles. His talons and fangs elongated, and he seemed to almost elevate himself on a cloud of darkness. Glowing eyes peered at his opponent, his chest heaving for breath, while his hands curled in balls.

Wait, he didn't have a weapon.

"As is customary, we will need a lightbringer to start the Red Battle." The announcer lifted a hand, pointing it at me.

Terror punched through me, and I froze on the spot. In seconds, a guard had burst into our balcony and bowed in front of me on one knee, both hands holding out two sticks.

I was so confused, yet I felt every single eye on me in the cavern.

"Pick them up," Ash whispered in my ear, which I did, even though I was trembling with nerves.

The crowds cheered, and I turned to face the arena once more.

"You are a guest in our home, so do us the honor of initiating the Red Battle." The announcer stared at me, waiting for me to do something I had no clue about.

"Rub the sticks together," Creed whispered. "It will ignite

a barrier around the arena to ensure the fight doesn't spill onto the audience."

I blinked up at him. "But I don't want Steele to fight."

"Pet, what other way would you have him prove his innocence? If he's right, then this is how we'll find out. And everyone is waiting, so please do the honors." He spoke tenderly, but there was firmness in his words.

Glancing up, I noted the golden monster had left the area where the two opponents waited for me. Steele was staring in my direction, giving me a tight smile, then he nodded for me to do it.

Reluctantly, I struck the sticks together, scraping them against one another.

Red sparks erupted from them instantaneously.

I yelped, flinching, yet managed to not drop them.

The red sparks jolted across the cavern and in seconds, a great red flame blew up, encasing the suspended platform.

My stomach trembled at the spectacle that had most in the crowd gasping.

The red flames died just as fast, though the perimeter of the platform glowed red. Ash collected the sticks from my hands and handed them to the guard who retreated.

Tempest and Seven both watched me intensely, and I couldn't tell if they were enjoying the show or just as devastated as me.

Despite everyone's excitement in the masses, to me, this was a dark day I'd never forget.

The gold monster stood between them, declaring, "If the accused survives, he'll be found not guilty."

I took Ash's and Creed's hands once more, a grip tightening around my chest.

"Fight," the golden monster abruptly yelled.

My heart thundered, driving all the fear into my veins.

Steele and Captain Vero lunged at one another, clashing spectacularly.

The spectators bellowed and screamed out ways to finish Steele quicker.

Tears came, stinging my eyes. I couldn't look away from the two of them, locked in a feral battle of growls, claws, and fangs. Steele suddenly flew across the platform, slamming into an invisible wall I'd set up with the sticks around the arena, then slumped to the floor. He sprung back just as fast, rushing into combat.

They pummeled one another, and it surprised me how powerful Vero was, when I'd seen Steele take on three of my monsters on his own.

But this wasn't a fair fight, was it? He was facing off against an undead.

Steele slid across the platform, thick blood slipping from a gash across his forehead. Vero charged him, knife raised, unstained by blood so far.

"Steele, get out of the way," I yelled, then swallowed hard to watch him roll out of the way at the last second.

Hate blazed through me, cold and boundless. Hate for this fucking fight, for the heartache that would shatter me.

Someone grabbed my arm, and I swung around to Creed guiding me to take a seat. But I shook my head. "This isn't entertainment for me, but something that's ripping me to shreds on the inside. I can't sit comfortably while he's out there fighting for his damn life and we're just chilled out," I cried.

Harsh tears blurred my vision, and I jerked away from Creed, clinging to the railing on the balcony, staring out at Steele. As much as it hurt me, I watched every strike, every scratch; it was the least I could do.

I wiped the tears that kept coming. *Don't die, Steele...don't you fucking die on me.*

Suddenly, four monsters came to stand by my side, and I appreciated their company more than they'd ever know.

The battle grew savage, the pair moving so fast, I couldn't

follow everything, but blood splashed on the floor and against the invisible wall.

My head pulsed with a headache, and the air was charged with electricity, with a hunger for blood, with my misery.

Steele suddenly delivered a blow, smashing his fist to the center of Vero's chest, sending him sprawling. My monster didn't hesitate but lunged after him, only to have his opponent kick him in the gut, so hard that even from our spot, we heard the pain in his grunt.

I died a little on the inside, but Vero wasn't holding back. He threw himself at a fallen Steele, blade glinting as it came down right for my lover's chest.

Creed's hand squeezed mine.

And the world seemed to slow down for me in those seconds.

"Watch out!" I yelled.

But nothing mattered.

The beast fell on him, the blade slamming into Steele's chest.

I screamed, my world spiraling out of control, tears drenching my cheeks.

My gaze remained glued on them, but something wasn't right...

I leaned forward right as the blade shattered in the monster's grasp, breaking apart like shards of glass. Then it burst outward.

Vero disintegrated into dust, as did the blade.

Steele groaned, rolling in the opposite direction to us. Was he dying?

Mouth gaping open, I wasn't sure what just happened.

But instead of cheers around me, the crowds had fallen deathly silent. Ash, on the other hand, shouted his cheers.

Desperately, I grasped onto his arm. "What's going on? Please tell me," I cried, unable to take another breath.

"He's not guilty," Creed boomed loud enough for

everyone in the cavern to hear. "Steele is not guilty of killing the Red Queen."

I screamed, mostly out of exhaustion, relief, and how strung up I felt. Then I found myself crying happy tears. Was he really not dead?

"How? Didn't the monster stab him?" I was so confused.

Ash leaned down to me. "The blade was the judgment the whole time. If it killed him, he was guilty. The fact that it fractured revealed his innocence."

Creed suddenly threw himself off the balcony, landing in front of the crowds, sticking the perfect landing. Then he marched over to the arena where the announcer tossed more gold at the invisible wall. The red around the perimeter faded instantly.

Creed hurriedly grabbed Steele from under his armpits and wrenched him to his feet, then raised one of his arms like this was a boxing match.

"Steele is not guilty. He is free!" Creed announced.

"Then who killed the queen?" someone called out from the crowd, but Creed ignored it and instead turned to Steele, who shoved himself away from the king. I witnessed the bloody and bruised anger on his face, the fury.

I couldn't hear the furious words they exchanged, but when Steele marched right out of the cavern without a single look our way, my blood curdled.

Behind me, murmurs rose about the queen's murderer still being out there.

I didn't listen to them though, I was just devastated for Steele. I couldn't even imagine what he must have gone through, being ostracised from his home, declared a killer by his family, all while being innocent and no one believing him.

Fuck. Was that worse than dying?

CHAPTER 12

BLAKE

"Fuck me, yes, fuck me harder," I cried out, bent over the table, taken ravenously from behind, a cock in my pussy, two fingers in my ass. "That's it, Ash, oh my god! I'm so close."

"Milk me, clench your sweet pussy around me. I could live with my dick buried inside you." He roared like a lion, pounding into me.

His cock hardened, and the ache of my orgasm fiercely claiming me hit hard. I screamed, my body rocking back and forth from the sheer force of Ash's thrusts. I thrashed beneath him as he brought himself to the ultimate climax, suddenly bursting within me, filling my pussy with his seed. His fingers in my ass never paused, working me as I kept squeezing him.

Primal arousal tightened my skin, and I panted for breath when he withdrew his fingers, and I could breathe easier.

When he finally drew that heavy cock out of me, he ran his finger up my leg, collecting his cum, and pushing it back inside me, his two fingers thrusting, tugging at my nerves.

Purring, I wriggled my ass at him, absolutely lost to my

lust. "It's almost like you're trying to get me pregnant." I half laughed, half moaned.

He growled, pumping his fingers into me faster, my body tingling, my nipples hardening. "I'm ready to fuck you when you're on all fours with a heavy pregnant tummy, breasts engorged, your greedy pussy desperate for me."

"You are?" I gasped from a combination of his words and him drawing out his slick fingers when I wasn't ready to finish. My insides twisted with a sense of excitement that he'd thought about having a baby with me, but yet terrified that I even contemplated the possibility. I mean...they were monsters!

He grinned, nodding as he returned his fingers to my throbbing channel, and I completely forgot what we were talking about.

Scorching heat swept over me. I might have asked more questions but when he pushed three fingers into me, I cried out. Another deep purr scratched over my throat because I couldn't get enough.

"Want me to stop, gorgeous?" he teased, kissing my ass cheeks.

"Don't you dare."

"Good, I want to see if you can take four fingers. Your pussy is so wet, so ready."

"No, that's too much."

He chuckled and bit into my ass, the pinch sharp. "My gorgeous girl, I've already got you so stretched, I might be able to get my hand in there."

I shivered, and when I shot him a glare, a growl ripped from me. "Now, you're being crazy."

"Am I?" He pumped into me faster, widening me, and I had no idea I could be so turned on, the burning hot walls clenching around his unrelenting fingers.

"Ash," I cried out, shifting to get him away from my pussy, but he just followed, refusing to let me go. Instead, he grasped my hip, fingers holding my love handles as he fingered me into Nirvana until I screamed down the castle from my fourth orgasm that morning.

———

By the time we'd finally collapsed into exhaustion and then showered, I thought of Steele again. I'd asked Ash to fuck my brains out to help me stop feeling like crap. No one had seen him since yesterday, and I knew he needed time, but it was killing me waiting to talk to him.

So after our little romp, Ash took me out to the local town square markets to try and distract me more. We walked along, and I searched the monsters we passed, wondering if we'd been able to provide the citizens of Wyld even a mere trickle of food, as it would be better than nothing at all.

The mystery of why the food had dwindled still remained unknown, though I knew Creed worked tirelessly to find a solution.

Ash came up to stand behind me, his hands on my waist, and I lifted my gaze to the stall of jewelry in front of us. Everything appeared to be made of hard, dried mud. Sure, it had been shaped into tear drops and crescent moons or a variety of other items, but it was still pottery at the end of the day.

"Is there anything you'd like from here?" he whispered.

The female with a frilled neck which kept inflating and deflating with each breath kept pointing at her bracelets, saying something to me I didn't understand.

"Maybe one of her bracelets," I suggested, picking up one that had tiny red stones in the mud circles, and was the prettiest of the lot.

Once he paid the woman who clasped the bracelet around my wrist, we kept moving to other stalls, each offering crafts, and one person barbecuing more of those slimy snails I'd seen in the cafe kitchen a few days ago. It smelled just as awful as it did then.

"The woman at the stand said the stones are garnets," Ash explained. "Which are said to protect the wearer from negativity and evil thoughts. She thinks it was made for you."

"Really?" I studied the piece, running the pad of my finger over a stone, noticing how it glinted a deep blood-red when the sunlight found its surface. "Well, that's pretty much what I need," I said sarcastically.

We kept walking, me taking in the sights. Some of the monsters we passed glared at us, but Ash had brought two spider guards with us. They kept their distance but watched in case someone decided I was fair game for starving them.

"Oh, look," I said, then felt stupid for saying that to a blind person. "They're selling the chocolate plants I love, and I could eat some now. Maybe we can buy a plant and I can just munch on the leaves?"

"Anything you want, I'll make it happen," Ash said smiling, and my insides tightened at the reminder of how much he brightened my life.

Before I knew it, he'd bought all the plants in the stall and had the merchant pluck the leaves and place them in a small bag for me. I blushed because I had no idea if they knew I was about to eat their precious plants. While they did this, I glanced around at an oversized fountain in the middle of the town square, with yellow water flowing. I didn't want to know what that was or touch it for that matter. But I was captivated by the beautiful statue of the woman with two heads holding onto a serpent, water flowing from its gaping mouth.

There were so many things in this world that were polar opposites, and yet they worked perfectly. Like whoever this woman had been, she either slayed snake monsters or was a maid killed by one to be forever remembered in statue form.

Kids were running around the water, splashing each other,

but something else grabbed my attention from the fountain. There was a red crown painted on the stone base of the fountain, just like the one I'd seen in the cavern of the Red Battle, and I was convinced I'd seen it elsewhere too.

At first, I assumed it was the creator's mark, but I wasn't too sure. It made more sense that it was a stamp of approval, perhaps from the Red Queen back in her day of reign. I found it interesting she'd placed her stamp of approval on items around the city.

Once Ash returned, we continued our tour through the markets. And by the time we got back to the castle, I was eating the leaves like a bag of chips.

Their chocolate taste left me salivating, and there was no way I could stop until I finished the whole bag. Ash had to leave for an errand for Creed, and seeing as I was alone, I found myself staring out the window, eating my leaves, thinking about the crown image I'd seen around. It made me wonder if the other place I saw it had been at the museum where they had the queen's head on display?

Stuffing my mouth with more leaves, I finally left them behind in my room and made my way to the museum, curiosity getting the better of me. Sitting around only had me overthinking where Steele was, how Seven kept his distance, and even Tempest's strange behavior lately.

By some small miracle, the elevator didn't try to kill me today–I only went three wrong places before making it to my intended destination. I made my way down the corridor where the mud-like walls were decorated with bones. Torches burned in wall brackets on my path, leading me to the familiar arched doorway made of entwined branches.

I knocked, but when no one answered, I pushed it open, greeted by the morbid display of severed heads encased in glass suspended from the ceiling by chains. Even if I had been there before, it still left me shuddering to have these dead eyes seeming to follow you around the room.

Once inside, I instantly spotted Boltaroy, the guardian of all the deceased as he'd once told me, a monster who wore black pressed suits with a white button-up shirt underneath. Currently, he had his nose inside a huge leather-bound book.

He stood lanky, skin whitish blue as though he was the one who was dead, and greasy black hair slicked off his face.

"Hello, Boltaroy," I said loud enough to grab his attention.

His head jerked up from this book, eyes wide. "Got an appointment?"

"I wanted to have a look around, if that's okay? You don't appear too busy and I won't be long."

He huffed with exasperation, his nostrils flaring. "Fine, but be quick. This isn't a place to pass time."

I wanted to laugh because technically it was. But without another word, I made my way around the clinical white room, quickly finding the Red Queen.

A beautiful woman with reddish skin, turquoise colored eyes, and thorns sticking out of her neck as though she wore them as a necklace. Except those things came out from her skin. Even her small silvery horns right over her temple added to her beauty, but her position of queen was exemplified by her jewel encrusted crown.

I circled her head, searching for anything showing the crown symbol perhaps on her crown, curious why it was so randomly placed around the city. More than likely, it meant nothing, but I also needed something to distract my thoughts.

When I came up blank on the symbol, I made my way around the room, seeing if I could find it again.

"What are you searching for?" Boltaroy asked, strolling toward me, his thick book tucked under his arm.

"I'm just looking," I answered generally.

"I recognize an inquisitive expression when I see it."

Considering he was now lingering alongside me, poking his nose at what I was doing, I figured there was no harm in asking him.

"I've been seeing around the city a red painted crown in the oddest of places," I explained.

"And you guessed it had something to do with the queen, so you came to find any evidence of it here?"

I eyed Boltaroy. Was he capable of reading minds? "So, you know what they mean?"

"Speculation only. You see, I've only seen it turn up right before the death of our queen. And nobody knows what it means. But the theory going around is that they are good luck charms and will bring prosperity to those near them."

I stared at him, unsure I believed him considering moments earlier he'd told me he had no idea.

"That's interesting."

"Well, the queen did dabble in the art of magic, so it made sense she'd bestow good fortune on her citizens. She loved us, after all."

I wasn't sure what to say. Part of me disliked the queen for the single fact that my monsters had been infatuated with her at one point. Another was probably related to the agony her death had brought Steele, tearing apart the circle who were once friends.

I suspected there was so much more going on that I didn't know, so I smiled at Boltaroy. "Thanks for letting me look around."

"Of course, but it really would be better if you made an appointment beforehand." He wandered back to the front of the museum, and I rolled my eyes at how pedantic he was.

Having found nothing new, and deciding it could be explained as the symbol being a good luck charm, I decided I'd make my way back upstairs. If I was lucky, I'd bump into one of the monsters because I wasn't really in the mood to be alone.

CHAPTER 13
BLAKE

I'd woken up in a mood.

My breasts were aching and swollen, I had a headache, and my vagina was on fire.

My period had started.

Being in this weird fantasy land had distracted me from real life. I hadn't had a period since coming here…and I'd been so caught up in all the craziness…that I hadn't thought once about it.

It probably should have been top of mind since I'd been fucked a million different ways lately, but what could I say… the monster dick had distracted me from the fact that I was in fact still a human woman…who did in fact bleed.

And it fucking sucked.

It was also probably dangerous, I thought, as I stared out my window and saw a flying monster zooming nearby…and the spider guards down below on one of the bridges.

I bet those fuckers would get one whiff of the blood and try and eat me alive.

I decided right then and there that I wasn't leaving the room without backup.

No sooner had I thought that, then a cramp started and I whimpered as it ricocheted through me.

Scratch that. I wasn't leaving my room. I also wasn't leaving my bed.

But what would I do about all the blood?

I'd always had terrible cramps. And I'd always been a heavy bleeder. It was the one reason I was allowed to skip school growing up. After I'd had too many periods where I would leak through the pads and tampons, staining my school uniform, they would usually let me take my heaviest day of my cycle at home...simply to avoid the gossip.

The house staff had made sure I had everything I needed. Hot pads and lots of Advil. Sometimes the cramps would get so bad that they would need to bring me more hardcore stuff...and I'd find myself hooked to an IV as they pumped medicine into me.

Fuck. This was one of those times I needed the hardcore stuff.

The hours passed in agony. Silent tears streamed down my face, soaking my pillow.

A knock sounded at the door.

"Go away," I grumbled, not wanting to see anyone or risk one of the household staff deciding I would make a good snack. I was in no condition to fight off anything.

"Blake?" Ash's concerned voice called through the door, and my body immediately relaxed. If there was anyone I'd want to see in this place feeling like this, it was him.

I sniffled, and the door suddenly flew open, rattling the room as it slammed against the wall. "What's wrong?" he demanded, his nose sniffing the air, panic all over his features. "Why do I smell blood? Who hurt you?" His voice was a roar by the time he was done, a slice of violence there I didn't usually see from my cute marshmallow monster.

"No one hurt me," I moaned pathetically. "It's just...my time of the month."

He cocked his head, his lips pursed in confusion. "Is this a special time? Should we be making a cake?"

A hysterical laugh squeaked out of me and his concern grew.

"A cake might be nice…but no it's not my special time. It's my period," I said, envisioning myself gorging on an entire chocolate cake.

A cramp rippled through me and I curled my knees to my chest, gritting my teeth and closing my eyes as I tried to breathe deeply and control the pain.

"A period," Ash murmured, and my eyes flew open to see him flipping through a tiny book, studying its contents intently, his fingers tracing along the bumps on the pages. Hmm. Monsters either could read braille, or they had their own system they used. "Aha! A period. 'Normal vaginal bleeding that occurs as part of a woman's monthly cycle. Every month, a woman's body prepares for pregnancy. If no pregnancy occurs, the uterus, or womb, sheds its lining. The menstrual blood is partly blood and partly tissue from inside the uterus. It passes out of the body through the vagina.'"

I stared at him in horror as he proceeded to give me an analytical description of my cycle. Evidently, his little book was some kind of human encyclopedia.

Ash finished reading and stared up at me proudly. "Okay. I've got this." He peered down at the book, continuing to follow along the lines with his fingers. "Human women often experience mood swings during this time of the month. Try massages, warm showers, and sweets to help alleviate symptoms."

"What the fuck is that book?" I spit out. Although, I had to admit that those three things sounded quite wonderful at the moment. What I really needed, though, was some Advil.

Another cramp hit me, and Ash panicked as he stared back down at his book. "Ok, where is it, the pain during period," he muttered. "Oh, here it is! 'During a human woman's period, their uterus contracts to help expel its lining. Hormone-like substances involved in pain and inflammation trigger the uterine muscle contractions.'" He read the rest of the sentence under his breath—thankfully—and then snapped the book shut, before glancing up at me proudly.

I stared at him dumbfounded. "Um…that's quite the book."

"As soon as I met you, I started to collect human resources so I could know all the things to make you happy."

I fucking swooned. I mean, how could I not? He was just too…cute. I had a stupid, silly grin on my face that I was glad he couldn't see. Because that would be embarrassing.

My smile slid off my face as another cramp pushed through me, and I whimpered, wanting the bed to swallow me because I couldn't handle this.

"Fuck. Okay. I have to get supplies. I'll be right back," he assured me before leaping out of the room.

I waited in misery, wondering what odd thing he'd return with…and hoping it would be something that actually helped. I was also hoping he didn't involve anyone else in his mission. If the rest of them came in and also pulled out little books about human periods, my ovaries would probably burst.

A few minutes later, he hustled into the room, lugging a large bag in his arms.

He hummed as he set it down on one of the armchairs in the room and rifled through it. Ash pulled out a large rock and practically ran towards the bed.

"Um…I don't think that book has the right information in it. I'm not thinking that—" My words cut off with a squeak as he flipped me to my back and then laid the rock right over my stomach…like the perfectly warm rock was a heating pad.

I moaned in relief and he grinned at me proudly. "The book says that heat helps with cramps. This Wyld rock will stay warm for however long you want it to."

"Amazing," I murmured as I sank into my pillows, a little relief strumming through my insides. But then another cramp hit. "Got any Advil in there?" I muttered through gritted teeth.

It was completely endearing how Ash ran back to the bag, searching through it frantically before he glanced up at me sheepishly.

"What exactly is Advil? That wasn't anywhere in my book."

"Pain medicine," I whimpered, pressing on the rock so the heat would seep into me more.

He brightened at that statement and went back to searching through the bag. "Here!" he announced triumphantly, holding up a…green plant. He walked back over to me, tearing leaves off the plant before handing them to me.

"Do I rub them over where I'm cramping? Do I eat them?" I asked desperately.

"Oh, right. You just chew them and they should help with the pain. Those leaves are the closest thing we've got to pain medicine here. They won't take all the pain away, but they should lessen it. Monsters don't actually find much use for the stuff."

"Right. Because you guys are all so bad ass," I huffed, tentatively stuffing one of the leaves in my mouth and chewing it. It was all I could do not to gag. It tasted like ground-up coffee beans…and sewage.

"I know it's gross…but I brought something to make it better!" Ash ran away again, but this time to the door. He threw it open with a flourish, revealing a cart with a giant, hopefully chocolate, cake sitting on a plate.

"If that's chocolate, I'm going to marry you," I announced, wincing as I swallowed the last of the leaves.

Ash's face lit up with absolute happiness, and I blushed. "I didn't mean—"

"I accept your marriage proposal," he said, totally taking my breath away.

Before we could go any further down that particular, confusing road…he grabbed the plate and walked it over to me, brandishing the whole cake proudly like it was an award he'd won.

I reached for the utensil to eat with, but he batted my hand away playfully and flopped on the bed, almost dropping the cake as he did so.

I gasped in horror at the thought of losing it. I was so desperate, I'd probably find myself eating it off the floor. Luckily…it didn't come to that. And he righted it before it could slide off the plate.

He scooped up a big bite of the cake and held it to my lips. Fuck, my insides were fluttering. And not because of my cramps. He was so freaking sweet. Like the best kind of candy.

Like this chocolate cake.

I moaned around the fork, enjoying the hunger in his gaze at the sound. Not that we could do anything about that hunger. I'd done a lot of things with these monsters, but sex during my period was a no-go.

"Thank god you have chocolate in this place," I purred as he eagerly scooped another bite, like he was enjoying this as much as I was.

The leaf stuff was starting to kick in. The cramps were still coming, but they were definitely less severe than they had been.

"We don't. I just know that it's your favorite, so I made sure to get some from your realm so we'd have it for you here."

I stared up at him…shocked. I mean, I shouldn't be shocked. He'd just told me he'd had a book made to help him understand me and my needs. And Ash had been nothing but a complete sweetheart since I'd arrived…and far longer if I thought back to my dreams.

But I wasn't used to being cherished. I wasn't used to someone giving a damn about my happiness. I wasn't sure I'd ever be used to it after the upbringing I had. Ash grinned down at me. He was in his human form today, like he was doing everything he could to make sure I had as relaxing of an experience as possible. Sitting here on the bed, while he fed me chocolate cake that tasted better than any chocolate cake I'd ever had, I could almost imagine I was a normal human girl, with her exceptionally hot boyfriend. I could almost imagine what it would have been like if I'd met him at Stanford and we'd fallen in love.

Ash would have been the dreamiest boyfriend to have in college. One you never would have wanted to let go.

"What does it taste like?" he asked curiously as he fed me another bite.

"You didn't sample it at all before you made it for me?"

"Well, I had our cook make it," he corrected. "If I had attempted to make it for you, it wouldn't have been edible."

"You could have licked the spatula," I said, lifting my eyebrows up and down like a dork…even though he couldn't see what I was doing.

"Spatula?" he muttered, and then he pulled out his book again.

I pushed it gently down, giggling. "Well, let's give you a taste then, shall we?"

His pale blue eyes stared at me intently…like he could actually see me as I took the utensil from him and grabbed a bite of the cake, bringing it to his lips.

Ash opened his mouth eagerly, totally trusting that whatever I was going to feed him, it would be amazing. I slid the cake into his mouth, shivering at the way he licked the chocolate off the utensil…almost sensually.

Eating chocolate cake had suddenly become foreplay.

"How is it?" I whispered, a rasp in my voice that definitely hadn't been there a second ago.

He leaned forward, until our noses were touching.

"Almost as sweet as your cunt."

My mouth dropped open, and another one of those embarrassing, hysterical giggles popped out. "I can't believe you said that."

"Why?" he asked with a shrug, grabbing the utensil out of my mouth and resuming feeding me.

"Because, well—" I couldn't think of anything to say. He'd completely broken my brain.

Another cramp hit me then, and although it was much better than the prior ones, I still groaned because, crap, it hurt.

"Alright, massage time," Ash sputtered, biting on his plush bottom lip like he was going through a checklist in his head of everything he could do to make me feel better.

He set the cake on a nightstand next to the bed…carefully, before removing the heated stone and then gently rolling me to my stomach. He set the stone on my lower back so it was still providing comfort, and then he went and grabbed a small bottle from his bag of tricks.

He straddled my ass, and then pushed my sleep shirt up to my neck. A second later, warm liquid hit my back.

"You're my favorite. Have I told you that lately?" I moaned as his hands worked the oil into my skin. His hands were magic. That was the only explanation for what a freaking incredible experience it was. I turned to putty under his ministrations. He paid close attention to my lower back, working on that area until my muscles finally relaxed.

"I think I might have died and gone to heaven," I murmured as his hands slid up my spine, taking away all the stress knots I'd developed there.

"Mmmh. You're never going to die, not unless I go with you too," he murmured fiercely. When he said things like that…I didn't know how to react. It was like he was in love with me.

I accept your marriage proposal.

What would it be like if he actually meant things like that?

All of a sudden, his hands slid to my sides, getting a whole lot of side-boob action. I yelped and he chuckled. "You know, there was something else on that list about a way to alleviate cramps." He said it casually, but there was an undercurrent to his words that felt very…dangerous.

"And what would that be?" I asked breathlessly. His hands had moved under me, and he was caressing and massaging my breasts, the pulls of his hand completely maddening.

"Orgasms," he purred as he plucked at my tender nipples. "Lots and lots of orgasms."

I stiffened. "Unless you're hiding a vibrator somewhere in this castle…I'm afraid orgasms aren't possible." Another cramp chose that moment to hit me, and I moaned…loudly.

Ash clucked his tongue. "I'd never allow a vibrator to do the work with me around."

"Ash," I said cautiously. "I mean it. I'm…bleeding a lot."

He flipped me over, and I yelped again as he hovered over me…looking like a perfectly delicious dark angel that I wanted to keep with me for the rest of my life.

Those are dangerous thoughts, girl, I cautioned myself.

"You should know, angel. One thing about monsters…we aren't afraid of a little blood."

I watched wide-eyed, as if I was a passenger in my own body, as he slid down my underwear. I'd stuffed a towel in between my thighs to try and catch the blood, and it was completely soaked.

Ash removed the cloth and brought it to his nose, taking a deep inhale as his pupils dilated, and a faint blush came to his cheeks.

I was a strange mixture of horrified and turned on as I stared at him getting off on my period soaked towel.

As far as I knew, most human men were very uncomfortable about periods.

Ash was…uncomfortably comfortable.

He set the towel on the bed next to him carefully, like he was saving it for a little snack later, and then he pulled aside my legs, carefully studying my bloodied folds like they were a rare specimen.

"Ash, I can't," I squeaked.

"Shhh, baby. You can. Let me make you feel good. There's nothing I want more." His fingers slid through my folds, already slick with my blood. He caught my clit with his thumb, rubbing against it leisurely, his head cocked like he was listening to my exhales and using them as clues to what I liked.

"I can't get enough of you. If you'd let me, we'd just stay in bed, and I'd spend all my days in your cunt." He leaned over me and then his lips were covering mine in a sweet kiss. "I want to make you as addicted to me as I am to you. I need you to need me the way I need you."

He sealed his lips over mine again, his fingers continuing their torturous movements between my legs.

This was an extremely heavy day. I could feel the blood drizzling out of me, and I was sure my cheeks were red from how embarrassed and horny he was making me. Ash leaned away and pulled his fingers out from between my legs. He held his bloody fingertips in front of his face and inhaled again, a look of deep fascination on his face.

"Ash…don't," I warned. But he didn't listen. Not one bit. He brought his bloody fingertips to his lips and his pink tongue darted out, licking the blood.

There was a low, pleased rattle emanating from his chest. "Fuck, that's good," he purred, his dick hardening even more against me as it grew.

"I can't believe you just did that," I hissed, trying to push him off me.

He chuckled but didn't let me move him even an inch. Instead, he stuck the rest of his fingers into his mouth and sucked on them until they popped out completely blood free.

"I'm convinced now there isn't a part of you that doesn't taste like perfection."

"You would know now," I retorted, a little grumpy because of how turned on I was.

"Don't worry, baby. I'm going to make you feel *all* better. It's just a bonus I get to eat while I do it."

"Ash!" That was all I could say as he slid his body down mine, making sure to replace his warmth with the rock again so I was taken care of.

He pried my legs open with both hands, gripping my inner thighs gently but firmly so I couldn't close them like I was trying to.

"I can't believe this. This is definitely not what my college boyfriend would be doing," I practically shouted nonsensically.

He chuckled against my skin, burying his nose near my pussy and simply breathing in like a crazy person.

Or monster.

"You want to play a little make-believe, sweetheart? Pretend it's a boring human between your thighs," he drawled. "I can guarantee a human boy wouldn't be able to make you feel half as good as I'm about to."

With that statement, he thrust his tongue between my folds, capturing all the blood as he licked and sucked my pussy.

I came instantly, the build-up was too much for me to hold back.

He lifted his face, a wide smile on his lips, and blood smeared all over his nose, lips, and chin.

A part of me perversely wished for a camera to capture the moment.

"That's one," he purred, before burying his face in my core once again. His tongue slid inside me in a thrusting rhythm, mimicking his cock. I whimpered in ecstasy, another orgasm already building.

"I've got you, sweetheart. Just let go. Let me make you feel good," he murmured in between licks.

I was forgetting the *bloody* situation with how good his tongue was feeling.

"I've never tasted anything better." He groaned hungrily and made a swallowing sound…and I realized he'd literally swallowed gulps of my blood.

Fuck.

I panted, and arched…and came…because evidently, I was a dirty bitch.

"That's two," he said breathlessly, diving back in.

My hands slid into his silky hair, pulling and pushing as I writhed against his face. It felt so good. He was eating me like it was his job, like it was his favorite thing in the world. His tongue slid and separated my folds as if he was chasing every drop of blood present there. Ash worked his way down to my *other* hole…circling the rim like he was trying to get every drop that escaped him.

"Ash, please," I panted, wiggling awkwardly. He slid two fingers inside me, his mouth going back to my clit as he summoned a third orgasm.

When he grinned at me and said "three," I snorted unsexily. His face lit up at the sound though, like I literally could do no wrong for him.

And then he dove right back in, resembling a serial killer with how much blood was all over him. And I mean all over him. It had dripped down his neck and onto his chest.

Like I said…it was a heavy day.

And as the orgasms continued, all of my cramps did indeed fade.

And I'd decided that having a monster for a boyfriend was much better than any regular college dude.

I was also realizing that I'd fallen hopelessly and completely in love with Ash.

I'd fallen asleep after Ash had worn me out with what felt like a million orgasms. When I finally woke up…I felt like a million bucks. I lazily stretched my arms over my head, realizing something silky and luxurious had been wrapped around me, and another small towel had been placed in between my legs. I must have been dead to the world to not notice Ash dressing me.

I blinked the sleep out of my eyes as I glanced around, wondering where Ash had gone.

I heard him before I saw him. He was humming in my closet. It was adorable.

So, I slid off the bed, amazed at how loose and relaxed I felt as I walked over to the closet.

I came to a screeching halt when I saw what he was doing.

First of all, he still had my blood all over him. And second of all…he'd built some kind of…bed in the closet.

"What exactly is all of this?" I asked, gesturing to the pile of odds and ends he'd put together…carefully, I might add. He seemed to have a specific method to his madness.

"I have a perfectly good bed out there, as you know," I teased.

He glanced up from his work happily. "I've made you a nest," he announced proudly, pointing to the mess on the floor.

A nest…I wasn't familiar with that.

"Is that a Wyld city thing? Because I've never heard of it."

His face didn't fall one bit at my confusion. "It's for you to cuddle in, now that you're officially breeding."

Breeding? W.T.F.

"I'm actually doing the opposite of breeding," I told him. "Human periods mean you aren't having a baby…remember?"

"The book's wrong," he said, peeling off his shirt and carefully tucking it into a crevice between a pillow…and a shoe.

"You've been here for months. And you haven't had your period. I think your body changed…like your hair. And you're actually breeding now."

I was absolutely sure he was wrong…or at least I was absolutely sure that I hoped he was wrong.

Before I could say anything, a pair of wings caught my eye. I leaned over and then grimaced when I realized there were white bugs sprinkled all over.

"What? Did I put something in the wrong spot?" Ash asked, clearly concerned.

"Yes," I said slowly. "You've put bugs in my nest."

"Oh," he said, sounding stumped. "Is that bad? Flufferhorn marges have very soft wings and a sweet scent."

I blew out a huff of air, hungry for some chocolate cake suddenly, anything to escape this conversation. "You should probably write in that book of yours that I'm decidedly anti all bugs. And definitely not where I'm resting…err, resting, I mean."

"Even flufferhorn marges?"

I did my best to hold in the laugh that was desperate to come out. "Yes, even those," I responded, keeping my gaze averted from the so-called flufferhorn creatures.

Ash was nodding his head like he was absorbing everything I was saying. He pulled out his book and wrote something in there, taking my request seriously. "I'll get rid of the bugs right away and redo the nest. Might take me a few hours more, but I'll get it done."

My giggle finally escaped because, seriously…he was standing there with my dried period blood all over his face, looking like a demonic dream. And he was building me a monster nest…because he thought I was breeding and would want one, apparently.

"How about we just cuddle…on the bed," I offered. "You can worry about the nest later."

He pursed his lips, clearly torn about leaving his project.

"We can eat more cake," I offered, taking a step back and hoping desperately he would follow me.

Ash perked up at that but still didn't move toward me.

"And then you'll let me eat you again…right, baby?" he finally purred, stalking towards me.

I mean, he already had blood all over his face…

"And then I'll let you eat me," I murmured, still embarrassed.

With that promise, he swept me up in his arms and prowled out of the closet and away from the nest.

And we did indeed eat cake and…other things…for the rest of the day.

I stood at the edge of the cage, watching the small monster huddled in the corner, carefully staring at his dirty feet like they held the secrets of the universe. There were other monsters and cages around him, some of them screaming in agony. But the boy didn't look up. I knew he wouldn't.

Not until they came.

He'd stayed in his own fractured world, because that was what he had to do to survive.

One of the monsters in the cage next to him began to violently retch all over the floor, the vomit a dark blood color that signaled his end was coming. I knew he was sick. There was always some kind of disease going around the camp. Special diseases of their own making since monsters would normally be invulnerable. The blue-skinned monster that was also in that cage eyed the bile carefully, plastering himself against the walls, knowing that if even a speck of the vomit got on him, he would die as well.

But the boy still didn't look up.

I heard the footsteps then, and my insides went cold, knowing what I was about to see. This scene was one my dreams took me to frequently. The day when the boy would completely fall apart, and *never be the same. I wanted to scream at him to run, to do anything he could to get away, but I knew it was useless. There wasn't an escape for him.*

They appeared then, outside the cage, terrifying creatures with long black snouts filled with razor-sharp teeth, and eyes that glowed a garish green color. They were enormous, even for monster standards, and they were scourges on the world. The Varicash.

"Ready to play?" one of them purred in a gravelly, scratchy voice that reminded me of nails against a metal wall.

Please wake up, please wake up, I chanted, not wanting to see this again. But of course, my mind kept me trapped in the dream. Watching.

The fact that the boy didn't look up only made them angry. The one who had spoken stepped into the cage and grabbed the boy by his rail-thin arm, giving him a shake to get his attention.

Still, he didn't look up.

"Maybe we've finally broken him." One of the others grinned, lime green spittle that almost matched the color of his eyes dripping from his teeth.

"Or maybe it means we haven't broken him enough," the other one answered, his groin tightening in anticipation of the horrors of what was to come.

"We will tonight." The room filled with the nasty sound of their laughter.

He dragged the boy from the cell. The monsters in the other cages didn't make a sound. They didn't call for help. They didn't protest. Even though they knew what his fate would be.

I was forced to follow the boy as they dragged him out of the warehouse and down a hallway with sterile white walls until they got to a gleaming ten-foot silver door that stood in stark contrast to the pristine perfectness of the connecting hallway. The one not holding the boy knocked twice, and a few seconds later, the door slid open with a groan, loud music and red light streaming from the room beyond it.

He dragged the boy inside, and I begged myself to wake up once again.

But of course, I didn't.

We walked into the room, where other male and female monsters were strung up on devices, being tortured for their Varicash masters' sexual gratification. He was the only child there, a place no child should ever be.

The monsters torturing the others stared at the little boy hungrily.

And then it began. And I watched as the boy was broken. I watched as the others came out of him.

I watched and I wanted to die.

It was a terrible thing to be forced to watch your rape over and over again every night in your dreams.

It was an even worse thing to know that because of it, you'd never be whole again, nor would you be able to be with the woman of your dreams. That those nightmarish creatures had won and the scars they'd left behind would ruin your entire life.

I woke up with a gasp, sweat-drenched, my chest heaving from the dream. I immediately leaned over and vomited over and over again, just as I always did when my mind forced me to relive the torture I'd experienced as a child.

After I'd finished throwing up, I flopped back into my chair, wondering why I'd let myself fall asleep at all.

It was an impossible thing. If I fell asleep, I had nightmares, but the more tired I became, the more likely it was that one of the others would come out to play, more likely that *he* would come out to play. And after what he'd done to Blake, I couldn't let that happen. Glancing around the fire in front of me, I rubbed my eyes in exhaustion, wondering for what felt like the millionth time if I was better off throwing myself into the flames and ending the agony once and for all.

What holds you back? he snarked.

I scoffed to myself, because *he* knew. *He* knew that I was too weak to do it, too selfish.

I didn't want to go somewhere where she wouldn't be. I thought back to that first night, when Creed had dragged us all along. I hadn't wanted to go. I had no interest. I had a date with death already planned and ready. What did I care of a little human girl?

But the second I'd seen her, all of me had wanted her. All of me had become completely obsessed. And every time I touched her, the obsession grew even worse. My demise was pushed back night after night, because I wanted to see Blake one more time.

We will have her again, he promised in my head, and I growled out loud, fully aware of how crazy I'd look if someone were to step in.

Then, as if I'd conjured him by my thoughts, Ash opened my door and peered in, a carefully blank look on his face that I knew was intentional. I'm sure I'd been screaming during my dream, and of course, he'd heard me—there wasn't anyone else with as well-developed hearing as Ash.

"You were dreaming again," he murmured, and I didn't bother answering him.

"Are they getting worse?" he asked, concerned. I waited before opening my mouth, kind of wanting to ignore him until he gave up and left. But then again – he'd never given up on me no matter how badly I'd treated him, no matter how much I'd pushed him away.

He never gave up.

I both hated and loved him for that.

"Maybe a bit worse than usual," I finally admitted.

"Is it because of her?"

I nodded reluctantly. Not that it was her fault, but worrying about my other selves coming out, worrying what they would do to her, worrying that *he* would give up our secrets…it was driving me even more mad than I already was.

"What if you just told her?" Ash asked after a pause, his body stiff, in case I decided to lunge at him for that suggestion.

I was tempted to. The idea made me furious. "I've already told you what he did when he got out around her. Why would I ever let that happen again?"

He chewed on his bottom lip. Ash was in his human form, as usual. While the rest of us preferred our monstrous forms, since the moment he'd met Blake, he'd switched to stay with his human face. I knew out of all of us, he was the most worried about what she thought of him. He truly was a monstrous creature, but I'd seen the looks she'd given him when he wasn't staring. And I didn't think our little human minded his monster form at all. But it was kind of nice to see my well-adjusted, cheerful, optimistic brother struggled with something, even though that made me a complete asshole.

"When are you going to make peace with *him*?" Ash finally asked.

"Peace with him?" I scoffed, throwing myself out of my chair and lashing my arms up in frustration. "Have you forgotten all the things he's done when he's taken control? The fights he's gotten into, how he almost got me thrown out of the castle after he fucked Creed's girlfriend. About how he almost ate Freddy? You want me to try and make peace with him?"

Ash sighed, an edge of exasperation in his breath. "Maybe he only does that because of how much you fight him. He's clearly as obsessed with Blake as you are—"

I scoffed as soon as the sentence came out of his mouth, but he only stared at me knowingly. For someone who couldn't see, it was almost terrifying how much he still managed to do it.

"I'm just saying. Maybe the two of you can come to some sort of truce. You're both interested in Blake. You're both invested in her happiness and her safety. So he goes about it in a rougher way…maybe that's not bad?"

"He tried to rape her!" I roared, the word sitting in the room with us like an ugly specter.

He was suspiciously silent inside of me, seeming to confirm what I'd said.

"Did he, though?" Ash asked softly. "With the way you described it, he may have overstepped some boundaries, but our little angel hasn't shied away from a bit of roughness. It might've scared her in the moment, but if you actually tried to talk to her about it, maybe she would have different thoughts about the situation and what you did."

I was already shaking my head before he finished, thinking of the fear and betrayal on her features when I'd taken back control. There was no part of her that had wanted that.

"What's the plan then?" Ash snapped, anger in his tone for the first time since he'd entered the room. Ash knew what had happened to me. I'd been rescued from the camps and come back to our household a broken shell of the brother I'd been before I'd left. I hadn't spoken for months, but Ash had never given up on me. He'd sat with me in the silence, he'd crawled into bed with me when my nightmares woke him up. Ever since that moment, he'd been the best brother and twin any creature could've asked for. The only other time he'd truly been mad at me was when he'd found a bottle of *shatra* in my room five years after my return from the camps, and he'd known I was planning on killing myself.

Ash deserved a better brother…everyone deserved better than me.

"You're doing it again. That 'woe is me' attitude where you give up on any chance of happiness in the world."

I stumbled back as if he'd put a knife in my chest. "My 'woe is me' attitude?" I whispered. "How can you say that?"

"Because you have the best chance of happiness that you've ever had right in front of you. What's the use in deciding to live if you're not actually going to *live*. Brother, I've watched you die a little more every day until Blake came into our lives. I know how happy she makes you. I know you're in love with her. And I won't let you ruin this for yourself," Ash said solemnly.

"What is that supposed to mean?" I growled, but he was already stalking out of the room, slamming my bedroom door behind him.

His words sounded ominous. What the fuck was my brother planning? I stumbled towards my bar as if I was already drunk, grabbing some particularly strong stuff to try and drown the night away.

"This is childish," my older grandpa-type demon chided inside me. But he was easy to ignore; they all were, except for *him*. None of the rest of them tried to take over, and three of them simply existed inside of me, letting me be aware of them, but never actually speaking to me.

I grabbed the bottle, not bothering to pour the liquid into the glass, and I threw it back, the burn as it passed down my throat exactly what I needed. I sat back in my chair and stared into the fire…and got more and more drunk. I couldn't help but think… What if Ash were right? What if there was a way for me to actually be happy?

———

Blake

Steele was gone, lost in the wind, so to speak. No one had seen him since that fight. I couldn't help but picture the look on his face, the one that spoke to the betrayal and pain he'd felt all these years when his so-called brothers had run him off and believed the worst of him. Every day he didn't show up, the panic inside me grew, wondering if he'd decided to leave for good, if he'd decided I wasn't worth the heartache and the pain of having to return to the home that betrayed him.

Ash said I was crazy to think like that, that no one could ever leave me voluntarily, but for a girl whose own parents hadn't even wanted her, the idea of another person I loved feeling the same way was a burning hole in my heart and mind that I couldn't get rid of.

I had taken to wandering the castle, hoping he would just pop out somewhere. I knew he probably hadn't stuck around, but there were so many mysteries still in this place that I held out hope. I tried to get the others to take me into the city to look for him, but all of them had wanted to give Steele his space. There were a lot of apologies to be had, but the stubborn, prideful fools didn't seem ready for it.

Today I found myself retracing my steps to the…unique monster café I'd found before. Unique was still the best way for me to put it. It had taken me a while to find the café again. The elevator had first taken me to some kind of fancy bathroom-type room where I'd been graced with the sight of what must've been a million-year-old monster judging by the kaleidoscope of wrinkles all over its gelatinous being. I was wondering if it was a relative of Freddy, judging by the slime she'd left behind… And I also wondered what the point of a shower was in the first place when you had slime like that for your skin.

The elevator had then taken me to a giant room that was literally soundless. I'd stepped out and it was as if I was caught in a vacuum of some sort. I'd begun to get lightheaded and almost fainted from whatever vibrations they had going in there that made it so silent you felt like you were going mad. I'd once read an article about a place like that on earth. The longest someone could stand in the room was four minutes before they started to go crazy. I imagined this place was like that on crack.

Somehow I made it back into the wretched elevator without fainting, and after two more tries, one in which it literally opened to a gray stone wall, I made it back to the freaky hallway with no windows and a dilapidated air to it.

I quickly walked down the hallway this time, excited when I made it to the arched double doors without getting lost. I knocked again and immediately felt a flicker of relief when Bane's voice called for me to come in.

He didn't seem surprised to see me when I walked in. I thought about how odd it was that the sight of the skeletal-looking monster actually had me feeling comfort and relief that I hadn't had in the days since Steele had disappeared.

"I wondered if you'd come back," he said in that casual way of his as he chopped what unfortunately resembled a giant eyeball into slivers.

"Couldn't keep away," I murmured, unable to take my gaze away from the sight of the eyeball being peeled away. I had the urge to cover my face for a minute and run, just in case the monsters at the café decided human eyeballs were next.

"It's the special of the day," he exclaimed as he artfully arranged it on a stone plate. He took a red sauce—that had the consistency of blood—and carefully spooned it over the slivers of eyeball. "This is from a rat-toothed horndog. It's a rarity, but one of the hunters found it lurking outside the city gates and I was able to serve it in the café today."

"A 'rat toothed horndog'?" I repeated. He had walked over to some books arranged on a shelf above the cooktop and selected one of the blue bound ones. Flipping open the pages, he stopped and showed me a picture of a creature that literally resembled an eyeball at least five times the size of my head with a skinny tail. "They use their tails to move around. They're quite rare, but they have a very unique flavor. I can charge five times as much for the daily special on days when I get my hands on one of these. Would you like to try it?"

No, I definitely did not want to try it, but I attempted to hold back my grimace and act polite at his gesture. "Thank you, but I just ate," I murmured after a second.

He nodded, thankfully not seeming bothered at all by my rejection, and then he walked out to the other side of the kitchen. I followed like a puppy, the shadows darkening again before we made it into the oversized room where customers were sitting eating. I waited there while he walked over and served a table the plate, both of the monsters looking absolutely thrilled with his offering. I watched as another couple made out over their plates, or should I say they both outstretched their thick blue tongues and rubbed them against each other. The gesture, although very alien to watch, had me thinking about Steele. Everything inside me was desperate to find him, like he had an integral part of me with him.

Bane returned from serving the couple, and we went back into the kitchen.

"Forgive me if I'm overstepping, but you seem a bit… down," Bane said in that quiet way of his, as he sliced more of the eyeball for another plate.

I was going to push his inquiry away and deny that anything was wrong, but then I wondered, if he'd been here for a while, would he have known Steele from before, perhaps?

"You've been in this place for quite a long time, right?" I was aiming for nonchalance, but when he lifted his face to me, it was like he could see right through me.

"For longer than I can remember."

I filed that tidbit away but pressed on.

"I assume you would have interacted with the king and his circle quite often, then."

He went back to slicing the eyeball, arranging more pieces on plates.

"I know some of the circle well. Others are not quite as interested in interacting."

"What about… Steele?"

"Steele is probably the member of the king's circle I'm closest to—was closest to," he corrected himself. He paused in his slicing for a moment. I held my breath, wondering what he was going to say or what questions I should ask.

"Towards the end of the Red Queen's rule, before she was killed, Steele would spend hours here with me. I got the sense that not all was well with the Red Queen." His words were careful, and I wondered what he would have said instead if we were friends and he trusted me.

"He's been missing since the fight, and I'm worried about him," I confessed.

He nodded, but he also chuckled as well. "The king and his monsters are not creatures you need to be worried about. But if you can't help yourself, there are some places that he might go."

I perked up at that pronouncement, feeling hopeful for the first time.

"Will you tell me where those places are? Please," I begged. "I'd really like to make sure he's all right."

He glanced up at me again. "You love him," he said matter-of-factly. Of course, just like any time that word was brought up, my first instinct was to immediately deny it, to run away from the very idea of it. I hesitated this time, images of Steele flicking through my mind, my chest warming as I thought about him, as I savored how he'd always treated me, and the words he'd said.

"I do," I finally said, the words tasting strange on my lips… But right at the same time.

Love was a dangerous thing, that I was sure of. But it was exhausting to keep trying to stay away from it.

He nodded again, in that funny way of his.

"There's a cave in the outer walls of the city. It was where the king and his circle would gather with the Red Queen. If he was anywhere, I bet he'd be there."

My stomach clenched at the mention of her name, just like it always did, hot jealousy spiking in my throat.

"Could you by chance give me some directions on how to get there? Is it safe for me to get there?" Maybe I shouldn't have been asking the question to basically a perfect stranger, but there was something about Bane that seemed so trustworthy. Something told me he meant me no harm and that he could be a great friend if I let him.

Proving my thoughts weren't absolutely crazy, he sat down his knife and wiped his hands on his apron.

"The king and the others would have me killed if I sent you to the caves alone. As much as we like to pretend that Wyld is a peaceful place, the Red Queen's death taught us otherwise." I could tell from the way he said the words, that he thought the killer was still out there, that he one hundred percent believed it wasn't Steele. Just another point in the pro column for liking Bane. A thought tried to push its way to the surface in my head, words being spoken by someone, but as soon as I tried to grasp onto the memory, my head started hurting so bad that I bent over in pain.

"Blake," Bane called out worriedly, hustling over and stopping a few feet away, obviously not knowing how close he was allowed to get to me.

I stood up shakily, rubbing my temple as the pain subsided. "Not sure what happened."

"Should I get you back to the king?"

I gritted my teeth, taking a few deep breaths as the pain

continued to subside. "No, I'd like to go check the cave," I insisted.

Bane's face was torn for a second, but he finally nodded and gestured back to the double doors that led to the hallway in the elevator. We both made our way through, and once we got to the elevator, he said, "the tunnels," in a calm, clear voice, and the elevator began to move.

I shook my head. "How do all of you manage to get it to do what you want?" I complained. "I end up in every place but the one I'm wanting to go to whenever I get in this thing."

He chuckled, nodding his head once again. "You thought about leaving this place, haven't you?" The way he said it wasn't really a question, more like a statement.

"I want to stay," I said slowly. "I think. But it wasn't my intention to ever come here in the first place, so I suppose deciding that I'm going to make it my home for good is a process."

He nodded again. "I think you'll find that your relationship with the elevator goes much smoother once you've made that decision."

I glanced at him in confusion. "The way that you're talking, it's as if the elevator is a sentient being," I mused.

He lifted an eyebrow, or at least he gave the appearance of lifting something. The way his skeletal features moved, you only got the gist of things. "Who said it wasn't?"

Before I could ask anything else, the elevator came to a halt and the doors opened. I blinked when I saw a stone tunnel in front of me.

Bane stepped out with confidence, but I left the elevator a bit more hesitantly. This place felt old and…powerful. That was the only way to describe it. I could feel the energy humming in the walls. He set off down the hallway and I followed, checking back every so often because it felt like there were eyes on us as we moved. This definitely wasn't my favorite place.

We seemed to walk forever, turning this way and that until there was a smooth wall in front of us, with nowhere else to go.

"Where do we go now?" I asked.

Bane didn't answer me, he just pressed on a tiny red symbol, and the wall instantly retracted, revealing a doorway. It opened up into an enormous cavern, and there, slumped against a wall…was Steele.

"I'll leave you to it, Blake," Bane said quietly, before heading back down the tunnel without another word. Steele was staring at me, his face perfectly blank, and I shifted in the doorway, wondering for the first time if I'd made a mistake and I should have just left him to return when he wanted…if he ever had. He certainly didn't look happy to see me right now.

Taking a deep breath, I stepped into the room.

"Hi," I said lamely, fidgeting nervously with the shirt I was wearing.

"Hi," he finally answered, after what seemed like forever.

When he didn't say anything else, my unease only grew. "I've been worried about you."

Steele gazed away from me then, staring up at the…starry ceiling of the cave?

My head began to hurt, the same excruciating pain as before. There was something in there, just out of my reach. Why did those stars look so familiar?

"Blake!" Steele called out frantically, leaping up from where he'd been sitting and sprinting over to where I was once again hunched over in pain. I waved him away as I tried to take a deep breath, the pain so intense it made me want to throw up.

"I'm fine," I said feebly.

"You're not fine. What's going on?"

"I'm not sure. This is the second time it's happened today. I don't know what's going on." The pain started to recede again, and I was able to breathe normally even if my insides were trembling in the aftermath. "I'm ok," I whispered.

Steele was now standing in front of me, and he lifted his hand as if he was going to touch my face before dropping it back to his side.

"Blake, why are you here?" he asked quietly.

He looked…wrecked. There were dark circles under his eyes, and an air of defeat surrounded him, even though he'd been a victor in the arena. But most of all, he looked…sad. Like all of the confidence and energy that usually surrounded him had been sucked out.

I remembered how brave he'd been in the battle how hard he'd fought, and it made me want to be brave too.

"I told you, I've been worried about you."

Okay, obviously I wasn't prepared to be *that* brave.

The stars flickered above me, but I found as long as I didn't try to think about them resembling something I'd seen before, the pain stayed away. I kept my gaze averted from Steele's intense one as I glanced around the room, noting it had a dark, beautiful quality to it. I could see why they'd want to spend time here, even if the knowledge of what they'd most likely done here made me want to scream and take a sledgehammer to the whole thing.

"Why?" Steele suddenly asked.

I glanced at him, confused.

"Why, what?"

"Why were you worried about me? You ought to know by now that I can take care of myself." He was really pressing me for answers, evidently.

My hand was trembling as I lifted it to his face, approaching his cheek slowly so he could move away if he didn't want my touch. He stayed completely still, and as soon as my skin touched his, he was nuzzling into my hand and making small groaning sounds like my touch was the comfort he'd been searching for.

"I was worried about you…because I love you," I whispered.

His face.

I would never forget it for as long as I lived. It was a look of awe and spellbinding beauty, like he couldn't believe it had come out of my mouth. Like he couldn't believe I could love him.

Didn't he know how perfect he was? Didn't he know he was the only ray of light for me while I'd been trapped in that awful asylum? That my sessions with him and glimpsing the sight of him in the hallway had been what kept me going. Every moment with Steele had bound him to me irrevocably, like our hearts had been stitched together. I never planned on falling in love with a monster, but there was no denying that I had.

"Say it again," he ordered, rough emotion in his voice.

"I love you," I said slower this time, making sure I enunciated every syllable so there was no misunderstanding. Suddenly, his hands were on my face and his lips were crashing against mine. The kiss felt like a promise, and my chest surged toward his until I was plastered against him. A wave of dizziness passed through me, and my heart jolted like it was restarting in my chest, re-born after this moment.

When he broke away from me, he appeared as dazed as I felt.

"What just happened?" I asked, my breath labored as my heart raced in my chest.

His face was alive again, like he'd been restarted as well. That same look of obsessive devotion was on his face, and I blushed from the intensity of it, wanting to wrap myself in it forever because I knew I'd always feel warm, I'd always feel safe, and I'd always feel loved as long as he continued to look at me like that.

"You just triggered our mating bond," he said in a very satisfied voice.

I would've reared back in shock, but everything inside me was wanting to plaster myself against him and never let him go.

"A what?" I squeaked, even though the rightness of the word he'd used flowed through me. A mate. Mine.

"You're my mate now. You're mine to love and protect and to have forever. You are the beginning and the end of my world. There is nothing that matters but you for me. And it will be that way forever."

I realized that my hands were clenched in the soft material of his top, almost desperately. And I was rubbing my face against his chest…like I'd been possessed.

I whimpered and tried to take a step away from him, but as soon as I did, panic and anxiety flared through me.

"Shhh, Angel, it's just the mating bond settling. I'll be like this for a day or so, and then you won't feel quite so desperate."

"Are you feeling this as well?"

"Like my heart will rip out of my chest if you take any more steps away from me? Yes, I am." He pulled me tight against him and I resumed my strange nuzzling into his chest.

"You can scent mark me all you want. I'm yours forever, baby."

I definitely liked the sound of that.

He tried to move his arm from around my waist, and I whimpered. This was really getting pathetic, but it almost felt like animal instinct, the need to be with him, to touch him, to own him.

He locked his other arm around me tighter but proceeded to pull a hand in front. "Look," he said proudly.

I glanced down, shocked when I saw a bracelet of infinity symbols around his wrist in sparkling gold ink, like he'd been tattooed.

"What is that?" I gasped.

"My mate mark." He sounded like a giddy, giggling schoolgirl with how proudly he stated that fact.

When I started scent marking him again, he scooped me up into his arms and walked to the other side of the cave, pressing on another red mark on the wall until another doorway opened, revealing a hidden bedroom in a smaller-sized cavern. There was a large black silk bed on the wall across from us.

Whatever nesting instinct had taken over me, I was desperate to get in that bed with him. The other part of me was balking though, because clearly, this was where they'd fucked their Red Queen. Just the thought of someone seeing Steele and his perfect body made me feel murderous, like if she was still living, I'd be the one chopping off her head. It said a lot for the madness that had overtaken me, because no part of me felt guilty about that thought.

"Baby, it's okay. I'm going to take such good care of you." I glanced down to see I was ripping his shirt, my hands having a mind of their own. It was all I could do to drag them away from him.

He stared at me in confusion. "We are not going in there," I spit out, my arms shooting forward against my will and grabbing onto his shirt again, tearing it in half this time.

"Why not?"

I was now rubbing my whole body against him, and over-whelming heat was spreading across my skin, the urge to have him take me completely overwhelming.

"Because that's where you used to touch her." The *her* came out venom laced, and his eyes widened before a spark of amusement lit them up.

"Creed had everything replaced in here, sweetheart. And this was never where I touched her—" a growl ripped from my throat, a red haze filling my vision as I pushed Steele towards the bed before he could say anything else.

Something had taken over my body. The heat had clearly

broken my mind. Steele didn't protest at all as I pushed him towards the bed and then threw him down on the black silk sheets.

His shirt was a shredded mess, and I made quick work of his pants as well, the ruined scraps of fabric fluttering somewhere behind me to the floor. He was unreal, flawless perfection made just for me. And he was mine, mine, mine. My hands traced over his stomach and chest, running along his arms and up his fingertips, admiring everything. I was going to run my tongue along every inch of him. He had become the altar I wanted to worship on. He was the embodiment of every desire I'd ever had.

"My perfect mate," he whispered, sounding completely mesmerized. *As he should be for his mate*, something thought inside of me. He abruptly flipped me over until I was on my back and he was straddling my legs, his hands beginning a slow slide up my thighs and my stomach, up under the blouse I'd been wearing. I moaned softly as he pulled it off, and then made quick work of my pants, needing our skin to touch. Why wasn't he moving faster? I moaned again, and he pressed a soft, sweet kiss to my lips.

"You're the most gorgeous creature I've ever seen. I'm going to take such good care of you... Forever." He leaned over until his mouth was capturing one of my sensitive nipples, his wet heat suckling and making my body arch and rise against him. This was what I wanted. This was what I needed. I didn't recognize the sound coming out of my mouth as he switched to my other nipple, my insides already tightening with pleasure from his efforts.

"I need more. Please," I cried, my own hands sliding between us and attempting to offer myself relief.

"No," he growled, ignoring the cries coming from my lips. "Only I make you come. You're mine." He gripped my wrist that was still inching its way to my clit and pushed it above my head, crawling further up my body until he covered me completely. His eyes were hot and hungry as he dragged his other hand from my neck, down in between my breasts, until he was finally, blissfully where I wanted him. He held it on my clit, but he didn't move, his chest heaving as he stared down at my desperate pussy.

"Look at you, sweet girl. You're dripping for me. You're going to feel so fucking good," he purred.

"Please," I begged again as his finger finally moved until he was slipping the tip of it into my opening. I thrusted my hips against his finger, his name coming out in a long, loud chant.

He growled as I moved, watching me fuck myself on his finger.

"My mate is so sexy. So fucking perfect."

My head was thrashing around, because what he was giving me wasn't enough. I needed to be joined with him. I needed his huge cock rutting in and out of me. I wanted him to own me.

"I'll give you everything you need," he rasped.

His lips met mine then, but the kiss was much too soft for what I needed. Didn't he feel this? Wasn't this madness coating his insides as well?

Steele made another hungry noise as he thrust two more fingers inside of me and finally began to fuck them into me roughly, turning his hand so the heel of it could grind into my clit with every movement. The world went white as a climax buzzed through me. His kiss continued against my lips, but I couldn't even kiss him back. My entire focus was on where his fingers were thrusting inside of me.

"Kiss me," he growled, his tongue sliding in and out of my mouth in time with his fingers. "And after you kiss me, you're going to let me mark you. You're going to let me cover you in my scent, in my touch, so there's no question who your mate is, baby."

His eyes were feral. That was what I needed. I needed him just as out of control as I felt.

"Give me another one. Squeeze my fingers with your greedy cunt again. Give it to me now."

I came again, like he controlled my body.

And he grinned savagely.

"My fingers aren't good enough for you, are they, my mate? Your sweet pussy needs my cock. You're desperate for it."

I was still recovering from the two orgasms he'd just given me, and words were a little hard at that moment.

"Tell me how much you want my cock," he growled.

"I want it," I mewled. "Please."

He pulled his fingers from my core and licked up every gleaming drop from his fingertips. Then he pushed my thighs wide, and slid in slowly, gently stretching me. It was at odds with the crazed gleam in his gaze. He was still in human form, but his dick was definitely not, because I could feel every crazy ridge on his monster cock, and after he d slid all the way inside, it started to vibrate and I immediately came.

His mouth pushed against mine, his demanding tongue rubbing against me. I whimpered as his hand went to my throat. He didn't squeeze, he just held it there, like he wanted to make sure I knew who owned me.

You do, everything inside me screamed, totally cool with what had transpired since I'd come to the cave. He watched my face closely as he slowly pulled out. I immediately felt empty. I ached for him.

Suddenly he slammed into me, throwing himself so hard forward that his balls bounced against my ass.

"You take me so well, mate. Such a perfect pussy for me to fuck forever."

As fucked me in earnest, I felt like I was having an out-of-body experience. I was definitely in the moment, but it felt like my mind was disassociating between everything that had happened *before* and everything that was happening now. Everything before I'd stepped into this cave felt like another life. I didn't know what crazy monster magic this was, but nothing had ever felt so right.

The bulging ridges on his cock hit me perfectly every time, and I lost count of how many times I came, sweat dripping down my body. I fell in and out of consciousness, but every time I came back to myself, my body was just as hungry for him as before. We fucked for hours. Or maybe we fucked for days. There was only this; nothing existed for me but him and what his body could do for me. He took me everywhere, and in every way.

And in every hole.

Being with him felt perfect. He'd been made for me. I'd never been more sure of anything in my entire life.

…

I blearily looked up, every part of my body sore, but the burning heat was gone. The constant need to have him inside me had finally disappeared. I was exhausted, but in a good way.

Something flickered in my chest, and I rubbed it, confused, realizing that I could feel something in there with me. I could feel him. A flash of amusement trickled through me, and I realized it wasn't my own.

"It's our bond. I can feel you inside me too," he murmured lazily next to me, extremely satisfied and well fucked. His hair was all over the place, and his lips were curled up in a sexy grin. If my body thought it was possible, it would've been ready for another round.

"Hmmm, how long has it been?" I asked in a raspy voice, rough from how much I'd been screaming.

"Three days," he commented smugly.

My eyes widened in disbelief. "Three days!" I sat up, staring around the room as if Creed and the others would appear from the shadows.

"They're probably trying to burn down the kingdom as we speak," he said wryly. The tone in his voice implied he clearly didn't care. He was much too well fucked to worry about the fate of his home, apparently.

"The mating haze lasted a little longer than it does when it's two monsters, but I'm not complaining."

I laid back in the bed, exhaustion overwhelming me. I probably needed to sleep now for three days, just to recover.

"I'm sure the idiots will figure it out soon."

"You don't sound as…angry and bitter as before," I commented, searching his face like I could see inside his mind. And it was true. It wasn't only his features and the tone of his voice I was listening to; I could feel it inside me, his contentment.

He shrugged and pulled me towards him. I was sure that I stunk to high heaven. Humans didn't exactly have the same features that my monsters seemed to have that made them smell amazing no matter what they'd been doing.

Steele didn't seem to mind my smell though. He touched my nose with his, and it was freaking adorable.

"I know they can't take you away from me anymore. They'll have to learn to share. And, I guess, all the shit that's happened doesn't seem quite as terrible as before, because it led me to you. It led me to this."

I blushed, though, for what reason, I wasn't quite sure. Maybe it was the earnestness in his expression. The way it seemed as if I'd become the sun in his sky.

"I'll give you my worst thought though, Blake. Even after everything that's happened, I'm glad *she* was killed. Because if I'd found you and she'd been alive, I probably *would* have been responsible for murder. Because nothing would've kept me from you."

Evidently, the mate bond had made me even more crazy, because simply the word "her" had me wanting to carve my name in his chest, so everyone knew he was out of bounds.

He smirked at me as if he could read my mind.

"You *can't* read my mind, right?" I clarified. He chuckled, and the sound reverberated through me.

"No, I can't, unfortunately. But there's nothing a mated monster likes more than feeling his mate's obsession." I squeezed my eyes shut, blushing even more.

"I can't help it. Everything inside me knows you're mine, and it doesn't like any reminders that you ever weren't."

"When I think back on before," he started carefully. "It's all gray. Everything in my life was grey before I met you. I think I've always belonged to you. I was born to be yours."

I swooned hearing my mate say that. Except…I kind of needed some information about what "a mate" even meant. Obviously, humans didn't have anything similar.

"Yeah, about the whole mate thing. I know that it means that you're mine, and I'm yours. But besides that…I'm kind of lost."

He smiled softly, and I could feel his bond inside of me, gleaming. It was happy about what I'd said about me being his.

"True mates are rare. In Shadowburn, the legend is that mates are two parts of a soul that somehow were separated. Most creatures don't have a true mate, and the ones that do, most of them will never find their true mates. They will always walk around with half of their soul in someone else. They say that you can tell the ones who have true mates out there, because they're doomed to never be all the way happy. They won't ever feel whole until they find their other half."

"And that's what we are? True mates?" His bond inside me fluttered again with happiness. Steele reached towards me and gently pushed a tendril of hair out of my face.

"Yes. That's what this mark means," he answered, holding up his wrist so I could see it. I frowned, examining my own bare wrist.

"Are you sure? Am I supposed to have one?" I asked, a

hint of panic in my voice that had him rubbing his own chest as my feelings flickered through him.

"You do have one, baby," he said reverently. His hand pointed to my chest, and I glanced down and gasped when I saw an infinity symbol in between my breasts. The sight of it made me crazily happy.

"And you said they can't take you away from me now?"

"Yes," he murmured, that sexy smugness back again. "True mates can't be without each other for long. If you died, I'd die, and vice versa. They can't do anything to me because it would hurt you. Which means there won't be anything that can keep us apart ever again."

I bit my bottom lip, glancing away.

"What is it?" he asked gently.

"Because we're true mates, does that mean…"

He was already shaking his head before I'd finished my sentence, and my voice trailed off.

"You're free to love whoever you want. As long as you still always love me."

A tear ran down my cheek and I felt awful at that statement. Maybe something was wrong with me that I could care for others when the other half of my soul was mere inches away from me.

"I don't know how you can be so understanding about it all. Just the idea of you being with anyone else makes me want to burn the world down," I admitted, a small sob in my voice.

He smiled softly, and it broke my heart even more. "I would assume it's because you're human. The true mate bond is different with us. I can feel your love for them in our bond. And I would never take that away from you. But just know, you won't ever have to worry about that."

I felt like I should say more, push back harder since he was being so understanding. But maybe I was a selfish bitch, because I wanted what he was offering me. I wanted them all…even Tempest, oddly enough.

Just then, a roar filled the cavern outside of the room and my heart leaped in my chest.

"Steele!" Creed rumbled, and there was banging on the wall outside of our room.

"I guess he found us," Steele said mildly, as if there wasn't a roaring monster king a few feet away.

"Are you sure he won't kill you?" I asked frantically, even though the idea of seeing Creed again was making my heart pound.

"Steele!" he roared again.

"Alright. This might get a little messy when he first comes in. But I'll be fine," Steele murmured reassuringly. My eyes widened, but before I could say anything else, Steele said, "Open," and an entry into the cavern appeared once again… immediately filled with Creed's furious, imposing figure. He was in full monster form, and I'd never seen him so angry before in my life.

"You're going to die, Steele. I don't care that you won the fight. How dare you try and take her from me," he spit. He lunged towards the bed, but right before he got to us, Steele held up his arm, the one with the mate bond around the wrist, his lips curled in amusement.

Creed came to a halt, and his mouth dropped open almost comically, revealing his sharp teeth. His gaze flickered from Steele's wrist to the mark between my breasts.

"It can't be," he whispered. "You're her true mate?" And it might've been my imagination, but I thought I almost saw a flash of deep disappointment in his gaze as he said it. But he blinked and whatever I'd seen disappeared.

"I am. And you and I will have to learn to get along, because I'm obviously not going anywhere."

"I'm not giving her up," Creed seethed immediately, the

malice in his voice so clear that goosebumps sprang on my skin.

Steele shot Creed a look of chastisement as he rubbed my arms, feeling the anxiety in my chest through our bond.

"I'm not expecting you to. I can feel…how strong her feelings are for you. For them."

My gaze dipped away. It was more than I'd ever said to Creed, and I didn't want to see how he was taking it.

When I finally glanced at Creed, his gaze was locked with Steele's and they almost appeared to be having a silent conversation, one that I definitely wasn't following.

"I've locked down the whole city searching for her over the last three days," Creed said carefully, the tightness in his voice clear. "You will both need to return to the castle now."

Steele seemed to be weighing his options, but finally, he gave a tight nod, slipping off the bed, not bothering to hide his nakedness.

"We can leave as soon as she's ready."

Creed nodded again, obviously displeased that he was having to take orders from Steele, but it must've been some sort of true mate hierarchy thing, because he disappeared out of the room without another word.

"Come on, baby. Let's get you some clothes. You can clean up once you get back to the castle," Steele soothed. I gave him a tentative smile and slipped from the bed, allowing him to pull a black silk robe around me.

Wait a minute… "Who's is this?" I asked, venom in my voice. Creed appeared in the doorway again. "Something I got for you," he said cautiously, like I was a feral monster he'd encountered in the wilderness.

The red haze that threatened to descend over my vision slowly flickered away, and I took a deep breath.

"Sorry about that," I said sheepishly. Creed and Steele exchanged another loaded stare.

"Come on, Pet. The others will be relieved to see you."

Creed held out his hand for me, and it kind of felt like a test, like he was really wondering if there was still room for him after my mate bond with Steele

I didn't hesitate though. I grabbed Steele's hand in one grip, and then I took Creed's hand in my other. And we all walked out of the room.

As we made our way through the other cavern to the wall I'd first come through, something made me look back. And as I glanced up to the ceiling, I saw a strange, red symbol.

And the pain began again in my head.

CHAPTER

ASH

"Where is she?" I growled to Seven, pacing the room as we waited for Creed's return. Tempest was out scouring the city somewhere. I'd been searching the city as well, but I'd found myself in Blake's room like a lovesick fool, hoping she would walk through the door any minute.

Seven was seated in an armchair by the window, staring out into the ashy landscape of the city.

His face was perfectly placid, like he didn't have a worry in the world. But I was spiraling.

"Did we do something wrong? Were we too rough with her? Did we scare her away?" My mind was filled with a million different things that we could have done differently. We always had guards around the outside of the castle, and somehow, none of them had seen her leave. I thought about Steele's continued absence. Did he have something to do with this?

I was a relatively easy-going monster despite my fierce appearance, but losing my obsession, my everything... It would push me over the edge.

"How can you be so calm about this?" I snarled at my

brother. The whole blasé attitude he had going was too much for me.

"It's probably better that she's gone," he finally said after a long moment, his morose attitude making me want to punch him in his stupid fucking face.

I stomped over to him.

"How can you say that? How can you be such a fucking asshole that you can't see what's right in front of you?"

It was the same argument we'd been having day after day, and I wasn't getting anywhere with it. But for some reason, it seemed imperative that I *did* get somewhere. Like the fact that we all weren't united together in a single-minded purpose to keep Blake with us forever and make her happy beyond her wildest dreams...my brain kept thinking that was why she left. I felt desperate to get my brother to pull his head out of his ass. I knew he'd experienced trauma. Trauma that I couldn't comprehend, and I'd always done my best to be patient with him, to help him, to love his most damaged self.

But Blake wasn't only my salvation. I believed with all of my heart that she was Seven's salvation as well. And to watch my brother give up on that...well, it was another thing I was having a lot of trouble with. It felt like I wouldn't be allowed to keep her if Seven didn't keep her as well. So it felt necessary to not only his happiness, but *my* happiness as well that he not drive Blake away.

The desperation had messed with my head, and when Seven simply huffed, I lost it. I lunged forward and punched him in the face, shocking us both. But when he recovered from the hit, it wasn't Seven who was there, it was *him*.

I'd actually had a lot more interaction with Seven's other selves than he knew about. He wasn't always aware when they surfaced, especially when *he* came out. Although he'd never given me his name, I referred to him as "George" in my head. It made him a little bit less fierce and terrifying. Have you ever met a mean George? I mean, the humans had that one king that they didn't like, but besides that, I thought George was a pretty friendly name.

He stared at me, a low growl building in his throat, and I made sure to stay perfectly still, not taking my eyes from his.

George was a predator through and through, an alpha male that could probably challenge Creed for dominance. The fact that he'd come out when I'd hit him wasn't a good thing. It meant Seven was breaking more than I was aware of.

Maybe that meant he cared more about Blake than he was letting on.

That was the other fear I had. I feared Seven would let Blake slip from his grasp, but I also feared that maybe I'd read the whole situation wrong, and he was actually so broken he wasn't able to fall in love with her like I had. That to me was worse, because it meant there wasn't a chance of being able to fix him.

"Why are we standing in this fucking room?" George growled.

I cocked my head, a little confused. I'd expected him to throw me through a window or something, not ask me a question. Before I could say anything, he went on. "Why aren't we burning this entire city down trying to find her?"

"Find… Blake?" I asked hesitantly.

He shot me a look that told me how much he valued my intellect. "Of course, you idiot. We should be rounding everyone up and locking them away, tearing the city apart until we find her."

Well, this was…quite unexpected. I mean, you always hoped your demons would feel the same way as you did, but George was a wild horse. When Seven had told me what he'd done to Blake, I'd been a bit nervous that maybe he'd done it in an attempt to torture her. I wasn't going to tell Seven that, but I had made a vow to monitor them closely…if Seven ever let himself get close to her again.

George stalked towards the door, and right then, it flew

open, revealing Creed holding a slumbering Blake, Steele standing next to him, his gaze locked on Blake's gorgeous face like she was the only wonder in the world.

"Blake," I gasped, but before I could get to her, George was there, snarling and grabbing Blake from a shocked Creed's grip. Steele moved to get her back, but Creed held up a hand. I was shocked when Steele actually listened to him.

Creed nodded his head respectfully at George, satisfying whatever George had been looking for. He held her tightly against him, his gaze darting around the room like any one of us was going to dart forward and steal her from him.

He reminded me of that creature in…what was the name of that human movie? Oh, right. *Lord of the Rings*. The gross Gollum creature that kept on saying "my precious". That was exactly how George appeared right now.

"Mine," he rasped, one of his hands stroking her hair methodically.

I'm sure all of our faces were identical. We didn't like that word coming out of his mouth. In our heads, we'd probably thought the word "mine" twenty-four-seven, even if it wasn't actually true.

George turned his back to us finally and went over to the bed. Instead of laying Blake down, he crawled onto the bed, keeping her in his arms. He hunched over her, rocking back and forth as he continued to play with her hair, his gaze flicking from her face to all of us.

"I'm not leaving her with him," snapped Steele.

"I'll stay and monitor the situation," I murmured, unable to look away from the scene on the bed.

Creed and Steele both seemed to think about that, and then they nodded and moved away. Creed practically pushed Steele out of the room and then, with one last glance at Blake, and another to me with a warning in his gaze, he left the room.

And then it was just the three of us, George, Blake, and

me. I walked over to the armchair Seven had abandoned earlier, and I sat down to take up watch. Everything in me wanted to scoop her out of his arms. My body was straining towards her, relief still flooding my veins.

She was actually here.

I wasn't sure if I'd believe that until I got to hold her. But I could sacrifice one more moment in time for my brother, like I'd been doing since he'd returned, a shell of the monster, when we were little children.

...

Blake

My eyelids felt like there was glue holding them together. I'd been so exhausted from my sex fest that I'd fallen asleep despite the circumstances almost as soon as Creed had scooped me into his arms and left the cave.

I jumped when I realized I was somehow in Seven's arms. And when I struggled to sit up, he wouldn't let me. His arms were wrapped around me, so tight that I could barely move an inch.

"Seven?" I asked. He only growled in response.

"It's not him," came Ash's voice. My gaze flicked over to the other side of the room, where Ash was perched in a blue velvet armchair, his gaze locked on the two of us.

"It isn't?" I asked, confused, until I glanced back at Seven and realized what he meant.

It was one of Seven's alter egos holding me. One of his demons. And judging by the feral look on his face, it was the one I'd already been introduced to.

"Ash...a little help?" I squeaked when he gripped me even tighter.

"Mine," Seven growled, his gaze running across my features obsessively.

"I don't think the two of you got a chance to formally meet," Ash drawled, his tone one of nonchalance, even though I could see the tension in the way he was gripping the arms of the chair, like he was prepared to leap out of it at any moment and save me if I needed it. That made me feel a lot better about the situation.

"We met alright, but I wouldn't call it a *formal* meeting."

"Blake, meet George."

I snorted, "George" sounding ridiculous coming from his lips, especially because I was sure it wasn't the name this version of Seven would give himself.

I was right, because Seven huffed and shot a death glare at Ash. The scary look didn't seem to faze him.

"What? You've never given us your name, so George is it."

"It's because I don't engage with cretins like you," he said haughtily, the tone of his voice so different from how Seven usually spoke.

I was still eyeing Seven warily. What would he do to me this time, especially with that look on his face?

"George, tell Blake you mean her no harm and you're in love with her," ordered Ash.

"Love," he scoffed, and something inside of me tightened with dismay. I knew it wasn't Seven there, but to hear a part of him say that was devastating.

"Love doesn't even begin to describe what I feel for her. Love is a simple word fools use. You couldn't possibly comprehend the depth of my feelings for her," George abruptly continued.

My mouth gaped open in shock. A quick look at Ash told me he was just as surprised, as evidenced by the fish face he was making.

"The last time I met you..." I carefully prodded.

He shook his head, confidence spread across his features. "Seven wasn't doing what was necessary to keep you. He was unwilling to give you what you needed, so I took over."

I thought through what had happened. I wasn't sure there was anything about that situation that I'd needed...

"And what exactly do you think I need?" I asked, not

feeling it was wise to argue with him when he had me in his grip like this. Maybe I would feel more comfortable talking when I was safely across the room.

"You need to be fucked. You need to have so much pleasure that you can't stand it. You need someone who watches you every minute, protecting and pleasing you above all else."

I was completely flabbergasted. At no point had I thought any of those words would come out of his mouth.

"I'm not sure that…Seven agrees with you," I finally said.

He ground his teeth in frustration, stroking my cheek much softer than I thought he was capable of. "Seven can't get out of his own way, and I am done with it. You're mine, and you'll always be mine."

The situation felt impossible. I had to admit, I was turned on by the aggressiveness of…George, but who I wanted, who I really wanted, was Seven. Seven…err, George, bent over suddenly and touched his forehead to mine and I was thrust into a dream…a memory.

Two little male monsters were playing in a field right outside a forest filled with crimson-colored pine trees. One of them was counting while the other one ran towards the forest. That one was a monster, who I immediately recognized as Seven. Those violet eyes of his were impossible to miss. Seven slid behind a tree, a huge grin on his face as he hid. As I watched him peek out from behind the trunk to watch for his brother, I could see a group of terrifying monsters with glowing green eyes approaching quietly from behind him. I opened my mouth to scream to him, but no matter how loud I tried to be, the child never glanced over his shoulder. He didn't notice them until they were right behind him, grabbing him with a hand over his mouth so he couldn't scream for help as his brother searched for him.

The scene changed. I was in a large warehouse. Seven was in a cage, dark circles under his eyes, face hollow, like he'd lost at least ten pounds. He was curled up in the corner, his gaze locked on his dirty feet. Staring around the room, I could see there were cages surrounding him, monsters of all shapes and sizes inside them, all in various stages of starvation and abuse. Seven was weeping quietly. My heart ached as I watched him. Metal screeching across metal filled the room. I turned towards the sound and saw a group of monsters in black uniforms with the same glowing, green eyes as the ones who'd found him in the woods walking inside. I watched as they headed directly to Seven's cage, taunted him...and then beat him...with their fists and with long black metal sticks that sparked at the ends. His screams filled the air as the scene faded...and then changed.

I was in a cage with little Seven again, and time had clearly passed. He was even smaller, and bruises, cuts, and scrapes peppered his skin. One of the monsters in a nearby cage vomited, but the little boy didn't look up; he kept staring at his feet. A few minutes after that, the monsters who'd kidnapped him came into the room. They dragged Seven from the cage and led him down a hallway, stopping in front of a large door. When the door opened, I saw all sorts of male and female monsters inside, strapped to various pieces of equipment I'd never seen before...The monsters were all being touched...or fucked in different ways. And none of them seemed to be getting any enjoyment out of what was happening, judging by their screams of pain that ripped through the air. I was screaming when they brought Seven into the room, inherently knowing what would happen. Whatever George had done, I was caught in that room with Seven, watching the terrible abuse he experienced.

And the memories didn't stop there; they went on and on until I felt almost as broken as Seven was.

The scene finally flicked away from the torture Seven had experienced as a child, and then I was seeing him, very similar to how he was today. Ash was dragging Seven from a battle, his recognizable scars all over him, but fresh. Deep wounds and lashes everywhere. Both of them were covered in dust and blood, and Ash was stumbling as he held Seven up and practically dragged him in front of her, *the beautiful monster I recognized as the Red Queen from the head in the museum. I watched as she refused to help him, ensuring he would be scarred like that forever. I heard Ash's screams as he begged on his brother's behalf. I saw Seven's spirit die even more.*

I was dragged from the dream then, the memories that had been shared with me. I was in Ash's arms, tears streaming down my face and wracking sobs echoing around the room. Nausea was stuck in my throat. It felt like all the happiness had been ripped from the world.

"Sweetheart, what happened?" Ash whispered softly as he stroked my hair. I couldn't answer him. I needed to find Seven or George or whoever he was at that moment. I'd never understood a person like I did Seven now, after seeing his past like that. As terrible as it was, it had changed something inside of me, like the mating bond had. You never really got the opportunity to see what made someone who they turned out to be, but I'd seen that with Seven. I felt like I almost knew him better than I knew myself.

"Where did he go?" I gasped, struggling out of Ash's arms.

He immediately let me go

"He left about an hour ago, when you were still unconscious..." Ash growled, "He laid you down on the bed and stormed out of the room." I whimpered, desperation bleeding in my veins. "What did George do? What happened?"

"I know what happened to him, Ash. George...showed me everything," I whispered hoarsely.

Ash's eyes closed, and his features curled up in pain. When he opened them, there was moisture gathered there.

"He would never have wanted you to see those things... But I'm glad you did," he finally murmured. "I think you're the best chance for my brother's happiness. I do. .but...I don't know how he'll face you knowing you've seen what happened to him. I only know because when they brought him back from the camps after saving him, I overheard our parents fighting about it every night. They didn't think he'd ever talk again. He was on suicide watch for years…he's still on suicide watch."

"I saw what that she-devil did to him too."

Ash's eyes closed again, and a shiver ripped through his body. When he opened them, I staggered backwards, because the sorrow in his gaze could have swallowed me whole. "I promise you, I did everything I could to help my brother. And after she did that to him, I never touched her again."

My fists were clenched so tightly that my nails broke the skin of my palms and blood flowed from the wounds. Ash sniffed the air and then stared down at me, alarmed, his hands searching for where I was bleeding. He picked up my palm, and then he…licked the blood. Of course I knew that Ash had an obsession with my blood, but the moment felt so tender, nothing sexual about it. It was just…comforting.

"Please don't ever hurt yourself for us," he pleaded. And a tear trickled from his pale blue, sightless eyes.

"I need to go to him." He nodded, resignation in his gaze.

"I'm sure he would've gone to his rooms. George wouldn't have let him disappear, not with you here."

"George is…intense." It still felt very weird to be calling him "George," but it made him a lot less scary.

"George is almost as obsessed with you as I am. It sounds a bit crazy to admit…but I kind of like the guy after all of this," Ash responded, a hint of a smirk on his full lips for the first time since I'd woken up. I couldn't resist laying a gentle kiss on them. They were too inviting. And then I slid off the bed to go find Seven. Ash followed behind me.

"I'll go with you to his room. But I'll wait outside. I just… have to be near you. You are the two most important beings in my life, and I need to make sure nothing happens we can't come back from."

It was a bit terrifying to think of all the things Seven…or George, that is, could do that we couldn't come back from, but after being held by him, I was confident for the first time.

His dark obsession…it called to me, like it did whenever I got a glimpse of my other monsters' need for me.

It made me wonder if it was possible to get what I wanted after all. The things that I tried to never think about.

Somewhere along the way, I'd decided I wanted to keep them all.

My bond tugged in my chest then. Steele checked in with me. I could only imagine the various emotions he'd been feeling over the past couple of hours. But I tried to picture… peace, and then I sent it through the bond, hoping that he would get it on his end.

A few moments later, the bond flickered in my chest.

"Steele's talking to you, isn't he?" Ash asked quietly, a thread of jealousy interwoven through his words.

"How did you know?"

"Your heart has a different pattern now, and sometimes it'll be a completely different beat even from that, like it's not actually *your* heart at that moment. It's something I've noticed in other true mates as well."

"It's the strangest thing I've experienced thus far…but I wouldn't trade it for anything," I admitted.

He nodded, and his jaw clenched as we continued to walk.

"Ash," I said softly, reaching out to touch his arm.

"It's fine, Blake. I know things are different now."

I shook my head frantically, even though he couldn't see it. "Nothing's changed, Ash. Yes, Steele is my true mate. But… I'm still yours too… If you want me?" Vulnerable. That was the best word to describe how I sounded just then. But he sounded vulnerable too.

I decided it was a beautiful thing when two creatures let down their walls and showed their true feelings. Just like it was a beautiful, devastating thing to see behind Seven's mask.

Ash froze in place, and I almost ran into him with how suddenly he'd stopped. He turned to face me, his hands lifting to my face, and his thumb gently brushing against my lips. "You really mean that, don't you?" he asked roughly.

I nodded, unable to say anything, but he felt the movement with his hands.

Abruptly he pulled me to him so I was plastered against his body. Slight tremors were buzzing between us, and his grip tightened and loosened over and over again like he was having to convince himself to be gentle with me.

"I —" he began before he stopped talking. Butterflies sprang in my chest, the words he wouldn't say floating in the air between us. "I want some time for us, time to talk about how we feel. But it's not right now, not when my brother needs you so much."

"Okay," I said hoarsely, a bit disappointed but understanding what he was saying as well. I saw him then, saw how Ash sacrificed for his twin. Maybe he was the happy-go-lucky one, because he had to be. Because Seven had always been the sad twin. I wondered about all the sacrifices that Ash had made in his life for his brother, and if his brother ever thought about those things.

"I see you, Ash," I murmured. And he was still for a long moment.

"You may be the only person who does."

Ash took my hand and led me down the hall again until Seven's bedroom was right ahead. I realized again how exhausted I was. Between my three-day rendezvous with Steele, and everything that had happened since then, my body hadn't been able to recover.

We stopped outside the doorway and I squeezed his hand. "He's in there," he announced, and I once again marveled at how fine-tuned his other senses were. "I'll be right out here."

I nodded and took a deep breath before opening the door. I was surprised when it flew right open. I'd expected he'd have it locked, but that was probably a good sign. Seven was sitting in a chair by the window, staring out at the moons that were rising in the sky.

Ash gave me an encouraging nod and then closed the door behind me once I was in.

There was silence. And it seemed to stretch on forever. It was the heavy kind of silence, the one that was actually loud, because it was filled with so many unspoken things.

Finally…Seven spoke.

"You know everything now," he stated in a hollow, destroyed voice that made me wince.

"I do. Your other self…he showed me…a lot." Tremors rocked through Seven's body and I took a step forward, desperate to soothe the agony he was obviously facing.

"How can you stand there, knowing what they did to me? What I let them do to me."

Shock ripped through me. That was how he felt?

"Seven, you were a child. There wasn't anything you could have done. It's a miracle you survived."

He trembled again.

"Seven. Nothing that happened to you was your fault." I took a step towards him, and then another. He still wasn't looking at me, all of his attention directed to the outside like it held the secrets of the universe. I kept walking until I was standing next to him. His body leaned towards me like he was desperate for the comfort but unwilling to let himself go.

"Seven," I murmured.

"You shouldn't be around me, Blake. I'm broken. I can't even control *him*. He could do anything to you, and I wouldn't be able to stop it. I'm weak." His voice was filled with so much self-loathing that I couldn't help but cry for him. I'd seen inside of him. I knew he was the strongest being that I'd ever met. The fact that he could survive what had happened to him and still make it through every day…it was a miracle.

"I think…you don't have to worry about George," I murmured, deciding to address that first.

…

Seven

I glanced up at her, a little taken aback that she was referring to him as "George" as well.

"What do you mean by that?"

She bit her lip in that cute way she always did when she was nervous.

"Well, I think he might be into me," she said after a long pause.

Obsessed. Obsessed is the word she's looking for, he whispered inside my head.

I can't believe you would show her those memories. They weren't yours to give away, I spit back at him.

There was silence, and Blake was staring at me, probably wondering if I'd lost my mind even more.

I knew you would never do what it takes to keep her. She knows everything, and yet she still loves us.

This was probably the most civil conversation I'd ever had with him, even knowing if he was standing in front of me right then, I'd be wringing his neck.

It struck me, what he'd said. *She still loves us.*

"You love me?" I asked, my chest burning with embarrassment at how pathetically I'd asked that. I was such a stupid idiot.

She raised her hand to my chest hesitantly. She was always so careful with me, just like Ash. When her hand touched my chest, she didn't say anything for a moment, or make any attempt to move, like she was waiting to see if I would push her away.

"I do love you. I love all of you," she whispered. I knew why she'd put her hand on my chest…because that was where the demons were a *piece* of me, but *not* me at the same time.

"You shouldn't love me. You shouldn't love *him*."

She has no choice, he snapped, and I growled. Her eyes widened and she moved her hand, thinking I'd growled at her, but I quickly reached out and hauled her onto my lap.

I would never be unbroken. Once you experienced what I had, the trauma didn't go away. If you were lucky, it simply faded. But it was a funny thing with Blake. Even though I knew I'd never be whole, the cracks in my soul seemed far less severe when she was with me. Her love felt like a glowing, living thing inside of me. The feeling was alien, but unlike my demons, it was one that I welcomed gladly.

Tell her you love her back, you idiot, he snapped.

My eyes widened, realizing that I hadn't said it back. Still, I hesitated. It felt like once I confessed it to her after she'd confessed it to me, she'd be locked in. Stuck. I'd never be able to let her go.

That's the whole point, he hissed.

Shut up.

"If I say it, you're mine, angel. You've seen the worst of me, and you're still here. If you give me this, if you give me hope, and you choose to leave, there won't be anything that can hold me together." There was a hitch in my voice, the truth of what I'd said settling in.

"I love you. I love all of you, even your broken, ruined pieces. Even your demons. They're all beautiful to me."

My eyes closed, that brightness in my chest growing until it felt like it could burst. When I opened them, I half expected her to be gone, for this all to be a dream. But there she was. Beautiful, perfect, and…exhausted.

We can fuck her to sleep, he commented.

That sounded kind of like a good idea, actually.

"I love you, Blake. And even the worst of me is obsessed with you. I'll never be good enough for you, I'll never be the whole monster that you deserve. But I promise I'll do my best every day. I promise to love you with all the different parts of me."

A hitched sob tore from her throat and she flung herself against me, burying her face in my neck.

Just then, the door creaked open, and Ash was standing there, a giant, stupid grin on his face.

"Oh, good, I have perfect timing. You finally got my brother to pull his head out of his ass."

Blake slowly lifted her face, and she was beaming. She was beaming at being mine. It was hard to comprehend that.

"He's perfect," she cried, squeezing me tighter.

I was sure she was wrong about that, but if she wanted to see me that way after everything she knew about me, I could work with that.

She loves us, he commented. And once again, we were in agreement.

Ash closed the door behind him and leaned against the wall, still smirking. "I can think of some ways we can celebrate," he offered.

"If you can unbreak my vagina, I'm all for it," she said with a cute giggle.

"Unbreak your…?" I asked, a little perplexed.

"It's a long story," she answered. "I'll explain it to you after."

"After…?"

Ash prowled towards her. "After we have some fun."

As we led Blake to my bed, intent on "unbreaking her vagina", I realized that I felt happy.

And I hadn't felt that way for a very, very long time.

CHAPTER 16

It was days later, and for some reason, Ash had built a new and improved nest in my closet. Something I was studiously avoiding.

I'd been lazy lately, mostly laying around and letting Ash and Seven entertain me. Surprisingly, the others hadn't interrupted our time together, and I wondered if Ash had come to some sort of deal with them.

A bloody deal, I snarked to myself.

But today, my solitude was going to end...because today...was Creed's birthday.

Ash had mentioned it casually, like it wasn't a big deal. Apparently, when you had the capacity to live forever, it really wasn't a big deal to celebrate another trip around the sun—err, suns, that is.

But I was determined to do something to celebrate the day. And I'd come up with just the thing. Instead of making a cake, I was going to make myself the cake. And although cakes weren't a thing here—Ash had to get creative when procuring one—I was about to make sure that Creed had a hankering for them from now on.

I'd gotten some of the chocolate from the kitchens, and

had the cook create a sweet cream with one of the random monsters they procured a milk-like substance from...and I was ready to go.

Taking my supplies, I went down the hallway towards Creed's chambers. Ash had promised to keep him from his room for another thirty minutes so I could have time to prepare.

Once I got to the room, I stripped and spread the cream around my breasts and my lower region...a la *Varsity Blues*. I dabbed some chocolate on my cheeks and across my stomach. And then I tried to arrange myself on his sheets in a sexy way, although I really had no idea how to do that.

It seemed to take forever, but eventually, I heard the door unlock...and a second later, Creed walked in, staring at a gemmed object in his hand.

He closed the door behind him, not yet looking up.

It took a moment for his nostrils to flare.

"And to what do I owe the pleasure?" he suddenly purred, his eyes heavy-lidded as they slowly lifted to the bed where I was lounging, widening when he saw me perched there in my...outfit.

"I thought I would surprise the birthday boy." I tried to stay confident as his gaze lazily ran over my skin.

"Mmmh. I don't see any boys in here, but your king is quite pleased with his gift."

I slid my finger through the chocolate on my stomach and then brought it to my lips, making a big deal of sucking it off...like I was pretending it was his dick.

His gaze flared, but he didn't make a move to walk towards me. Instead, he crossed his arms and leaned back against the door.

"You are fucking sexy, Pet," he growled.

Enjoying the adoring heat of his stare, I circled my finger around my nipples this time, wiping some of the cream off so the rosy skin peeked through. He bit down on his full bottom lip, his fangs peeking out.

He was so freaking sexy.

I held out the cream to him. "Come taste this."

"Come taste this, what?" he taunted.

I shivered, our eyes locking as I used my other hand to dip into the cream around my clit.

"Come taste this, Daddy," I murmured.

I'd never called him that before, but it fit his big dick energy. If there ever was a "daddy", it was Daddy Creed.

Creed must have been a big fan of my nickname because it finally got him moving away from the door and stalking towards me.

He stopped in front of me and leaned over me until I had no choice but to fall back on the bed. His tongue swept out and he licked at my still outstretched finger, suckling on it so sensually that my core fluttered.

"Say it again," he ordered after he'd let my finger go.

I grinned smugly before obeying.

"Fuck me, Daddy."

His golden eyes seemed to glow as he slowly dropped to his knees, pushing my thighs apart as he moved. My breaths were coming out in gasps in anticipation of what he was about to do, and I could feel that my inner thighs were already a mess of my cum and cream. Watching me closely, he slid two fingers through my folds, capturing the cream on his fingers. He made a big show of bringing them to his mouth and slowly sucking the sweetness off.

"Just when I thought you couldn't taste better."

"Do you want me to eat you, baby? Do you want me to cover my face in your juices? Swallow it down because it's the only thing that can truly satisfy me?"

My brain had short-circuited at his dirty mouth, and his face wore a pleased expression that he'd stunned me. When I didn't answer, he plunged two fingers inside me, eliciting a scream that echoed around the room. "Got an answer for me, Pet?"

"Yes. Yes, I want that."

"Yes, I want that, what?" he goaded.

"Yes, I want that…Daddy," I breathed.

And he rewarded me by caressing my clit as his other fingers worked on that special spot inside of me that my monsters found so easily.

He worked his fingers in and out of me, biting down sexily on his lip again, his gaze watching me intently, adjusting to every sound I made so I was constantly on the edge of pleasure.

"Fuck," I panted, my voice a high-pitched keen as I fell over the edge.

He didn't give me time to recover. He withdrew his fingers and covered my core with his mouth. He sucked and licked, his movements messy as his tongue captured every taste of the cream in my folds. His finger slid through the chocolate on my stomach and he spread it around my clit, his tongue following his finger so he was getting every bit of the chocolate as well.

I was holding onto his horns, fucking myself against his face. His cheeks hollowed out as he sucked, his gaze never moving from mine.

It might as well have been my birthday, because this was a true fucking gift. Pleas streamed from my mouth. Pleas for him to keep going, to never stop, to let me cum again. He swiped the chocolate once more and brought it to the entrance of my sex, his tongue spearing in and fucking me as he lapped at the chocolate and my juices.

I screamed as tremors flashed through my body, the orgasm so intense that my vision briefly went black. Creed growled in response, yanking his tongue out and standing, his face shiny with my pleasure and smeared with chocolate.

"You're such a good girl, cumming on your daddy's tongue like that. Such a good fucking girl."

I'd lost the ability to speak, and he didn't seem to mind as he moved between my legs, bending over me as he sealed his lips over mine. I moaned as I tasted myself, the salty flavor mixed in with bits of cream and chocolate.

Delicious.

He was messy with his kiss, like he wanted my face to be as covered as his. His tongue lapped at my mouth, his teeth grazing my skin as he moved my face exactly where he wanted it.

I was so distracted by his kiss that I wasn't prepared when he pressed my hips even wider and then pushed into my dripping core.

"Yes," I huffed out.

He had no interest in slow today. He immediately started rutting into me like he'd been possessed. The fit was so tight. Every time. It was obvious my body would never adjust to his two-headed cock.

I was so far stretched beyond my comfort level that it was hard to breathe.

"You have such a tight fucking pussy. Look at it, so pink and perfectly stretched around my cock. I'm so fucking lucky."

In the back of my mind, I thought about the three other words I wished he would say to me. But as soon as the thought came to mind, I pushed it away.

Those were three words I would never hear from him. It didn't do any good to wish for them.

Creed was holding me completely still on the bed so I could do nothing but feel him thrusting into me. My breasts bounced with every push, bits of cream flicking off with the force.

"Come on my cock, Blake," he ordered. "Come on my big fucking cock."

He didn't need to ask again. I was so turned on, it took nothing to get me exploding once again.

"Creed," I moaned, my hands reaching up to my favorite place…his horns, to hold onto them and keep myself from floating away.

My body was on fire, searing pleasure coursing through every inch of me.

I might never own him. But there was no denying, he owned me.

"We're going to cum together this time, Pet. Your sweet pussy is choking my dick. I can't hold out any longer. You're going to be my good girl and cum when I say."

"Yes, Daddy," I breathed.

"Fuck, yeah, you're a good girl. Cum for me right now," he purred as his rhythm faltered from its pounding pace and his hot liquid gushed into me as I came again.

He fell forward onto his forearms, taking just enough of his weight so he didn't crush me as he lay on me, the cream and chocolate squishing in between us.

"How does sex get better with you every time?" he asked, a hint of wonder in his voice.

Of all the things that happened so far that day, *that* was what made me blush.

"Happy Birthday, Creed," I murmured as we stared into each other's eyes.

"Best birthday ever, Blake," he responded, something in the depths of his gaze unfathomable and almost…emotional.

It would be enough to have him like this if it was all I could ever get from him.

And that was another lie I told myself to survive my time there.

———

A knock sounded on the door, and it flew open before I could ask who it was.

Creed stood there.

Because of course the monster king wouldn't deign to ask permission before entering a room. I was surprised he'd knocked at all.

It had been a week since his birthday, and for some reason, I felt shy standing there.

I hated how much I'd missed him. Hated how my gaze devoured his handsome features eagerly, desperate for his golden gaze to meet mine. I was so busy staring at him that it took a second for me to see he was holding some sort of see-through gossamer fabric in his hands.

"Hello, Pet," he murmured, looking quite pleased to see me judging by the way his gaze was devouring my face and body as eagerly as mine had done to him.

"Hi," I answered, not sure why I felt so shy under his stare.

"The other cities' leaders will all be coming in for a celebration next week. I've brought the gown you're going to wear."

"What's the celebration for?" I asked, tensing a bit, thinking of a huge group of unfamiliar monsters all staring at me. I wondered if I could find a way to get out of it.

He didn't answer me, just unraveled the dress so I could see the whole thing.

It was made of a sparkling, freaking gorgeous material.

It was also completely see-through.

"I'm not wearing that," I announced.

A smirk graced his lips, like he'd been expecting some sort of pushback. His golden gaze seemed to glow as he stalked towards me…every inch the predator.

"This is the dress that a queen of Wyld would wear. You will wear this, Blake."

"Well, I think you must have me confused for someone

else. Because I'm not your queen," I snapped back, feeling irrationally angry.

Angry at the thought of being bared like that in front of the whole party.

Angry at the thought of him mocking me by having me go to such a party in the first place.

Just…angry.

I turned my back to him and crossed my arms while I walked towards the window, intent on ignoring him.

He may be king, used to getting his way, but this was one thing he wouldn't win.

"Why are you pouting like a petulant child?" he asked calmly…only stoking the flames of my fury further.

"I can't believe you would want me to wear that. To be bared like that in front of everyone important in your world.

I heard his footsteps behind me as he walked towards me, obviously not willing to allow the little hissy fit I was currently throwing.

"By wearing this dress, you are ensuring that everyone knows who their queen is. It's a gown of honor. No one is allowed to wear it except for the queen."

He slid his claw gently down my nape and across my neck, sending shivers through my spine.

"I don't want to be made a fool," I whispered, realizing why I was so upset.

Because I would be nothing but a figurehead, a joke as I met all the dignitaries.

"And why exactly do you think you would look like a fool? You know by now that nudity means nothing to our kind."

"Because I'll never be your queen," I finally cried, turning to face him. "I'll be your mistress. Your pet. But I'll never be anything more to you."

"What are you talking about?" he huffed.

"You don't love me," I said, my voice shaking. "Somewhere

along this crazy ride you've put me on, I fell in love with you. But you'll never love me back. I'll be your food source, your toy…your pet. But I'll never get what I want."

I was suddenly against the wall, his clawed hand around my neck, his golden eyes glowing.

"And who says I don't love you, Blake? Who told you that? I'll kill them."

I froze, my mind having trouble wrapping around his words, what he was saying.

"What did you say?"

His grip tightened and he rolled his eyes.

"Blake, I've been fucking you for over three years. I've been inside your head. I know every inch of your body. I know every inch of your heart. Three years of that…and I've been in love with you almost that long."

I lost the ability to speak. Never in a million years had I thought he would say it. I know I'd wanted him to say it, obviously, but the reality was so much more than I could've imagined.

His face was smug now as his tongue slipped out and lapped at my lips. "Are you going to say it back?"

I probably should have, but the more I thought about it, the more I was mad he hadn't told me before this. He'd let me go all these years thinking I was just a toy to him.

He needed to work for it.

"No. I don't think I am," I said stubbornly.

His annoying grin widened.

Creed winked, his claws ripping at the front of the dress I was wearing. "I know you love me, Pet. But you can have this moment if you'd like. You can tell me when you're ready. It won't change anything for me." He tore more of my dress, so it slid completely off me, and indeed, he didn't ask me to say it again. But he fucked me so hard against the wall, I was pretty sure I was screaming it by the end anyway.

CHAPTER 17

BLAKE

News was spreading about more deaths in the city as a result of starvation.

Sharp pain twinged across my insides. Nothing we did improved the situation, the copious amounts of sex we'd been having provided nothing but a sliver of sustenance to the population.

Creed had declared a visit to Pariah, a sex club located in the very epicenter of Wyld, as another effort to make energy for Wyld. Energy has always been collected there, I'd been told. Evidently, having sex there could help amplify the feeding energy for the city.

And I was up for trying anything…and a little excited about it.

As if on cue, Creed strolled into my room, rubbing a hand over his jawline, looking like he carried the world on his shoulders. He had that brooding vibe about him, and something about seeing him that way left me burning up. I kept thinking back to him telling me he loved me, and my heart skipped a beat, loving him so much that I almost lost my breath.

His gaze lifted, finally looking at me, and he grinned.

"That dress is gorgeous on you. But I hope you're wearing something more appropriate underneath?" The corner of his mouth curled upward in a sinfully sexy way.

I laughed, nodding. "It'll be a surprise."

With Creed still eyeing my dress, or perhaps it was the low neckline, I said, "I gave the seamstress a sketch of what I wanted to wear and she made it almost identical to my design. She also made me this dress." I ran my hand over the emerald green sundress. The fabrics in Wyld always surprised me because so many were woven from spider webs, making them close to impossible to tear, but also soft as satin.

He crossed the room in two long strides, his fingers sliding along my jawline and to my chin, where he tilted my head back to meet his stare. My knees melted as I softened against him, his touch sending a flare of desire through me. "If I didn't have to go on an errand, I'd take my time exploring exactly what you've got hiding underneath, but it'll have to wait for later." I shivered as he growled hungrily.

"Wait, so we're not going to Pariah, then?" I reared back a little.

"I'm sorry, Pet, but there's been a slight change in plans," he murmured, frustration flickering in his eyes. "I have a few crucial things I need to get done first, so I'll meet you there, okay?"

"Sure, I'll go with Steele, Seven, or Ash," I explained, glancing around for my shoes, well aware I'd still get to spend the night with him.

"They're with me, so Tempest will take good care of you until we arrive."

I stiffened.

Maybe I'd simply had enough drama to last me a lifetime, or I wanted a night off, which meant not dealing with a sarcastic, grumpy monster. I glanced up, about to protest to Creed that I could as easily wait until they were ready and head over there with them, but he was pushing my door open wider. Tempest stood in the corridor. He had his back to the wall, hands deep in the pockets of his black pants, giving me a toothy grin in his human form.

Oh, great, this would be loads of fun then.

Creed cupped my face, kissing me to the point where my toes curled, and a slight burst of slick dampened me. With a final lick across my lips, my handsome monster broke our kiss and drew back. "I'll be seeing you soon."

He turned and marched out of the room too quickly for my liking. I wanted to keep kissing him.

Then it was just Tempest and me. He wasn't moving from the corridor either, and while I contemplated shutting the door, it was also selfish of me to not head to the club to help feed Wyld.

I moved around the bedroom, finally tracking down my flats because I wasn't strolling through the city and swinging bridges with heels. Once I slipped them on, I headed out of my room.

Tempest was licking a cut on his bottom lip, then pushed himself off the wall.

Once we stepped into the elevator, I asked, "How'd you cut your lip?"

"Got into a fight," he answered before commanding the elevator to take us to the ground floor. "This pisser monster got in my face about being hungry. I get everyone's situation sucks, but I'm also not taking their aggression."

I wasn't sure I wanted to ask what a "pisser monster" was, and assumed it might be the one I'd seen recently, urinating on the street while kids played under it like a sprinkler. I shivered at the memory.

"Guessing he ended up in a worse condition than you with a busted lip?" I murmured.

He shrugged. "It was either getting a few bruises, or the guards were ready to take him down permanently. It's a death sentence to attack anyone from the royal circle."

"I'm surprised you cared." The moment the words left my mouth, I cringed at how spiteful I sounded. "That came out wrong. I mean—"

"You don't need to explain yourself to me. I know I'm a fucking asshole." He soothed a loose strand of hair hanging over his eye back into place, his sharp emerald green gaze blazing at me. "I'll always be honest whether someone likes it or not, so I don't expect you to hold back. Like now, by telling you that you're wearing the wrong outfit for our trip."

As my mouth opened with a response, the elevator doors pulled apart, and he stepped out.

"What's your problem?" I stated, my stomach tightening as I followed him. "Nope, don't worry about it. I think I've worked you out."

"Yeah, enlighten me," he said with a glance over his shoulder at me, that evil grin spreading his lips once more. The kind of expression I imagined on a serial killer, sending a ripple of fear through me. And yet I still found myself swooning at how incredibly gorgeous Tempest was, how my body responded to him and craved him.

That was the thing about him. He brought out fear in me, dread, all while I burst with arousal.

"You love being an asshole so you don't have to get close to anyone or open up, because it's so much easier that way. But are you any different from the rest of us? I guess the only difference is that you hide your pain behind hurtful and sarcastic comments. But in the end, you're as fucking ruined as everyone else"

His deadpan expression made me smile because I'd gotten to him, so I offered him a grin and strolled right past him, pushing open the door to the outside world. Yep, I could give as good as he gave, and I was enjoying this new brazen side of myself.

But right as I emerged at the yard in front of the castle, I yelped at the sight before me.

Two of those horny water buffalo horses stood there, strapped with saddles, reins attached to a ring in the middle of their noses held by two of the castle guards.

They all glanced at me, the biggest beast beating his front hoof into the ground, smoke floating from his flaring nostrils.

"Told you that you're wearing the wrong thing," Tempest grunted with too much glee in his voice as he paused next to me.

"We're not riding those."

"Oh, we definitely are," he stated, suddenly sweeping me off my feet.

I cried out from shock. "Put me down," I growled, thrashing against him, furious and terrified all rolled into one. But just as quickly, I was suddenly straddling a huge freaking beast, and I panicked, snatching Tempest's shirt, fisting it with my life, holding him close to me. "I'm not kidding. Get me off here, now!" I growled.

"Why? You're a brave girl now, and if you intend to live in Wyld, then nothing should scare you."

"You're an asshole."

"You'll be safe, you'll see." His voice was so casual… meanwhile it felt like my heart was attempting to break out of my chest. He turned to the guards who handed him the reins before looping them over the beast's head, then placed them in front of me.

"I told you, I'm not riding this thing. I've never even ridden a horse…or a pony in my life. I'm not ready to start rodeo riding a flame-throwing beast."

"Derins are gentle animals." He pried my fingers from his shirt and pushed the leather reins into my hands. "Do you trust me?"

"Fuck no!"

"You break my heart, Blake," he said dryly.

"Fuck you."

"I'll take a rain check on that." With a sly grin, he stepped back and slapped a palm to the animal's rump.

The Derins beneath me grunted, unleashing a fiery snort, and suddenly took off.

I screamed, my hands scrambling to hold onto the reins before I tumbled off and got trampled on. Heart thundering, my adrenaline surged through my veins, and I was completely in survival mode, my body going numb.

Muscles tight, I held on with dear life, my legs clamped around the beast, my knuckles white.

I had zero idea how to stop a horse, so I went with instinct and started pulling back the reins. The problem was, every time I did that, the creature snorted flames, sending a plume of unbearable heat over me.

We rushed forward, hooves hitting the ground and crossing bridges. The motion and wind shoved my dress up to my waist, fluttering madly as I flashed everyone.

Some monsters dove out of our path, sneering at me. "I'm sorry, sorry, I can't control it," I shouted back.

We took left and right turns, like the animal knew exactly where it was going.

Then something flew into my mouth, and I choked. *Oh my god,* I'd swallowed a monster fly. I was going to die after it laid eggs inside me. Hacking up my lungs, I finally spat something small and black out. "Oh hell." *Keeping my mouth shut from now on.*

A whistle rang out from behind me, and I twisted my head to find Tempest flying up behind us on his own charge.

Smiling again, he caught up to me fast. "Are you even wearing underwear?"

I rolled my eyes at him. "Get me off this thing."

"Can't do that," he answered with fake sincerity. "You see, once you tell a Derins where to go, it doesn't stop until it reaches its destination."

I blinked at him, then glanced at my creature darting

forward over a thin bridge, not perturbed in the slightest by how easily it could slip off the edge.

"I hate you," I called out over my shoulder. "You go out of your way to piss me off."

He caught up to me, and we traveled over a long stretch of lanes created by closely connected towers. "But aren't we having fun yet?"

I gave him the death glare, while he studied me with that smug demeanor he'd mastered.

"What's wrong with you?" I demanded. "Why do you hate me so much, when you've known me for years? What did I do to you?"

He didn't respond for a long time, and we kept on traveling in a direction that seemed to be farther away from the center of the city as I attempted to push my dress down.

"Sometimes you remind me of her," he said, both of us side by side, bouncing on our beasts.

"Who?"

"The queen."

I sucked in a sharp breath. "I'm insulted you'd think I was anything like her."

"That's not what I said. I'm referring to how I tried my hardest to pull away from you both, and yet I still found myself drawn to you both. And in the end, just like with her, it'll fuck me."

I blinked at him. "And that's a bad thing to be drawn to me?"

He shook his head like somehow his thoughts had sent him somewhere he didn't want to go. "It is when it brings pain."

"I bring you pain?"

"The queen was someone who despised me, who tortured me, and who I couldn't leave. I'd been sworn into her guard since I was a child. Told that when I grew up, I'd take my place to feed the city. I had no say. Leaving my post would get me killed, and really, I stayed for Creed, Ash, Seven, and Steele. They were my found family, but her...she was a fucking psychopath. And she reminded me of it any chance she got."

"Didn't you help her feed the city though? She must have felt something more for you." He spoke with so much venom in his voice when he mentioned her.

He scoffed, his face twisting with hatred. "When someone hurts you for simply existing, over and over, you learn to shut out emotions. A fuck is just a fuck," he growled.

He suddenly took off with his creature ahead of me, leaving me completely puzzled. And slightly hurt. Was that how he saw me when we had sex? That I was nothing more than a hole he fucked? I couldn't deny that left a bruise on my soul, because even if he scared me and always kept me at arm's reach, I'd never detested him.

I'd been hearing so many conflicted things about the queen around the city. There were those who were absolutely loyal to her to a fault...even after all these years. And then there were others who absolutely...hated her.

Kicking my heels into the beast, I sped up and realized that riding this animal wasn't really that bad. Just as Tempest had said. I even managed to pull my dress down to cover my ass, tucking it underneath me. I finally caught up to him.

After a while of not talking, I murmured, "My parents were assholes too–beyond assholes. I was in that asylum in the first place because I walked in on my father fucking...not only his secretary but also his *male* chief of staff...and our gardener...at the same time. Even now, the image makes me want to puke. But...I think there are just evil dicks in the world who enjoy hurting others. You know, my father once said to me that the evil that exists in the world lives in the shadows of each one of us. I actually think he was talking about himself, acknowledging what an awful person he was. When he died...I didn't feel an ounce of pity for him."

A muscle in his jaw tightened, and I expected some hurtful remark. I readied for it. But when he said nothing, I took that as a step forward to having our first real conversation.

"So, why were you promised to be by the queen's side from such a young age?" I asked. "Is your family royalty?"

He chuckled, sounding bitter. "If only that had been the case, then I could have walked away from her a long time ago. My family had accumulated an enormous debt with some nasty monsters who happened to be guards to the queen, so when it came time to pay up and they were short, they sold me into servitude. When I came of age, they packed my bags and sent me to the castle."

"Oh fuck," I mumbled, feeling slightly heartbroken thinking of Tempest as a child. It didn't excuse him for always acting like a dick…but he'd obviously been rejected his whole life. Something like that messed with your head.

I knew that from experience.

I was not a fan of the fact my monsters had been treated so poorly in life.

"It's the past, and I don't want your pity."

"And you won't get any from me," I said gently. "I know what it feels like to be fucked up by family. It burns…like acid." A sharp sensation deepened in my throat, then drifted to my chest. "Have you seen your parents since?"

"Only once. I was young and desperate to leave the castle after the queen wrongly accused me of theft, and whipped me publicly. When she found the real culprit, she laughed in my face. My parents weren't any better though. I had snuck back, desperate for them to take me from the Queen. I spied on them through the window, not sure how they would react. And then, I found my fucker of a father drunk and beating my mother to death. Exactly as he'd done to me growing up."

He paused, shadows darkening his features, a pained,

dead expression in his gaze. My chest was tight, and moisture pooled in my eyes picturing his story.

"What did you do?" I finally asked, when he hadn't continued.

"I attacked him…but it was too late for my mother. I left my father gasping for air in a pool of his own blood. I never went back to find out if he survived. As far as I'm concerned, he's dead."

"I'm sorry we both have such shitty parents," I whispered, knowing nothing I said would be enough.

He shrugged, evidently unbothered. "It may not seem like it most of the time, but I like having you in Wyld."

"Thanks," I gasped, surprise bubbling in my chest at his words. I would have never expected that to fall from his lips.

We rode the rest of the trip to the club in a comfortable silence, while I reeled the whole time that Tempest gave me a compliment that wasn't sexually related.

It also left me thinking that if Tempest let me in more, we could…get along. With his sarcastic attitude, it could be fun. Maybe it wasn't too late for us. I studied him from the corner of my eye, my heart fluttering. Despite all the crap he'd pulled…I definitely wasn't repelled by him—quite the opposite.

I was starting to slowly understand some of the reasons for his behavior. Steele was a good example of it too. They always behaved like strong, protective monsters around me, always trying to be more. But maybe they needed someone to remind them they were perfect as they were.

We finally reached Pariah, the club that resembled a gothic, Greek cathedral, shrouded in darkness.

Tempest climbed off his beast, then he came and lifted me off mine, setting me gently on my feet. Except, my legs had become like jelly on the ride over, so I crashed into Tempest.

He laughed, grabbing hold of me, that ache from his eyes gone, replaced by the usual dark mask he wore.

"You can't go in with that dress," he told me.

"Yep, I know."

He was staring down at me, but I wasn't going to feel intimidated to change into something more revealing. I was trying to remember that nudity in this realm was normal.

Without another thought, I stepped away from the building where I was alone and pulled my dress up and over my head. I was left standing in a leather, teddy lingerie, and my skin rippled with goosebumps at how much I was exposing.

The bra cups were non-existent, completely exposing my breasts. I had covered my nipples with a small patch of fabric I'd had the seamstress create, held in place mostly by moisture, so I hoped they didn't fall off. The bottom half was a high bikini which was crotchless…well, at least when I spread my legs; otherwise, the leather was just enough to hide all the essential bits.

I unlatched the thin choker I had tucked into the bodysuit and wrapped it around my neck for a full effect. It even had a metal ring on it should one of the men want to lead me around on a leash. Something I knew my monsters would love.

But standing out in public dressed like this was something else. And like my first visit to the club, I felt nauseous with nerves.

My cheeks blushed when I glanced up to Tempest's gaze. He stood near a pole where he'd tied up the buffalo creatures, already in his huge shadowy monster form--clawed hands, long fangs--wearing a black leather loincloth. And I hated to admit it, but he was hot as fuck.

I wasn't the only one impressed, because his mouth hung half open at the sight of me, eyes wide and drowning with lust. The dead giveaway he was a slave to his lust as much as me…the huge bulge behind his loincloth, which did little to cover all of him.

I flicked a lock of pink hair over my shoulder, then tossed him my balled-up dress. "I thought you said you were taking a rain check on fucking me," I teased. "Your eyes are telling a different story."

He rapidly tucked my dress into a compartment on the saddle, then practically threw himself at my side. His clawed hands grasped my hips, and he studied me up and down, his nostrils flaring, a long, forked tongue licking his lips.

"We're going to have fun tonight," he growled.

"You bet we will," I replied saucily, slapping his ass, and then winking at him as he raised an eyebrow.

I felt different around Tempest after glimpsing behind his mask, and I wanted our relationship to improve. Something I'd work on with him. He'd finally opened up to me today, made me feel like I was important to him.

We were greeted by a spider guard beyond the dark opening of the building, bowing its head low. "Your party has been expected, sir," he said gruffly to Tempest, not paying me any attention.

"Good," Tempest muttered and pushed past, keeping me close to him by the arm he'd thrown around my waist.

Darkness swallowed the large room, and red smoke pumped out from the walls, making it feel like we walked through a cloud of blood. The red spotlights hanging from the ceiling gave everyone a reddish glow.

I was in such a haze from the trip and my talk with Tempest, that I barely noticed all the eyes on us as we entered the place. But now…I felt their heaviness, their hunger.

Monsters were everywhere--big ass-hairy ones, reptilian ones, freaky horned beasts, and all manner of things that would terrify me normally. But there was no such thing in the city of Wyld. Anything went. Then there was the moth-man creature leaning against the bar as a female with one eye was sucking his huge, purple dick.

Across the room, the suspended cages had couples having sex in them, most rocking wildly.

"Did you want a drink?" Tempest asked, glancing at the busy bar.

I instantly shook my head, remembering the last time I'd drank their radioactive colored cocktails…how strange I'd felt afterwards.

Tempest walked me past the bar, his fingers almost digging into my side with how hard he held onto me. He snarled at any monster who leered at me, sending them reeling from us.

"Every single one of them wants to fuck you," he whispered. "But I'd kill each of them before I let them lay a hand on you."

"That's very white knight of you," I drawled.

"I don't know what that is, but white doesn't work for me." He clicked his fingers at the bartender, sending him some hand signal that meant nothing to me.

"Yeah, you're right. You're definitely more of a dark knight," I mused, knowing he had no idea what I was saying.

Then he drew us up a set of stairs to the second floor, and into a large room with sofas and a coffee table.

The flooring was made of something transparent because I could see right into the floor below us where there was an oversized bed covered in red silk sheets.

"Are we going to be watching someone have sex?" I murmured, not really turned on at the thought, which was hypocritical of me, seeing how I loved my men fucking me in their various forms.

"If you want," Tempest said. "But once the others arrive, we were toying with the idea that we'd take turns fucking you down there, while the rest of us watch." He spoke with his back to me as he strolled across the room to where he jabbed his fingers into a screen on the wall.

"Oh," I gasped, wondering exactly how often they had

conversations about fucking me. "That's new...How long before Creed and the rest of them show up?"

Music began to play, something with strange beats and harmonies, but it wasn't unpleasant.

"Interesting music," I said, crossing the room and crashing down on the sofa when an oversized beetle entered the room, carrying a black tray on its back with four glass bowls filled with what appeared to be candy.

"Oh, what are those?" I leaned forward as Tempest collected them and placed them on the table in front of me. Once the beetle scuttled out of the room, Tempest kicked the door shut and threw himself next to me.

"Let's play a game," he offered.

"I'll be honest, your idea of games scares me slightly."

He laughed and pushed the four bowls in front of me. Each one was filled with what reminded me of rock candy, with a different color in each bowl–blue, red, purple, and orange.

"Okay, how does this work?" I reluctantly asked, knowing I'd regret it later.

"Each color represents a different element of arousal, and when eaten, you will experience heightened sensation. The game is about how long you can last without giving in to your desires."

I blinked at him, feeling like I'd stepped into a sex-warped version of *Harry Potter* with their Bertie Botts Every Flavor Beans. "Why would anyone play this?"

"For fun, because it'll bring you the hottest orgasms you've ever experienced." His eyes darkened, staring at me as he licked his lips, waiting to see what I'd do.

I couldn't deny, I *was* curious about the candies...and we were at a sex club after all...to feed the population. I threw caution to the wind and reached down, picking up an orange one.

It tasted slightly bitter, but then spread across the back of my throat with a creamy texture. I glanced at Tempest who was grinning.

"I don't feel anything," I said after a few moments.

"You need to eat more than one. That's part of the game. How many can you eat before it becomes too much for you?"

His hand slid over to my thigh, and a dangerously captivating anticipation surged through me. I took a handful of the little orange balls and popped them into my mouth.

"What happens if I take all the colors at the same time?" I licked my lips, growing rather fond of the taste, but resisting the urge to eat more.

"Give it a try." He studied me carefully, but I wasn't that gullible.

"Maybe let's see how the orange ones affect me first."

When his hands slid up my thigh, arousal soared through me. "I'm glad it's the two of us. I want you all to myself, to lock you up in this room with me so you're only mine. All mine."

"I guess you'll have to take advantage of our time alone," I murmured, rubbing my nipples that kept itching.

He was chuckling again, the sound dark, his fingers crawling between my thighs. I clenched them tight, even though I was starting to feel super hot.

I kept rubbing my breasts with my forearm, and Tempest watched my every move.

"Maybe we should remove those circles from your nipples. Let them breathe."

A tingle came again, seeming to rush around my breasts with the sensation of someone trailing a feather over them. A moan slipped over my throat, and the moment Tempest trailed the pad of his fingers just beneath them, my chest thrust out toward him, the rush of my pulse thundering in my ears, an inferno sliding over me.

Oh, that was strange…and slightly alarming.

"What are all the different things the candies do exactly?"

I asked breathlessly, startled at how strong my reaction to his touch had been. Did I eat too many already, perhaps?

"Let me see. One makes you desperate to have your cunt licked. Then there's one for being spanked. Another will have you begging for your tits to be sucked, and then the fourth creates a hungry desire to have your toes sucked until you orgasm."

My eyes widened with shock, because as he said that, a strange tingle ran across my feet.

"Oh my god, please tell me it's not the last one. I have the tickliest feet, and I might die if it's that one."

Tempest grinned, studying me like I was the most beautiful thing he'd ever seen. "Guess we'll find out together."

I shot to my feet instantly, walking around and wiggling my toes…but now my ass was feeling strange. "Which craving was the orange candy?"

Because it felt like I was feeling more than one thing…

I stood in the middle of the room, the rising pleasure in me fizzing my brain into panic.

Tempest was on his feet too, ripping off the loincloth and tossing it aside.

His cock was huge and black, like his shadows.

I backed away, my breaths coming in gasps.

"Do you have any idea what you do to me?" He kept coming toward me, and when my back hit the soft padded wall, he pinned me in place.

"There's only one way to find out what arousal you've triggered," he teased. He was enjoying this too much as he fell to his knees in front of me. "I'll help you." Tender hands pushed my legs apart, the rush of wetness coming in waves like something was building inside me.

"You smell fucking incredible." He leaned closer, pulling apart my crotchless bodysuit, grinning to himself. "You need to wear these from now on. I'll have your other panties thrown out."

"What? No—"

His tongue suddenly lapped at my pussy, sliding between my swollen folds, and I moaned as the heat of his mouth latched onto my clit. My legs trembled. Nothing compared to having a monster between my legs, eating me savagely.

Plastered to the wall, my hips rocked. I needed more. My hands were in his hair, and I was ready to burst when he abruptly pulled back and stood.

"That's not it," he declared, his tongue dragging over his glistening lips.

"I beg to differ," I stated. "It felt like the real deal to me. Maybe you should try again." I reached for his shoulder to push him back to his knees, but he moved with such speed, I lost my breath. In the span of a heartbeat, he'd placed me over his bent knees on the sofa.

Before I could even protest, a clawed hand came down hard on my ass.

"Ouch," I protested, wriggling to escape, but the asshole wasn't letting me go, spanking me two more times before finally conceding that wasn't the candy I'd eaten either.

Stumbling away from him, I rubbed my rear, and another wave of arousal pulsed through me because I didn't want to admit it, but I did enjoy the spanking.

"What's wrong with you? Clearly, you know the right color, and you're toying with me."

"Are you enjoying yourself?" He rose before me, tall and monstrous, while he palmed his huge cock, staring down at my feet.

"Well, I'm not hating it, but no, you're not touching my feet."

Suddenly, he lunged for me. I screamed, but he moved like the wind and in seconds, he had me pinned up against the wall again, ripping both of the covers from my nipples off. They were erect and aching. *God, were they swollen?*

He latched onto one, taking it deep into his mouth as his

other hand toyed with my free nipple. I screamed with pleasure instantly, fire streaking across my breasts with a brief flare of pain.

I shuddered as desire soared through me. Barely a few seconds in of him sucking hard, his fangs gently biting against my flesh and pinching my nipples, I yelled with the world's fastest orgasm.

He didn't let me go while I trembled, exploded, and screamed. Slick gushed down my inner thighs, my breaths heavy.

Tempest released my nipples from his perfect torture, his erection poking me in the stomach as he came up for air.

"What are you doing to me?" he groaned, his hips rocking into me, his hands sliding to my ass, spreading my legs so I wrapped them around his hips.

"What am I doing to you? What are you doing to me!"

His cock pushed at my entrance, and I tensed. "You're in my head, little human. I can't get the scent of your pussy out of my nostrils. I crave to lick your slick constantly." He thrusted into me unceremoniously.

I moaned loudly, grasping onto his strong round shoulders.

"I guess it's just a fuck for you," I murmured, unsure why I said that, or why his earlier words still played on my mind.

"Blake," he growled, hammering into me. "Don't you dare fucking think I meant you when I said that. You've been my light, my survival in a dark world I've always sought escape from. Fucking you has been the only thing that keeps me alive. It terrifies me that you've made me feel like that…"

I moaned, my body jumping up and down on his cock. Emotions gripped me, and his hand pressed tenderly to my throat as he kept on fucking me harder, his eyes never leaving me. He stared at me, conflicted, his gaze suspiciously shiny, and for the first time, it felt like he'd opened up to me…and I was able to finally stare into his soul. A place dark, twisted, and completely heartbroken.

"You're all I've ever wanted, but you deserve more than someone as destroyed as me. Someone who doesn't break everything he touches. Someone who everyone detests. You deserve so much more…"

"Tempest," I breathed, my chest hurting because the pain in his voice strangled me.

"I'm ruined, and you'll never see me as anything but the real monster who hurt you, who's done things that will make you hate me…things you won't forgive me for."

We fucked harder, my pussy clenching his huge cock. His words left me slightly distressed though.

"W-what are you talking about?"

But he never paused. He kept rutting me like a wild animal, grunting, when he finally groaned hotly in my ear, "Some days I fucking hate you for making me love you. Other days, I feel like I'll die without you."

I shuddered at his words, tears collecting in my eyes as he banged into me with that ache he'd been living with for too long.

I wanted to hug him, to whisper that even if his world was upside down, things could never be so bad they couldn't be fixed. But the things he said stabbed at my heart.

Something was different about Tempest. Where before he'd been the demon who fucked me for the sake of it, now I saw him as the shadow who'd emerged into the sunlight, who was drowning in his secrets.

It scared me, and something told me that once I found out what else was in his shadows…I'd never be the same again.

CHAPTER 18

BLAKE

I was in the kitchen with Bane, attempting to have him teach me how to make a meal. I'd decided if we were all going to make this work, we needed to have some bonding moments with all of the guys that didn't involve my bedroom—although I really liked those bonding moments too.

Regardless...I decided that family dinners would be a thing.

What I hadn't taken into account was how much their food grossed me out. Steele was currently perched on a stool, a smirk on his handsome face while he watched me cook. I was definitely putting on a show.

Bane was surprisingly patient, and seemed to not be taking offense at the fact I had to take breaks every couple of minutes because I was afraid I would throw up with every dish he taught me how to prepare.

The one I was currently working on was considered another delicacy. There were alot of those, evidently. I was a little worried I was in fact preparing Freddy, because what I was currently rolling into small balls was a gross, gray-colored goo, the same shade as him.

"A little smaller," Bane commented as I worked on rolling one of the balls. We were going to fry them in oil after dipping them in the scales of a sea monster. It was supposedly one of Seven's favorite dishes.

I'd come up with the brilliant idea of making a favorite dish for each of them, so after this, I had to cut the eyeball I'd seen last time I was in here into slices.

I didn't know yet what I would make for the others, but I considered this an extreme act of love.

"You're looking a little…green," Steele teased, his bond fluttering in my chest with his amusement.

I shot him a dirty glare as I dropped the grey ball of goo into the scales, rolling it around so the entire outside was covered.

"The oil's ready," Bane announced, and I picked up the ball and plopped it in the basket. The fact that it was oil was where the similarities ended between their frying process and humans'. The oil was actually a gland from another kind of monster, and it smelled…like rotten cheese.

"What's your favorite dish again?" I asked Steele, wishing I had some sort of gas mask to block out the smell of the oil, and maybe a blindfold as well so I didn't have to see what I was doing. The eyeball dish was next, and it was sitting on the plate on the other side of the counter…staring at me.

"Macaroni and cheese," Steele said with a sly grin. I nodded, before his words sunk in. I glanced up at him hopefully, because macaroni and cheese happened to be one of my favorite dishes as well. And although the food that was prepared for me here was less monstrous than the dishes I was currently preparing, they were still nothing like human food. Thinking of macaroni and cheese had my mouth watering.

"Really?" I gasped, seeing Bane frowning out of the corner of my eye, as though we'd mortally offended him. Evidently, gagging over his monster food was acceptable, but suggesting we cook human food was offensive.

"Can we by chance make that...?" I joked, not thinking it would be possible.

Steele walked over to the fridge that was more like an old-school ice box and opened it up. He pulled out ingredients, and my squeal filled the kitchen as I actually recognized what the items were.

Cheese. And noodles. And milk. Okay, I was pretty sure the milk was not from a cow, but there was still cheese and noodles.

"How did you get those?"

"I slipped back to your realm to grab some things I thought you'd like. I remembered how you would smile on macaroni and cheese day."

I lunged forward and threw myself at him, belatedly realizing I had the gray goo all over my hands still.

"All right, we're making this next. But you'll have to take the dish away from me as soon as it's done, because I don't have enough willpower to not eat the whole thing before we get to dinner."

Steele's gaze filled me with butterflies as I pulled away. It was so besotted looking, that I would've thought it was fake had I not felt him inside of me. Out of all of them, he stayed by me the most. And I didn't mind that at all.

"I'll just finish these...ball thingies," I murmured, turning back to the gross dish. Bane appeared next to me and pushed me to the side gently with his hip.

"You obviously have no taste, and neither does your mate, but regardless, I'm not sure you'll be able to concentrate on my cooking lessons until you've made that monstrosity. And we wouldn't want the Perverian balls to be ruined. Seven would have my hide. I'll finish these up."

I didn't argue with him. I figured that rolling the balls and getting them in the oil counted as making Seven's favorite dish.

Steele set the ingredients on the counter, and then he pulled on an apron that was only slightly different from the ones you wore in the kitchen on earth. It was hilarious on his huge monster form.

"You're going to help me?" I asked.

"I need to learn to make my mate's favorite dish," he said seriously, and I swooned.

"I thought I was your favorite dish."

The look he gave me could've impregnated me right there.

"All right, the secret to good macaroni and cheese is that you have to boil the noodles in the milk and that helps add to the creaminess."

Steele nodded, studying the noodles and milk intensely, but not moving towards them. Almost as if he expected them to start cooking themselves.

"Will you grab that pot?" I finally asked, and he nodded sheepishly before darting to it and setting it in front of me like an offering. I managed to hold in my giggle.

Who knew cooking could be so much fun?

He watched as I carefully poured the milk into a clay bowl roughly the size of a measuring cup.

"I think we'll need at least eight scoops of the noodles." Bane snorted at my comment, not trying to hide it at all. I gave him the side eye.

"My monsters have big appetites, and I want to make sure there's enough for me," I explained haughtily.

He held up his hands in front of him. "I wasn't saying anything," he responded, the mirth in his voice clear.

Ignoring his attitude, I resumed working on my macaroni and cheese. I went over to the stove, which was more of a fire than anything else, and I placed the pot of milk on top of it. Steele popped one of the raw noodles into his mouth, grimacing as he crunched down. "Something's wrong with the noodles. I think I got the wrong kind," he growled, annoyed.

This time, I couldn't hold in my laugh. "There's nothing wrong with the noodles. They just have to be cooked before they taste good, and even then, you have to smother them with cheese to get the right effect."

There was a slight flush to his cheeks, and I cocked my head, examining his embarrassment.

"You lived on earth for *a while*. What did you do to survive?"

His blush deepened. "A lot of take out," he finally drawled. "I tried to cook once, but I burned down my apartment, so after that, it was easier to buy premade food. I know absolutely nothing about cooking."

For a second, I imagined how we could have been on earth, living in an apartment or a house, cooking in our kitchen together like this. It was a beautiful thought, and one I'd had often when I'd been on earth, but the idea wasn't as bright as it once had been.

Somehow, standing here in this monster kitchen, with eyeballs and gray balls of goo, and Steele in his monster form…it seemed much better than what I'd once envisioned.

My life had certainly changed.

"What are you thinking about?" he asked softly, as the milk popped with bubbles and I poured in the noodles to cook.

"I used to imagine moments like this. I'd see you in the cafeteria and I'd pretend we were actually eating together. And then, of course, my thoughts would spiral from there, and all of a sudden, I'd be daydreaming about us in our own house."

Steele's answering grin was beautiful. He was clearly happy to hear me admitting how much I'd thought about him.

"I never imagined it would come true like this. But

somehow it's even better than what I used to dream." I bit my lip and stared down at the frothing milk. "Did you ever think about things like that?"

I didn't know why I felt so weird asking the question, but I did. Our mating bond meant I could feel how true his feelings were, but it would probably take years for my brain to get on the same level as my heart…thanks to my terrible upbringing.

"I never dreamed of cooking with you simply because I didn't cook…But I thought about doing everything else with you. You were all I ever thought about. I lived for those moments when I saw your face. I'm sure you weren't even aware I was watching you most of the time."

I leaned against him, absentmindedly stirring the noodles so they wouldn't clump together. "It still feels unreal that you're here." He took my face in his hands and brushed a kiss across my lips.

"And now I get to do my best to make sure your whole life is a dream."

Bane snorted nearby, breaking the moment. My cheeks flushed, and I glanced at him, embarrassed.

"You're both making me sick, and you're ruining your dish," he offered calmly.

I cursed when I realized he was right, and the noodles were almost too done. I took it off the fire and then grabbed the cheese we'd already shredded, sprinkling it into the milky noodle mixture and stirring slowly. Steele hadn't known all the things to get, but luckily Bane had some spices that, while not exactly the same, were similar enough that I could finish the dish. I poured the cheese and noodle mixture into another pot, and then stuck it in the oven to bake. Steele had tried to grab bites the entire time, but luckily my food was mostly intact. He'd seen I was a bit feral about the dish.

I went back to helping Bane with the other meals, finally stopping and letting him take over when I cut into some kind of slug and it squirted green juice all over me.

Bane was much more efficient than I was, and by the time the macaroni and cheese was done, and he'd taken over, the rest of the dishes were finished in a flash.

"Ready to go?" I asked. Steele nodded, his face slightly pained. I rubbed my chest, the tightness in his bond catching me off guard.

"What's wrong?" I asked.

He wrinkled his nose. "Sometimes I forget that the bond works both ways."

I poked his chest and he sighed. "I'm not sure that this is ever going to be comfortable. I can remember clearly how it used to be, and I miss it every time I'm around them."

I picked up the macaroni and cheese and Steele carried the other tray loaded down with dishes. I wasn't going to let anyone else be in charge of my noodles. I would hate to kill my mate because he ruined my meal.

I was joking, of course. Kind of.

"We were once brothers. Creed and I were closer than close. The loss is still with me, ya know?"

He was staring straight ahead as we walked, and it was definitely intentional. He balanced the tray in one hand and then wiped at his face suspiciously. My heart throbbed seeing that show of emotion.

Unfortunately, I was pretty sure time was the only thing that could heal the group's relationship with Steele Although he'd been the one wronged, he seemed much more able to forgive than them.

Another reason why this family dinner was so important.

We got to the dining room, and my jaw dropped. I was really wishing for my camera. The other four were all seated at the table, dressed in their best. They'd gotten ahold of human tuxedos and it was like they'd stepped out of a fashion magazine as they sat there. Even Tempest was early, which was a surprise, because the look on his face told me he'd rather be tearing his eyes out than attending this dinner.

Baby steps, right?

I had Steele set down the tray, and then I put all the dishes on the table, making sure to place my mac and cheese nearest to me, of course.

Ash inhaled deeply and groaned in ecstasy. "You had fleming's stew made."

"She *made* fleming's stew," Steele corrected.

You would've thought I'd made all of Ash's dreams come true by the sappy, enthralled look on his face. That had been the dish that spewed green stuff all over me. And I had indeed thrown up in the trashcan afterwards.

But now, it was all worth it. I'd make it for him every day of the week if it would make him happy like that.

All of them talked over themselves, telling me how good everything looked. Except for Tempest, of course. He was staring down at his dish with a strange expression on his face. Like the sight of it was hurting him.

"Steele told me that was your favorite, but I can make you something else," I offered, unable to keep the disappointment from my voice.

That shook him out of whatever daze he was in. His eyes snapped to mine and he shook his head vigorously. "It's great. Thank you," he rumbled, but there was clearly still something off about him. Steele didn't seem to notice Tempest's attitude, and he led me to my seat in between Creed and him and pulled out my chair to sit like the perfect mate he was.

"Pet, don't forget about last night," Creed drawled. "You should be staring at *me* like that." I flushed and stared down at my plate, feeling everyone's interested gazes on me. I didn't even remember half of last night. He'd done things to me I was still feeling today.

Seven scooped a couple of the balls onto my plate eagerly, obviously trying to get my attention. But there was no way I would be trying it. I flashed him a broad grin anyway though, because it was cute.

Rubbing my hands together, I scooped a heaping spoonful of the macaroni and cheese on my plate. Not even taking a second to see if everyone else was eating, I needed to get it in my mouth now. I moaned…loudly as it hit my taste buds. I was sure if I compared it to the dish made on earth, it would be completely lacking. But right then, it was the best thing I'd ever tasted.

"Don't make those noises, Blake, if you don't want to become the main course," growled Ash. I glanced up at him and dropped my fork with a clatter when I saw how hungrily they were all staring at me.

"No. This is a sex-free meal. We are going to eat and talk and become closer. Don't distract me with your sexy faces."

Seven snorted, and the stern face I'd been trying for fell, because I couldn't help but be ridiculously happy I'd made my usually morose monster laugh.

"Sex-free meal, hmmm? Not sure if I like that."

I stuck my tongue at him before going back to shoveling the macaroni and cheese into my mouth. I was only half aware of Creed scooping some of it onto his plate. But I definitely heard it when he tasted it. He started gagging, pushing his chair away from the table and hurling up what he'd just tried. I stared at him in horror.

"That is without a doubt the worst thing I've ever tasted. Are you trying to poison me?" he growled, sounding slightly hysterical.

The word "poison" had my gaze flicking to Tempest for some reason, and I found his eyes locked on me. I dragged my eyes from his and then took another bite of the noodles, in case there was another part of it that didn't taste right or something. It tasted amazing though, and Steele was still eating it eagerly.

"It can't be that bad if she made it," offered Ash, leaning over and grabbing a spoonful of the dish.

As soon as the spoon slid past his lips, he was gagging

and spitting it out as well. I snorted as Tempest and Seven both had the same reactions. I exchanged an amused glance with Steele and shrugged my shoulders. "More for us," I drawled, scooping more of it onto my plate unrepentantly as the others stared in disgust. At least I'd gotten sex off their minds. Now they were thinking about how gross my macaroni and cheese was.

They eventually resumed eating their other dishes, but they weren't really talking to one another. I shot Steele a look and he rolled his eyes, but finally, he set his utensil down.

"So, Creed, been fishing lately?"

Creed froze, staring at Steele incredulously. The question was so ridiculous considering everything that had happened since Steele's return, and I started laughing hysterically. Tears were streaming down my face. I couldn't think of a more crazy question he could've asked.

Ash started laughing next, the sound of it playful and fun, like he was. The rest of them followed suit, and suddenly, all six of us were almost falling out of our chairs. The laughter was extremely overdone for the question Steele had asked, but it was like we were all releasing our locked-up emotions at once.

It was an amazing thing, but after we'd finally calmed down, the conversation went much more easily. Creed even joked with Steele about how he'd managed to convince humans he was actually a therapist when he was so messed up in the head himself.

I knew I was watching them with a stupid grin on my face, but I couldn't help it. The scene gave me hope for the first time that maybe the six of us could work, that Steele and the others could coexist peacefully, and maybe even be friends again someday. My insides swooned when I saw Creed and Steele exchanging an amused glance after Tempest said something assholish, and I realized they were sharing an inside joke that they'd probably had before.

Both of them quickly glanced away when they realized what they'd been doing, but it was a start.

It was the perfect day, and I did in fact finish the entire pot of macaroni and cheese.

And I loved every bite of it.

Just like I loved every bit of them.

CHAPTER 19

BLAKE

I should get some kind of warning before my men burst into my room like charging bulls.

Half the time, I jumped out of my skin, half expecting to find out it was the end of the world. Over time, I'd learned that their actions were normal monstrous behaviors. Not an emergency reaction. I couldn't really tell the difference.

So, when Ash charged into my room like the city was on fire, I didn't panic but kept on combing my hair, well aware we had a date today. Or more like he'd be showing me the city so I became familiar with my surroundings should I find myself lost.

Feeding was still a huge issue and something that Creed was working on by attempting to source temporary feeding energy for the population from the neighboring city if things didn't improve.

In the meantime, the sex marathons continued, and somehow, amid the darkness, I started to feel a tiny sliver of hope that maybe…we'd find a way to fix everything.

My gorgeous monsters were coming together again. Well, except for Tempest, but I was still holding out hope for him after our night at the sex club. I'd seen a new side to him there. One that scared me, but also made me want to patch things up between us.

"I have a surprise for you," Ash announced, and only then did I notice he was holding a wicker basket, which looked strangely delicate held by such a muscular man.

"We're going on a picnic?" I asked, suddenly excited for our outing.

"It's the location that'll be the surprise."

I strolled over to him, staring at the basket, curious what a monster packed in a picnic basket, but he pulled it away from me. "Then I'm ready to go."

And with that response, he took my hand and whirled me out of the room, me dropping my comb behind me.

For a change, the sky shone a lighter hue of red, and strangely, the city was starting to feel familiar, like I knew my way across nearby bridges and belonged there. It wasn't as though I had a welcoming party to return back to earth. Wyld was growing on me with each passing day. Even the oppressive heat from the lava was becoming normal, which was saying a lot.

"Maybe we should have asked the others to join us," I suggested, walking hand in hand with Ash.

"That wasn't going to happen, beautiful one. I couldn't sleep last night in anticipation of our day together, thinking of where to take you, and exactly where I'm going to kiss you."

I raised my eyebrows, smiling at him, even if he couldn't see. "You were planning where to kiss me?" I snorted.

"Oh, did you think we were only kissing?" he said. "That's just the taster. We'll definitely fuck too," he muttered, loud enough that the couple slithering past glanced at us, nodding at me with encouragement to get it done already.

I laughed at Ash because he was adorable.

But having the whole city pushing me to keep having sex was something I'd never get used to. There were still riots in areas, but with our increased sex workouts, the population felt a slight increase in the trickle of feeding, so they knew we were trying. Though I wasn't sure we could take it up to the next level without me permanently having a dick inside me.

We strolled onward, past pod-like towers, crossing all manner of bridges, and most of the monsters we passed kept a wide berth.

Ash suddenly drew me into a black tower and then an elevator, where we soon emerged into a foyer made of marble, and I immediately recognized the place.

"Oh, we're going back to the lake? Where you said it was illegal to swim in clothes. I love that place."

"Not quite." He drew me against him and walked me right past the entrance to the lake, while I kept glancing back, pouting.

I rolled my eyes at him, and he chuckled, drawing my hand to his mouth. "Just because I can't see what you're doing, don't assume I can't tell when you're rolling your eyes."

"How do you know I'm doing anything?" I stuck my tongue out at him.

"Heightened senses, and I pick up on the smallest of sounds like your mouth parting…that sweet tongue sliding out."

When he drew us into another foyer made of stone and decorated with suspended faux moths, a spider guard quickly greeted us, bowing as low as its front, spidery legs allowed.

"Welcome, sir. Your reserved spot is ready for you."

My skin crawled at being so close to that huge, bulbous black body, with thin legs covered in spiky hair, a tiny head with dozens of eyes, and fangs that seemed to be dripping green venom on the floor.

I bumped into Ash in my attempt to be as far from the guard as possible because they really freaked me out.

With a chuckle under his breath, Ash drew me into a dimly lit hallway that seemed to go forever.

"You really dislike the guards, don't you? They won't harm you and they keep you protected."

"I know, but they look like the creepy crawly spiders we have back home, and everyone hates them. They bite and are venomous. I would kill any one I came across, smacking it with my shoe."

He made a gasping sound. "How hard did you strike it for it to die from a single hit of your shoe? They're known for having especially hard heads."

I bumped my shoulder into his arm playfully. "They're not huge like these ones, or everyone on earth would have already burned down the planet and moved to Mars. They're as small as my palm. Some are tinier…but did you hear me say they carry venom in their fangs and can kill you?"

His nose scrunched up. "And you're scared of something that small?"

"You have no idea," I rasped with a shiver running down my back. "They love hiding in cars and jumping out at you, crawling through your window, and living in your shoes. And sometimes they even charge at you when they're threatened."

Ash was hollering with laughter. "Humans are such a fearful race."

I slapped his arm. "Trust me, if you encountered one, you'd scream like a baby."

"Highly doubtful. I'd pick it up and eat it."

Okay, I wasn't expecting that response.

At the end of the hallway, he pushed open a set of doors and an explosion of light poured over us. We stepped outside into a lush, green park. A field of yellow and purple flowers spread out as far as the eye could see. Trees peppered the grounds, bursting with reddish leaves, the branches laden with violet, globe-like fruits.

Please let them be plums.

There were a few monsters in the garden too, walking

around, others under trees, and one couple with long beaks were kissing super awkwardly.

But aside from that, I was in heaven.

"Wow," I gushed, enjoying the light breeze ruffling the skirt of my dress, the freshness in the air, the scenery. I might have stepped through the Narnia wardrobe because this felt like a completely different world. "This is so beautiful."

Releasing Ash's hand, I rushed forward, running through the flowers, wanting to know why I hadn't known this place existed until now. Twisting around on the spot, I called out to Ash who strolled towards a small hill by a massive tree over-flowing with branches and those purple fruit. I chased after him.

"You told me before that the lake next door was run by Creed's circle. Does he own this too?"

"Of course. The places are open to all who work at the castle, and that's why we have royal guards patrolling the entrances."

At the top of the hill, we found a blanket already laid out under a tree, and I took a seat, crossing my legs, staring out at the landscape. "We need to come here more often because I keep discovering places I'm loving in the city. Not everything is towers and bridges and lava heat. This is paradise."

"This city is incredible, and I want you to fall in love with it like I have. To see why we fight so hard to hold onto it. This is my home, your home, and there are so many things I can show you. I love hearing your reactions."

"I can't wait." I grew jittery. "So, what's for lunch then?"

Ash opened the basket and started pulling out food. The first was long white worms tangled together and wrapped up in plastic.

"Eww, I'll pass on whatever that is."

"Intestines. I heard they are a delicacy on earth."

"Where did you hear that? From your little book? If so, cross it out forever."

He chuckled, and I watched in amusement as this man, who belonged on the cover of a fashion magazine, unpacked the picnic basket he'd made for me. I was swooning hard, something inside me tightening because I could easily see myself spending the rest of my life with him. Which was crazy, but I was completely smitten. Was it possible to fall for someone so hard that you'd even consider eating strange intestines if it made him happy?

By the look of the array of foods he'd brought, there were only two edible items.

A salad. And more of those delicious chocolate leaves I couldn't get enough of.

I passed on the dish that resembled grey lungs, and especially the gelatinous slimy slug cubes that told me Bane prepared this picnic basket. I dove into the salad though. It came with little blue tomatoes and something white sliced into matchsticks. They tasted like radish, only sweeter.

"I love it here," I murmured with a mouthful of salad, while Ash picked up the bowl of gelatinous cubes. Why did he have to go with that one first?

"Just so you know, before you eat those things, I may never be able to kiss you again," I teased. And I kind of wasn't lying…I didn't want to think about slime while kissing my gorgeous god-like monster.

His face suddenly fell at my words like I'd insulted him, and he stuffed the plate back into the basket. "Oh."

My heart broke because I thought I hurt him.

"Ash, I'm only joking. You can eat them," I cooed, hating myself for saying that.

"No, no, it's all good. I'm not that hungry anyway." He leaned back on his arm, while guilt was killing me.

I set my salad down and crawled over to him, then pulled out the bowl from the basket. "Please, I'm sorry, I shouldn't have said that. Sometimes I have major foot-in-mouth problems."

Grabbing a squishy cube with two fingers, I brought it to his mouth. "I promise I'll kiss you after you have one. Will you do me the honor?" I tried my best to sound playful, but truthfully, I felt like crap.

"It's okay, I understand. Things will take time for you to get used to them." He smiled at me, but he sounded strained.

"Yeah, but I was rude and I feel l like shit, and—"

But just then, Ash twisted to get up, bumping into me from his sheer momentum, knocking me over, the cube flinging into the air. He came right after me to catch me, both of us now tangled and bursting out laughing at the chaos as we rolled on the grass.

It also happened to be exactly when the cube dropped right into my open, laughing mouth. I choked, frantically trying to twist around to spit it out, except I ended up biting into it. And I was ready to start vomiting.

"Babe, are you okay?"

"I-I…" A burst of flavor exploded across my tongue, like the sweetest pineapple in the world. I moaned, chewing it, half grossed out that I'd eaten a slimy snail…and another part wanting more. To my surprise, it slid down my throat without me gagging. "O.M.G. I swallowed it."

"Oh, did you die?" Ash said sarcastically, holding me in his arms as we both lay in the field of flowers. "Was it as disgusting as you thought it was?"

"I'm going to keep eating my words today, aren't I? Because it was actually freaking delicious. Why the hell does a slimy slug taste good? That's so…weird."

Ash was laughing hysterically at this point.

I felt like I'd won a major prize as I listened to his laughter. I flopped onto my back among the flowers, him on his side next to me. "You're very fortunate that you enjoyed the praqex cubes…I don't think I could continue loving someone who didn't." He pulled a hilarious face at me.

My heart soared in my chest, but I tried my best to remain

calm, to still the excited trembling. "Ash, did you just say you loved me?"

"Well, of course, but it comes with conditions."

I couldn't help myself and pushed towards him with such exhilaration that I drove him onto his back, me on top of his chest, staring down at that angelic face. "And what are these conditions? Because I have a few of my own."

"Why would you have conditions? You haven't declared your love."

I laughed, feeling like I might burst from the precious feelings surging through me. Then I kissed him, showing him exactly how much he meant to me.

"I love you with all my heart," I announced with a shaky breath because it suddenly felt as if I was floating, passion blooming inside me.

Ash kissed me back, his breaths rushed as he embraced me. "You own my soul, and you've owned it since the first time I met you in our first dream together. I knew that I loved you…even back then. I knew I'd lose my heart to you, and that one day we'd end up together forever. I love you so much, Blake."

"Forever is a very long time." I kissed the corners of his mouth, absolutely adoring this monster.

My heartbeat accelerated, and I considered pinching myself to check I wasn't dreaming.

"Well, forever is one of my conditions so every day I can tell you how much I love you, kiss your sweet lips, and lick your pussy. Oh and then I can breed you obviously."

I chuckled. "So, then one of my conditions is that you give me a foot massage every night."

"Done."

I embraced him, bringing him back over my body. The next thing I knew though, we were rolling down the hill, me laughing hysterically. If there was such a thing as a perfect day, I'd found it. There were still so many problems to fix, but

I let myself have that moment with Ash, to enjoy the feeling of being loved by another one of my monsters.

I was the luckiest girl in the world.

By the time we were about to leave, I told Ash I wanted to collect a bunch of the flowers for my room.

I wandered around the hill, unable to stop smiling, and already planning to take Ash back to my room to really show him how much I loved him.

But as I bent over to pick up a blue flower, a strangling sound came from behind me.

I jolted up and spun around, unsure what I was staring at for a moment.

One of the spider guards was shedding his skin, and he was on the ground squirming, making that horrid sound as it attempted to pull itself free from its old flesh.

I pulled a face at what I was witnessing, yet I couldn't look away.

He used the beautiful flowers to drag his body across and finally wrenched himself out of his gross skin.

My heart thundered, a scream pressing on my throat at the monstrosity I witnessed as he finally stood up on hairy legs, so much bigger than the other guards.

I gasped as he shook himself. He glanced at me and tipped his head forward as if I hadn't observed the grossest thing ever.

Except, I'd been so wrong.

As he scuttled away in his new bigger body, another jelly-like monster, reminding me so much of Freddy, rushed over and then threw himself down at the spider husk left behind. He plunged his face into it, jelly hands greedily snatching at the remains.

I gagged, bile hitting the back of my throat.

It slobbered all over the husk, hungrily tearing into the skin, clawing at it, and shaking it in its mouth. He was eating it, swallowing it down in huge chunks.

I was going to be sick.

Just then, a big dollop of slobber flung directly at me. It hit me right across my chest, the wet sloppiness revolting.

I screamed that time, frantically using the flowers in my hand to wipe it off me.

Ash was at my side instantly. "What's wrong?"

"Get it off me, get it off," I cried, batting at the slobber, but I still felt it as if it slid over my skin.

Ash wiped the rest off my chest with his hand, not bothered by the mess. "It's just a bit of slime from the guard molting his skin."

Horrifying slurping sounds continued from the monster eating it, and I gagged once more, about to vomit. Yet I kept wiping at my chest. "I can still feel it, like it's wriggling on me. Please, Ash, get it off me." I desperately clawed at his arm, pleading for his help.

He lifted me into his arms, and we were running across the field. "We'll go wash it off, hold on. The lake is made of purified water that cleanses anything. But you know the spider skin is a delicacy to many...it's not going to hurt you."

"Stop telling me thinks are delicacies," I all but screeched, my skin itching with a gross feeling.

When Ash finally set me on my feet, they sank into cool water. We were in the paradise lake and I didn't waste a moment, throwing myself into its embrace.

The cold water was a shock to the system, and I frantically rubbed at my chest to get the slime off.

Bright lights popped suddenly behind my eyes, and a sharp pain cut through me. I curled up, terrified.

Then it started...memories flashing across my mind, coming so fast that my underwater world spun.

I was in a cave with Tempest. Him healing my wound from the sandworms, and I had cried in pain from where it bit me all because Tempest had thrown me out of the city to kill me. Then he fucked me, revealing all his secrets, then cursed me to forget it all. And he told me things he never wanted me to know. And now they were running wild in my mind.

I wanted to cry, to scream.

All my lost memories rushed over me, slamming into me, tearing at my heart. And when it all settled into my brain, terror clung to me.

I threw myself up through the water for air, my head breaching the surface, panic in my veins, and the words on my lips flew out at Ash, my words splattering out.

"I remember it all. Oh fuck, Tempest killed The Red Queen. And he tried to kill me!"

CHAPTER 20

TEMPEST

"Tempest, are you coming in?" Queen Eruthria called in her sweet voice that had me grinding my teeth. She never beckoned me unless she was in one of her moods, and it sure as hell wasn't a call to fuck me. Feeding the population was reserved for her favorites—King Creed, Ash, Seven, and Steele. But me, I was the asshole she kicked.

I entered her chamber because no one said no to the queen of Wyld. For a long time, I'd believed I loved her, and that with time, she would feel the same way toward me.

I was stupid for holding onto hope.

Lifting my gaze from my monster form, I met eyes of every infinite hue of blue. One glance, a light tug of the corners of her lips upward, and I fell once more for her charm, a lifetime of desire built up inside me that had rarely been put into use. But maybe today she'd see me for me. She'd welcome me to her bed instead of the occasional quickie. She'd whisper those words I'd longed for…that she loved me too.

She lounged on her throne in the great hall, the walls carved with monstrous depictions of our ancestors, and herself…but I couldn't take my eyes off her beauty.

Caramel red skin glowed beneath the burning torches, and

watching my approach, thorns pushed out of the flesh around her neck, flaring in aggression like they always did in my company.

Small silvery horns at her temples stood out amid thick curls that tumbled over her shoulders and to her waist.

She was naked and absolutely spectacular. I reminded myself to not expect anything. Then she couldn't disappoint me. But keeping my gaze away from her full breasts, from her silver-tipped nipples, became unbearable. Sitting cross-legged, she tapped her fingers on the armrest of her throne.

"Hurry, boy," she chided.

I fell to my knees before her, but she scoffed. "For Darkevers' sake, stand up. I'm not in a patient mood today."

"Your majesty," I bowed my head instead. "How may I serve you?"

"Well you see, that's the thing. I've been hearing rumors from my guards that you stole from me." I twisted my head to her Guard Captain, Vero, smirking in my direction.

Fucking liar. We all knew he lusted after the queen, and I was just another pebble in his shoe.

I raised my head up to my queen, my pulse thundering. "I would never. Who—" I choked on a sudden coldness thickening my throat.

"Don't lie to me," she spoke with a deep voice, one I recognized too well.

"This is the fourth time this week I've been accused, and each time I proved I took nothing." I knew the moment I replied, I'd set her off.

Fucking idiot! Shut your mouth.

Her face twisted into something ugly, into the real beast. The one who lived behind that beautiful face that fooled me into believing she might one day be who I longed for.

"Are you calling your queen a liar?"

Captain Vero stepped closer, shoulders broad, a growl on his throat. My ribs still stung from last week's beating where he broke three.

I swallowed hard, biting my tongue, retreating. Her eyes darkened, narrowing on me.

An icy chill swept over my skin with a single blink of her eyes. I shuddered as the cold deepened, seeping into my bones and stealing my breath.

Her magic was a cruel whip she used on me too often.

"Stop it, please," I pleaded, resisting the urge to retreat. That only made her angrier.

Lips peeling back over her fangs, the hair on my nape stood up as she climbed to her feet, standing before me, showing me everything I craved. Everything that reminded me I was worthless.

The freezing touch of her power rushed over me. Teeth chattering, I reached for her. "Make it stop."

The floor was iced over, and the air I drew in with every breath grew colder and colder in my lungs.

She strolled around me as the cold seeped into my marrow, the feeling from my body fading, and all I kept thinking was that this time she'd finally kill me. She'd push it too far.

Sharp stabbing pain bled through me, and I hugged my arms around myself, trembling so hard, I couldn't see straight.

My queen approached me. "You have never been my favorite, Tempest." She reached down and ran her fingers over my hanging cock. Heat burned everywhere she touched, the pain like shards of ice slicing my dick.

I hollered, liquid agony pouring over me, and I somehow managed to take a step back from her touch.

Eyes flaring, she came after me, snatching my cock in her fist, her hand on fire from her magic, and I shouted in agony while she laughed in my face. But the longer she held onto me, the more her warmth spread over me, chasing away the cold. I leaned forward, desperate for more, aching for her touch.

Her nose scrunched up at my reaction in disgust. She'd never enjoyed touching me; even the times she'd taken me as a necessity to feed her population, she scratched and bit me, leaving me hating myself worse.

"Listen here, you piece of shit. I brought you into my home as a favor, a promise to keep you in my servitude, but nothing about you is good enough for me."

She squeezed my cock, and tears ran down my face as I squirmed, teetering on passing out and falling over.

"So…if I say you stole from me, then you fall to your knees and apologize. If I ask you to fuck my steed in the barn, then you'll do it." She sneered. "You think I enjoy having to fuck all five of you pathetic monsters? I feel dirty and sick to my stomach each time I do, but I play a role. And so will you, Worm."

I gritted my teeth and thrust my chin forward, meeting her gaze. It burned into me. Maybe she saw something behind my eyes that she approved of, because she finally released me. I bit back a pained moan as the cold raced over my cock once more; the rest of my body frozen from the inside out.

"The worm has a spine, can you believe that?" she said over her shoulder to Captain Vero.

"Your majesty, did you want me to chop off his cock so he never touches you with it again?" he growled, staring death daggers at me.

She was prodding her chin. "Tempting, but I think our worm has learned his lesson."

I stood trembling, the sensation of icicles stabbing me deepening.

"Actually, no, I changed my mind," she purred with a sound that scared me. "Vero, leave us alone. Out. Now!" she demanded.

"I've been feeling rather aroused lately, and no one seems to have fanned my flames. But be a good worm and don't go anywhere." She walked around me, her hand running across my chest, my arm, my back, heat stealing the cold, and I moaned, craving the warmth.

"Yes, please," I murmured, picturing her wrapped around me, soaking in her heat.

Her laughter sang in my ears, and I rocked on my feet, following her, craving her but completely loathing myself for it.

"You know every day you breathe is a gift…I should have killed you ages ago." She paused in front of me, her eyes on fire.

My stomach churned as I balanced on the edge of completely passing out from the cold.

"Do it," I spat the words, meaning it because I'd had enough of her tortures, of beatings, of being belittled by her and her guards.

"What fun would that be?" She cupped the side of my face, warmth bringing feeling to my face once more, and I leaned against her touch, frantically needing that heat, but she ripped it away just as fast. "Your family rejected you, so what makes you think I'd see you as anything but worthless?"

She stepped away from me, making her way to her throne as the cold spread through me, over me, securing my feet to the floor.

"I smell your fear," she muttered. "And I like how it makes me feel." She flopped down on her throne and spread her legs for me. "Let me show you something you'll never have again because I've decided you'll no longer fuck me. You won't step foot in my throne room ever again. I won't see you or hear your voice because you're moving out in the back with the animals. So, call this your parting gift."

Heart hammering, I grew fucking dizzy, my vision patchy.

But her words played on my mind, and with them, something feral rose up. It licked my insides, a heavy feeling in the pit of my stomach that I couldn't ignore. One of primal rage.

Watching her tug her tits and spread her pussy in front of me as she fingered herself did nothing for me. I screamed on the inside with agony, iced over like a fucking animal. I didn't think I could take this another day.

Her moan rang across the room. "Watch me," she purred, rubbing her clit faster. I couldn't look away, as the bitch had fucking froze me.

Anger accelerated through my veins, my mind thrashing against the impossible cold. It wasn't long before it became too much, and when my world blackened, I thanked whatever miserable god had put me out of my misery.

———

I flipped open my eyes to running water rushing over me, the stench of something putrid filling my nostrils. Groaning, I pushed myself up, rubbing my eyes to work out where the hell I was.

It became evident fast the guards had dumped me into the sewage drains at the rear of the castle.

Seething, something snapped inside me…something dark licked at my spine. My whole life I'd been kicked around, pushed down, from my father to the queen.

I wasn't her "worm".

I wasn't hers at all.

I smacked a fist to my head, over and over, wanting her voice out of my mind. Wanting it gone. A prickle of awareness tugged at my thoughts, but I shoved them aside and embraced my monster side. The one where I'd no longer be the laughing stock, the garbage others kicked around.

I shook with anger, my mind blurring with a maddening frenzy. I threw myself back into the castle, knowing my way well enough to avoid the guards, to stick to the shadows. Making a quick detour to my room, I snatched the knife I'd been hiding and sprinted back to the throne room. I wasn't an idiot and used the side entrance when I heard voices from inside.

Pausing at the doorway, I pressed close and pushed the door only slightly open. The queen was being fucked over her throne by a blue monster with ivory spikes that ran from the middle of his head all the way down his spine, his body explosive with muscles. She roared while having her ass fucked ruthlessly, both of them grunting like those horny Derins who humped anything they could mount.

I recognized the monster. It was Kurden, the king of one of our enemy cities, who'd already waged war against us once. What the fuck was he doing here? What the fuck was she doing?

"Kurden, you shouldn't have come," the queen whined in a sweet voice, and I ground my teeth with irritation.

He licked her face with a thick, blue tongue. "I'll make this quick. Tomorrow, my army and I arrive before dawn, and I'll destroy those idiots you fuck, who touch you like you're theirs. I'll start with Creed and chop him up before feeding him to the Gazen."

She moaned in ecstasy at his words.

"Then I'm taking over Wyld with you at my side. You've got everything in place, right?"

She nodded eagerly. "The explosives are set around the city, painted with my red magic. No one will know what hit them."

My blood ran colder than when the queen had encased me in ice. She was going to betray her own monsters, and give our city over to our enemy, all for blue cock in her ass.

That fucking bitch. It shouldn't surprise me, but even this was low for the cunt. My breath shuddered, my rational brain screaming for me to tell the others, to warn them. But who'd believe a worm like me?

I slammed my fist to my head to shut off my thoughts.

Heavy footfalls grew louder, and I jerked my attention to find them both coming my way.

Panicked, I frantically threw myself down the hall and into a side corridor. Flat back to the wall, I didn't make a sound, didn't breathe. My ears were alert, and I listened to her pushing him out the back door and instructing Captain Vero to get them out safely and fast.

By the time she returned to the throne room, I went after her in silence, only to spy Steele entering the throne room.

Fuck. Shit timing.

I waited in the shadows outside the room and kept checking over my shoulder, not even hearing their discussion with how loud my heart thumped in my ears. But when he strolled out, I made my move and entered the room silently so she wouldn't see me.

My nerve endings were all twitchy, my brain popping with adrenaline.

What she proposed was treason. Killing my brothers, and the rest of Wyld.

I stalked her, my head not my own, but one made of fury and retribution. I would do the right thing, no matter the cost.

I learned a long time ago that the only person I could rely on in life was me. So I slid along the walls in my shadow form, slipping unnoticed, as the queen dropped into her throne, laughing maniacally.

The sound grated on my nerves. It brought back the hundreds of times she'd hurt me. The memories of her refusing to heal Seven after his torture. When she purposefully hurt Ash by placing things in his path so he tripped and lost confidence in being blind. To mocking Steele, and even undermining her king, Creed, by cheating on him and planning his death.

My blade gripped tight in my grasp, I heaved for breath, rage building inside me.

She had her back to me in her seat, and I lunged forward.

I sliced through the room, and all I heard in my head was her voice.

Worm. Worm. Worm. Worthless worm.

I hurled myself up and over the back of her throne.

One hand grabbed a fistful of hair, wrenching her head back, my blade biting into her throat.

Her eyes shot up with surprise in the exact same moment that I crouched on the back of her seat.

"Worm," she growled, the slight prick of magic already slipping over my skin, but I didn't give her the chance to hurt me.

She'd had too many already.

"You've got to ask yourself, why didn't you see this coming, bitch?" I aggressively swiped my knife across her throat. Blood splashed down her body, and I didn't stop at one. I hacked a few more times until her head lopped right off.

"Die, you fucking bitch, because I'm making sure you can't come back."

But in a blur, something huge rushed across the room and slammed into me, throwing me off the throne, the queen's head slipping out of my grasp. It went flinging somewhere in the room.

I hit the floor with a grunt, the blade falling from my grip.

Seconds was all it took for me to come face-to-face with Captain Vero. He roared in my face, fury bleeding behind his eyes, and he went wild on me. Punching, hitting, biting…but I wasn't the worm anymore.

Not now. And not ever again.

She was gone.

I sure as fuck wouldn't let this bastard ruin the good I'd finally done for this city. One day, everyone would see the queen for who she really was. They'd cheer that I killed her, thank me for removing the virus from the city's lifeline.

So I did what any hero would: I kneed the prick in the balls and shoved him off me. And then I scrambled to grab my blade.

Right as I swung around, Vero rose to his feet, and I swiped my hand with the weapon across the air between us, catching him across the throat, slicing deeply. He stumbled and gurgled, and blood splattered everywhere. He hit the floor like a sack of sand and died after a few choking sounds.

I grinned savagely, knowing blood coated my features.

Tucking my blade in the back of my pants, I picked up the queen's gown she'd left on the floor, using it to grab the knife from his pocket. I smeared it in the queen's blood and tossed it back to the floor, to make it look like he turned against his queen.

I'd tell Creed about the attack in the morning, and we'd be ready.

As I released the most calming breath of my life, the loud thud of boots echoed outside the main doors into the throne room.

Fuck, someone was coming in.

I flew across the room to the side door, checked the hallway was empty, then vanished into the shadows.

And for the first time since being born, I felt like I served a purpose in life.

CHAPTER 21

BLAKE

The saddest part about being betrayed was that it rarely came from enemies. It came from family, from friends…from lovers.

Something I should have known all too well.

But I'd never expected my world to crumble like this… right when we'd just started finding a good place between my monsters and me.

And now the truth was about to ruin us.

Tempest had been lying to us, letting Steele take the blame. He'd also tried to kill me…and then cursed me to forget him doing it.

Opening my eyes on a heavy sigh, I stared out across the city of Wyld from the balcony, hugging myself because I'd been crying and shaking with anger since we'd left the lake in the paradise gardens.

I was terrified now that the truth was out, the circle of my monsters would be torn apart.

Growing close to Tempest made me believe him when he said he loved me at the club, but every thought kept returning to the cave where he spilled the real truth. I guessed it must have felt good for him to finally tell someone.

Just like now, despite feeling like things could never be completely happy again, the air felt lighter. It had been this way ever since I burst out of the lake and I suspected whatever curse was on me by Tempest had also blocked our feeding of the city.

"Blake, we have him," Creed announced, pulling me out of my thoughts. "They'd tracked Tempest and brought him in."

Dread flared over me as I turned to my king.

"What will you do to him?" I asked, my voice brittle. How much more tragedy could a girl take?

"Justice," Creed answered stoically, holding himself solid, but I knew him well enough to see the deepening lines at the corners of his eyes from his frown, to hear the ache behind his voice. "He has a lot to answer for."

Collecting my hand in his, we made a quick path to the throne room, a grand place I rarely visited. The enormous room was empty, with only the huge throne at one end, perched on a platform of stairs. No other furniture, only monster carvings in the wall. It always felt clinical there and unwelcoming.

My gaze fell on Tempest who was shirtless and kneeling, his head down to the floor, forced there by Ash's foot on his back.

Tempest had his hands free yet he wasn't fighting.

My mouth went dry as my gaze remained trained on him. We were the only ones in the throne room, which gave me hope that Creed wanted to find a way to solve this before announcing to the city they'd found the real killer.

We approached them, my stomach doing somersaults with anxiety.

Tempest twisted his head to look at me, his gaze burning with terrifying agony, his cheeks pale.

I shivered all over. He had the face of a man caught red-handed, but it was so much more than that. He was remorseful; I could see it scribbled all over his mournful expression. If he didn't care, he'd fight back. He'd swear at us until he was blue in the face, declaring he was innocent.

After all, it was his word against mine. Yet he was accepting his fate.

"I'm sorry," he murmured lowly at me, two words that suffocated me, because he'd never said them before.

An uncomfortable silence fell over the room as Creed moved to stand in front of Tempest and flicked his hand for Ash and Seven to lift him to his feet. Steele took his place by Creed's side, and I remained close to them. I trembled, unsure what to expect.

Creed cleared his throat. "Confess your sins against the kingdom of Wyld."

I was frozen, watching, breaking apart on the inside, but also furious at Tempest.

He raised his head towards his king. "You don't need to do formalities, Creed, I'll openly confess. I killed the bitch queen, and I'd do it again in a heartbeat." The truth that finally spilled from his mouth completely stunned the rest of the circle.

"You fucking asshole." Steele lunged at Tempest, slamming a fist into his face, then another and another. Everyone stood back.

"Get it out of your system. Hurt me," Tempest groaned, bleeding from his nose, a bruise already forming under an eye. "Make me bleed more if that'll make you feel better. I deserve it. I get it. I'm nothing but dirt, a worm."

The way he said "worm," it made me sick. Because he said it like he believed that's what he was.

Tempest flung his arms out on either side of him, blood dripping over his chin. "I never intended for you to get blamed. You were in the wrong place at the wrong time. The few times I tried to tell Creed, he was too busy for me, grieving for his queen. He didn't speak to anyone for months.

But that doesn't excuse me, so for that, I don't expect you to forgive me."

Steele roared and threw his fist out, clipping him so hard across the head that it sent Tempest flat onto his back. He groaned, giving way to agony raging across his face.

I winced but watched every strike, preparing for the storm to come. Tempest deserved it all, and he took it. Not fighting back, not doing a fucking thing.

And it felt wrong. If he spent all these years concealing his crime, cursing me just the same, why wasn't he fighting back?

"Why did you do it?" I asked, needing to understand what was going on in his head.

"Fuck that, let's finish this. I can't stand looking at his face a second longer." Steele's shoulders rose and fell with how heavily he breathed; I could feel his pain, and the betrayal he felt, pulsing in our bond. It was enough to almost knock me over.

Tempest got to his feet without a word, running the back of his hand across the bleeding cut on his brow.

"Agreed," Creed boomed, taking me off guard. "Shave his head and get him prepared for the sword."

I stilled, my heart hammering, breath sawing out of my lungs. "Wait, shouldn't we hear his side first?" I didn't even understand why I was standing up for Tempest when he'd betrayed my mate, and then tried to kill me. Sure, he'd then saved me, but that didn't make him any less of a villain.

Tempest's eyes widened in response, then determination flared in his gaze, like my words had sparked something inside him. "Creed, it isn't what you think."

"Then fucking talk," he snapped, while Ash and Seven snatched his arms, kicking his legs out from under him so he fell to his hands and knees.

My throat tightened, and I moved forward, a sense of urgency warning me this was escalating too quickly.

"I had no choice but to kill her," he finally groaned, and I could feel his agony pulsing around the room like a living, breathing thing.

I grabbed Creed's sleeve. "Don't do anything rash. Hear him out completely, please, for me. A guilty man fights back, but Tempest isn't."

Creed didn't even glance at me, and the truth of his fury was a cold reality. I understood his anger, but like with Steele's alleged guilt, something didn't feel right.

"There's so much you don't understand, Creed, so much I'd kept from you because I knew you wouldn't believe me. You were so fucking infatuated with the queen while she led you by your dick. But behind your back, we were nothing to her, she hated our touch."

The air thickened at his words, those he once called friends lingering closer, ready to rip him to shreds.

"You're lying," Seven roared and grabbed the back of Tempest's neck, shoving his head to the ground while collecting a blade from his pocket. "He fucking dies now!"

I flinched, convinced he'd stab him in the head.

The men were beside themselves at hearing the queen never wanted them. Jealousy whipped up inside me, but I didn't say a thing. I kept my green monster inside. This wasn't about me.

Seven grabbed Tempest's hair and shaved it all off. Ash and Steele held him down, and I felt sick to my stomach.

"Fuck, listen to me," Tempest pleaded, but his gaze was locked on mine, like I was the one he needed to convince. "She was having an affair with Kurden. I saw them, heard them plotting to take over Wyld. She'd set up explosives around the city as a distraction for when she snuck the enemy into our home to take us over. Kurden promised to murder each one of us." He gasped for air. "I freaked out because we were going to die, so I eradicated the problem."

I tried to process it all, but it was hard to picture the life they'd once led. The queen they'd once loved. Anxiety flowed like a river untapped through me.

"Let's test him to see if he's telling the truth," Steele declared bitterly, still hacking at shaving his head, never ceasing. "Let *him* fight an undead."

Creed stepped up to Tempest, snatching the patch of hair he had left and dragging him to his feet. Tempest appeared pitiful, blood and tears covering his face. A soft groan in his throat was him being submissive to Creed.

That wasn't the Tempest I knew, but someone completely ruined.

"Why the fuck didn't you come and tell me?" Creed roared, his voice echoing, booming off the walls.

Tempest was shaking, his arms tight by his side, hands in fists. "Because you wouldn't have believed me! You were so fucking angry at her death, and I felt like no one would listen to me. You knew how much she hated me and tortured me, so you'd have blamed my action on wanting revenge. Fuck, Creed, you were all so infatuated with her, you were blind to the truth. She did nothing wrong in your eyes." He spoke quickly, sounding panicked.

A snarl rumbled in Creed's chest.

The other men watching Tempest appeared ready to throw themselves forward and finish him.

"The enemy was attacking the next day. I didn't have time to waste trying to convince you or have you alert her that we knew of her plans. So, I took care of business, wanting to show everyone that I wasn't fucking useless."

Listening to it all, I couldn't breathe, couldn't think, but when Seven snatched Tempest by the throat to shove him back down to his knees, I noticed a red mark on the back of his head where there'd once been hair.

"Wait. What's that?" I stepped closer to Tempest.

Creed and Steele doing the same.

"You have a mark on the back of your head, did you know that?" I continued.

He was reaching for the back of his head, fingers running over a symbol I recognized instantly.

It was the red crown mark I'd seen in random places around the city.

"Wait!" I murmured, the wheels spinning in my mind with all the information I'd just learned. "Tempest, you said the queen set up explosives around the city. Did they ever go off?"

Creed shook his head. "Definitely not."

"I've seen that crown mark from Tempest's head in the Cliff of Doom cavern, in the town square, in caves. That's too much of a coincidence, wouldn't you think? What if they're the locations of her explosive spells?"

Creed blinked down at me, his forehead furrowed. Everyone fell silent, only the rasp of quickened breaths sounded.

They were finally realizing that Tempest might be telling the truth.

"I don't feel the mark, but I shouldn't have anything there. What the fuck is it?" Tempest groaned, still rubbing his fingers across the back of his head frantically.

My heart broke for him, tears gathering in my eyes, because if my theory was right, he was telling the truth and the queen made him one of her explosives. Her death must have deactivated the bombs, otherwise they would have gone off already. I embraced the small miracle amid the chaos.

Moving towards Tempest, I reached up to his arm. "She marked you with her crown symbol."

Tempest trembled, a cruel, sorrowful mask slid over his face. One of vulnerability. "That fucking bitch was going to blow my head off."

I choked on a breath, but right then the front doors to the room burst open, coming off their hinges.

I screamed, recoiling.

Creed grabbed my arm and threw me behind him, shielding me from the rain of splintering wood.

A dozen monsters all wearing a red sash around their arm charged into the throne room. Most were huge as though they'd been lifting weights with tree trunks. Solid, muscular beasts who were sneering at us.

"What the fuck's going on?" spit Creed, stepping forward, Steele taking his place in keeping me covered behind him.

"Who the fuck are you to break into *my* throne room?" His words echoed off the walls, while my head was stuck in panic mode, frozen.

Creed snapped into his monster form in seconds, his men following suit, the air thick with fury and danger.

A beast stepped forward, standing on hind legs, covered in black, matted fur, with a long snout and a mouth dripping with pointed teeth.

His gaze locked on Tempest. "We found the cunt who killed our queen." Then they charged him without pause.

Alarm jolted through me, coming hot and fast. All the monsters threw themselves forward to fight the intruders, except for Steele, who snatched my arm and rushed to the back of the room. Behind me, the explosion of fighting and thundering footfalls escalated.

"Who the fuck are those monsters?" I cried out, my heart thundering, terror coming at me in waves.

"I'll find out." Steele opened a compartment in the wall, which had me blinking at the small storage room with empty shelves. "But you need to stay here. Lock it from the inside, please. I can't lose you, not after everything, but I have to help them."

He turned to leave, but I grabbed his hand with my shaky one, stopping him. "I think Tempest was telling the truth about the Queen, and I know it doesn't excuse him for letting you take the blame, but..." I wasn't sure what I wanted to say or how to ask him to be gentle to an old friend he hated and wanted to murder.

Steele gave my hand a light squeeze, pushed me into the tiny closet, and shut me inside. I quickly locked it and backed away.

The sounds from the room were amplified in the closet, thunderous, deafening, and I heard every grunt, punch, and slam against the walls.

My back hit the wall of shelves, and I slid to the floor, hugging my knees in the darkness. I kept going over every word Tempest said, the mark on the back of his head, the same ones I'd see around the city, every damn thing I'd ever learned about the queen.

Fingers curled, I fisted my hands as the pain in my chest deepened. For the anguish and hurt the Red Queen had brought my monsters.

And now, with those monsters barging in, going after Tempest, all wearing a red sash, I had no doubt in my head that they were the queen's supporters. Had they been hiding in the city this whole time?

I had no idea how Tempest survived her reign, how he didn't go insane. Well, maybe he had, it would explain his mood swings…his aggression…the fact he'd tried to kill me. I didn't blame him one bit for how he'd felt about me though. Not after *her*.

The room shuddered, dust raining down on me from the ceiling, but that time, the shuddering didn't cease. The walls around me creaked, and something hard smacked me in the face. A piercing scream invaded my space from the throne room.

Alarmed, I scrambled out before I ended up buried alive. A chunk of the wall dropped inches from where I stood. I leapt sideways, then threw a terrified glance to the gaping hole where one of the attacking monsters had crashed right through the wall.

I winced, hurrying out of the hiding spot to complete chaos. The room had been destroyed, holes covered the walls and the ceiling, blood and bodies were everywhere, but it took me a few moments to realize our team might be winning this battle.

Creed roared, lifting a monster over his head before dropping him onto his bent knee. The loud snap of its spine was audible enough to make me cringe. Creed shoved the enemy aside and got up, covered in blood, like the rest of them.

Something dark fell over me, and as fast as it rose, a powerful arm lashed out and latched around my throat, wrenching me back against a wall of muscle.

I thrashed, kicking my heels back, crying out with a raspy voice. The asshole squeezed tighter though, and I lost all ability to breathe.

Panic swirled in my head, my lungs screaming for air. Sudden terror carried through me that, despite everything, this would be the day I died.

"Whore," a monster snarled in my ear. "I'll make sure you watch us butcher your lovers as I fuck you to death."

Hatred seared through me, and I drove my heel back hard. The bastard groaned. I shoved out of his grip.

I spun on my heels, just as something dark flew right past me, throwing my hair into my face. Rapidly backing away, I shoved my hair out of my eyes to find Tempest had ferociously slammed into the man. It took barely a few seconds for him to dispose of him, for the walls to be splattered in his blood.

Throwing the body away, splashed with blood, he rushed over, as did the other monsters. "Are you hurt?" he asked, eyeing me head to toe. The hurt in his eyes that I'd been injured melted me. Despite his best efforts…he cared

"I'm fine," I murmured.

"You're bleeding," he groaned, wiping the blood underneath my nose from being whacked in the face.

"I'm okay. But were those monsters really the queen's guards still in the city?" My words were rambling as I stared up at Creed, slowly being surrounded by my other monsters who were reaching out to touch me as if they couldn't believe I survived that. All except Tempest who pulled back.

Then he muttered, "She had some very loyal followers, monsters who hated everything about us. They most likely supported her decision to hand over our city to the enemy. There might even be more of them in Wild."

"Fucking bitch," Creed growled, and I couldn't agree more.

Ash was clenching his jaw. "I believed her. All that time, I told myself everything she did was for the city, for us."

"I should have known better, should have fucked her up a long time ago," Seven grunted. "I did nothing but blame myself."

Creed's breaths sped up, fists balled. "This is my fault. I was too fucking blind, believing anything she told me. You weren't wrong, Tempest. I excused her behavior, I didn't stop her from torturing you." His lips pinched tight in pain and regret, the muscles in his neck flexing.

"So what now?" Steele barked, wiping the blood from his mouth, sounding exasperated with Creed. Then he stared at Tempest. "I get that you did what you thought was best for the city…I can't even fault you on it, but fuck, I'm still struggling with being the fall guy."

"And I was her punching bag, her fucking explosive…so we both have issues to get over," Tempest muttered with a stupid lopsided grin, his attempt at humor falling flat.

I laughed, and then cried at the same time. "You can't let her destroy us this long after her death. Somehow, we have to find a place of forgiveness." I had no idea if I was overstepping their boundaries, but after everything we'd all endured, I couldn't be blamed for trying.

Tempest stepped forward, then dropped to his knees in front of us, head bowed.

"I don't expect any of you to forgive me, just your acknowledgment that I tried so hard to do the right thing for us." He glanced up at us. "For years, I wanted a family who didn't beat me or remind me of how worthless I'd been. I was struggling for a long time to find peace while carrying the burden of what I'd done to Steele, and at hiding the city's secrets. And I admit, it changed me. I was constantly angry, and I wanted others to hurt as much as I did. I'm sorry for everything." He lowered his head. "And if you want to punish me for it, I won't stop you. I'll grovel for your forgiveness if that's what it takes."

"Fuck yeah, I need you to grovel more, maybe kiss my feet," Steele retorted.

"Steele." I rolled my eyes at him.

Silence descended, and I felt as though I couldn't breathe from the emotions choking my throat. I took a step toward Tempest, then another to stand in front of him. "I don't think I could hate you…even after everything you've done."

"I'm sorry, Blake, for trying to kill you, for hurting you. I never wanted those things for you, but my head was so stupid. The things I've felt for you, the way you were always kind to me, I kept telling myself you'd hurt me in the end, so I had to do it first." Tears glistened in his eyes. "But I fucking love you so much that it'll destroy me if I lose you."

Tears raced down my cheeks. Pain was ripping through my soul for what my monsters had endured, and how the Red Queen had ripped them apart.

I wanted to fix this. And that meant starting somewhere my heart led me.

I got to my knees in front of Tempest, and stared him in the eyes. *She'd* been a fool. This beautiful monster deserved so much more than what the world had given him.

"I forgive you, Tempest," I whispered. "I might even love

you." His head shot up, a fresh tear tracking down his cheek. "Things feel terrible now, but it'll get better. It always does, and I'll be there to help."

"Blake," he rasped and drew me into his arms. "That's all I ever wanted to hear."

It didn't take long for the others to join us, getting on their knees and moving in closer, embracing us, with Tempest and me in the middle.

"It'll take time," Creed said. "But I'm not giving up on you, Tempest. Just no more fucking secrets."

"I swear on my life," he stated, all teary and smiling in a way I hadn't seen since I'd met him. It warmed my soul.

"I forgive you," Ash and Seven said in unison, before both glanced at each other with a growl and the rest of us burst out laughing.

"And you, Steele?" Creed asked.

Steele was shoulder to shoulder with me, a deep frown creasing the bridge of his nose. "I feel completely outnumbered," he teased flippantly. "I don't hate you, Tempest, and over time, I'll find a way to forgive you. That's all I can give you right now."

"That's all I want," he croaked.

There was still tension between them—when wasn't there in this world?—but on the bright side, we were making baby steps towards progress. I leaned over and kissed Steele on the cheek, offering him a knowing smile as I felt his bond flicker in my chest with what suspiciously felt like…happiness.

"I have an idea," I said, turning to them all. "You've already started the demolition in this place," I pointed to the ruined room around us, "let's redo it in a way that's us…and not her."

Creed laughed at me, drawing me into his arms. "Whatever you want, you can have, Pet."

"I say we replace the thrones with a big bed," Ash suggested, and I giggled.

My heart fluttered and I burrowed into the warmth of my surrounding men, feeling safe for the first time ever. The kind of safety that came with knowing I had someone to rely on when the world started to burn, and that I was one of the lucky ones who'd found true happiness.

I was exactly where I wanted to be. In love with five monsters who desperately wanted me.

CHAPTER 22

BLAKE

It was a month after everything had happened. And today was finally the gathering Creed had threatened me with weeks ago, where all the leaders of the other major cities and Shadowburn would be coming to meet Wyld's new queen.

Me.

At first, I felt weird adopting the "Queen" title, especially considering how evil the last one had been, but then Creed put a crown on me and fucked me within an inch of my life… and I began to think differently.

Okay, that was a lie, but all of my monsters had been showing me the influence I could have on the city, outside of the feeding I provided, and slowly, I was changing my mind about it.

"You look beautiful, Pet," Creed growled, barging into my room as usual. Not that one of them wasn't always in the room with me. I'm not even sure why we called it "mine" at this point.

I was wearing *the dress*, and wearing it felt like I'd officially left my human upbringing behind. You could see everything… And I meant everything. I would feel awkward all day, but Ash and Steele had assured me that Creed wasn't being an asshole. The dress was ceremonial and what the other leaders would expect.

So there I was, wearing a see-through gown with a gorgeous silver crown perched on my head with blue stones bigger than my eyes scattered throughout it.

"I'm nervous," I blurted out.

"Blake, you've been going over everything with Ash for the last month," he reminded me.

I nodded, thinking of all the sessions we'd had where he'd walked me through court behavior. It was a lot. Evidently, there was more to being a queen besides fucking.

"You know, I think you need a stress reliever," he mused, stalking towards me, his eyes glued on mine in the mirror I was standing in front of.

"You have Xanax?" I joked, and he smirked, his golden eyes happy and free. Solving the city's inability to eat had taken a huge stress off his shoulders. And while he was still a crazy, possessive bastard, there was a happiness to him that had never been there before.

"I think I have something better," he growled roughly as his chest hit my back and his clawed hands settled on my hips.

Oh…I immediately realized what he was referring to.

"Not happening," I hissed, trying to take a step away, but his claws pinned me in place.

"Creed!" I couldn't go out there, in this dress, and have every monster in the room be able to…smell me.

He chuckled darkly, his tail whipping back and forth behind him as if it was excited too.

He buried his face in my neck, and I watched in the mirror as he took a deep inhale.

"Creed," I panted again as his fingers moved the dress up, until my pussy was completely bared to him. He stroked his finger through my folds teasingly, and of course, when he moved his finger away, it was glistening with my wetness.

My breaths were coming out in gasps as I watched him.

I mean, they *were* going to see everything. What would it matter if they knew I was well taken care of by *my* monsters?

I'd obviously gone mad.

"Let your king serve his queen," he murmured, as he slid his finger into his mouth, my gaze locked with his golden ones in the mirror. He groaned, like he hadn't tasted me a million times before. I thought he would continue what he'd been doing, but Creed shocked me when he slid around my front and dropped down to his knees, moving me so we were sideways to the mirror, and we both could see everything.

It was beyond arousing, seeing him lower himself to the ground in front of me and seeing him in the mirror as well.

He admired my bare skin for a minute. "Such a beautiful, perfect pussy," he growled, separating the folds with his fingers so my clit was visible, the cool air brushing against it.

I purred, and he grinned, wearing that familiar sharp-toothed smirk that drove me wild. He continued to examine me, which only made me hotter, before finally leaning forward and flicking his tongue against it. I bit down on my lip, trying to hold in the scream pressing at my lips in case there were guests nearby.

Creed growled when he saw what I was doing.

"Give it to me, Blake. I want to hear your perfect cries."

He dove back in, and judging by the exuberant way he was eating and licking at me, he obviously wanted to make me scream as loud as possible.

I was riding his face when the door opened and Steele appeared in the entryway, not looking surprised at all by what he was seeing.

He stepped inside and closed the door, before walking over to a chair and sprawling on it. Creed didn't even look up, which said a lot for the comfortableness they'd regained the past few months. It was clear it still wasn't like it was, but every day brought more progress.

Creed speared me with his tongue, pushing any thoughts I had away, and my moan ripped through the air.

"Such a perfect mate, letting her king take care of her," Steele drawled.

Creed continued, his fingers joining his efforts. Right before I came, he pulled away and grinned, my juices coating his face in a decadent way.

"More," I demanded, and he went back to work, finally letting me fall off the edge, pleasure coursing through my body so intensely, my gaze darkened. Creed bit down on my inner thigh, bringing me back to the present before I blacked out.

I stared at him in shock, and he grinned unrepentantly.

"How do you feel, sweetheart?" purred Steele appearing behind me.

I felt…amazing. My nerves were almost completely gone. It was incredible what a good orgasm could do.

I felt Steele's hardness behind me, and I could see evidence of Creed's, but neither made any attempts to further anything. Creed rose from the ground gracefully and then took my face in his claw-tipped hand, sealing his lips on mine in a slow, leisurely kiss that had me tasting myself.

"Ready to go?" he murmured.

"Yes," I whispered.

"Now kiss your mate and let us show off our queen," Creed commanded.

Steele spun me around and pressed his lips against mine, taking my breath away with the promise of later I could practically taste.

"My queen," he murmured, and I flushed as they both took my hands and led me out the door.

This felt like the first day of the rest of my life, and thanks to Creed's magical tongue...I was now feeling much more ready for it.

Creed opened his mouth to direct the elevator, but I slapped a hand over his face, eliciting confused stares from both him and Steele.

"I want to do it," I exclaimed.

"Okay," Steele drawled. I was sure he could feel the way my heart was thumping in my chest and the nervous energy floating through our bond, but he probably wouldn't understand why.

"The Valencia Room," I ordered the elevator softly.

At first, we didn't move, and my heart sank because if it didn't work now, it was never going to work. Bane had said the elevator would work when I'd decided to stay, but—I squeaked when the elevator moved, and a second later opened up into the enormous ballroom-type area where the gathering was being held.

"It worked," I whispered, moisture pooling into my eyes.

"Well, if that didn't prove you loved us, I'm not sure what would," quipped Steele. Creed was his normal, cocky self. But he did grab me and give me a blistering kiss before we stepped out of the elevator.

Only then did I remember he hadn't washed up after having his face drenched. Not only were the monsters in the room going to smell me...they were also going to smell me on him.

Staring at a beautiful monster who was eyeing Creed and Steele hungrily...I decided that was a good thing. We might need to have an intermission so Steele could be appropriately marked as well...

Creed let me go and stepped out of the elevator. Steele bowed to me, much more formal than he'd ever been, and motioned for me to walk out ahead of him.

Oh, right. Ash had mentioned the rest of them would act

more subservient at the gathering. Only Creed would be able to act as my equal because he was the king.

I hated that, but they'd all insisted it was how it had to be done.

There were black gossamer banners strung along the ceiling, and a large one in the center, this one pink.. in honor of my hair, I suppose. There had to be at least three hundred monsters in the room, all of them so different from each other, I could spend hours studying them.

One of the women had orange tentacles coming out of her head, and when I stared at her, eyes appeared on each leg, staring right back. Another emerald green monster had four arms and there were pincers at the end of each one.

Freddy appeared out of nowhere, sliding in front of Creed, his usual trail of goo running behind him. I was stunned to see a once dead Freddy, now very much alive, joining our ceremony, and I could only guess his revival had something to do with the curse over the city having been lifted. Something I'd have to ask about later.

"All hail Queen Blake!" he called out, and the entire room echoed him, sending chills across my skin. The crowd parted as Creed took a step to the side and bowed low.

This was where I had to walk up the middle of the room, to where our thrones were, in my see-through dress.

Lovely.

All eyes were on me, and I'd never felt so exposed.

Luckily, Ash, Seven, and Tempest were situated down the aisle so I could keep one of them in my viewpoint my entire walk. Pride gleamed in their gazes, and they eyed me hungrily as I approached.

Which, of course, only made the situation worse because my nipples hardened into points and my thighs became slick with need.

I was never not a horny bitch around them. But it would have been nice if I could have avoided that today.

I finally made it to the front of the enormous room where two thrones were set up. Both of them were made out of a black branch-type material around the outside of the red brocade seat. The black branches were covered in thorns.

They were quite intimidating, and I wasn't sure I lived up to the dangerous vibe they were giving off.

But I could try to be badass today.

I settled into my throne and tried to stare imperiously at all the monsters. Creed stopped a few feet in front of the throne and knelt down on one knee. The rest of my monsters mirrored his pose a foot behind him.

"Maxsala mensueta chargogin," Creed began. "I swear my blood, my power, and my loyalty to my queen, from this day, to forever."

The rest of them repeated the oath as well.

Chills were sliding down my spine as I watched them. And I made a vow to them and myself…that I would always be deserving of this oath.

Creed snatched a long, fierce black dagger and slashed at his other hand, his blood dripping from the wound. He wiped it across his chest, leaving a long bloody streak there, and then he handed the knife to Steele. Creed rose from the ground and walked the remaining few steps.

And, of course, it got more intense. Because now, in my see-through dress, I had to drink from Creed and the others' blood. He reached out his hand, his golden eyes glowing, and I took his hand gently in mine, pressing my mouth on the wound and lapping at the blood.

Heat flooded my insides, and I could feel his life force moving inside of me. Right next to Steele's bond, another one arose.

I gasped and stared at Creed, and he nodded knowingly.

It was all I could do not to cry as I drank from the others' hands.

Ash's bond felt like pure sunshine, and a hitched sob tore from my throat as I felt him there, my ray of sunshine.

Seven's was dark and protective; it settled inside me, seeming to fasten onto my heart so I could never lose track of it.

And Tempest's…Tempest's was the one that had tears streaming down my face. It was full of longing and devotion, and the promise that he'd never hurt me again. It told me all the things he wasn't able to say.

Their four bonds fit right in with Steele's perfect one.

After their vows, it was time for mine. I stood up, trying for confidence, and cast my gaze around the room.

"Maxsala mensueta chargogin," I began, having practiced the traditional start to the vows with Ash over and over again so I could say them correctly. "I swear my blood, my power, and my loyalty to Wyld, from this day, to forever."

The room answered my vow with a roar and shook the walls. Creed handed me the same dagger they had used, and I took a small pause before I cut into my hand. I dragged the blood across the top of my breasts, and then across my abdomen. This was supposed to symbolize the life I would provide Wyld.

"All hail Queen Blake," the crowd cheered again.

Haunting music started up and I breathed a sigh of relief that the ceremonial part of the evening was over. It was now time for the celebration.

Guests lined up to meet me as others danced and ate.

A particularly gruesome blue monster, with spikes running down the middle of his head all the way down his spine, stepped in front of our thrones almost immediately. Creed and Steele tensed. Creed's face was perfectly placid, but he was gripping the arm of his throne so tightly, it was amazing it didn't shatter.

"Kurden," Creed clipped, and the monster gave us a mocking bow. My eyes widened. This was who Tempest had told us about. The one who had the affair with the she-bitch and had tried to take over Wyld.

He even looked like an asshole. I couldn't believe he had the balls to show his face in this kingdom after what he'd done.

"If you ever get tired of them, my door is always open, Your Majesty," the asshole purred.

Tempest lunged forward, only stopped by Seven grabbing his arm and yanking him back.

I didn't like that. Not at all.

"You can be leaving now," I drawled, and my monsters glanced at me in surprise. Kurden's mouth was gaping open like a fish. Evidently, I wasn't supposed to say that.

Creed was the first to recover. "You heard our queen, Kurden," Creed said with a fierce, sharp-toothed smile.

Kurden was about to say something else, but Tempest stepped in front of him, his hand settling on the dagger in his own belt.

"I'll kill you myself, if he doesn't," I spit out, not sure how I'd manage it, but liking the threat nonetheless.

Kurden stared at us, hatred in his eyes, before he finally growled and stalked from the room. Creed sent soldiers to escort him out of Wyld, but I made a mental note that he needed to be dealt with soon…in a permanent way.

"You're amazing, my queen," Creed rasped as he picked up my hand and kissed my palm.

Before I could say anything, there was another monster in front of him. But this one…this one had a beautiful human girl with him.

A beautiful human girl he had collared and was dragging behind him with a long black chain.

She didn't look like she'd been abused though. Her skin was unmarked, and her long blonde hair had been carefully styled. She was wearing a tiny blue dress that barely covered the important parts.

I was jealous of the coverage, which was hilarious because that dress was tinier than anything I would have worn on earth.

Look at me now, showing my goods to everyone.

The monster was enormous, his skin a dark charcoal color that blended in with the dark shadows circling his body. He was almost a cross between Tempest and Creed. His cocky smile certainly was.

"Titan," Creed acknowledged, his tone friendly and welcoming.

"Creed, it's good to be here celebrating your queen. A much better one than the she-bitch."

Okay…he did have his girl collared, but he also clearly had good taste since he appeared to hate the Red Queen.

"This is Trinity," he said, nodding his head fondly at the girl shooting daggers at him.

"Are you from—" I asked.

"I am," she spit out fiercely, yanking the chain viciously… which only made Titan chuckle. "This fucking asshole stole me from my home in the middle of the night."

I glanced at Creed with wide eyes…her story sounded a bit familiar.

"Let it go, Pet," he purred, and I wrinkled my nose at him.

"I'm—sorry to hear that?" I asked, biting my lip in awkwardness.

Titan lunged towards her and pulled her tight to his body. Her cheeks flushed…maybe from anger…but maybe—

"Lust. Definitely lust," Ash murmured from where he was set up behind me.

"If you touch me, I will stab you in your sleep," Trinity hissed at Titan. He just grinned at her, like she'd said the sweetest endearment to him.

"Growing pains," Titan said to us with a shrug. "But she'll love me soon enough."

"Over my dead body," Trinity growled, and I couldn't help but snort.

She glared at me too, like I'd betrayed her by laughing, but I waved as Titan led her away.

"That will be fun to watch," mused Steele.

It would indeed.

The night went on. I danced with each of my monsters, and smiled and nodded at hundreds of others. The party raged into the night, and then into the morning when the suns began to rise in the sky.

And all night, my monsters had been torturing me.

A touch here, and a touch there. Their bodies too close to mine while we danced. Their hard dicks rubbing up against me. They fed me from their fingers and sipped from my cup where my lips had been. They stared at me like they wanted to eat me alive.

And finally…I'd had enough.

"Take me to bed. Now," I ordered. "I don't care that the party's not done. I want orgasms. A million of them."

I sounded whiny, but it was their fault.

Creed chuckled darkly and stood up from his throne, reaching out a claw-tipped hand for me to take.

"Your wish is our command," he said mockingly, and I rolled my eyes at him.

The others crowded around me as Creed led me across the room. There weren't nearly as many eyes as before. Most of the crowd was drunk and engaged in all sorts of debauchery…including Trinity and her monster, whose head was currently between her legs in the corner.

It felt like I could breathe again when we made it into the elevator and Creed ordered it to take us to his rooms.

As the doors opened, Seven scooped me into his arms and rushed towards the bed. "I'm first, fuckers."

"I think we know Blake likes all of her holes filled,"

drawled Tempest, ever the asshole. I stuck out my tongue at him, and he winked as Seven lowered me to the bed.

I noticed Ash transforming into his human self and I held up a hand. "I want you as a monster tonight," I purred. His face was unsure for a moment. "I want to hold onto those horns as you fuck me."

Ash's face was pure unadulterated pleasure, and a second later, he'd shifted back into his fierce form.

And as my monsters all gathered around me on the bed, I couldn't help but think of the scared girl I'd once been.

Who knew that the monsters waiting in the dark would be the ones to free me from the monsters on earth who walked in the light?

Creed fucked my core with his tongue earnestly, and I moaned, staring into his eyes.

"Keep going, Daddy, you're going to be my good boy, aren't you?" I teased.

His eyes flashed as his tongue movements intensified.

And as their hands, and cocks, and teeth, and tails worked my body...all I could think was how incredible it was that after everything I'd experienced...I would actually have a beautiful life.

EPILOGUE

BLAKE

I was choking on Seven's dick as Ash fucked me from behind. The brothers were always finding me when I was alone and demanding playtime.

Lucky for them…I loved to play.

"Yes, that's it. Give me that fucking greedy pussy," Ash purred. I moaned around Seven's cock and he thrust down my throat harder, like he was trying to make sure my attention was on him.

Seven's features were strained, and his cock hammered into me relentlessly.

"Care for another dick?" growled Steele from the doorway. I couldn't do anything but moan around Seven's dick, but he got the point.

I was always up for his dick. Any of their dicks honestly, if they were willing to give them to me.

Ash pulled out abruptly and then sprawled next to me. Him and Seven somehow finagled me so I was on top of Ash, riding him as Seven readjusted his position without losing much momentum right above Ash's head.

"Try not to hit me in the face with your balls," Ash drawled, and I snorted around Seven's dick.

Ash's hands gripped my ass cheeks, spreading them open…and I flushed…because he was basically offering my asshole to Steele.

Okay then.

"Love your fucking ass," Steele murmured as he spit onto my hole. I didn't need that, honestly…my juices from Ash's efforts had made me plenty slick enough. Steele pushed a finger in and began stretching me as Ash fucked up into me.

"She likes that," Ash moaned. "She's choking my cock with her hot little cunt."

Steele slid into me, and I cried out around Seven's dick, who was sputtering a handful of dirty words that were making me wetter.

I clung onto Ash's biceps, writhing as Steele and Ash found their rhythm.

"I'm gonna cum all over your face and those pretty, perfect tits," growled Seven as he thrust even deeper.

"Do it," Creed's voice ordered. My eyes cracked open, meeting his golden ones at the side of the bed. "Look at you, our gorgeous, fucking queen. Taking our cocks like such a good girl. You love being filled up, don't you, Pet? You can't get enough."

I moaned in response, because fuck…it was true.

His tail slid across the bed, moving across the sharp points of my chest and then wrapping around my neck.

"But you know who your king is, don't you, my sweet?" he purred.

Tears streamed down my face as Seven fucked into my throat one more time…viciously, before pulling out and cumming all over my chin and my chest.

I gasped, not having any time to recover as Creed's tail tightened, making sure I knew who was really in control. He stroked his two-headed cock slowly, the tip an angry, red pulsing color as he moved his hand.

Steele chose that moment to start his vibrations…and Ash chose that moment to…grow.

I came instantly, so overwhelmed the room spun. "Yes, yes, yes," I chanted as another dick tapped my lips.

Tempest was there, a smirk on his lips as his shadows played with my nipples. Ash groaned, and I felt his hot liquid release, filling my insides.

"So fucking perfect," murmured Ash, pushing Tempest aside as he kissed my lips…

It was a good thing I'd already licked off Seven's cum.

"Come one more time for me," urged Steele in a strained voice, his finger rubbing my clit vigorously as he turned his vibration on and off…spiraling me higher.

I was a good girl and did as I was told, my screams echoing around the room as Steele coated my insides. He slapped my ass cheek as he withdrew. "Such a good girl."

Tempest suddenly flipped me back on all fours, and then he slid underneath me to devour me…not caring about the cum leaking from my holes. His hot wet tongue speared through me, fucking me over and over. It was nasty and dirty…and I loved it.

Tempest's cock was hovering right in front of me, so I leaned forward and captured it in my mouth. He groaned as I deep-throated him, his shadows pulling harder at my nipples.

"Fuck my face while you choke on my cock," he murmured against my folds as he thrust harshly into my mouth.

And then Creed was sliding into my ass, the fit so tight I squeaked. He didn't give me a second to recover; instead, he immediately slid in and out at a devastatingly slow pace.

"You taste so good," moaned Tempest. "Cum on my face."

And I came again.

"Look at you, Pet. So fucking sexy. So fucking perfect." His hand slid around my hips to my stomach. "I'm going to breed you. We all will. We're going to fuck you until our seed is gushing inside you, filling you all the way up. I'm going to drink from your breasts after you feed our child. Fuck. I can't wait."

Tempest must have thought Creed's mouth was hot too, because he came with a gasp, his seed flooding my mouth.

I swallowed, of course, and then he slipped from between my lips, giving me one last, long lick through my folds.

And then it was just my king…while the others watched.

He pounded my ass, murmuring so many filthy words I was sure I'd be cumming even if he wasn't hitting every spot perfectly. His tail rubbed my clit as his clawed hands kneaded and massaged my breasts.

He fucked me for hours, it seemed, until my voice was hoarse from my screams.

I was cumming when I finally blacked out, the warmth of his cum as it filled me the last thing I was aware of.

SECOND EPILOGUE

Find out what Blake and her monsters are up to five years later by signing up for our newsletters: https://dl.bookfunnel.com/7es6k8dqyp

And turn the page for an exciting look at our next project in the Shadowburn world....

MONSTER'S DARLING

LOOK AT ME MONSTER, BOOK 1

The Monster God is going to ruin me…

The seductive spin off series set in the same world as the Monster & Me duet.

Grab your copy today: http://books2read.com/lookatmemonster1

BLAKE'S MONSTER MAC & CHEESE

Ingredients:

5 cups Whole Milk Or 2% (Lite)

3 cups Elbow or Small Shell Noodles

1 ½ tsp Dry Mustard

½ - 1tsp Black Pepper or to taste

1tsp Salt or to taste

5T (tbsp) Butter

⅛ tsp Nutmeg

3 cups Sharp Cheddar Cheese (Reserve ¼-½ c for topping)

1 cup Shredded Mozzarella

Directions:

1. Preheat Oven to 400°F

2. Add milk and butter to a large pot and bring to a soft boil stirring frequently to not scald the milk.

3. Add noodles and stir frequently. Slow and steady so milk doesn't curdle.

4. Cook until just shy of al dente.

5. Take the pot off the heat and stir in the rest of the ingredients. Cheese Last! Don't forget to reserve some cheese for the topping.

6. Transfer mac and cheese into a greased 9X9 baking dish. Top with remaining cheese and bake for 10min at 400 °F uncovered or until cheese is melted and mixture is bubbly.

7. Let rest for 5 min and enjoy!

RAPTURE
STANDALONE BOOK

While you wait for Monster's Darling to launch, dive into Rapture, our sinfully dark, Peter Pan retelling…

They saved me…only to sacrifice me…

To him.

They call it the Rapture, when the vampire king comes.

And this time, he's come for me.

Just as he's come every ten years for so long, no one can even remember when it all began.

He's the villain in my story, I see that right away.

But when his teeth sink into my skin…something happens.

Something that isn't supposed to.

Instead of draining me like all the others…

He changes me.

Makes me like him.

Now I'm trapped in his kingdom of monsters.

Completely unrecognizable from the girl I once was.

He and his lost boys have changed the rules of the game.

But the more time that passes, the more I realize…I still want to play.

Prologue

GWENDOLYN

I'd woken to my parents arguing again, and this time it wasn't just a disagreement. This was a full-on screaming match filled with slamming doors and harsh, cutting words. It left me shaking in bed, convinced they were finally done for good.

My father lost his job at the local fishery port several days ago, and ever since, there'd been no peace in the house. The hushed, worried whispers had grown louder every day, to the point their arguments could be heard clearly through the walls. My mother would try to hide her tears, but I'd walked in on her more than once to find them streaming down her face. It was clear we were in trouble, and I could barely sleep.

Especially when I'd overheard them this morning, discussing how we were close to losing our home…

I'd been slipping out of bed in the early hours, trekking up the hill to hunt with my bow and arrow. My father had fashioned it out of oak for me, and he'd worked on it for days before giving it to me on my birthday.

If I caught enough rabbits, I could sell their fur at the markets. And I'd hunt every day if I needed to until Father got another job. Anything to stop the arguing and keep our home.

I spotted a grey-furred rabbit hopping through the field of blue and white flowers and sprinted forward on silent feet behind it. This wasn't my first time hunting. My father always liked to brag that he'd been hunting deer when he was my age. No time like the present to brush up on my skills before I moved on to bigger game.

I glided quickly through the meadow, my hands tightening around the bow and arrow, when the animal paused.

I followed suit, my heart drumming in my chest, imagining the smile on my parents' faces when I showed them what I'd managed.

The animal lifted its nose in the air, sniffing

Had it caught my scent?

As a wolf shifter, I could easily hunt it in animal form, but then I'd risk losing control and devouring it. I hadn't exactly gained strong dominance over her yet, even if she was an omega, but Father was always telling me that I needed to build my skills both with and without my wolf. To be adaptable, because life was never steady. It could change in a heartbeat.

I understood, and now it was time to make him proud.

I lifted my weapon, straightened my spine, and pointed the bow down as I notched the arrow to the string. Aiming for the rabbit, I tried to steady my breath and arms.

A smoky breeze suddenly got caught in my throat as I inhaled through my nose.

I turned my head toward the village down in the valley, and the sight sank deep inside me, freezing me to my bones.

Fire was engulfing the village.

The sky grew darker with black smoke, brutal amber flames blazing across the huts. It hungrily licked the sky, and people were madly running around to put out the fire with buckets of water.

I gasped out loud, causing the rabbit to scramble madly away from me. But I didn't bother trying to go after it again, not with the sight in front of me.

Sparks of dread flared in my heart.

Dropping the bow and arrow, I turned and ran down the hill. The wind whipped against me, the downward momentum pushing me to go faster. A sob slipped past my throat as the crackle of fire sang on the wind blowing past me.

I ran faster, my sight narrowing to the right of the village where my home was, where I'd last seen my parents.

Howls came from all around me, and terror rose in the back of my throat, a scream pressing forward. Townspeople were already in their wolf forms, scrambling away from the growing inferno.

My foot suddenly caught on a root, and I went flying. The ground came rushing toward me as I smacked into it so hard, all the air swooshed out of my lungs, and I cried out in shock.

Fear tightened in my chest. My parents…they were all I had. "Please be alive, please." I began to sob with terror at what awaited me in the village.

The fire grew worse, and even from my position, I felt its heat on my face, the smoke stinging my nostrils.

With renewed panic, I scrambled to my feet, pushing past the pain in my knees and shoulder that I'd crashed down on.

Our town was ruled by the wolf shifters who lived there, with guards to keep us safe. How did this happen?

More howls came, and the fires raged higher.

Crackling and snapping, sparks flew in every direction.

Leaving the hill behind, I darted frantically to the village while people ran past me, yelling at me to turn around.

I didn't listen to them. I couldn't.

I cut across the pebbled street where the smoke grew thick. My eyes stung, but I covered my nose and mouth with my sleeve and ran madly. Fire roared all around me, flames bursting out of windows, licking the walls, scorching them with burn marks.

People were screaming, most running away. The blaze was giant, towering over the town. Some homes were completely engulfed, others untouched.

I sprinted across the open marketplace where people were rushing in every direction, frantically yelling for help.

Bodies lay in front of some homes, burned to the point where I couldn't recognize them. Smoke curled up from their bodies, and a scream got caught in my throat from seeing them.

I forced myself to look away while tears filled my eyes and smoke assaulted my senses.

I finally came upon my family cottage. A small brown building that was perfect for the three of us. By some miracle, it hadn't caught alight yet. The only reason I could guess was that we were located at the rear of the village, backing onto the woods.

The blaze behind me heightened, the gust of wind lashing at my hair, engulfing me with the stench of smoke. I coughed, the pain like acid on my throat.

But I kept going, rushing past the open front gates, and I burst into the house.

"Mama," I frantically yelled. "Papa!"

I ran into one room and the next, my pulse speeding. Had they escaped?

Outside the window, the neighbors' house glinted orange with the fire.

Darting into the kitchen, I tripped over something. I moved too fast to catch myself and fell forward, landing on my hands and knees. The faint scent of blood found me, and I tasted it on the back of my tongue.

Crying out, I swiftly twisted around to find exactly what I'd fallen over.

"Papa," I cried, fear piercing my chest.

He lay on his back on the tiles in a pool of blood. Wide open eyes, he stared at the ceiling. Blood gushed from his slashed throat. It spilled from him, running down the side of his neck.

My heart struck my ribcage, and I desperately shoved myself back across the floor until my heels hit the iron stove.

Tears rushed down my face, and I curled in on myself, hugging my knees, my head spinning.

My mind screamed to run out of there, but I couldn't move.

I struggled to breathe, unable to call out for help.

Shutting my eyes, I couldn't erase the image of my father savagely killed, torn apart and left to die.

In a flash, the thumping of footsteps resonated somewhere in the house, growing louder as whatever it was moved closer to the kitchen.

I flinched, trying to squeeze myself into the crevice between the stove and wall, wanting to disappear. What if Papa's killers were still in the house?

A figure filled the kitchen doorway and I screamed, tears blurring my vision.

Soft hands were suddenly on my arms, words reaching me. "Hush, Gwendolyn. You can't make a sound."

Eyes widening, I wiped the tears away. "Mama!'" Her face was scared, her eyes rimmed red from crying.

I threw myself into her arms, sobbing uncontrollably. She lifted me into her embrace and walked me out of the kitchen.

"Now listen carefully. I need you to do something for me, Gwendolyn. Can you do that?"

I nodded, trying to stifle my tears as she lowered me to my feet. We were in the living area with the fireplace and two couches covered in knitted blankets. She was opening up the cabinet doors where she kept the linen. We didn't own a lot, but she pushed a bed sheet and blanket aside and then looked at me.

"You have to get inside now, Gwen. And don't say a word." Her voice trembled, and she kept glancing over her shoulder.

Straining for breath in the smoke-infused air, I stared at her. "What's happening? Who killed Papa? The fire will be here soon." My words were running fast out of my mouth.

"Please, sweetie. You need to get inside. They're already putting the fires out, but something more dangerous is coming back for us."

"Who?" I choked on my breath, and before I knew it, she'd gotten me to climb into the cabinet that offered me enough space to sit upright.

"Don't make any sounds. Can you do this for me, Darling?" she whispered in a pleading voice just as a loud bang sounded so near, it might have been inside the house.

Mama flinched, her wide, terrified stare glancing to the hallway, and her hands trembled as she gripped the doors.

"I'm scared," I whispered.

"They're here," she mumbled under her breath, then fiddled with the ring on her finger. She took it off and gave it to me. "This is yours now, Gwen. It's our family ring and you must treasure it. It will always remind you of me."

She curled my fingers around the ring, then smiled softly and traced a hand over my cheek. "I love you so much, Gwen. I'll always be with you in your heart, no matter what happens. Please, remember to always fight for what you want. I love you, my sweet angel. Now, cover your ears."

Without another word, she shut the cabinet doors, and darkness closed in around me. I quickly pushed the ring into the pocket of my pants. But panic engulfed me as my mind raced with who was coming back. The same people who hurt my father?

Thunderous footfalls sounded, and I hugged my knees tightly to my chest.

A sharp screech came from somewhere in the house, and I pressed myself into the corner, shaking.

The floorboards creaked in the hallway, like they always did when anyone heavy walked over them.

Tears rolled down my cheeks, the urge to scream in the back of my throat. But Mama's words blared in my head.

Don't make any sounds.

A crashing of wood splintering came from somewhere nearby, followed by my mother's scream. Glass shattered and I flinched, tears rolling down my face.

Mama! I almost cried out.

Don't make any sounds.

A loud thump came, like something hit the floor, followed by a squelching, wet noise and a thunderous growl.

I trembled, my breathing see-sawing in and out of me, my vision blurred. To stop myself from screaming, I clamped a hand over my mouth and sat there, frozen and terrified, picturing my mother left to die just like my father.

A gurgling came next, and then the pounding footfalls seemed to run through the house.

Something more dangerous is coming back for us.

Shaking, I didn't dare move and remained that way long after the sounds vanished. So much so that I must have passed out, because when I opened my eyes again, the door was being pried open and a man with the kindest eyes I'd ever seen was staring at me.

"Hello there," he soothed. "I'm not going to hurt you."

Even delayed, the shock startled me, and I flinched backward, screaming with dread.

He had strawberry blond hair that was graying at the temples, and somehow, he got me out of the cabinet.

My pulse raced through my veins, my knees so numb from being cramped up that I couldn't stand on my own.

The man held me and smoothed the hair out of my face, studying me with the softest brown eyes. "You're safe now, little one. The fire's been put out. We're searching for survivors."

I blinked at the man I instantly recognized as a shifter by his heavy wolf scent.

"My parents," I gasped, peering over to the hallway where all I saw were bloody drag lines. Remembered horror pounded in my mind, and fresh tears fell from my puffy eyes.

I tried to stand on my own but stumbled, and the man held onto my arms to steady me. "It's only you in the house. I don't know what happened here, but you're not alone anymore." He stared at me with pity in his gaze. "My name's Caleb and I've been helping with the clean-up of this town, rescuing who's left. What's your name?"

Everything was too much, too confusing, and still, my name slipped past my lips in a whisper, "Gwendolyn. But where's my mama?"

The bridge of his nose pinched. "There's no one else in the house. But you don't have to be alone anymore. I have a large home, and there's always room for one more; you can stay until your mama comes back." Even as the words slipped from his lips, I knew he thought she was dead.

Without warning, he lifted me in his arms and carried me out to the hallway where there was indeed no sign of my mother. Only blood. So much of it was on the floor, and more was splashed on the walls.

I cried, trembling in the man's arms.

A sliver of sunlight caught my eyes once we stepped outside the house, the smoke clearing, and I gazed up to the bright sky. It heated my face, and I was certain I heard my mother's whisper in my ear.

I will always be with you in your heart.

"I have a large garden you can play in, and a family who will love to have you there, so you'll never be alone. Okay, Gwendolyn?" Caleb said, distracting me.

I wasn't sure how to respond because I wanted *my* family, not a different one.

Around us, the fires were out. Only wisps of smoke curled from the charred remains that were once homes. Most of the huts were destroyed. Those that remained, like mine, were black on the outside from how close the fire got, but there were maybe only half a dozen of those remaining.

We reached a white SUV by the side of the dirt road where Caleb set me on my feet. I kept staring at my home, at the village that had been obliterated. A few people searching the burned homes in the distance remained, but I didn't recognize them.

Caleb collected a blanket from the backseat, and wrapped it around my shoulders. "We can wait to see if you recognize anyone in the village who might have information about your family."

His words were soft, and every time I looked at him, I saw my father in his kind eyes. He offered me a bottle of water.

I nodded, wiping at my tears. "Okay."

"I won't be long; I have to go speak with my friends." He walked quickly to the others nearby, without waiting for my response. He paused to talk to two females, then soon returned, announcing, "They're going to ask around for your mama."

I nodded, hugging myself with the blanket just as a distraught couple came over to us.

The woman with reddish hair offered me a soft smile and asked for the man's details in case they needed to get hold of me if they found my parents. They gave me pitiful looks after that, and then they left. I didn't know them, but neither of them offered to take me with them.

Caleb turned to me, and I stared at him, too choked up to reply. "Should we head out?" Black soot stained his face and arms from having searched for survivors in their burned homes. He was a kind person, I could see that clearly. He would have gotten along well with my father.

"Yes." The tears fell and my chin trembled.

He opened the back door for me and I slid inside. Before closing the door, Caleb paused, his lips pinching, and I saw the pain etched in his eyes. "I don't think anything I say can ease your pain from today, but my grandfather once said something to me that has always stayed with me."

I blinked the tears away. "What was it?"

"That sometimes the universe will challenge us. It will take away everything. But every one of us has the power to change our fate. You just have to fight for what you want no matter how much it hurts."

With a small smile, he closed the door and got into the driver's seat, and started the car. But his saying brought back my mother's last words.

Remember to always fight for what you want.

Grief burned through me, and I dropped my face into my hands, crying.

"I'm really sorry this happened to you, Gwendolyn," he murmured. "I heard from friends about your village going up in smoke, and we all came quickly so we could lend a helping hand. But we didn't get here quick enough."

I wanted to say something about this not being his fault, but no words came. As we began to drive away from the village, I stared out my window, up at the sky, watching the ash blowing in the wind like snow.

Ashes of where I'd once belonged, and the life I'd lost.

Forever.

Get your copy of Rapture today!

ACKNOWLEDGMENTS

What a finish…am I right? Monster's has probably been one of the funnest stories we've ever written. Creating a fantasy land like that left everything open. There's little bits of our life interwoven into the tale though. I think that's what I like the most about writing…hiding my own stories where you least expect them.

All Hail Queen Blake!!!

We have *a lot* more planned for Shadowburn…so buckle up. But first…a few thank you's.

Leah-My girl. Thank you so much for your work. I know it's always last minute, and basically shoved down your throat. And you're just gorgeous for putting up with it and helping make our words shine. Love you to pieces.

Caitlin-My bff for life. Love you and I'm so appreciative of you. You are such a light in my life!

Asheley, Janie, Brook, Angela-thank you so much for stepping in and beta reading for us. Thanks for your comments and your willingness to always help out and ensure we get the best story possible. You ladies are amazing!

Jasmine-you're a goddess. I tell you this every time, but your efforts are seen and appreciated. Thank you for what you do for our book babies!

And last…thanks to you. I wake up every day, in disbelief of the gift you've given me of reading our words. I never take it for granted. Not a single day.

BOOKS BY C.R. JANE

www.crjanebooks.com

The Fated Wings Series
First Impressions
Forgotten Specters
The Fallen One (a Fated Wings Novella)
Forbidden Queens
Frightful Beginnings (a Fated Wings Short Story)
Faded Realms
Faithless Dreams
Fabled Kingdoms
Fated Wings 8
The Rock God (a Fated Wings Novella)

The Darkest Curse Series
Forget Me
Lost Passions

The Sounds of Us Contemporary Series (complete series)

Remember Us This Way
Remember You This Way
Remember Me This Way

Broken Hearts Academy Series (complete duet)

Heartbreak Prince

Heartbreak Lover

Ugly Hearts Series Contemporary Series
Ugly Hearts

Hades Redemption Series
The Darkest Lover
The Darkest Kingdom

Academy of Souls Co-write with Mila Young (complete series)
School of Broken Souls
School of Broken Hearts
School of Broken Dreams
School of Broken Wings

Fallen World Series Co-write with Mila Young (complete series)
Bound
Broken
Betrayed
Belong

Thief of Hearts Co-write with Mila Young (complete series)
Siren Condemned
Siren Sacrificed
Siren Awakened
Siren Redeemed

Kingdom of Wolves Co-write with Mila Young
Wild Moon
Wild Heart
Wild Girl
Wild Love

Stupid Boys Series Co-write with Rebecca Royce

Stupid Boys

Dumb Girl

Crazy Love

Breathe Me Duet Co-write with Ivy Fox (complete)

Breathe Me

Breathe You

Rich Demons of Darkwood Series Co-write with May Dawson

Make Me Lie

ABOUT C.R. JANE

A Texas girl living in Utah now, I'm a wife, mother, lawyer, and now author. My stories have been floating around in my head for years, and it has been a relief to finally get them down on paper. I'm a huge Dallas Cowboys fan and I primarily listen to Taylor Swift and hip hop…don't lie and say you don't too.

My love of reading started probably when I was three and it only made sense that I would start to create my own worlds since I was always getting lost in others'.

I like heroines who have to grow in order to become badasses, happy endings, and swoon-worthy, devoted, (and hot) male characters. If this sounds like you, I'm pretty sure we'll be friends.

I'm so glad to have you on my team…check out the links below for ways to hang out with me and more of my books you can read!

Visit my **Facebook** page to get updates.

Visit my Website.

Sign up for my newsletter to stay updated on new releases, find out random facts about me, and get access to different points of view from my characters.

ABOUT MILA YOUNG

Best-selling author, Mila Young tackles everything with the zeal and bravado of the fairytale heroes she grew up reading about. She slays monsters, real and imaginary, like there's no tomorrow. By day she rocks a keyboard as a marketing extraordinaire. At night she battles with her mighty pen-sword, creating fairytale retellings, and sexy ever after tales.

Ready to read more and more from Mila Young? Subscribe today here.

Join Mila's **Wicked Readers group** for exclusive content, latest news, and giveaway. Click here.

For more information…
mila@milayoungbooks.com